What people are saying about ...

JADED

"Small-town flavor, real-life issues, romantic, funny, and poignant—hope with a hint of a drawl. Denman's fresh voice is a delight, and her debut is a winner."

Candace Calvert, bestselling author of *By Your Side*

"In her debut novel, Varina Denman tackles tough subjects in a contemporary setting as she weaves a story of memorable characters with the secrets that haunt them. With touches of humor and an air of mystery, *Jaded* may trigger a few of your own questions about spiritual truths and the accountability of church leaders. A nicely paced small town tale. I look forward to more stories from this gifted storyteller.

Carla Stewart, award-winning author of *Stardust* and *The Hatmaker's Heart*

"A compelling story with truth tightly woven at the core, Ruth Ann and Dodd's journey will stay in your mind long after the last word is read, and it will challenge you to look at others and the world through different eyes. A powerful debut novel."

Anne Mateer, author of *Playing by Heart*

"Varina Denman's *Jaded* showcases the talent of an author who is unafraid to inflict truth upon her characters as they journey from prejudice and naïveté toward acceptance and the rawness of knowledge gained through pain. Relevant and real, this emotive debut subtly strikes at the heart of what keeps so many people at arm's length from God and provides a satisfying romance that keeps the pages turning toward its hoped-for happy ever after."

Serena Chase, author of *The Ryn* and contributor of the *Happy Ever After* blog at *USA Today*

"*Jaded* is a poignant story of old scars and new hope. Through the journey of one wounded family, the transformational powers of forgiveness and genuine faith become clear. Varina Denman's fictional small town could be any town, and many readers will recognize the all-too-human challenges facing today's churches."

Lisa Wingate, international bestselling author of *The Prayer Box* and *The Story Keeper*

"Varina captures your heart in this journey of love, pain, and intrigue. Captivated by the town's mysterious past, caught up in the suspense, and lost in forbidden romance, you'll never be prepared for what happens next. Read this book. You will not regret it."

Don Brobst, MD, author

"*Jaded* is not only a soul-stirring tale of transformational love, but it's also a bridge—one that stretches the delicate divide between hurt and hope. The empathy and grace of Denman's skilled pen will carry far beyond these characters and into the hearts of her readers."

Nicole Deese, author of the Letting Go series and *A Cliché Christmas*

"*Jaded* is an emotionally-charged masterpiece that sinks into your soul and challenges you to see beyond the pitfalls of religion. The small-town setting, remarkably real characters, and meaningful theme of forgiveness makes this book a 2015 must-read."

T. L. Gray, Kindle bestselling author
of the Winsor and Set Apart series

"Trapp, Texas, is a town where football and gossip are king and queen, secrets are kept and told, and nothing changes—until it does. Denman has given us a story as rich as a chocolate sheath cake with characters as familiar as an old pickup truck and with grace as broad as the flat fields of cotton. Recommended!"

Bill Higgs, author

JADED

A NOVEL

VARINA DENMAN

JADED
Published by David C Cook
4050 Lee Vance View
Colorado Springs, CO 80918 U.S.A.

David C Cook Distribution Canada
55 Woodslee Avenue, Paris, Ontario, Canada N3L 3E5

David C Cook U.K., Kingsway Communications
Eastbourne, East Sussex BN23 6NT, England

The graphic circle C logo is a registered trademark of David C Cook.

LCCN 2014948814
ISBN 978-1-4347-0837-3
eISBN 978-0-7814-1288-9

The Team: Ingrid Beck, Jamie Chavez, Nick Lee, Jennifer
Lonas, Helen Macdonald, Karen Athen
Cover Design: Amy Konyndyk
Cover Photos: Getty Images (Thomas Barwick), Veer Images, iStockphoto

Printed in the United States of America
First Edition 2015

1 2 3 4 5 6 7 8 9 10

123114

For those who long for heaven

Let any one of you who is without sin
be the first to throw a stone at her.

John 8:7 NIV

PROLOGUE

I last attended worship service on a blustery Sunday in March, the year I turned seven. I'm certain of the date because I still have the bulletin from that morning. Momma wadded the paper into a fist-clenched ball, but I pressed it between the pages of an old dictionary to flatten the wrinkles and later hid it in my chest of drawers beneath my sweatpants.

That morning, we took our usual spot in the musty building, fifth pew from the back, and my best friend, Fawn Blaylock, sat with her parents in front of us. Fawn turned around to make funny faces at me, so I was giggling when Momma snatched my arm and dragged me out the door. Fawn's comical expression morphed into surprise, but her parents, oddly enough, never looked at us.

Our silver hatchback careened through town as Momma put a death grip on the steering wheel, and by the time she pulled under our carport, the muscles in her face and neck resembled polished marble. Mind you, Momma never cried. No matter what she was feeling, every emotion manifested itself as anger. Even when Daddy left, she bottled up her grief like one of those homemade bombs you make with a Coke bottle. So when she read that notice in the church bulletin, her emotions ignited into an explosion the likes of which I never saw before or since. When her rage petered out, she locked herself in her bedroom and stayed there until supper.

Fawn Blaylock stopped being my friend before the Monday morning Pledge of Allegiance, and Momma's church friends looked the other way whenever we'd pass them in town. It didn't seem to matter that Daddy was the one who ran off. Nobody asked for details before they branded Momma with a scarlet letter.

We became invisible to our church family, and after a visit from one of the elders, I knew we would never return to worship services. No more Saturday night plastic curlers, which I wouldn't miss. No more Sunday morning ruffled socks, which I would. And for all practical purposes, no more Momma. She stopped smiling, socializing, living. My seven-year-old immaturity convinced me the church had pulled her away from me, and I wondered if, in some way, they had taken Daddy, too. I resolved to steer clear of Christians, and over the years, the baptized believers never gave me cause to reconsider.

Thirteen years later, my callous determination had grown fierce, and when the Cunninghams moved to town with their charm and good intentions, I figured they were nothing more than a fancy version of the same old rigmarole.

CHAPTER ONE

"Ruthie, did you hear? There's a new kid up at the school." My cousin, JohnScott, called through the window of his step-side pickup as I pushed a squeaky shopping cart across the parking lot of the United grocery store—my second job. For my day job, I worked full-time as attendance clerk at the high school, so I knew for a fact we hadn't gotten a new student in three years. I could almost taste my curiosity.

The truck idled in front of the store, and I stopped to lean on the rusty driver's door. "What are you talking about? I left the school an hour ago, and I didn't see anybody."

"Let me think ..." He rubbed a palm across his five o'clock shadow. "Seems like the name was Cunningham."

"Any relation to the new middle school teacher who's supposed to be showing up any day?" I smiled as I inhaled the scent of his truck, a mixture of cheap cologne, cattle feed, and West Texas sand. "Out with it, JohnScott."

"It may take a minute for me to recollect. I remember going to the office to turn in some grades ..." He squinted at the sky.

"If you talk, I'll get Blue Bell Ice Cream from the back freezer."

"No charge?"

"My treat."

He killed the ignition. "You're too easy, Ruthie. I would've talked for less."

I grinned as his goading washed over me like the sugary smell in a donut shop. JohnScott would do anything for me. We had practically been raised as brother and sister, because in childhood I spent more time at my aunt and uncle's house than my own. Now that we were grown, my cousin teased me a lot, but I knew I could count on the man.

"What's his name?" I quizzed JohnScott as we stood shoulder to shoulder in the walk-in refrigerator at the back of the store.

"Grady Cunningham. He's a senior. He was touring the school with his mother. And yes, she's teaching. Couldn't come two weeks ago because she was giving notice at her old job."

I nodded as the refrigerated air sent chill bumps across my neck, but JohnScott could not be rushed.

He peeled away the lid of the ice-cream container, studying the contents. "Surely he'll play football, right? I mean, why wouldn't he?" Since JohnScott was the head coach of the high school football team, his conversations tended to gravitate toward the pigskin sport. "You think he could take Tinker's place?"

"Maybe." Football made little sense to me. I slipped into a huge jacket that hung on a hook by the refrigerator door, and a whiff of sour milk enveloped me along with the jacket's warmth. "He's only missed a few games."

"Good thing we've got a bye tonight or he'd be missing another one." JohnScott scratched behind his ear. "I guess he's a city boy. Comes from Fort Worth."

"So the dad's not a farmer?"

"I don't think the dad's in the picture, but the mother seemed nice. She's short, like you."

"What's that got to do with anything?"

He clicked the plastic spoon against his teeth, licking the frozen chocolate. "I don't know, but she looked awful small next to the boy."

"So he's tall."

"Smidgen taller than me, I guess. Might be good on offense."

"A new family with a son who plays football?" I shook my head and mumbled, "That news will spread faster than a grass fire in a drought."

My cousin looked at me out of the corner of his eye. "Mom will be all over this, you know."

I cringed. Aunt Velma meant well, but her advice always ended with me getting married. I'd do that too, if it meant getting out of Trapp, but most of the men I knew planned to spend the rest of their lives here. "For crying out loud, JohnScott, the kid's in high school."

"Not ideal, but he'll grow up."

"I'm not planning to hang around that long."

"He's a looker …"

I laughed. "Then you date him. I don't need a babysitting job. Besides, he can't be handsome enough for me to risk losing my job at the school."

"His older brother might be, though."

I bumped a pile of egg cartons, then reached to steady them. "Older brother?"

"The boy mentioned him. I figure he's home from college for the weekend." JohnScott wrinkled his forehead. "Could be older."

I smiled. Other than my cousin, Trapp boasted four eligible bachelors, all of whom repeatedly asked me out, and none of whom understood the concept of antiperspirant. I shivered, partly from the temperature in the refrigerator and partly from the possibilities this older brother presented. "Tell Aunt Velma I'll marry that one."

"Done."

I stacked three milk crates and told myself not to get my hopes up. Reality rarely matched my daydreams, so I steered the conversation away from my impending marriage plans. "I got my acceptance letter."

"Tech or A&M?" JohnScott finished his Rocky Road and crushed the carton.

"Tech. I gave up on College Station."

We fell silent as my mind cluttered with thoughts of the future. Before I could desert Momma, a series of complications would have to be overcome, the greatest being the need for a scholarship. So far I'd had no luck.

The refrigerator door opened with a wave of warm air, and the manager leaned in. "I need you on checkout, Ruthie."

"Be right there." The door closed again, and I sighed, wishing my breaks were longer.

"Mind if I stick around a while, little cousin?"

"You just want to listen to gossip." I slipped off the jacket and hung it on the hook.

"Is that a yes?"

"If you'll bag groceries for me, you can stay as long as you like."

He followed me down the dog-food aisle to the front of the store, and I punched my employee code into the register while he readied the plastic-bag dispensers. Two elderly women rambled to the counter, chattering nonstop. I recognized them as sisters who lived forty-five minutes outside of Trapp and came to town every few weeks to stock up on groceries and town news. I could never keep their names straight, so I referred to them secretly as Blue and Gray—because of their hair colors.

I greeted them and began scanning items while listening to their prattle.

"He's a rapist, you know."

"I heard it was statutory."

"It's all the same in my book."

I faltered. *What in the world?* Rape was not a common topic of conversation at the United, especially between two little old ladies.

I glanced at JohnScott and knew he wondered the same thing. "Are you talking about that Cunningham family?" I asked.

"Lawd, no." Gray's hunched back made it seem as if she shared a great secret. "Clyde Felton. You two remember the likes of the Feltons?"

I shook my head, but JohnScott mumbled, "Seems like I've heard the name."

"They've been gone nigh on fifteen years now, but Clyde—"

Blue wagged a crooked finger. "It's been twenty years if it's been a day."

Gray scrunched her eyes so tight, her nose got involved. "You may be right, Sister." She focused her attention back on JohnScott and me. "But anyhoo, Clyde Felton just got out of prison. Drove into town this afternoon."

I hesitated with a box of Rice-A-Roni in my hand. "He's in Trapp?"

"Rented the old, yellow trailer house over on Third," Blue said. "Who owns that thing anyway, Sister? Why would they rent it to a convict?"

"Can't say as I know." Gray reached for the reading glasses she wore around her neck, the chain jingling as she held them above her nose, and appeared captivated by the fine print on a magazine cover.

After sliding a bag of potatoes to my frowning cousin, I wiped grit off my hands. The United grocery served as the hub of community gossip, but I hoped the sweet sisters had their facts wrong. The thought of a convicted rapist living a few streets over from Momma and me sent a tremor down my spine like a low-grade earthquake.

Blue took a step toward me and giggled. "I bet you can't wait to meet 'im, girlie."

"Clyde Felton?" I dropped a container of pimento cheese but didn't bend to pick it up until Blue answered.

"Lawd, no. I mean that new boy. Does he play ball, Coach?"

Lowering my head as I made change, I ignored JohnScott, who stifled a chuckle behind his response. *Good grief.* The female shoppers at the United would have me married to a teenager before the end of the month. It was bad enough I still checked groceries at the United at twenty, but even worse, many of the customers fancied me the town's matchmaking project.

Using the intercom, I called a boy from the back to carry out the groceries, while the women jumped back into their conversation.

"I hear they came in a big U-Haul, pulling an El Camino."

"An El Camino? You don't say."

"Never knew a widow to drive a truck."

"Don't seem right, does it?"

JohnScott hefted a watermelon into their cart. "Actually, the mother drives an SUV."

Silence followed for five seconds until Gray seemed unable to stand it any longer. "The mother?"

"Yep, must be one of the sons drives the El Camino."

"Ah ..." Gray smacked her lips. "The son drives the El Camino."

"Best we make a stop at the post office after this, Sister. They're sure to know about that El Camino over there." The women meandered toward the door.

"Bye, now." Blue waved her receipt over her shoulder.

"Have a good day." I smiled, but JohnScott crossed his arms, appraising Blue and Gray as they made their way to their car.

"You thinking about Clyde Felton?" I asked.

"Mm-hmm."

Goose bumps crept up my arms, but I busied myself changing the receipt paper in the register. "And to think I traipse all over town by myself."

"Maybe we should change that."

"If you pick me up after work, I'll tell you what he looks like."

JohnScott stiffened. "You figuring to meet him?"

"I work at the United, JohnScott."

He eyed me for a moment. "I can stay longer."

The idea comforted me like warm milk with honey, but practicality overruled my fear. "Aunt Velma will tan your hide if you're not home for dinner."

His shoulders relaxed, and his voice took on a patient whine. "I've got my own place now."

I remembered good and well his double-wide in Aunt Velma and Uncle Ansel's pasture, but I also remembered my aunt's admission that he never missed one of her home-cooked meals. "If you say so." I winked, knowing my teasing didn't pack a punch, since I truly did still live with my mother.

"I'll pick you up at ten, and I want to hear everything."

I followed him to the door, blinking against the late-afternoon sun. "We've gone years without anyone moving to town, and now we have two at once. What are the odds?"

"About one in a million. See you later, little cousin."

As the door closed behind him, I had mixed feelings. Dread about the rapist coming to the store, and butterflies about the Cunninghams doing so. Strangers made me nervous, but I'd better get ready, because the odds of either Clyde Felton or the Cunninghams making an appearance at the United before closing time beat a million to one, of that I was certain.

CHAPTER TWO

Miles of cotton fields and sprawling ranches had given Dodd Cunningham an uneasy feeling that afternoon, even before he passed the *Welcome to Trapp, Texas! Home of the Panthers!* road sign, but he figured small-town life would grow on him. The sense of security his mother felt being near her old friends, the Mendozas, made up for the petty discomforts nagging him.

"Dodd?" His younger brother, Grady, rolled down the passenger window of the El Camino, speaking over the moan of the glass. "Does anyone live in this town?"

"Well, there was the guy back at the gas station."

"You think he killed the rest of them?"

Dodd cut his eyes toward Grady and chuckled. "Possibly."

"Well, I think the high school principal could be in on it."

"Tell me he's not that bad."

Grady stuck his head out the window and shook his hair in the wind. "I guess you'll find out Monday morning, won't you?"

Dodd smiled as he eased to a stop behind the orange-and-white moving truck in his driveway. He and Grady climbed out of the car to stand on the cracked sidewalk, surveying the pink siding of the shoebox-sized house for the second time that day. Dodd took a deep breath and realized Trapp even smelled strange. Like baked dirt. "I have a funny feeling about this place."

"Funny like hysterical?" Grady said. "Like maniacal laughter?"

Dodd glanced at puffy, white clouds, finding comfort in their familiarity. Funny like how did I end up here. He flinched. His primary goal was to be an encouragement to Grady and his mother, so he forced a lighter mood. "Funny like you never know what God has up His sleeve."

Grady strode to the chain-link fence at the side of the house. "You can't pray about a move as much as we have and doubt whether it's right. Obviously God wants you here or He wouldn't keep dumping job interviews on you." He leaned against the top rail, the wire mesh clinking in protest. "I thought no big trees grew out here."

Dodd joined him, leaning his forearms on the warm metal. "Grady, that tree is dead."

"Yet they left it here as a memorial."

Grady frowned at the oak in their backyard, but Dodd didn't doubt his brother's enthusiasm for their new home. Even at eighteen, Grady had the markings of a natural missionary, and Dodd envied the ease with which his brother adapted to new situations. Their mother had signed a contract to teach at the middle school two weeks ago, and at the last minute, Dodd decided to come with them. He hadn't yet gotten used to the idea of living in Nowhere, USA, and his confidence was sprinting to catch up to his good intentions.

Their mother called from the front porch. "What do you think of the place?"

"You've got to be kidding me." Grady pushed away from the fence.

"Just wait until Fawn Blaylock introduces you to some of the kids," she said.

"Mom ...," Grady whined. "We don't even know her. Isn't she old?"

"I think she's twenty. That's not old. Besides, Charlie says she knows all the teenagers in town."

Dodd followed his brother to the moving truck and shoved the door up with a clatter. Wednesday night, the Trapp elders had come to Fort Worth for a brief interview, and Dodd had met Fawn's father, Neil Blaylock. Polished boots, starched jeans, broad smile. In some ways, the complete opposite of Charlie Mendoza, his mother's old friend from college, who was a softer version of cowboy. The third elder, Lee Roy Goodnight, could've been their grandfather.

Dodd looked at Grady and gently crossed his eyes.

"We don't want no hick girlfriends, Mom." Grady hooked his thumbs on his tank top.

"I didn't mean to imply you did." She retrieved a mop and pail from the back of her SUV. "Before you know it, Trapp will feel like home."

She smiled, but Dodd detected a hint of apprehension in her voice that echoed his own. He took the cleaning supplies as a breeze swept red sand down the street and with it, the odor of manure. "This town will take some getting used to, Mom." He kissed the top of her head. "But the important thing is the people."

Grady cleared his throat. "Both of them."

Forty-five minutes and several dozen boxes later, sweat soaked Dodd's shirt and stung his eyes. He paused to analyze how they would get the refrigerator off the truck. "Of all the vans on the rental lot, I end up with one whose ramps are stuck."

"What do you suggest?" Grady asked.

Dodd gauged the distance from the truck bed to the ground. "What if you lean the chunky girl all the way back so she's almost lying on her side, then ease her over the edge." He rubbed the nape of his neck. "If you pull back when she slides down, I think I can support her weight until she reaches the driveway."

Grady scratched his head. "So you want me to pitch her down to you? Just like that?"

Dodd pushed up the sleeves of his T-shirt with deliberate movements, flexed, then laughed. "Okay, so it might not be the most practical idea, but I don't see any other option."

"Cool." Grady clambered into the truck. "I may get my own room after all." He dragged the appliance across the bed of the truck as the screech of metal on metal echoed down the street. "That's as near as I can get it. I'll tilt it back and slip the edge off the side."

Dodd wiped sweat out of his eyes. "Rotate it ninety degrees to take advantage of the smooth side. As it is now, you'll be sliding against the back tubing."

"But that'll scratch the finish."

Dodd looked past Grady. "Grab a blanket from behind you."

Grady dug through a box, then flared the bedding like a bullfighter. "You ready, then?"

"Bring it on." Dodd grinned at his brother, glad of the time they were spending together, a bittersweet result of their father's death. If all had gone according to plan, they would have still been hundreds of miles apart—Grady working foreign missions with their parents while Dodd labored stateside, sending money to support them.

Grady angled the appliance until the bottom edge lay even with the truck floor. "I'll pull back as I send her over. Here comes the princess."

Dodd braced himself against the bottom of the fridge and said a quick prayer.

Together they scooted the bulk over the edge, but too late Dodd realized the blanket would cause the appliance to slide too easily.

Grady stammered, "My hands are slipping. Sweaty."

"Not yet. Two more feet."

"I can't."

The top of the refrigerator crashed against the inside wall of the truck, and Dodd buckled under the added weight. "Grady, do something!"

"There's nothing to hold on to."

Dodd heard running footfalls, and the fridge shifted before gliding to the ground. He rose slowly, massaging a sore spot where the door handle had gouged his inner arm. That would be a substantial bruise, but it could have been so much worse. He breathed heavily as he stepped around the appliance and came face-to-face with one of the largest men he'd ever seen. Several inches taller than Dodd and twice as broad, the stranger was a modern-day Hercules … in a tattered Led Zeppelin T-shirt.

"You came along just in time." Dodd extended his hand. "I'm Dodd Cunningham."

The man's gaze swept the street before he gripped Dodd's hand and answered in a deep bass tone. "Just moving in myself."

Grady sat on the bed of the truck, his legs dangling over the side. "You saved my brother from getting smashed by four hundred pounds of Maytag." He grinned. "I'm Grady. What's your name?"

The stranger hesitated. "Clyde. Clyde Felton."

"I'm not above bribing you, Mr. Felton," Grady said. "If you help lug this old thing into the house, we'd be more than happy to assist with your own belongings."

"Place came furnished." Clyde scrutinized the pink shoebox of a house as if it were a nest of scorpions. "I guess I can help real quick."

Most likely Clyde could have transported the appliance on his own, but together the three of them maneuvered it toward the porch, and all the while Clyde glanced up and down the street. Dodd wondered if the other neighbors would be so skeptical. So far he'd received a hearty small-town welcome, but this guy was new in town too. Maybe he felt as out of place as Dodd.

With the fridge installed in the corner of the kitchen, Clyde said shortly, "No dolly?"

Dodd's mother entered from the backyard, where she had been shaking out rugs. "My son gets carried away pinching pennies. I'm Milla Cunningham."

"Ma'am."

Her gaze bounced from their neighbor to the floor and back again, and Dodd knew his mother was having just as much trouble figuring him out as Dodd. The man seemed lost, like a toddler separated from his mother in a toy store—a peculiar blend of angst and excitement.

"I wish I could offer you a glass of iced tea," Milla said, "but tap water will have to do for now." She dug through a cardboard box for a stack of foam cups as Clyde shuffled toward the door, his outdated Adidas dragging across the gritty linoleum.

"Water's fine."

The man made his way to the front porch one step at a time as he dodged questions from Milla. Eventually she would crack the poor guy, and they'd be friends, but Dodd opted for a slower approach, figuring it might take a while to earn his trust.

Grady motioned to the weeds in Clyde's yard across the street, then the tall grass in his own. "I'll be mowing tomorrow. I'll make a swipe through your place as well."

Clyde's eyes jerked toward the teenager. "No need."

"It's the least I can do for the man who saved my brother's life." Grady slapped Dodd on the back.

"Best stay away from my place."

Dodd tensed at Clyde's tone, wondering if the crusty neighbor intended the remark as an underlying threat, but his concern evaporated as an older pickup stopped on the street.

"There's Charlie, late as usual," Milla said, in an obvious attempt to lighten the mood.

His mother's old friend folded himself out of the truck with a broad grin. His boisterous voice boomed, belying his thin frame. "About time you made it to Trapp, Milla Vanilla."

"I haven't heard that nickname in twenty-five years—Charlie *Women*doza."

"Hey, now." He pointed an index finger at her as he strode across the yard.

The way Charlie put his mother at ease lessened Dodd's doubts about their new home but reminded him of his father's absence.

Dodd would give anything to be able to ask his dad's advice about his new job at the church.

"Neil asked if he could tag along." Charlie gestured toward the truck.

Neil Blaylock, tall and tan, swept a cream-colored cowboy hat onto his head as he walked toward them.

Dodd shook the man's hand. "Good to see you again, Mr. Blaylock."

"Welcome to Trapp, son. From what I hear, your father would be right proud of you for all you've taken on. Right proud."

"Thank you, sir."

"It's good to see the old El Camino." Charlie gazed wistfully at the car. "I can't believe it's still running. Your daddy and I had some adventures back in school."

Milla peered at Neil and Charlie. "You didn't bring your wives?"

"Not this time." Neil flashed a smile. "But they'll be at the ranch tomorrow night for the cookout."

Dodd's stomach tightened uncomfortably. He wanted to impress the church members yet felt underqualified. His measly experience didn't make up for his lack of education, and he was even more ill-prepared to lead his family. He was grateful to have Charlie—and hopefully Neil—as a source of encouragement and guidance.

"Everything go all right with the move, son?" Charlie's large hand gripped Dodd's shoulder.

"Smooth sailing until Grady and I tried to unload the refrigerator by ourselves, but a neighbor came to our rescue."

"Neighbor?"

"Clyde Felton. He lives across the street." Dodd motioned toward the porch, but sometime during the conversation, Clyde had slipped away.

"Whoa," Grady said. "Where'd he go?"

Neil adjusted his hat with a frown. "Clyde Felton was here?"

"Until a second ago." Grady grinned. "Dodd would be smashed right now if not for him."

Dodd wondered at the man's abrupt disappearance, but Milla waved away the discussion. "Come on in," she said. "I'll show you what we've done with the place."

"That shouldn't take long," Grady mumbled.

As his mother and brother entered the house with Charlie and Neil, Dodd surveyed the old trailer house across the street. A light shone in one of the windows, but he could detect no movement. The evening breeze carried the trill of a distant train whistle, and Dodd once again inhaled the odor of cattle. He would be accustomed to the scent in a day or two, along with hundreds of other unexpected differences of small-town life, and by the time he fulfilled his three-year commitment to preach part-time at the Trapp congregation, he might even beg to stay. In the meantime, he decided it would serve him well to get to know his neighbors.

Especially Clyde Felton.

CHAPTER THREE

"What do you think the new kid's like, Ruthie?"

I spent all evening ringing up groceries and listening to housewives chatter about Grady Cunningham, and while I hadn't learned anything new, the family's biography changed several times during my shift. By closing time, the older brother had evolved from an unknown Fort Worth man into a rich Montana rancher planning a takeover of the local grain elevator. A few bold shoppers even speculated that he had been in the penitentiary with Clyde Felton.

The question from the stock boy shouldn't have irritated me, but after working fourteen hours straight between my day job at the school and my night job at the United, I'd had all I could take. I glared at him where I crouched to retrieve a wadded sales page under the counter, my shoulder grinding against the rough edge of the shelving. "Luis, don't ask. I'm sick of hearing about those people."

"Well, excuse me for living." He flipped through a magazine, not looking up.

"Do you suppose you could help me?"

He turned another page. "What do you need?"

"Toss this in the trash and hand me a box of plastic bags."

He took his time, then leaned against the counter as I spied more trash. The swishing suction of the door signaled an entering shopper, and I looked over my shoulder. A blond teenage boy, head held high, strolled past the greeting-card display. He paused in front of the water fountain and peered back at the door.

Following his gaze, I glimpsed a dark-haired man. Undoubtedly, the blond was Grady Cunningham, JohnScott's football hopeful, and the man was his mysterious older brother. I jerked back around, but not before unintentionally making eye contact with the brunet.

JohnScott may have exaggerated a teensy bit, but Grady Cunningham was indeed handsome. The older brother, also attractive, looked like something out of the L.L.Bean mail-order catalogs in Aunt Velma's guest bath, but neither of them struck me as knockout gorgeous. The quality of their clothing, the length of their hair, even their posture, said city folk.

Luis stared at them, trancelike, so I finished the bags on my own, rising as they came through the checkout with a bottle of Gatorade and a Dr Pepper.

I scanned the drinks, ignoring the appealing scent of cologne-over-sweat, and dropped change into the man's palm. "Have a good day." Store policy dictated I speak.

Luis's gaze made a slow sweep across the man's V-neck shirt and blue jeans, and then my juvenile coworker craned his neck to get a better view of the boy's fancy athletic shoes. "Y'all must be new in town."

"I'm Grady Cunningham," the blond said, "and this is my brother, Dodd." The boy held his hand toward Luis, who gazed at it blankly before shaking it.

"I'm Luis. This is Ruthie. You play football?"

Now that I had seen him, I understood why JohnScott assumed Grady played. He and his brother moved with the graceful air of athletes.

The teenager gently tossed his bangs out of his eyes. "I played in junior high, but I haven't decided yet. Do you play?"

"Starting freshman," Luis boasted.

"What grade are you in?" the man asked. His voice held the authoritative tone of a businessman, and I wondered what he did for a living. Banker, maybe?

I grabbed a bottle of Windex and drenched the spotless counter as the spray bottle honked. Why had the older Cunningham asked Luis what grade he was in? The freshman just mentioned his classification.

I wiped the counter with paper towels, wishing they would leave, but when I looked up, three pairs of eyes waited for my answer.

My nerves hummed like Uncle Ansel's hot-wire fence. "Oh. I'm out of school." I dropped the cleaner.

Real smooth, Ruthie.

Dodd smiled apologetically. "Have you worked here long?"

Luis answered. "Naw, about a month. Ruthie's been here a couple years, though. She's gotta work two jobs 'cause her dad ran off, and her mom can't hold down a job."

I scrubbed a sticky substance on the side of the register, using my thumbnail to scrape the last bit. Actually, I had worked at the United over *four* years. But still.

"You starting school?" Luis asked.

"Monday morning," Grady said.

Dodd stepped past Luis and around the counter, and I wondered how a man could look so uppity dressed in Levi's. Maybe it was the way he moved. I'd never be able to properly describe this guy to JohnScott.

Grady bent down until we were face-to-face. "Good to meet you, Ruthie." He flashed a smile before following his brother.

Luis pattered after them like a puppy, asking Grady what position he played.

When the door swooshed behind my back, the hot-wire fence cooled, my nerves relaxed, and I embraced a few minutes of sheltered privacy. Lifting my hair off my shoulders, I held it to the top of my head. My neck had been stiff all evening, and when I moved it from side to side, I felt a muted crackle like rice cereal. As soon as Luis came back in, I'd turn off the lights and clock out. JohnScott would be here to pick me up in a few minutes, and I had a lot to tell him.

Pivoting to lean against the counter, I froze.

Dodd Cunningham stood ten feet away, watching me curiously as though I were on display behind a Plexiglas wall at the zoo.

I dropped my hair protectively around my shoulders. "Can I help you?"

"I didn't mean to startle you, ma'am."

Ma'am?

He took a step toward me and rubbed a palm across the back of his neck. "I only came back in to say it was nice to meet you." He exhaled but didn't turn away.

What happened to Mister Executive? I picked up the damp paper towel. "So you're from Fort Worth."

"You've heard about us?" He stepped to the empty register adjacent to mine and placed an elbow on the check-writing ledge.

"I'd say by now everybody in town's heard about you."

"Is that typical?"

I frowned, leaning my hips against the counter. "Everybody knowing everything you do? Yes, I'd say that's overwhelmingly typical. Welcome to Trapp."

He sighed, then twisted the cap off his Dr Pepper. As he took a drink, I inspected a curl nestled behind his ear.

"How do you stand it?" he asked.

My mind whirled.

"People talking about you, I mean."

"Oh, that. No choice but to stand it." I shrugged. "That's just how things are."

He scrutinized the store, focusing on the cash register, the fluorescent lights overhead, the signs hanging from chains above each aisle. Then his gaze returned to me, and the corners of his mouth lifted. "I'd better get used to it, then."

"You might as well."

A car horn honked, and Dodd glanced toward the parking lot. "That's Grady." He took a step but turned back, the executive tone returning to his voice. "It was good to meet you."

"You, too."

When he got to the door, he looked back yet again.

I had never been a fan of flirting, but suddenly it seemed like an opportunity I shouldn't pass up. I smiled and tilted my head.

He reached for the door handle but missed. Chuckling, he glanced at me one last time before sheepishly putting a shoulder against the glass and walking effortlessly through the doorway.

Warmth slid from my scalp to my shoulders, as though chocolate pudding were being spooned onto the top of my head.

I crept to the window to spy on Dodd from behind the Coke machine, absentmindedly wiping fingerprints off the selection buttons with the towel still clenched in my hand.

Grady stood at the passenger side of the ugliest car I had ever seen—an old navy El Camino that wanted to be a truck but couldn't quite make it out of the car category. Luis had his foot on the hood, leaning an elbow on his knee. It might have been a suave position for him if the hood hadn't been so high.

Dodd, on the other hand, walked to the driver's side as he gulped his Dr Pepper with fluid movements, reminding me of a graceful buck JohnScott and I had admired from a deer blind the fall before. The animal poised so close, we could see muscles rippling in his shoulders, until I frightened him away with an explosive sneeze.

Luis and both of the Cunninghams turned as Fawn Blaylock's Mustang sped into the otherwise-empty parking lot and pulled into the space next to the truck wannabe, right in front of my hiding place.

I groaned. Fawn hadn't truly spoken to me in thirteen years. Not since Momma and I left the church. Even though the church members still ignored me whenever they'd see me in town, I had enjoyed a two-year respite from Fawn while she was away at college. Her untimely arrival sucked the joy from whatever daydreams I might have entertained about Dodd Cunningham.

She flounced her blonde curls and perched on the hood of the El Camino, leaning toward Dodd as he spoke. I couldn't make out their words because of the hum of the Coke machine, but I heard the lilt of their voices.

Why was Fawn flirting? She had a boyfriend.

Dodd capped his empty bottle and tossed it in the back of the car. He smiled at Fawn but glanced up the street while she chattered. Grady took a few sips of his Gatorade and nodded. Luis seemed to be the only one playing up to her. She paused, then bubbled laughter as though she were telling a joke, and just as she came to the punch line, the Coke machine shut off, and I was able to hear her last word. *Tramp*. She flicked her hand toward the store, and all three males looked through the window. Directly at me.

I ducked behind the machine as anger struck like a rattlesnake. It was one thing for Fawn to treat me like pond scum when it was just her and me, but she had no business talking about me to strangers. Reaching behind the Coke machine, I slammed light switches one after another while two images flashed across my mind. Dodd Cunningham leaning against the counter smiling at me. And Dodd Cunningham standing by his El Camino peering at me doubtfully. I could have ripped every blonde strand from Fawn's arrogant head right then, but as I walked to the back of the store, I realized my anger wouldn't change her one bit. Fawn was a Blaylock, and that was that.

By the time the store surrendered to darkness and I slumped into the break room, my anger once again lay coiled in hibernation.

"Those guys are great," Luis said as he shuffled into the room smelling like a third grader after recess. "I told Grady he can hang out with me and my friends on Monday."

The thought of Grady Cunningham and Luis Vega hanging out together should have evoked an automatic eye roll, but his statement barely registered with me. "Did you see JohnScott out there?" I asked.

"Parking lot's deserted." He pulled his shoulders back. "Fawn and I shot the breeze for a while after the Cunninghams took off."

It couldn't have been more than a few seconds, but I didn't mention that to Luis. Instead, I grilled him for information. "So, Grady's brother? He's in college or something?"

Luis sighed dramatically. "Dodd's twenty-six, Ruthie."

JohnScott's age.

I weighed the possibility of the man living with his parents, but the image didn't fit. More likely he came to help the family move in, with the intention of returning to his job as CEO in a Fort Worth high-rise.

But maybe he was staying in Trapp.

I chewed a hangnail. What if he came in the store every evening, leaned against the register, and smiled at me?

As the ice machine dumped its load with a clatter, I reached for my purse. "So Fawn just met them?"

"Yeah, but she already heard about them from her dad and the church."

The muscles in my neck tightened. "What do you mean?"

"Duh, Ruthie." He slapped his hand against his forehead. "Dodd's the new preacher."

I turned away as my skin prickled, starting at my elbows and pulsing all the way down to the soles of my feet. Probably it was goose bumps, but it felt more like hives, or pox, or tangible dread.

How could that man be the new *preacher*? It was impossible. I stared at the bulletin board, pretending to study next week's work schedule and willing my voice not to quiver. "You mean their *dad's* the new preacher."

"No, Ruthie, the dad kicked off a year ago. It's them and their mom." He reached past me to hang his box cutter on a hook.

The image of Dodd Cunningham behind a pulpit didn't compute, and instead, I pictured him leaning on the check-writing ledge. He had seemed so sincere when he asked, "How do you stand it?"

Suddenly my brain connected the dots.

Dodd was the preacher, so of course he had heard about my history with the church. All about Daddy and Momma's scandal. All about how everybody down at the church shunned us. *He knew.* That's what he meant.

I felt as though someone had punched me in the stomach. The goose bumps tickling across my skin melted into a heated tension that made me short-winded. I didn't know whether to be irritated or furious, but I was definitely suspicious.

Lapsing into reflex mode, I moved through darkened aisles to the front of the store as Luis went in search of the manager to ask what needed to be done out back. My mind clouded in a dust storm of anger and humiliation, but I relaxed when I saw JohnScott outside the entrance. My cousin leaned out the window of his truck, studying a playbook under the purring glow of the store lights. I pushed through the doorway as though pushing through a wall of quicksand.

"You see him?" JohnScott queried while I locked up.

For a split second I wondered if he somehow heard I made a bumbling idiot of myself in front of Dodd Cunningham, but then I realized he was only fishing for information about our town's recently returned rapist.

"Clyde Felton? No, but all the women say he's huge and scary." I picked up two stray cash-register receipts and a sticky soft-drink can from the sidewalk and tossed them in the trash barrel before opening the truck door.

"So they've seen him?"

"I doubt it." I slid onto the seat next to him. "You can't believe everything you hear at the United."

He studied me. "There's something wrong. What's up?"

I could never hide my feelings from JohnScott and seldom had reason to try. Resting my head against the back window, I let the tension drain from my body. "Grady Cunningham's brother is the new preacher at the church."

JohnScott's nose wrinkled as if he smelled a stinkbug, but the expression slipped away so quickly, I wondered if I'd imagined it. "You sure?"

"They were talking to Fawn Blaylock." I rubbed my thumb against the worn vinyl of the seat, snagging my nail on a spot of exposed stuffing.

JohnScott studied his fist where it rested on the stick shift. He stayed that way for several seconds before shoving the truck into gear with a thud. "Well, little cousin, I guess this means your wedding's off."

CHAPTER FOUR

Dodd shifted his weight, trying to find a position that would prevent his shoulder blades from grating against the wooden pew. He had preached on the topic of fellowship, an easy segue into the luncheon planned after the worship service, and he felt good about his first sermon. The congregation seemed responsive—not too many yawns—but Dodd knew it would take a while to prove himself. Not only was he unknown to these people, but he was young. Very young. While he joined the congregation in singing "Shall We Gather at the River?" Dodd observed the people sitting around him.

Fawn Blaylock sat across the aisle with her boyfriend, Tyler Cruz, who lived in the neighboring town of Snyder. Dodd liked Fawn, but he couldn't quite figure her out. She hadn't mentioned her boyfriend in two days, and Dodd was startled when Tyler showed up at services that morning, but that wasn't the only thing that surprised him about Fawn. Every so often, the girl would throw out a comment about someone, not necessarily disrespectful, but close.

His glance fell on Emily Sanders, Fawn's shadow, perched on the pew in front of him. Every few minutes, the girl looked over her shoulder. Dodd couldn't tell if she was looking at him or Grady or both. Hopefully Grady, since Emily was in high school.

Two middle school boys rustled in the corner, but Dodd couldn't remember their names. From the looks of it, they whispered about Grady's and his clothing. Dodd checked Grady's tie for breakfast cereal, then took a survey of the males around him, discovering the appropriate attire for the Trapp congregation consisted of button-down shirts, starched Wranglers, and polished boots.

Down the aisle from him, Neil Blaylock and his wife sat like statues. In fact, most of the congregants lent a serious tone to their worship. Dodd wished he could've heard the previous minister once or twice, just to know what the church was used to, but no matter, he'd preach where the Lord led him. Dodd smiled. He had been curious about the Trapp elders hiring him without ever hearing him preach, but now he marveled at himself accepting the job without asking if the pews were cushioned.

Twenty minutes later, two eight-foot-long tables laden with casserole dishes occupied the front sidewalk, and Charlie Mendoza stood nearby, preparing to address the congregation with the other two elders. The night before at the Blaylocks' cookout, Dodd had gotten to know all of them better as Charlie supplied a running narrative, boasting that all three men had been members of the congregation since the cradle-roll class. Dodd went home that night knowing more about the church leaders than some of his own cousins.

Eighty-three-year-old Lee Roy Goodnight, the oldest of the three, had been an elder for thirty-five years. According to Charlie, his health might be failing, but not his heart or mind. Lee Roy grasped a cane with one wrinkled hand and raised the other to get everyone's attention. As conversations tapered, Dodd strained to hear the man's raspy voice. "We welcome Dodd Cunningham to our fellowship today, along with his mother, Milla, and brother, Grady. Dodd, you have a pair of big shoes to fill, but after such a fine sermon, I'd say the Trapp congregation is blessed to have you in our pulpit." His speech seemed to tire him, and he wiped the corner of his mouth with a cloth handkerchief.

Neil Blaylock spoke next, standing straight with one thumb hooked through a loop near his silver belt buckle. "I've gotten to know Dodd over the past few days, and I'm impressed with the man." He grinned, white teeth against tan skin. "He may be young, but that's to our advantage, because we can raise him like we want."

The congregation tittered, but Charlie's voice carried over them. "Dodd's daddy and I attended college together, and I can vouch he comes from good people. Don't take my word for it, though. Get to know him. I'd say the man can take care of himself. Amen?"

He received a chorus of responses, giving Dodd yet another reason to like him.

"Since we all agree the new preacher is a dandy," Charlie said, "let's get down to business and pray for the cooking." He paused, then lowered his voice. "Dear Lord, we thank You for this food, and we ask that You would bless it. In Jesus's name. Amen."

Dodd barely had time to bow his head before the prayer ended. "That's my kind of blessing," he mumbled. As he stood in the churchyard, the herbaceous scent of lasagna caused his stomach to protest, and he stepped toward Lee Roy as the line dwindled. "I'm overwhelmed by the church's response, Lee Roy."

The older man waved a gnarled hand. “You won’t find a better group of people on the whole of God’s green earth.”

“I believe you’re right.” Dodd stepped to Lee Roy’s other side to avoid a red-ant bed.

“And don’t worry, you’ll pick up on how we do things here. You’re young and adaptable.”

Dodd hesitated. “Anything in particular?”

“It’s a fact we read from the King James here in Trapp.” He leaned heavily on his cane, and Dodd noticed the old man had stirred the ants into a maelstrom. “If it was good enough for Paul, it’s good enough for us.” Lee Roy chuckled at his own cleverness.

“I like the NIV myself,” Dodd said, steering Lee Roy to a safer location. “But sometimes I pull out the King James or the Revised Standard for comparison.”

Lee Roy blinked twice. “We use the King James.”

“Um … yes, sir.”

A whiff of yeast washed between them as Emily Sanders appeared at his elbow, pulling apart a roll. She bit off a minuscule section.

Lee Roy nodded at Dodd, frowned at Emily, then hobbled away.

“Aren’t you eating?” Emily swung from side to side as she nibbled.

“I was just getting in line.” When Emily followed, he did his best to make small talk. “So, have Fawn and Tyler been dating long?”

“Forever. They’re perfect together. Everybody says so. Dad calls them two peas in a pod, them having so much in common. Or their families, that is. Mom says Byron Cruz is as powerful in Scurry County as Neil Blaylock is here in Garza County.” Her speech accelerated. “Sometimes I wonder at them ever getting married. Not that they are, but can you imagine? It would be like thunder and lightning, or firecrackers and sparklers, or … or … Prince William and Kate." She smiled dreamily before she gasped, possibly realizing her show of emotion had gone overboard. "I'll go save you a seat." She scampered away.

Dodd picked up a paper plate and fanned himself as he loosened his tie. The unofficial dress code might not be a bad idea after all. As he loaded his plate with lasagna, green-bean casserole, and fried chicken, Emily's mother—an older, plumper version of Emily—positioned herself across the table, filling her own plate with seconds.

"I see you've taken notice of my sweet Emily," she said.

Dodd reached for a deviled egg, opting to keep his mouth shut.

"She's a good student, mostly As and Bs, and she can cook better than I could at that age. I don't know where she gets it." The woman paused long enough to heap a spoonful of mashed potatoes on her plate. "She's been helping with the toddler's Sunday school class for two years now, babysitting for four."

Dodd hesitated at the napkins and worked one out from under the glass casserole lid that prevented the stack from blowing to New Mexico. "I'm sure you're proud of your daughter, Mrs. Sanders."

"She'll make a fine wife." The woman hit a serving spoon firmly against a dish to release a blob of macaroni and cheese. "She'll be graduating this year. Been thinking of going on to college, but she'd rather just settle down with a strong Christian man and birth a houseful of little ones."

Dodd's paper plate wobbled. "I'll be working at the high school, Mrs. Sanders. I don't think it's appropriate—"

"Excellent sermon this morning, Brother Cunningham." She grinned knowingly as she sailed away from him.

Dodd reached for a plastic fork and stabbed it into his lasagna. Trapp, Texas, with all its quirks, was going to take some getting used to, but he was determined to make the best of it. He chuckled, thinking he'd be more at home on Mars, but people were the same no matter what planet they called home, so he didn't doubt he could do the Lord's work. He lifted his chin and walked confidently toward Charlie Mendoza and Neil Blaylock.

"I'm expected to use the King James Version," Dodd said as he backed his mother's SUV out of the parking space. "I don't mind, of course." He scratched his head. "Apparently the NIV isn't allowed."

"Neither are slacks," his mother said.

"Wranglers and boots," added Grady from the backseat. "We may need to go shopping."

She clucked her tongue. "I'd hate to commit a social blunder so soon."

Grady thrust his head over the front seat. "Like preaching from the NIV in your first sermon? Talk about a bad impression."

Milla thumped him, but Grady stayed where he was, resting his elbows on the back of her seat.

"Mom, did you hear? Dodd's dating Emily Sanders."

Dodd groaned. His brother's words were meant to tease, but anxiety washed across him in waves.

"Grady, leave your brother alone. He has enough on his mind without worrying about an immature girl." Milla snapped her sun visor down and found him in the mirror. "By the way, aren't you glad you'll know a few people on the first day at your new school?"

"It will help." The leather of the seat cushion made a shushing sound as Grady slouched back.

Dodd welcomed the change in topic. "We met a football player at the grocery store the other night. Luis is in ninth grade, so he won't be in Grady's classes, but at least he'll be another familiar face."

"The girl's the one I want in my classes," Grady said, "but she's out of school. What was her name?"

Ruthie. The woman had scrubbed that cash register as though it were infested with anthrax. And as she worked, her dark hair swung just above her waist. Dodd cleared his throat. "Ruth, I think."

"That's not right," Grady said. "I remember thinking it wasn't quite biblical." He snapped his fingers. "Ruthie. Almost biblical, but not quite." He quieted as they made a right turn at the town's lone traffic light. "She seemed a little prickly."

Prickly might not be the best word to describe Ruthie, but as Dodd parked the SUV in front of the little pink house, he entertained more appropriate adjectives. Like *captivating*. He grabbed his Bible from the console and slammed the door, realizing the best word to describe her was *gorgeous*, in an unaware, small-town way.

His mother and Grady went in the house, but Dodd sat on the stoop and rested his Bible on the cool cement next to him. He needed to sort things out. His mother and Grady? Top priorities. The church? Equally important. His new job? Paramount. But women? He'd been so consumed with responsibilities lately, he hadn't had time to consider the opposite sex. Too many people were depending on him.

But as he remembered Ruthie lifting her hair off her slender neck and tilting her head from side to side, he decided it wouldn't hurt to get to know her. Even though she hadn't been at church that morning, she still might be a believer. And if he didn't do something just for himself, the pressure of his responsibilities would buckle him.

He reached for his Bible. Tomorrow afternoon he'd go by the United, and with a little luck, he might run into Ruthie again.

CHAPTER FIVE

"Morning, little cousin. Ever see the ex-convict?"

The scent of hazelnut coffee filled the high school office as JohnScott set his travel mug on my desk. "Not a sign of him all weekend." Swiveling in my office chair, I reached for the mug, knocking my name plaque to the floor.

Ruthie Turner—attendance clerk.

Darn that faux-wood block. Not only did it represent my shallow attempt to enter the business world, but it also served as proof I still resided in Trapp, still worked two jobs, and still lived at home. As JohnScott returned the plastic reminder to my desk, I sipped from his mug and told myself to be proud I had a name plaque at all.

He shuffled to his teacher mailbox and sifted through its contents. "Maybe Clyde Felton doesn't eat food."

"Maybe he came in the store on my off hours."

"Maybe he's an alien, brain-sucking zombie."

I smiled at my cousin. He was the first person I saw every morning. The hall lights would flicker, one at a time, and I would know he had entered the building, unlocking the doors and getting the air running in the gym before coming by the office to check on me. He treated me like a child, but I didn't mind. He was six years older and had been checking on me since elementary school. In fact, the hardest years of my life came when JohnScott attended college, and I still thanked the Lord he hadn't gone farther than Lubbock.

JohnScott inclined his head toward the door behind my desk and raised an eyebrow.

"He's early today."

Surprisingly, the principal had arrived before either of us and shut himself in his office. Judging by the muffled drone coming from under his door, I assumed he was already on the phone.

JohnScott sat on the corner of my desk and crossed his arms "Did I miss any news this weekend?"

"Not really. I think Friday's megagossip event exhausted the merry citizens."

"Might be a blessing."

I waved an interoffice memo. "The school board finally hired a math teacher to replace Mr. Rodriguez."

"About time. School started two weeks ago." He reached for a pen and clicked it with his thumb. "That substitute was a sweet lady, but she didn't know the first thing about calculus or trig. So who'd they hire? The woman from Sweetwater?"

"Doesn't say, but I figure either her or Wilmer's oldest son."

JohnScott clicked the pen repeatedly until I swatted him in annoyance, and then he tossed it back on the desk. "Neither of them will do a lick to increase our test scores, but they're better than nothing. By the way, you saw the Cunningham boy Friday night. He could replace Tinker, right?"

At the mention of the name Cunningham, dread settled over me like a swarm of gnats. "Like I would know."

"Well, he's obviously athletic. Even if he's never played ball before, I could train him to run."

"Oh, he's played before."

JohnScott raised his palms. "You were saying?"

I dug through my desk drawer, searching for a nail file and wishing we could talk about something else. Even though I had told JohnScott about Dodd being the preacher, I never got around to telling him about our conversation. Or my sappy smile. It was simply too humiliating, even for JohnScott.

I located an emery board. "I don't know anything about football or Tinker or replacements, but I heard Grady Cunningham tell Luis Vega he played in junior high but hadn't decided if he wanted to play for us or not."

"In that case, he will." JohnScott took a swig of coffee. "What can I bribe him with?"

I focused on a fingernail, running the file lightly across a rough spot. "You could offer him a free haircut. Both he and the preacher are shaggy."

"Yeah, that's the city. It'll wear off."

The principal, closeted in his office behind me, burst into laughter, causing me to wonder who was on the phone with him so early in the morning.

JohnScott moved to the other side of the counter, leaned on his elbows, and scrutinized me. "What do you want on your homecoming mum? The usual bells and whistles?"

My hands fell to my lap. The homecoming game would be the hoopla of the football season, and every female under thirty would be wearing a huge white flower bedecked with glitter, beads, and braided ribbon. "I told you I don't want one. It's a high school thing."

"No, it's not. The college girls have them too."

"I'm not a college girl."

"Well, Mom's made you a mum every year since you were thirteen. She's not stopping now."

"She didn't my sophomore year. I had a date."

"I wouldn't count that kid as a date, and his flower barely classified as a mum, but whatever you say."

Behind me, the office door opened, but I didn't turn around. I was too busy frowning at JohnScott.

Nelson Andrews, our gray-haired principal, breezed past my desk. "Ruthie, I apologize for the short notice, but could you get our new math teacher the necessary forms for insurance and what have you?" Nelson greeted JohnScott with a brief "Coach" before turning to face me. But he looked over my head to his office door behind my back. "Mr. Cunningham, this is Ruthie Turner. She keeps our attendance records, organizes employee files, and performs a million other tasks. She'll get you fixed up."

What did he say?

The principal gazed at me expectantly, and when I didn't react, he motioned to his office door. "Ruthie, like I said, this is our new math teacher."

Ice water flooded my veins as I rotated my chair.

Sure enough, Dodd Cunningham stood in the doorway behind me, dressed in khakis and a black polo. From his expression, I'd say he was as surprised to see me as I was to see him.

"Hi." I felt small and insignificant.

"Hello again." He spoke in his CEO tone, but a bothersome smile played at his lips. It disappeared when he looked at Nelson. "We've met."

"Oh, right … the United," the principal said. "Anyway, this is JohnScott Pickett, history teacher slash football coach. Couldn't survive without him."

JohnScott stepped forward and extended his hand while Dodd said, "Dodd Cunningham. Good to meet you."

As the three men talked, I calmed my racing nerves. So the new preacher would be working at the high school. No big deal. I could handle this.

Slipping to the filing cabinet where the employee documents were kept, I considered the preacher's actions on Friday night. I still couldn't make sense of him talking to me, and I speculated on his motives. Probably he was simply being nosy, probing my sinful heart out of curiosity and making fun of me in the process. That was only a half step beyond the treatment I normally received from the local Christians. Still, the thought made me as furious as Uncle Ansel's Angus bull.

Retrieving the forms from a file folder, I slid the drawer closed with a clank, drawing Dodd's attention. He smiled at me before returning his gaze to the principal.

Nelson tapped the counter with a knuckle. "By the way, Coach, the jerseys came in, but I think they're wrong again." He reached for the door. "The shipment's in the library. Let's take a look before I notify the Booster Club. They're likely to throw a hissy fit."

"Can hardly blame them." JohnScott followed the principal but winked at me, wordlessly conveying, *We'll talk later, little cousin*. Then he called over his shoulder, "Welcome to Trapp High School, Dodd."

"Thank you." The preacher studied the door as it closed behind JohnScott, then looked at me curiously. "Miss Turner, is it?"

Nobody called me Miss Turner except the kindergartners down at the elementary school, but I didn't bother explaining. It didn't feel right for him to call me Ruthie anyway. Too familiar. I held a document toward him. "Here's the form to sign up for medical, dental, and vision."

He took the paper from me, not looking at it. "Does the district offer life-insurance coverage?" His eyes twinkled.

I lifted another paper. "Life insurance and accidental death."

He studied the page before lifting his gaze. "Those two always seem backward." He chuckled. "If life insurance pays when you die, shouldn't it be called death insurance?"

I'd heard that one before.

"And accidental death? That's death insurance for when I *accidentally* die. As though life insurance only pays if I die on purpose, which of course, is the one time it wouldn't pay." He narrowed his eyes. "Doesn't make sense, really."

With a sinking feeling, I realized he was still strangely conversational. *What a twist.* After thirteen years of despising the way church people ignored me, I now wished one of them would. I thrust another paper at him. "Here's the form for cancer coverage."

"Ah, cancer." His voice suddenly returned to business, but he didn't take the paper.

Oh great. His dad probably died from cancer. That would explain the insurance jokes. I shuffled the form to the bottom of the pile. "And here's a form to have your paycheck automatically deposited into your checking account, but only if you bank here in town."

He nodded.

"Have you opened an account downtown?" I felt obliged to draw him out of his shadowy mood even if I didn't like him. "You'll actually get your money a day earlier that way."

"I'll add it to the top of my to-do list. Right along with getting extra keys made and purchasing adequate window coverings."

I smiled to myself when I thought about the current window coverings in the parsonage. Apparently Old Man Dunbar and his wife saw no reason to bother with privacy in their living areas. Maybe they thought it gave their house a welcoming glow, but anytime I walked past at nighttime, I would see them in there, leaning back in matching recliners or hobbling around in bathrobes. Once I even saw them kissing, which was not as titillating as it sounds, since they were already in their eighties.

"Window coverings?" I said. "Walmart over in Lubbock carries vinyl miniblinds for five bucks a pop."

"I like that price tag." He perched on the corner of my desk I habitually kept cleared for JohnScott. "In the meantime, we're using Grady's old Buzz Lightyear sheets from his preschool days. To think Mom almost threw them out before the move."

I raised an eyebrow. "That would only take care of two windows. Tell the truth. Whose sheets are covering the others?"

He leaned his head back. "All right, I confess. My Ninja Turtle sheets might be on the kitchen windows."

"All right, then."

He crossed his arms and peered down at me, but said nothing. Then he briefly inspected the items on my desk before glancing at the computer screen, all the while smiling like Curious George.

Oh my goodness. He was doing it again. Watching me. Studying me. Talking to me until my defenses were down. And I had fallen for it again.

I bent over the bottom drawer of my desk, letting my hair fall around my face. "Here's a folder for your forms." I said it curtly, refusing to return his invasive smile. "And I've included a pamphlet that explains the details of the insurance coverage." I held the folder toward him, but when it trembled in my hand, I tossed it quickly on the desk next to his hip. "There's also a website. And you can sign up online if you don't want to fill out the papers."

"Thank you." He said the words cautiously as though sensing my mood change, then stood and distanced himself from my desk.

"That should be everything, Mr. Cunningham." I lifted a corner of my mouth, not able to muster a complete smile. "Let me know if you need anything else." I focused on my computer screen, but he didn't move.

"Um … Miss Turner?"

The way he said *Miss Turner* grated on my nerves. "What is it?"

"I apologize, but I haven't the slightest idea where my classroom is."

Shame immediately replaced my tension. Of course he wouldn't know his way around the school, and it was my job to make him feel welcome. "It's on the left, past the teachers' lounge."

His eyes laughed. "And where might the teachers' lounge be?"

I glanced at the wall clock and stood, giving in. "Sounds like you need the ten-cent tour."

He opened the door, then followed me into the hall, where I stood in front of the trophy cases. Only a few minutes remained before the bell, so I would have to make this quick. "The library is on the left halfway down the side hall." I pointed. "Past the library, all the way to the end, is the gym. The students gather there before the first bell rings, and teachers take turns monitoring them each morning. I'll add you to the rotation."

He nodded. "What's the high school enrollment?"

"Around two hundred." I motioned toward the gym again. "If you go out that door, you'll be headed toward the ag barn and the baseball field. Beyond that is the middle school and elementary." I paused as JohnScott and Nelson came out the library door and turned toward the gym. "Any questions?"

Dodd watched the two men. "Nothing to speak of. So what's down the front hall?"

He followed me a quarter of the way down the hall as I jangled my keys to unlock a door. "Teachers' lounge." When he nodded, I closed the door and motioned to a nook just past the doorway. "Vending machines."

"Score," he said under his breath.

"Like soft drinks, do you?" I opened his classroom door.

"If you cut me, I'd bleed Dr Pepper." He scanned the room before walking to the teacher's desk. He pulled open a side drawer, found it empty, and inserted his benefits folder. Next he opened the middle drawer and discovered a lesson-plan book. "Right where Mr. Andrews said it would be." He laid the book in the middle of the desk and gave it three soft pats before returning to my side. "I feel like I've got my security blanket now. So what else is down this hallway?"

We stood outside his room, and I pointed again. "The Family and Consumer Science kitchen is three doors down."

"That could be interesting."

I smiled without pausing. "The cafeteria is at the end of the hall, on the right, and if you exit the door at the end, the field house is around the corner. The weight room is in a separate, smaller building adjacent to it."

My gaze fell to his bicep, where I noticed a bruise, but his loose shirtsleeves prevented me from assessing his muscles.

For crying out loud. Why would I want to anyway? This man was the preacher. The last person on earth I should be casing. I glanced back to his face—a safe place to rest my gaze—but his eyes seemed to be making a slow circuit from my forehead to my ear to my chin. I might not have dated often or lately, but I recognized that look.

Disgust welled inside me, and I had the urge to spit in his face. Did he think because of Momma's reputation, I would melt into his arms like common trash? I gritted my teeth.

He took a step back and coughed. "Thanks for the tour, Miss Turner. I'd better look over my lesson plans before the students arrive."

"Probably a good idea." I spun on my heel and marched back to the office.

CHAPTER SIX

My jack-of-all-trades job at the school kept me running across our small campus, sometimes from the elementary building all the way to the middle school, but at lunchtime I always made it back to the high school teachers' lounge to eat my sack lunch with JohnScott. Typically, only a handful of teachers joined us, since most ate in their classrooms, but on that day, at least eight showed up to check out the new math teacher.

When Dodd entered the room carrying a Dr Pepper and a cafeteria hamburger, he glanced at me. His eye contact sent a shiver across my shoulders, but I ignored it and unwrapped my tuna sandwich. The preacher's pretty face may have given me a gut reaction, but his alleged faith rendered a much stronger negative one.

My idiot cousin called to him. "Hey, Dodd Cunningham, new math teacher. Meet Lonnie Lombard, old ag teacher."

"I'm not that old." The ag teacher, sitting across from JohnScott, reached up to shake Dodd's hand. "Not much older than you, JohnScott. And even if I was, I look younger by a long shot."

JohnScott rubbed the top of Lonnie's bald head. "You keep telling yourself that."

Lonnie laughed. "Dodd, have a seat, why don't ya?"

I glared at my tuna. If Dodd sat down with us, I would fabricate a stomachache and leave.

He hesitated. "Thank you, but I believe someone's keeping an open seat for me at the back table."

"Well, don't be a stranger," JohnScott said. "Come back and visit occasionally."

As Dodd walked away, JohnScott gave me a disapproving frown. I knew what my cousin was thinking. Even though the preacher somehow reminded me of thirteen years of animosity with the church, JohnScott would insist I treat the man civilly. I didn't intend to be rude, but I certainly planned to keep a comfortable distance, so I looked straight into JohnScott's eyes and bit my sandwich forcefully.

Dodd sat at the back table, surrounded by women, only one of whom was single. Maria Fuentes, the thirty-something Family and Consumer Science teacher, appeared to be working a plan. The rest of the women exhibited curiosity laced with self-control that prevented them from gawking.

Sipping my canned Sprite, I studied the man. Maybe he was more attractive than I'd given him credit for. His hair had that nice, almost-curly look—even if it did need a trim—and his clothes suited him. The black polo set off his dark hair.

The preacher's eyes met mine, and he returned my smile.

Horrified, I immediately scowled, but much to my irritation, his demeanor only faded slightly and took on an amused tint.

Turning to JohnScott and Lonnie, I focused on their discussion with rapt attention. My cousin and I spent many lunch hours with the ag teacher, who loved to needle our conservative views, so it only took a few seconds for me to catch the gist of their debate. Today's topic was World War II Germany.

"… but the Nazis thought they were doing the right thing." Lonnie laughed as he spoke to JohnScott. "They had good intentions and were honestly trying to make the world a better place. They were nuts, of course, but you have to give them credit for sticking to their beliefs."

I shook my head. "That's absurd. The Nazis lost all concept of right and wrong, trying to boost themselves to a higher status."

Lonnie scrutinized me out of the corner of his eye. "But, Ruthie, who are you to say what's right and wrong?"

"I don't have to say it." I gripped my sandwich baggie. "There's an unspoken authority dictating moral values. Any six-year-old would know what the Nazis did was atrocious."

He shrugged. "I don't believe in all that God stuff."

"I didn't mention God, but I see you recognize it for what it is."

JohnScott whistled. "Now you've got her wound up. We'll never get her to hush."

I stuck out my tongue at my cousin as the crowd at the back table burst into laughter. They passed a cell phone around, looking at something on the screen, but Dodd paid no attention. In fact, he seemed lost in thought. And he was studying *me*.

Surely this wouldn't be my high school nightmare all over again. Fawn snubbing me in the cafeteria. Dodd snubbing me in the teachers' lounge. I crumpled my paper sack as Lonnie left the room.

As soon as we were alone at our table, JohnScott leaned toward me. "The Cunninghams don't look like a typical preacher's family, do they?"

"What do preachers' families look like?"

"Dorky, I guess."

"Coke-bottle glasses?"

He smiled and shook his head. "The Cunninghams appear almost normal."

"Almost?"

"Well, I don't know if Grady's playing football."

I shoved him and thoughtlessly glanced to the back of the room. The Family and Consumer Science teacher seemed to be trying to keep the preacher's attention, but he paid her no mind. Instead, his gaze traveled back and forth between JohnScott and me as though he were analyzing a trigonometry problem.

"Hey there, Ruthie-the-checker-girl." Grady Cunningham took the computer next to mine in Mrs. Steen's fifth period Information Systems class, and I cringed. Working as a teacher's aide, where I quietly graded homework, was usually a welcome respite, but as Grady slid into the station next to mine, dismay pressed on my shoulders like Aunt Velma's polyester shawl. I jiggled the mouse until my old monitor crackled to life, but Grady continued. "The teacher says I should sit here so you can help me catch up with the rest of the class."

I reached for a file folder containing the teacher's grading sheet and jerked the paper so briskly that it sliced the tip of my finger. "Why are you even in this class?" It didn't come out like I intended, but Information Systems was generally for freshmen and sophomores, and Grady was a senior.

His mouth curved in an easy smile. "We lived in a small town in Mexico my freshman and sophomore years, and computer classes weren't an option."

I studied him silently, putting all the pieces together.

"Well, not Dodd," he added. "He never lived in Mexico."

I dropped my gaze to the answer sheet, but when Grady didn't turn away, curiosity compelled me to ask, "Why did you live there?"

"We were serving as missionaries. My dad had a love for the Mexican people." A dismal expression fell over him, but then he perked up again. "I guess you heard my ugly brother is Trapp High School's new math teacher."

My face warmed, and then the warmth slid down to my shoulders.

Grady chuckled. "Or don't you think he's ugly?"

The bell rang to begin class. *Thank God.*

After Mrs. Steen lectured, Grady began his assignment but soon stretched his legs and positioned his high-dollar sneakers on the edge of my chair as though settling in for a comfortable interview.

I concentrated on grading.

"This school is different from my old school, but I like it. How long have you lived here?" He talked as funny as his brother, enunciating every word.

"Always."

"No kidding? It would be great to live in one place your whole life. We've moved around, what with my dad's work and all." He cleared his throat. "Have you ever been to church?"

Did he truly just ask me that? By now he'd undoubtedly heard about my past with the church—the accusations against Momma, the informal expulsion, the mounting rumors—so his question rubbed like a saddle sore. I met his gaze. "I've been there."

"I guess in a town as small as Trapp, everybody comes to church sometime, right?"

While he finally focused on his assignment, I stared blindly at my computer screen and contemplated the kid. He and his brother couldn't be more different. Grady chattered nonstop like a lifelong friend, but Dodd spoke deliberately and observed my reactions. *And watched me.*

With a sigh, I shut out all thoughts of the preacher and his brother. One more hour, and I could leave the high school and head to my evening job. At least at the United, I'd be free from the Cunningham frenzy.

Or so I thought.

CHAPTER SEVEN

When I arrived at the store, Aunt Velma stood in the produce section in her seersucker housedress, and I rubbed my hand across her back, inhaling the scent of Pond's cold cream.

"Girl, you coming to our house this weekend?" she asked.

"I've got to work Saturday morning, and besides I don't want you to make an extra trip to town, just to bring me in."

"Don't have much else to do."

That wasn't true. Aunt Velma and Uncle Ansel had a farm with more than enough work, even with JohnScott's help. Besides, my uncle was pushing seventy and moved slower than a horned lizard on a cold day.

I smiled at Velma and consented. "Pick me up after work on Saturday."

"Bring your momma, you hear?"

A nice thought, but we both knew it wouldn't happen. Every evening, Momma came home from the diner, plopped in front of the television, and watched reality TV until bedtime. But I wasn't complaining. She'd been waitressing at the diner for five months, and I thought maybe she'd finally found a good fit.

Emily Sanders, one of Fawn's churchy young groupies, pushed a cart past us, checking items off her mother's list. Her eyes slid over me, but she grinned at my aunt.

Velma pointed with a banana. "Emily, honey, those peaches over by the water fountain are nice and ripe. You get some so your mother can make you a peach cobbler."

"Thanks, Ms. Pickett."

"But watch out for the cantaloupe 'cause they're squishy. Won't last till suppertime."

I tied my apron around my waist. "Time for me to man the register. See you in a minute."

When I turned, I almost collided with a woman in a light-blue pantsuit. *A pantsuit?* I instantly recognized the stranger as Mrs. Cunningham. Even if I hadn't been able to identify her by the process of elimination, I would've known her because she looked so much like Grady. I excused myself and strode to the register twenty feet away, where I grabbed a handful of coupons and pretended to be busy.

My aunt scanned the woman up and down. "Bless your heart. You must be the minister's mother."

"Yes." The woman stuck out her hand, but Velma didn't notice. Women didn't really shake hands in Trapp, and Mrs. Cunningham was bound to figure that out soon enough.

"Velma Pickett," my aunt said with a nod. "My husband Ansel's a farmer-rancher. Your boys will know my son, JohnScott, from school. Coach Pickett? Anyhow, I've got eight more kids grown. We're not churchgoers but don't begrudge those who are." She stretched the truth with that last statement, but Velma always said what people didn't know wouldn't hurt them.

Mrs. Cunningham had Grady's smile, but her speech wasn't as attention-deficit as her son's. "My name is Milla Cunningham," she said. "We're from Fort Worth, but my husband and I worked as missionaries for several years."

"Husband?"

Milla rustled her shopping list. "He died last year."

"Sorry to hear that." Velma's attitude softened, and she lowered her head in condolence while the preacher's mother seemed to force a smile.

"Things sure are different here."

"That so?" Velma said. "I bet you'll get used to it directly."

I peeked over the edge of a coupon and watched as Milla Cunningham steeled herself.

She leaned toward Velma and was about to say something when Emily charged around the corner, sending an apple rolling across the floor.

"Mrs. Cunningham, how are you?" Emily bubbled. "Are you getting settled?"

Velma shoved her grocery cart toward the okra and away from the ensuing hugs.

"Well, the boxes are unpacked."

Emily stood so close that I thought she might knock the lady down. "My parents raved about the sermon yesterday. They said Dodd made the Bible easy to understand." She giggled. "Dad said he's going to be a better preacher than Brother Dunbar."

"Oh my." Milla fumbled with her necklace.

"Is it all right for me to call him Dodd?" asked Emily. "Because if you think I should call him Brother Cunningham, you say the word.

Or Mr. Cunningham, if that's best. Though Mom insisted we know each other well enough to go by first names. But whatever you think is what I'll do, Milla."

The woman's silence accentuated Emily's rant, and I almost laughed. To cover, I studied an expiration date on a Tide coupon.

Milla seemed sorry to rain on Emily's infatuation parade. "I suppose 'Mr. Cunningham' might be more appropriate, since he's one of your teachers now."

"Oh my goodness, you're right. It's just that I don't think of him that way, you know?"

Milla's expression was utter patience, but the way her left hand gripped the shopping cart made me think she wouldn't mind grabbing Emily by the shoulders and giving her a shake.

The teenager blubbered on. "I heard you and your husband went to college with Charlie Mendoza back in the day. He and his wife are so sweet. And now you've met the Blaylocks, too. Mom says Neil Blaylock is as close to an apostle as you can get—"

Fortunately, another shopper came to check out, providing a reason for me to ignore the rest of Emily's drivel. By the time I had the customer out the door, Milla Cunningham had disappeared into the depths of the store, and Emily stood in front of me.

"Good afternoon," I said. "Did you find everything all right?"

"Mm-hmm."

Not so talkative now.

Emily craned her neck to search out the window at nothing and then studied a pack of gum as if she was memorizing the content label. When her gaze bounced from the label to me, I pretended not to notice.

I felt sorry for her in a way. She didn't have a mean thought in her empty head, but she had always been a follower, and she'd jump off the Caprock Escarpment if everyone else decided to. She habitually ignored me, of course, but I always felt her heart wasn't in it.

"That'll be seventeen dollars and twelve cents."

Emily handed me a twenty and mumbled, "Keep the change."

She scooped up her plastic bags and sped out the door before my brain processed what she had said. *Keep the change?* That would be almost three dollars. Enough for a burger from the Dairy Queen. As I stuffed the money in the front pocket of my jeans, I considered whether Emily was trying to be nice or simply wanted to get out of the store and away from me.

"That girl's a mess." Velma rattled her shopping cart toward me. "Talked the Cunningham woman's ears clean off."

I scanned a can of pork and beans as Velma lowered her voice. "The preacher's mother seems like a nice lady, but you can't judge the buttermilk by the color of the cow. Could still be soured." She leaned toward me. "What are the sons like?"

I pictured Dodd sitting on the corner of my desk, but I forced the image away with a shrug. "The same."

"Boy hidy," Velma muttered. "I bet they caused fruit-basket turnover up at the school."

"You'd have thought they were painted fluorescent orange the way everyone carried on."

She dug through her handbag. "You heard whether the kid's playing ball?"

"No idea." Her groceries filled six plastic bags. "You want me to call Luis to take these out for you? He's hiding in the back."

"That boy …" Velma reached across the counter to push the Talk button on the intercom. "Luis Vega, you get yourself out here and help an old woman with her bags, you hear?"

At the back of the store, the swinging metal door slammed against the freezer case.

"Coming, Mizz Pickett!"

Velma snapped her purse closed. "I'll see you on Saturday, Ruthie. Peach cobbler." Then she swept out the door, with Luis running to catch up.

What would I do without Aunt Velma? Since my childhood, she had comforted my tears and praised my successes. She taught me to cook, enlightened me about the birds and the bees, and educated me on proper dating etiquette. My heart warmed as she stomped across the parking lot in her Crocs, and I turned to smile at my newest customer.

Milla Cunningham eased her basket onto the counter, then clasped her hands at her waist. "You must be Ruthie."

A muscle on the side of my neck twitched.

None of the employees at the United wore nametags—why would we?—so I wondered at her knowing my name. "Yes, ma'am." I hurried with her groceries, setting my face in an expression of deep concentration as though I couldn't be interrupted. It didn't work.

"I'm Milla Cunningham."

She waited for me to speak, and I racked my mind for something to say. *You make me uncomfortable. What have you heard about me, other than my name? Would you mind shopping when I'm not on duty?* I opted for something more civil. "Hi."

"I've heard about you."

That much was obvious.

"From my sons," she added. "They said they met you Friday night."

Her groceries fit into two bags, and I positioned them on the end of the counter. "That'll be twenty dollars and seventy-six cents."

She scanned a debit card and punched in her PIN. "See you later, Ruthie."

"Have a good evening, ma'am."

I fiddled with the plastic-bag dispenser until she was out the door, and then I watched her walk to her car, a dark-red SUV. She was a pretty woman with a stylish haircut that immediately put her out of place in Trapp, but she wasn't made up fake, and her pantsuit wasn't overly fancy.

She seemed harmless enough, but I wasn't about to trust her. I couldn't help remembering Velma's buttermilk comment.

Time would tell.

CHAPTER EIGHT

JohnScott was the best cousin in the world. Even though I had yet to lay eyes on Clyde Felton, the rumors still made me nervous, and I saw no reason to risk running into the rapist on my own. So at closing time, my cousin picked me up again. As he eased his truck down Main Street, one hand on the steering wheel, the other lolling out the open window, he looked sideways at me. "What do you think of the new family?"

Truth be told, the name Cunningham was beginning to nauseate me. "This town is obsessed."

JohnScott read my thoughts. "It's sort of nauseating, but I get the feeling they're good people."

He pulled to the curb in front of my house and killed the ignition. We sat in silence while I contemplated the overly friendly behavior of all three Cunninghams and wondered *why they were so nice to me.*

"I like the math teacher." JohnScott spoke as though he were thinking out loud. "But I can't figure him being a preacher."

I didn't answer.

"That bother you?" he asked.

"Should it?" The breeze tossed a strand of my hair across my neck, and I flicked it over my shoulder.

"That answers my question, I guess."

Sometimes it seemed pointless for JohnScott and me to bother speaking. We understood each other without words.

"Little cousin ..." He gave me a reproachful look.

"What?"

"Today at lunch. Nazis? Really?"

I examined the house. Momma had forgotten the porch light again. "Nazis, Christians, whatever."

He sighed. "Not the same, Ruthie."

"Okay, but if the Cunninghams are so nice, why do I feel like they're talking about me?"

He grazed his palm along the steering wheel. "I don't know about that. They're just different somehow, but I can't decide if they're different in a good way or a bad way." He shifted to lean against the door, laying his arm across the back of the dusty seat. "You know, today at practice, Grady paraded around the field house meeting all the guys, even the ones most players ignore."

"The kid could talk a hole in a cement block."

"Yeah, but it's more than that. He was trying to remember everyone's name and position."

The porch light flicked on, illuminating the sparse grass and weedy flower bed, and Momma opened the door, still wearing her brown polyester uniform from the diner. Her long hair was wadded into a messy bun on top of her head, and she wore house shoes. "Is that you and JohnScott, Ruth Ann?"

The truck sat fifteen feet from the porch, so I answered without raising my voice. "It's us, Momma."

Ambling across the yard, she asked, "You hear about the new folks?" She rested one hand on the rearview mirror outside my window, the other on her hip.

I grunted. "And nothing else."

She crossed her arms, exhaustion showing in her eyes. "You kids be careful with them."

"Aw, Aunt Lynda," JohnScott teased, "we don't even know them yet."

"All I'm saying is watch out. I don't want no family of mine getting dragged through the mud."

I squeezed the handle that rolled up the window. Even though I agreed with her, I wished she would stop treating me like a teenager. "We know, Momma."

She gave me a final lingering look before turning toward the house.

JohnScott called after her, "Thanks, Aunt Lynda."

She paused at the door but didn't turn around, and then the screen slammed behind her.

That was Momma. A living Eeyore. Except Momma was beautiful on the outside. She attracted lots of attention from men in town, which only made her more grumpy, since most of them were married.

I rested my elbow on the doorframe of the truck. "Remember when she was happy?"

JohnScott reached across the truck to finger a strand of my hair, tugging gently.

We sat in silence. Moths already swarmed the porch light, tapping against the glass, desperately wanting what they couldn't have. I took a deep breath and let it out, spying a tarantula picking his way across the yard on rubber-band stilts.

JohnScott murmured, “Speak of the Devil.”

I glanced at him questioningly, then noticed Dodd and Grady jogging toward us, running at a steady pace as they talked.

I reached for the door handle, but JohnScott snapped, “Ruthie, don’t.”

As the Cunninghams approached the driver’s side of the truck, Dodd called, “It’s JohnScott, right? Is this where you live?”

“Naw, this is Ruthie’s house.” JohnScott pointed his thumb toward me, and Dodd and Grady bent to look into the truck.

The preacher glanced at me, making brief eye contact before focusing his attention on something down the street.

Well, that was subtle.

Grady grinned. “Hey there, Ruthie-the-checker-girl. We meet again. I didn’t know you lived here. Our house is just a few streets over.”

He sounded ridiculous. Not only did everyone in Trapp live a few streets over, but the church had used the same house as a parsonage for as long as I could remember.

“Right, Grady,” I answered. “I know where you live.”

JohnScott tapped his fingers on the seat, warning me to behave.

“Can I ask you guys a question?” Grady said. “What’s the deal with all those cows on the edge of town?”

“You mean the feedlot?” asked JohnScott.

“That’s quite a smell you’ve got there, Coach Pickett,” Grady said.

JohnScott bobbed his head. “When the wind blows just right, it’ll knock you down.”

Grady snickered. "Maybe this town should've been named Crap instead of Trapp."

JohnScott's shoulders shook with stifled laughter, not because of what Grady said—we'd heard it a million times—but because it came from Grady. The goody-goody preacher's brother saying a dirty word. JohnScott collected himself. "You ready for the game on Friday?"

"The jury's still out," Grady admitted. "I'm not big on football, but it appears I ought to play regardless."

"Yeah," replied JohnScott. "Everybody who's anybody plays football. In Trapp, at least. No pressure or anything."

"Oh no. No pressure at all." Grady smiled. "I'm thinking it's a good deal, though. Dodd said it'll be like becoming all things to all men."

JohnScott looked from Grady to Dodd. "I'm not following you."

The screen door thumped, and Momma appeared in the doorway, sending a surge of condemnation from her heart to mine. "Ruth Ann, come in the house. Now."

Grady poked his head into the truck and whispered, "Is that your mom, Ruthie? I'd love to meet her." But the screen door had already slapped against the frame, prompting Grady to hurriedly add, "Never mind, maybe later."

I slid out of the truck, miffed at Momma but grateful to have a reason to get away. As I tramped across the yard, JohnScott and Grady continued their conversation. The teenager asked if JohnScott had ever been to church, and my cousin replied, no, his family wasn't the churchgoing type. Apparently this was Grady's standard break-the-ice question.

I looped my finger through the cool metal handle of the screen door and glanced over my shoulder. Grady leaned against the driver's-side door, but Dodd still hovered a few feet away. When our eyes met, the preacher held my gaze, as though he was going to say something, and a ripple of raw curiosity sloshed through my nerve endings, sickening me. But I waited a second or two, not wanting to seem bad mannered.

Sweat had dampened his hair, and he breathed irregularly because he'd been running. He took a half step toward me but appeared to change his mind and moved to the shadows of the truck, where he could join the discussion.

I entered the house with a shrug.

Momma lay on the couch watching a rerun. "Stay away from them, Ruth Ann."

"I will."

"They're nothing but trouble."

Getting irritated with her always produced more problems, so I perched on the arm of the couch. "Everything go all right at the diner today?"

Her eyes flashed as though I'd accused her of shoplifting. "Work went fine. Just like every other day." She grabbed the remote and punched the volume up a notch.

Why even try? Momma's depression prevented her from carrying on a normal conversation.

I moseyed into the kitchen to scrounge up a snack, settling for a bowl of Rice Krispies. After that I soaked in the bathtub until I wrinkled, then brushed my teeth and slipped on an oversize T-shirt before sliding between the bedsheets, where I lay awake pondering the day's events.

School would be back to normal tomorrow. Or at least the day after. Soon everyone would get used to the Cunninghams and stop paying them any mind. It might take longer at the United, since most of the customers didn't interact with the Cunninghams every day. They'd have to jabber the new family out of their systems. The thought made me pull my pillow over my head, but even then, Dodd Cunningham's face appeared. I pictured him as he peered in the truck at JohnScott and me.

And then he clammed up.

His silence irked me. Not because I wanted to talk to him but because he hadn't had any trouble speaking to me at the United. Or that morning in the office. And certainly not during our tour. No, he only ignored me when other people were around. A familiar cloud of inferiority pressed me into the mattress.

What was it he expected from me when nobody was around? At first I thought he considered me loose, but now I wasn't so sure. He didn't seem the type to act on that knowledge, even if it were true. Which it wasn't.

Grady, on the other hand, caused me a different dilemma. Why so chummy? Friendliness could be tricky when I didn't know what motivated it, and I suspected his kindness held underlying motives.

An hour later, as I stared at the ceiling with my jaw clenched tight, I heard JohnScott rev his truck and pull away from the house.

CHAPTER NINE

The next day JohnScott acted odd. If I hadn't known he'd talked to the preacher for so long the night before, I wouldn't have thought anything of it, but by the time I slid into his truck for our speedy shuttle to the United before practice, I was fed up with his aloof behavior.

"By the way ..." I didn't even wait until we were out of the parking lot. "I never asked you about your extended conversation with the Cunninghams last night in front of my house. Pushing two hours."

"Was it that long?" He tilted his head away from me as he made a left turn. "I guess they're the sort of people you feel like you've known for years."

"Give me a break."

"I know what you're thinking, Ruthie, but they're different."

"Like you said, that's the city. It'll wear off." I fumbled with the zipper on my purse, unzipping it a half inch, then zipping it. "So what did you talk about?"

"They were telling me about the Bible."

He said this as though it was the most normal event in the world—like the sun rising in the east and setting in the west.

"They're trying to get you to go to church."

"Honestly, they didn't mention church at all."

The thought of JohnScott sitting in a pew contradicted everything I had ever known about him, but I had to ask anyway. "Do you want to go to their church?"

He whistled through his teeth. "Of course not."

As he pulled into the United parking lot, I pondered his words. The preacher's family impressed JohnScott, which was weird. After all, we had pretty much been raised by the same woman, and Velma always warned us to tread cautiously anywhere the Bible might be lurking. "What did they say about Momma and me?"

"Nothing."

I opened the door, and the fall breeze whipped my hair across my face, slapping reality against my cheeks. "But they will."

By the time I clocked out that evening, thoughts of my cousin churned through my mind until I thought I might be sick. When I locked the United's front door behind me, I breathed deeply of the cool night air and felt an odd sense of relief that JohnScott hadn't arrived on time to pick me up. I could do without another religious confrontation. The parking lot was deserted, other than an old sedan I didn't recognize, so I took off across the asphalt at a steady clip, knowing JohnScott would see the darkened store and realize I had gone on home.

I hurried past the sedan and angled toward Fifth Street—not the shortest route to my house, but the best way to avoid JohnScott when he finally showed up. As I stepped into the shadows between streetlamps, shame niggled at my conscience, and I almost turned back. I stood motionless in the middle of the street, giving myself a pep talk. JohnScott was my best friend, but even if he was, he wasn't necessarily acting like it.

Behind me a car door moaned. Someone was in that old sedan, after all, but who? Trapp shut down on weeknights. Friday and Saturday would boast late-night activity as teenagers and young adults met in town to entertain themselves, but Tuesdays were quiet like the dead. Everyone in town knew the routine, except the Cunninghams and—

Goose bumps fingered across my neck. An out-of-style tennis shoe emerged from the car, then another, gravel gritting against asphalt as the owner pulled himself up to tower above the vehicle. *Clyde Felton.*

The humming outdoor lights of the United, partially dimmed for the evening, failed to adequately reveal the man's appearance. I could clearly see his forehead, but not his eyes. His cheekbones, but not his chin. His biceps and broad shoulders, but not his elbows or hands. He nudged the car door, closing it with an echo, then glanced casually around the parking lot before rotating his neck to examine the darkness where I stood.

Could he see me?

Slowly I backed away until my thighs pressed against the bumper of an RV parked at the curb. *But good grief.* Just because Clyde had attacked a woman before didn't mean he would do it again. Still, the shivers running down my spine compelled me to run. Compelled me to get away from him, to find JohnScott, to save myself. But my limbs were frozen.

I searched for the darkest shadow while Clyde slumped against his car, lit a cigarette, slowly lifted a hand in my direction.

The fact the rapist waved at me barely registered. He knew where I was. A streetlamp illuminated an area of pavement in front of the camper, so I slipped into the blackness behind it. Most likely, Clyde Felton could outrun me—I'd never been much of an athlete—so I crouched behind the RV as sweat trickled down my sides. One hand rested on the smooth bumper, the other splayed in sandy grit on the street.

When Clyde shoved his weight back to his feet, my nerves exploded, and I inched toward an acrid-scented plant on my left. Peeking between the fronds, I watched him drag the soles of his shoes across the pavement, covering ground rapidly because of the length of his gait. Already he approached the streetlamp, swaying toward the RV.

Ice shot through my heart when his deep, garbled voice called out, "That camper don't hide you none."

I'm not sure why I didn't scream. It would have been logical, resulting in porch lights being flicked on and sleepy residents coming outdoors in their pajamas, but fear paralyzed reasoning, and my primal reflex was *escape*.

"Lord, help me." The words came out of my mouth in a strangled moan, more reflex than intent, but I found myself wondering if God Almighty might notice anyway.

Five blocks separated me from my home, so I pushed away from the bumper and stumbled toward the safety of brighter streetlights one block over on Main. My legs, numb from squatting, behaved in a nightmarishly sluggish manner, and I lost my footing, landing on all fours among a cluster of potholes. My palms stung, and my right knee burst into pain, moistening my jeans as they rubbed across a fresh wound.

A skinned knee.

When I was five, I bloodied both knees jumping rope, but Fawn held wet paper towels against my skin until the bleeding stopped. I wondered where she was tonight.

With my cheek close to the pavement, I peered under the camper to see Clyde's tattered tennis shoes making their way past the front passenger tire. A whimper flipped my lungs into a deep, ragged breath as I leaped into a stumbling sprint, careening past a low hedge, which clawed at my clothing. My muscles turned to clay, and my feet to sandstone slabs, and when I rounded the corner at the stop sign, a brick flower-bed border sent me sprawling across the sidewalk just as a car turned from Main, its headlights blinding me where I lay.

JohnScott.

The recognition of my cousin's truck finally pulled a scream from my throat, and I crawled, then ran, slamming against the passenger door before scratching for the door handle. I scurried inside and yanked the door shut as Clyde staggered to the corner, balancing himself against the stop sign.

JohnScott sped away, but I stared at Clyde through the back window, his menacing gaze following the truck until we were out of sight.

CHAPTER TEN

After my scare with Clyde Felton, I no longer attempted to traipse around town by myself. JohnScott had snatched me up, driven me home, and talked in soothing tones until I calmed, but I still panicked whenever I thought about the rapist. My cousin kept reminding me that nothing actually happened, but I knew he was just as alarmed as I was.

Regardless of his comforting words, the tension brewing between JohnScott and me was worse, and I wasn't about to broach the topic of the Cunninghams. Even though JohnScott acknowledged my fear of Clyde, he probably wouldn't approve of my apprehension about Dodd. I chose to remain silent, but of course he knew something was up, and by the weekend, we had established an elephant in the room rapport.

After Velma's big dinner on Saturday night, our options for entertainment were sparse, and JohnScott and I ended up in the parking lot of the Mighty Clean Car Wash, licking dipped cones from the Dairy Queen. While John Mayer sang from the cab of JohnScott's truck, I sat on the tailgate swinging my legs and gazing up and down the street. "It's quiet tonight."

JohnScott chuckled. "Next week will be rowdy, what with the homecoming game."

"I hope you've got your boys ready. I hear Denver City's tough this year." I bit a chunk of chocolate from my cone, and ice cream trickled toward my thumb.

"They'll give us more of a challenge than we got last night, that's for sure." JohnScott smiled at me, and I almost felt like things were back to normal. If only we could sit on his tailgate at the car wash every evening and ignore the rest of the town. A car engine revved behind us, and JohnScott's brow wrinkled. "Watch out now."

His eyes never left his cone as Fawn Blaylock's Mustang pulled into the side entrance of the car wash. She eased through a washing bay, then sped out the front entrance after she glanced at us. Gravel showered the change machine, killing my hopes for a peaceful evening with my cousin.

JohnScott stuck out his bottom lip. "Too bad she couldn't stick around."

I contemplated her tinted windows as she stopped at the intersection. "You think Tyler's in there with her?"

"Without a doubt." JohnScott cocked his head as the Mustang turned the corner. "How do they decide which awesome vehicle to drive?"

"Maybe they flip a coin."

The corners of his mouth dropped. "When I taught your history class, Fawn bragged about her car so much I thought I'd scream." He repositioned his ball cap. "But I confess, I'm jealous of Tyler's truck."

"Why's Fawn taking the year off from school?"

"I heard she's expecting a marriage proposal from Tyler now that he graduated."

"Is she working?"

He snickered. "Why would she? Her daddy has more money than God."

JohnScott didn't often insult people, even in jest, and the light acid in his voice revealed his bitterness toward anyone who didn't work to support themselves. I enjoyed the momentary meeting of the minds, but then he chuckled. "Well, looky there. Miss Blaylock may change her mind and come back now."

Any warm fuzzies I felt toward JohnScott vanished when Dodd's El Camino stopped at the red light. The preacher was quickly becoming JohnScott's idol, and I recalled my bitter envy back in first grade when Fawn got mad at me and spent an entire recess playing with Wendy Bly. Hurt and fury had overcome me at being so easily replaced.

This was worse.

JohnScott lifted his cone in greeting as Dodd and Grady pulled into the parking lot, but then he leaned toward me with his face directly in front of mine. "Can you be nice?"

"Polite, yet distant. That's the best I can do."

"I'll take it."

Dodd eased to a stop next to JohnScott's step-side pickup and called through the open window. "So this is the Trapp high life? Ice cream in a gravel parking lot?"

"Don't knock it." JohnScott rose to lean against the side of his truck as Dodd killed his engine. "You should see it in the dead of winter."

"It couldn't be worse than this." Grady stepped out of the car. "Where is everybody?"

"Home watching *CSI* probably, but all the cool people are down at the car wash."

Dodd's eye caught mine as he slowly shut his car door. He sucked a straw in a Dairy Queen cup, and from the gentle curve of his cheeks, I guessed he had a milkshake. I looked away.

"Ruthie-the-checker-girl." Grady dropped to the tailgate next to me. "Can I call you that? Because Miss-Turner-the-checker-lady doesn't have the same ring to it."

Why did they have to come? The night had been so normal up until then. "I'm not a teacher, so I don't see how it matters."

Dodd lowered the tailgate of the El Camino and sat sideways, leaning against the inside of the bed with one knee bent. "Do you have a degree, Miss Turner?"

Good grief. "No, Mr. Cunningham, but I'll be going to college next fall."

He looked perplexed. "I thought you were older."

"Did you now?"

A vehicle with an amplified muffler approached, drowning out my acidic remark, but it was probably for the best. JohnScott would be all over me if I kept this up. I glanced toward the street, and anxiety prickled across my skin like poison ivy. Clyde Felton's beat-up sedan crawled toward the red light, then accelerated without stopping. His engine, growling like an angry hound, could be heard long after the car sped away.

JohnScott whistled low, but Grady, of course, smiled.

"That's Clyde Felton. He lives across the street from us. I guess you know him?"

My cousin shook his head. "I know of his family, but Clyde only just got out of prison."

"No way." Grady's smile tapered. "What did he do?"

JohnScott glanced at me, then lowered his voice. "Served twenty years for rape."

Dodd's elbow slipped off its perch on the edge of the El Camino, and Grady's mouth fell open.

Scooting back in the truck, I hugged my thighs to my chest, and my skinned knee protested as my jeans tightened across the scab.

"So, Dodd …" JohnScott moved to stand behind me at the side of the truck. "How did your first week at the high school go?"

Dodd nodded slightly, acknowledging the change in topic. "Blessedly uneventful." He took a draw from his milkshake and watched the two of us. "Not a single drug bust."

JohnScott whooped. "Drug bust? Was that normal in Fort Worth?"

"Not every day, but a couple times a semester."

My pulse still raced faster than a jackrabbit, but I figured I would relax more quickly if I forgot about the convict and joined the conversation. "Did you preach in Fort Worth, too?"

"Yes, Miss Turner, but I only filled in at my home congregation and a few other churches in the area. I've never preached full-time."

"Did you have to go to Bible college or something?" I hoped I didn't sound too interested, but I wanted to figure this guy out.

"No, I just started giving little sermon talks when I was in high school, and it snowballed into summer internships and random speaking gigs."

"What's your degree in?" JohnScott asked.

"Mathematics." A corner of his mouth lifted. "But I changed my mind a million times. Couldn't decide what I wanted to be when I grew up."

"So, Coach Pickett," Grady interrupted. "How'd you land the head coaching job at your age? You can't be much older than Dodd."

"Small-town politics." JohnScott grinned. "I guess you could say I know the right people. All of them."

"Not to mention he was Trapp's star kicker, went to Tech on a full-ride, and"—I paused for dramatic effect—"only missed five field goals."

Grady ducked his head, clearly not impressed but wishing he could be. "Five field goals in four years?"

"No," I said. "Five field goals in ten years. College, high school, middle school, only five misses."

I lobbed the remainder of my forgotten cone into a trash barrel three yards away as a honk drew our attention to a black Jeep stopped at the traffic light. Luis Vega leaned his head out the window and yelled, "Party at the elevator, Grady!" Then he squealed his tires and sped away.

Grady pointed after the Jeep, deep in thought, before snapping his fingers. "Luis Vega. Freshman tackle. Works at the United with Ruthie-the-checker-girl. Lives two doors down from the elementary school." He grinned. "Did he say something about an elevator?"

"The grain elevator on the south edge of town," JohnScott explained. "It's where college kids go to drink. Apparently Luis is crashing the party." He stood and walked to the curb, reminiscing aloud. "I haven't been down there in years."

Grady jerked his head and peered at his older brother.

"No." Dodd said firmly, finishing his milkshake with a slurping rattle.

"But, Dodd, it would be a great place to rub elbows with the community."

"Grady, the church would never approve of their minister socializing at the town watering trough."

I stifled a laugh as I pictured holier-than-thou Dodd Cunningham drinking beer with the locals, but my cousin still focused on the blinking-red traffic light, where Luis had called to us. He lifted his ball cap and ran his fingers through his curls. "Maybe it's time I went down there again."

"Really?" Grady bounced to his feet. "Can I go with you, Coach?"

"Settle," Dodd said.

"He's not going to the elevator," I insisted. "JohnScott, tell the kid you're joking. He's about to bust a gut."

JohnScott's expression softened, but his puppy-dog eyes trained on me, not Grady. "Ruthie, Luis is down there, and as his coach, I've either got to go keep an eye on him or call his parents."

A weighted breath caught in my lungs as I realized Luis Vega's parents wouldn't care what their son did. "Fine," I said, "but there's no way I'm going with you. I'll walk home."

"Not with Clyde Felton on the move, you won't."

My throat tightened, convincing me to stay put.

"Can I go with you?" Grady repeated in a stage whisper.

JohnScott looked at the preacher and shrugged a shoulder. "What do you say?"

"You're just getting Luis, then coming straight back?"

"I don't want to stay down there any longer than I have to."

Dodd sighed. "All right, Grady, but be good."

The teenager bounded to the passenger side of the truck, as irritation slapped my patience. Just when JohnScott and I were managing the elephant in the room, our evening was yanked away from us. Luis was obviously responsible, but my dander ruffled against the Cunninghams.

JohnScott motioned for me to get up before he slammed the tailgate. "I'll be right back, Ruthie."

Surely he was kidding. "Wait—take me home first."

He stopped with one leg in the cab. "Ruthie, I need to get on down there. I'll only be gone a second." He looked at Dodd. "Can she stay here with you for ten minutes?"

"Of course."

My throat constricted into a solid mass of petrified wood. "No!"

"Ten minutes, Ruthie, that's all."

Before I could protest again, my moronic cousin pulled the door closed and drove away, leaving me alone in the middle of town, short of breath and steaming from disbelief.

With the preacher by my side.

CHAPTER ELEVEN

I could have boxed JohnScott on the ear.

Whenever he switched into coach-of-the-year mode, all he thought about were his players. And if they needed him, he would bend over backward to help. I respected him for that, but it rubbed.

Leaning a hip against the side front of the El Camino, I wrinkled my nose at Dodd's back. He still sat on the tailgate, gazing down the street as if a parade might stroll past any minute. If I had this man figured out, he'd start talking up a storm any minute.

He looked over his shoulder and smiled in a way that made me think he was laughing at me. When I frowned, he turned back around with a shrug.

Okay, so maybe I was being rude. And if I thought about it, maybe I'd been rude all week. "Thanks for staying with me." As soon as I said it, I realized how inaccurate the statement was. He wasn't staying with me. He was staying away from the elevator.

"No problem." He didn't turn around again, and I got the feeling he was suggesting I sit with him on the tailgate, which, of course, would've been the normal thing to do. But this was not a normal situation. Surely he recognized that.

The El Camino was still warm, and I laid my palms flat on the hood. I was lucky things were somewhat quiet in town. Probably everyone who typically would have been cruising up and down Main Street was down at the elevator getting bombed. Hopefully JohnScott and Grady would get back before anyone else drove by. The four of us sitting at the car wash wouldn't be worthy of gossip. Dodd and I alone? That would make the front page of the Trapp Times.

He cleared his throat. "Did JohnScott tell you Grady decided to play football after watching last night's game?"

"At least ten times. Runner, right?"

"We like to call him a receiver." He looked at me again, and this time he shifted sideways without breaking eye contact. "And JohnScott convinced me to help with the coaching."

I raised an eyebrow. "Do you know football?"

"Know it but don't love it." He gazed down the street.

"Well, if you're helping with football, you'll have fewer discipline problems in your classes. From the boys, at least. They think coaches are the best thing since sliced bread."

Dodd's shoulders jiggled silently.

"Why is that funny?"

He shook his head but continued laughing. "You're right, and I couldn't agree more. But it was the *sliced-bread* comment. You sound like my grandmother. In fact, most people here talk like her."

"Like hicks?"

He was silent for a second, and I realized he smiled as much as Grady. Only quieter. "No, just old-fashioned."

Another car approached the stoplight, its engine running rough with a familiar sputter that sprayed panic from my eardrums to the depths of my soul. I dropped to my knees at the front bumper of the El Camino before Momma's hatchback made it to the light. She *could not* see me with this man. Her mental health couldn't take a hit like that.

"Hey, isn't that your—"

Evidently Dodd noticed my disappearance. The car shifted as he rose from the tailgate, stepped to the side of the car, and rested his hand on the hood, where mine had been only moments before. He would be able to see me out of the corner of his eye, but he didn't look my way. Instead, his head swept slowly from left to right as he watched Momma drive past.

I stared at the change machine, wondering how to explain my actions.

When the hatchback rattled down the street, Dodd stooped down and tilted his head to study me. "Everything all right over here?" When I didn't answer, he added, "Miss Turner?"

The panic that had thoroughly soaked my heart, now solidified with the speed of quick-set cement, leaving a hard outer shell of unbearable annoyance.

"For goodness' sake, it's *Ruthie*."

He leaned his elbow on the front bumper. "I don't suppose we could stand up now, could we?"

"No."

"Why not?"

I spoke slowly, my words cracking the concrete one syllable at a time. "She was headed to the Dairy Queen for a cheeseburger. She'll be back by any minute." I decided to change the subject. "What's up with Grady?"

"What do you mean?"

"A week sitting next to him in Information Systems is the equivalent of three months with a person of average linguistic skills. Is he seriously that talkative, or is he trying to prove something?"

"Average linguistic skills?" Dodd lifted his eyebrows as he sat lightly on the hood. "You don't always talk like my grandmother."

My breathing felt deliberate, as if I would suffocate if I didn't make a conscious effort to keep inhaling, so I calmed my lungs until my chest rose and fell at appropriate, staggered intervals, and I could almost forget I had to try. "So I'm not a hick after all?"

He shook his head slowly. "No, you're still a hick."

Before I could catch myself, I slapped his shin. As much as I hated to admit it, the preacher reminded me of JohnScott. But just a little.

A car stopped at the curb ten yards from us, and I tensed, not having heard it approach.

When Dodd glanced in that direction, I thought he flinched ever so slightly before stepping toward the street.

I cocked my head. Who could put the preacher on edge like that?

A low hum told me an automatic window was being lowered.

Dodd cleared his throat. "Hello, Brother Goodnight, what brings you out this late?"

Lee Roy Goodnight. Probably the oldest fuddy-duddy at the church. He and his wife weren't bad people, just set in their ways. And their ways would never allow their young preacher to be seen with someone who practically had a scarlet letter tattooed on her chest.

"Just driving in from Lubbock." Lee Roy paused before adding, "You?"

"Waiting for Grady. Coach Pickett took him to see something, but I expect they'll be back any minute."

Another pause. "Well, okay, son. I'll see you on Sunday."

"Yes, sir. Sunday."

The window hummed to its original position before the car eased away from the curb. A few seconds later, Dodd appeared next to me. He clasped both hands behind his neck and sighed.

When he looked down, I lifted my eyebrows in an I-told-you-so challenge and gestured to the ground next to me.

He slid all the way down till his backside met the gravel. "I'm sorry. I was so concerned about not going to the elevator, I didn't stop to think how it would look for me to be here with a single woman. I'm not sure the church would approve of that, either."

"I understand." *Perfectly.*

A rock dug into my thigh through my jeans, and I shifted to relieve the discomfort as I considered the irony of the situation. Because of the church, I was avoiding being seen by Momma, hiding with the preacher who was avoiding being seen by anyone in town … because of the church.

I was going to kill my cousin.

Momma's hatchback sputtered past us again, and Dodd lifted his head, listening. He peered at me with a question in his eyes, but he seemed to let it go in lieu of a safer one. "So, you don't drink?"

I bounced a pebble from palm to palm. "No, I don't. My daddy drank when I was small, and I don't see any use for it."

"Does your dad live around here?"

I slung the pebble against the metal siding of the washing bay, but it only made a light ping. "Weren't we talking about Grady?"

He lifted both palms. "Should I just take you home? I don't know why that didn't occur to me sooner."

"Absolutely not." I answered too quickly, but heaven forbid I should pull up to my house in the preacher's car. I tried to soften my reaction. "Thanks, though." I picked up another pebble. "JohnScott's been gone longer than ten minutes."

"More like thirty." Dodd pulled out his cell phone, swiped the screen, and immediately became enthralled with the contraption.

I rolled the small rock between my palms like a ball of Play-Doh. "Checking the weather? Surfing Facebook? Playing a mindless game?"

His fingers stilled. "Texting JohnScott."

I let the pebble slip to the ground. "Oh … What did he say?"

"Didn't reply." Dodd turned his phone off but didn't put it away. "You don't have a handheld device?"

A giggle slipped from my throat, and I shook my head slightly, thinking the preacher sounded like an advertisement for an electronics store. "You mean a cell phone? No, I don't have one. I've got better things to spend my money on."

"Yeah, Grady doesn't have one either. When we moved, that's one of the things we cut from the budget."

I peeked at him out of the corner of my eye, surprised his teenage brother would give up his cell phone for the good of the family. I wondered what else had been shaved off their expenses.

Dodd punched a button, and the screen lit up again. "I'm addicted to Candy Crush." He smiled tightly, as though ashamed.

"What's Candy Crush?"

"A stupid game. What was the adjective you used?" He nodded. "Mindless."

"It can't be that bad if *you're* addicted to it. Show me." I leaned toward him but kept a comfortable distance.

He held the phone toward me, swiping here and there as a happy tune played. "You just match the candies and try to get three in a row."

I was supposed to be watching him play the game, but instead I inspected his square palm. Hardly any calluses. Long fingers. Neatly trimmed nails. And for some reason, his hands seemed … kind.

But that was absurd.

Hands were not kind. Hands had no personality traits whatsoever, and even if they did, I had no reason to trust Dodd Cunningham's.

I turned my head away. "You're right. That's stupid."

He chuckled. "Grady says I need a twelve-step program."

"Not a bad idea. I think JohnScott might be addicted to ESPN. He checks scores more often than he eats and drinks."

"He certainly loves the game of football." Dodd went to work on his phone again. "Check out this app I found. It shows you the stars."

"It can't be better than Candy Crush," I said flatly.

He wagged a finger back and forth an inch in front of my nose. "Just you wait."

Dodd Cunningham may have been a jerk, but he had extraordinary people skills. Even though I despised him, he somehow kept drawing me out of myself, and only part of me wanted to get away from him. "I can't believe I'm doing this."

He shrugged. "I don't think JohnScott would feel threatened by it."

JohnScott wouldn't feel threatened no matter who I played games with. Not that I had tested that theory lately. Picking up a handful of gravel, I let it sift through my fingers.

"See?" Dodd held the phone above his head, pointing at the screen. "It shows you the stars and constellations that are above you."

I rested one palm on the ground behind his hip and cautiously leaned in to get a closer look.

"And you can move it around." He demonstrated. "Whatever direction you choose, it shows you what's there."

"Too bad it's so cloudy tonight. I'd like to see the real stars now that I know what I'm looking for." I nudged his hand, sweeping the device slowly across the night sky, and then I put my finger and thumb on each side of his wrist, stilling his movements. I tilted my head, squinting to read a caption about a satellite.

I heard a tentative sniff just before Dodd's breath brushed my ear.

Was he smelling my hair?

I stared blindly at the stars on the screen—his thumb partially obscuring the words—and in a split second, I racked my brain for an appropriate course of action.

None came.

I turned my head slightly, and his eyes studied my lips before traveling upward to meet my gaze.

I held my breath. A dormant longing awakened inside me, and a pleasant shiver rippled across my shoulders. At the same time, the tolerance I'd been nurturing began to curdle into a soured knot of contempt.

"I should go." I shoved away from him, knocking my elbow against the taillight as I jumped to my feet and stumbled from behind the El Camino.

For crying out loud, I could walk home. I could run home. I could flag down a passing car and get a ride.

"Ruthie, wait."

Dodd's voice did nothing except propel me forward in a frantic attempt to distance myself. But just as I made it to the sidewalk, Clyde Felton's sedan came to a stop at the red light. My movements caught the convict's attention, and when his eyes locked with mine, I felt the burning urge to release a guttural cry like a trapped animal. *God has quite the sense of humor.*

Instantly weighing the lesser of two evils, I spun around and slammed into Dodd's chest, knocking both of us off balance.

He wrapped an arm around my waist to steady me.

The sensation of his embrace startled me, and I couldn't move. Could barely breathe. Could think of nothing except the heat of his arm on my back, seeping through my T-shirt to warm my skin.

"Watch it!" I convulsed away from him.

"Ruthie, I … I'm sorry."

"Take me to JohnScott."

The preacher's eyes widened. "Miss Turner, you know I can't go down there."

I trembled with rage and angst and acute embarrassment. "Oh, that's right. You can't be seen at the elevator where there's alcohol, but you can hide out at the car wash trying to seduce a single woman. That makes perfect sense."

"That's not what happened," he said forcefully.

"Take me to JohnScott," I demanded. *"Now."*

CHAPTER TWELVE

As Dodd and I pulled into the white-rock lot adjacent to the grain elevator, I attempted to get my bearings while the headlights still shone. We were away from streetlights, and the place would fall into darkness as soon as Dodd killed his headlights. Hence the desirable location.

Luis's Jeep angled near us, with a handful of vehicles around it. Seven or eight people holding beer bottles and wine coolers squinted into the brightness, and on the far side, Fawn Blaylock perched on the hood of her Mustang with Tyler standing next to her, his arm around her waist. JohnScott and Grady leaned against the step-side, and as we pulled up, Grady floated toward the El Camino with his palms up.

I had the car door open before we came to a complete stop and was halfway to JohnScott's truck when Dodd turned off his headlights. Instant blackness fell over me, and I stopped, hoping my eyes would adjust to the darkness.

"Over here, Ruthie." JohnScott opened his cell phone, creating a beacon of light. "You must have pitched a fit to get Dodd down here. Grady was just telling me how much pressure he feels to be the perfect preacher."

"Perfect?"

"Do I detect a hint of sarcasm?"

I had no intention of relaying Dodd's and my star-gazing experiment, or the tangle following, even though Dodd insisted he would understand if I told JohnScott. *Really?* Did he think JohnScott was my guardian?

I bumped my cousin's shoulder with my own. "Why are you still here? I thought the plan was to get Luis and meet me back at the car wash. Ten minutes tops."

"The twit won't leave." JohnScott sighed. "When I suggested we go, he made a scene. Loudly." From JohnScott's tone, I knew Luis would be running laps on Monday. "So my search-and-rescue mission got downgraded to basic childcare."

Muffled words coming from the direction of the El Camino told me Dodd and Grady were in disagreement about their next move. I'm sure Dodd had planned to get Grady and hightail it out of the vicinity, but apparently he was having as much luck with Grady as JohnScott had with Luis.

JohnScott pulled me to the back of the truck, where he lowered the tailgate. I could hear a few other conversations, none of which were loud enough to understand. Most people were keeping to themselves, probably huddled in small groups, and without a doubt, couples slipped away occasionally for privacy.

The sickeningly sweet scent of beer reminded me of my daddy. I rested my thighs on the squeaky tailgate, scooting back until my feet lifted off the ground, and I thought how nice it would be to keep inching back, crawling to a place where memories couldn't reach me.

A low roar transformed my melancholy into alarm, as headlights illuminated the lot around me. It was Clyde Felton's loud car, and my spine tingled as exhaust fumes temporarily eclipsed the odor of alcohol. "JohnScott?"

"It's all right, Ruthie. Stay with me, and you'll be fine."

Clyde's door screeched as it opened, and the interior of the car lit, revealing the hulk of a man. He pulled himself up and gazed around him before slamming the door.

I clenched JohnScott's elbow. *Unbelievable.* We were hobnobbing at the elevator with a convicted rapist and a bunch of drunks. Suddenly I could feel the darkness. It lay over me like a suffocating tent, trapping me on the tailgate of JohnScott's truck while I listened for any tiny sound that might alert me to Clyde's whereabouts.

Dodd, breaking his silence, called a greeting, but Clyde didn't acknowledge him.

Silence hovered over the lot, indicating my cousin and I weren't the only ones who had heard the rumors. Several phones lit up the darkness, but they only managed to identify their owners.

A loud belch broke the silence, and Luis drawled, "Anybody need another beer?"

When a deep voice answered, I recoiled. Clyde stood at the front bumper of JohnScott's truck, not eight feet away. "Throw me one, kid."

JohnScott flinched when a bottle bounced off the side of his truck.

"What'd you do that for?" Clyde's speech slurred.

My cousin slipped off the tailgate as another bottle crashed.

I rested my hand on the metal where JohnScott had been sitting and tried to absorb any confidence that might be lingering there. I would be fine. JohnScott wouldn't let anything happen. There were people everywhere.

But when I heard a scuffle and the truck shook from being bumped on the passenger side, I jerked to my feet, stumbling along the far side with a hand raised. A tremor shook my knees, but I figured as long as I knew where Clyde was, I could keep the truck between him and me.

My hand touched skin, and I jumped back. "Grady?" I whispered. "Is that you?"

"Came to check on you, Ruthie-the-checker-girl." He gripped my forearm.

Dodd's voice crooned from across the bed of the truck. "Go on away from here now. Go on."

"Get your hands off me, preacher man." Garbled speech dampened the menacing tone of Clyde's voice.

Someone produced a flashlight and shined it toward the commotion. Dodd had his hand resting on Clyde's shoulder, and JohnScott had moved between him and Luis.

Dodd repeated, "Go on back home. You don't want to be here anyway."

Clyde gazed over Dodd's shoulder, glaring not at Luis but into the darkness toward Fawn's Mustang. "No, I suppose I got no reason to be here."

He jerked away from Dodd, and soon his car thundered to life. I expected him to speed away, pelting us with gravel, but instead he eased back, letting his headlights shine on the lovebirds. Fawn turned her head to avoid the glare, but Tyler raised his chin and scowled.

I peered after Clyde's taillights as he wove toward town, and only then did I retreat to the familiarity of the pickup's cab. I took several deep breaths, inhaling the comforting scent of my cousin and his mundane life while slamming the door on alcohol fumes and danger.

The El Camino pulled away, and as I watched Dodd and Grady turn toward town, I realized that as much as I hated it, Dodd Cunningham's cool behavior settled my nerves. An hour before, I was so angry I wanted to do the man bodily harm, but after seeing him with Clyde, I didn't know what to think.

In the end, I let it go. It didn't really matter if Dodd was a nice guy or a jerk. He was still the preacher. I was still me. The two didn't mix, and I knew I couldn't trust him.

CHAPTER THIRTEEN

"Meet me outside the field house, little cousin. I'll bring your mum before I start the boys stretching. Mom wants you to have it on before you hit the stands." JohnScott's telephone call should have lifted my spirits, but it only served to remind me how pitiful I was. *A mum from my aunt? Delivered by my cousin?*

"Will do." In spite of my humiliation, I wore my favorite blue jeans and hoodie, even a little makeup, for the big game. As I walked briskly through the parking lot, I passed Fawn and Tyler arguing. She turned her pointed nose away from him, but he snatched her by the arm, pulling her back. The victimized look on her face sent a tiny ray of justice streaking across my hardened heart. The bully was getting a mouthful of her own medicine.

JohnScott was waiting for me by the brick wall of the field house. He bent down, then raised the lid of a white box and pulled out a large chrysanthemum draped with yards of blue-and-white ribbon and scores of trinkets.

I lifted it to my shoulder, fingering a tiny cowbell as the cool petals nestled my neck. "Smells like homecoming."

He rubbed his chin as I pinned and repinned the mum. "Everything hitched up all right?"

"That should do it." The mum held secure at my shoulder, with ribbons falling down to my waist. I gave him a sideways hug. "Thanks, JohnScott."

He leaned so close I could smell the mint of his toothpaste. "You're welcome."

I picked up the box as Dodd jogged past, diverting his gaze as though embarrassed to look our way.

"Ignore me, then," JohnScott called after him. "I'm hurt. I'm cut to the core."

Dodd pivoted, walking backward. "You'll learn to live with the disappointment, J.S. Carry on."

The two coaches pushed through the door of the field house, leaving me perplexed. The Cunninghams had been in Trapp only two weeks, and already the preacher had a nickname for my cousin. It didn't seem natural. JohnScott hadn't been to church a day in his life. I'm not sure any of the Picketts had. Momma only ever went to church because Daddy led her there.

I wandered toward the bleachers while the band's warm-up tones bubbled across the field. Uncle Ansel and Aunt Velma were camped on the fifty-yard line, already settled into their folding bleacher seats. My aunt nestled under a quilt, and my uncle held an empty Dr Pepper can in which to spit tobacco juice, but my mood soured when I saw the Blaylocks right behind them. I wouldn't have paid them any mind, but when I went to sit down by Velma, Neil's boot perched on the edge of my seat.

"Excuse me," I said, keeping my eyes on his footwear.

He waited a good five seconds before sliding his boot out of my way, and the gritty scrape rubbed my pride like sandstone rock against an open blister.

Velma patted my knee as I sat. "Ruthie, you want to share my quilt?"

"I'm all right. And I love the mum, Aunt Velma. Thank you."

"Aw, it was nothing." She waved her hand through the air as though swatting a horsefly. "Looks right nice on you, though."

Ansel didn't speak, but he leaned forward and smiled. My uncle didn't use many words to convey his thoughts, but I knew his smile meant *Good to see you, sweetheart.*

I smiled back.

Twenty minutes later, we rose to our feet while the band played the national anthem, and we remained standing for a prayer led by none other than Trapp's new preacher. But he didn't pray like a preacher at all. In fact, he sounded like he did any other time, citified and stuffy. I didn't pay attention to the entire speech, but I heard him mention something about forgiveness. *Strange.* Most of the men prayed for safety and sportsmanship. Occasionally one of them would be so bold as to request a win. Forgiveness was something new.

I put it out of my mind until I spotted Milla Cunningham headed toward our section of the bleachers. She climbed toward us, but I studied the field, assuming she would ignore me right along with the Blaylocks. No such luck.

On the contrary, she slipped her arm around me and gave my shoulders a light squeeze. I instantly imagined a blaring megaphone instructing every fan to look my way and make note of the irony of the situation. "Hello again, Ruthie," she said.

Her hug startled me, and from Velma's expression, I'd say it surprised her as well.

"Hello, Velma." Milla reached across to grope my aunt's hand and then focused her attention behind us.

"Thanks for saving me a seat, Neil."

"Oh, sure, sure," he said as he traded places with his wife so the women could sit together. Milla hugged both of them before sitting down, and I giggled under my breath. I hadn't witnessed such a public display of affection since the rodeo dance last summer.

Milla settled onto the bench. "Do you guys know Ruthie?"

My back straightened, and my ears became high-powered radio antennae tuned to the most sensitive frequency.

Neither of the Blaylocks replied, so Milla repeated herself. "Are you acquainted with Ruthie? I bet Fawn knew her in school."

After an endless silence, I peeked back.

Neil studied the scoreboard as if he had never seen one in his life, and his wife dug frantically through her oversize handbag. Milla's gaze volleyed from them to me, her face a mask of confusion.

The nerves in my stomach exploded. "We know each other." Maybe Milla Cunningham could read lips, because I'm certain no sound came from my mouth.

Facing forward once again, I exhaled as Velma muttered under her breath. "Pay 'em no mind, Ruthie. Not worth the trouble."

Charlie Mendoza and his wife, Ellen, brushed against me as they moved from another section of the bleachers to squeeze in next to Milla. The five of them immediately fell into an obnoxious discussion about everything from Sunday fellowship meals to Saturday elder meetings.

I tuned them out to enjoy the game.

The sights, sounds, and smells of football exemplified the spirit of Trapp. The band played the school song, the cheerleaders chanted rhymes, and the buttery scent of popcorn wafted through the stands.

Laughter.

I thought about next year, and where I would be at homecoming time. When I got away from Trapp, I might not ever come back. Even though I enjoyed homecoming, one night at a football game didn't make up for endless days working to support Momma. But she seemed to be getting better all the time, and by next fall, I'd be able to leave.

In the meantime, I enjoyed the evening with Velma. At halftime, we took a bathroom break, then waited in line for nachos, soft drinks, and a pickle for Ansel. When we returned to our seats, the group behind us hadn't even stopped for breath, but their current discussion caught my interest.

"… in junior high school when he lost his hearing." Milla was speaking. "He had hearing aids in both ears, and the doctors labeled it permanent damage. Claimed they couldn't do anything. I tell you, his father gave them what for. He took the boy to specialist after specialist until he found someone to help."

"What did they do? Surgery of some sort?" asked Charlie.

"That's right. They repaired one eardrum, then six months later, the other. Now he has near-perfect hearing."

"How bad was it before?"

"He could hear nothing at all for most of his seventh-grade year and half of eighth." Milla's voice trembled. "Now he says God allowed it to happen so he would have greater compassion for others."

Yeah, right. I swiped the last of my nacho cheese with my finger as Ellen crooned, "Dodd is an amazing man, Milla."

My attention snapped. *Dodd?*

I never would have dreamed Dodd Cunningham had been deaf at any time in his life. The man's demeanor screamed confidence and capability. What must it have been like? Middle school is hard enough without a disability.

I located Dodd on the sideline. JohnScott had outfitted him in knit coaching pants and a school polo shirt a size smaller than the preacher normally wore. He stood with his hands on his hips, scanning the field. As I considered his medical history, I imagined myself unable to hear the band, the cheerleaders, the announcer, even the annoying voices behind me. Eerie.

Velma nudged me, drawing my thoughts back to the game. The team was lining up for the final play with ten seconds remaining on the clock. "Ansel says they're running the Slide Ten, which always pushes us into the end zone."

"Is that where they do the dipsy-doodle and run around to the side?"

"Sure enough."

Ansel's football intuition proved true. The Slide Ten resulted in a Panther touchdown as the final buzzer sounded, and our side of the stadium went berserk. Air horns screeched, fans screamed, and the band struck up the fight song as the remaining team members stormed the field. Bending over, I gathered my trash, but the clamor around me subsided like a wind-up music box running down.

Velma shuffled her Naturalizers next to me. "Ansel …"

I shoved a nacho container into my mum box, but when I stood to search the field, my heart stopped.

JohnScott lay motionless in the end zone.

My aunt and uncle pushed past me as I surveyed the scene through a fog. Grady sprinted across the field, followed by the medic, while the rest of the team clustered in a silent huddle. I became aware of Milla jostling my shoulder, but when she spoke, I couldn't hear her over the ringing in my ears. Maybe that's what it would be like to be deaf. Instinctively I found Dodd on the sideline, sitting on the bench with his forehead resting on clenched fists.

I gaped at him incoherently until I realized he was praying.

CHAPTER FOURTEEN

On Saturday morning, Dodd Cunningham hunkered down in the driver's seat of his El Camino, examining the grocery store while he tried to think of something to buy. A reason to go in.

An old woman hobbled out, and Ruthie crept behind her pushing a grocery cart. The woman talked as she unlocked her trunk, and Ruthie leaned in to hear her soft words. As Ruthie placed the bags in the trunk, Dodd heard the tones of their laughter floating across the lot in the morning air. Ruthie shut the trunk with a gentle snap and rested her elbows on the cart as the woman poked her shoulder. Ruthie opened the driver's door and waited while the woman lumbered in, and then she pressed the door closed and fluttered her hand in a wave.

Only then did Ruthie hurry, shoving the cart toward the entrance and jogging a few steps before settling into a steady pace. As she neared the building, she moved in front of the cart, walking backward to pull it through the doors, and just as she stepped into the store and out of view, she glanced at Dodd.

His insides tightened as if he'd been punched.

What had he been thinking? Of course she would notice him. Most likely he drove the only El Camino within a fifty-mile radius.

He grabbed the car door handle and jerked so hard it snapped off in his hand. With a grumble, he tossed the mangled metal onto the floorboard and rolled down the window noisily, reaching outside to free himself.

Ruthie didn't pause when he entered the store but continued with her work, swishing a broom around the registers.

"Good morning, Miss Turn—Ruthie."

She lifted her chin in greeting but didn't look at him. He wasn't surprised. She'd been giving him the cold shoulder ever since the unfortunate incident with his cell phone last week.

"Have you seen JohnScott yet?" he asked.

"He sat in the emergency room half the night. He's probably sleeping in." She worked her way across the front of the store, sweeping dust into a pile while Dodd pretended to study the magazine display. He had seen her mother sweeping the floor at the diner, and their similarities were remarkable. Petite with dark eyes and long hair. Same smile.

Dodd shoved his hands into his pockets. "I hope JohnScott makes practice next week."

"Mm-hmm."

Luis sauntered toward them and sprawled on the counter. "The players make the team, not the coach."

Ruthie jerked upright. "Then why have the Panthers improved every year since JohnScott's been here?"

"Well, yeah. There's always that point of view," Luis said, dodging the question. "But I don't see why he can't come to practice."

Dodd squinted. "Most likely he'll be back at practice on Monday, but because of the concussion, he's got to take things easy."

"What about the broken ribs?" Ruthie stored the broom behind the Coke machine. "Think if he got hit again."

"Broken ribs are no big deal." Luis pulled himself up from the counter, evidently tired of the conversation. He stalked away from them, calling over his shoulder. "They don't even put a cast on them."

Dodd cringed at the thought of JohnScott taking another hit. His friend had given everyone a scare the night before. After the final touchdown, the opposing team's frustration got the best of them, and they began taking shots at the Panthers. JohnScott attempted to stop the fight and got smashed between two players in full pads. The medic revived him within seconds, but because he was disoriented, an ambulance whisked him away to the emergency room in Lubbock.

The door slapped open, and a pigtailed girl ran in. "Ruthie, Ruthie!"

"Hey there, Bethany."

"I got new shoes." The girl stomped her feet, and lights blinked near her soles.

"Well, they're precious, aren't they?" Ruthie placed a quick kiss on top of Bethany's head as her mother called her away.

"You like kids?" Dodd asked.

Ruthie took a deep breath and blew it out with a huff before looking him straight in the eye. She only made eye contact for a fraction of a heartbeat, but it still caused Dodd's stomach to do a somersault—even though he suspected she gritted her teeth.

She was so much like her mother. Whenever Lynda waited on him at the diner, she had the same disdainful attitude as Ruthie. Dodd had a feeling it had something to do with the Blaylocks, and he sensed Lynda's animosity transferred to his own family by association. Ruthie's mother didn't even attempt to hide her enmity, and Ruthie barely did.

Ruthie removed an empty Snickers display box from a display on the front wall, then stretched for a replacement carton on the top shelf, standing on tiptoes to nudge the corner.

Dodd reached above her head and handed her the box, noticing her hair smelled of strawberry shampoo. "So, about JohnScott … You guys are pretty close, right?" He hated himself for asking. Hated himself for wanting to know. His plan had been to stay away from Coach Pickett's girlfriend. Some plan. He hadn't figured on Ruthie's strawberry-scented hair … or her defiantly masked fragility.

He might as well find out how things stood between her and JohnScott. Find out if he even had a chance. He glanced at the ponytail falling down the back of her United shirt and held his breath as he waited for her answer.

He didn't get one. They were interrupted by the coach himself, pushing through the glass door, and Dodd wondered for the hundredth time why he didn't simply ask his friend. Maybe he feared losing him. Maybe he feared the answer. Definitely he feared exposing himself.

Ruthie gasped when she saw JohnScott hunched forward, protecting his rib cage with his left hand.

It hurt to look at him.

She crept forward, placing one of her delicate hands on each side of JohnScott's battered face. "You have not been a good boy, JohnScott Pickett."

He glanced at Dodd. "She's such a mother hen. Let's call her Henny Penny, shall we?" And then in falsetto, he drawled, "I am going to bake some bread. Will Ducky Lucky help me?"

When he put his hands in his armpits and flapped like a chicken, Ruthie slapped him gently on the shoulder.

"Hey, woman." JohnScott's mouth hung open in feigned shock. "How dare you hit an injured man—and in front of a witness, too." He turned to Dodd. "Sir, may I call you to testify in my defense?"

"I am forever at your service." Dodd waved an arm in the air and bowed.

"Don't encourage him." Ruthie's gaze bounced between the two of them before her smile melted.

Dodd got the impression Ruthie disapproved of JohnScott's friendship with him, but he didn't understand why. What did she have against him?

JohnScott leaned against the counter next to her. That should have been answer enough to Dodd's question. He suddenly felt intrusive. "I'd better be going."

"See you Monday," the coach said.

Five minutes later, Dodd found himself in the El Camino, fingering the rough nub of handle left on the door and contemplating the Ten Commandments. When he learned them as a child, the tenth commandment, *do not covet*, had always meant he shouldn't want his friends' Hot Wheels cars. At twenty-six, it meant he shouldn't want their real cars. And he didn't. He took pride in being content with what he had, but as he peered through the plate-glass windows of the United grocery, where Ruthie laughed at something JohnScott said, the tenth commandment took on a whole new meaning, and he felt as guilty as any convicted felon.

He coveted something belonging to JohnScott Pickett.

CHAPTER FIFTEEN

Wednesday I planned to discuss my college plans and desperate scholarship search with JohnScott, but when I nudged the teachers' lounge door open at noon, I saw my cousin huddled at the back table with Dodd and the ag teacher. Right where he'd been every day this week. JohnScott caught my eye and beckoned me to join them, and Dodd looked between the two of us with that curious expression he seemed to reserve just for me.

I waved my fingers and stationed myself at the front table instead. A radio rested on the counter, and I tuned in a Lubbock station to drown out their conversation. I didn't care what the men were talking about, but as I tapped my foot, I considered the possibilities. On Monday I had speculated they were discussing football—JohnScott's number-one topic of conversation at any given time—but on Tuesday I ruled it out. If they'd focused solely on sports, the ag teacher would have bailed already. Now that Wednesday had rolled around, several other options ran through my mind. Politics, education, women.

As I picked at my bologna sandwich, Maria Fuentes came through the door balancing a cafeteria tray. The Family and Consumer Science teacher hovered near the corner of my table and evaluated the three men, but when none of them noticed her, she turned and settled into a chair across from me with her back to that side of the room. Bless her heart. Of all the female teachers who had come to spy on Dodd that first day, she was the only one who hadn't returned to her usual routine. I took a sip of Sprite. "Hey, Maria."

"What's up, Ruthie?" Her tone screamed, *No offense, but I'd rather be sitting with the men.*

"Thinking about the pile of work I have to do this afternoon."

"Not enough hours in the day, that's what I say." She picked up a small paper cup of ketchup, squeezed its contents into a bowl of gravy, and stirred the mixture with a chicken strip. "They don't pay us enough for all we're expected to do."

I hummed in agreement as I monitored the back table. JohnScott leaned on both elbows listening to Dodd, while the ag teacher shook his head. The preacher had finally gotten a haircut that made him look less citified, and his new coaching pants made him look more athletic. The changes didn't necessarily suit him, because he was losing his mysterious executive air.

Maria glanced over her shoulder. "What do you suppose they're talking about?"

"Football," I lied.

"They're not."

Tearing off a corner of my sandwich, I asked, "What makes you so sure?"

"Their hand gestures."

I raised an eyebrow.

She dipped three french fries in her pink gravy before stuffing them in her mouth and speaking around them. "They can't be talking about football because their gestures are all wrong." She swallowed the mouthful of food like it was a horse vitamin. "First you throw the ball across to the receiver." She held her arms apart and motioned like she was throwing a ball. "Then the receiver runs down the field." She hunched with one arm curled against her stomach. "Then he gets tackled by the huge line-whatever, and they do it all again." She circled one finger in the air, tornado-style.

Apparently Dodd noticed her dramatic attempt to gain his attention, and his gaze slid into mine as his lips curved up. Was it my imagination, or did he roll his eyes ever so slightly?

I pretended I didn't notice.

"You're right. They're only waving their palms back and forth." I looked her in the eye. "Health-care reform?"

"Yeah, maybe. Or terrorism." She bit half a chicken strip. "So, Ruthie, is your cousin dating anybody?"

JohnScott continued to sit with Dodd and the ag teacher, and by Friday morning I had come to expect it. A sensation burned in my gut, which I first labeled as jealousy but soon recognized as fear—the unfathomable fear of losing my cousin. JohnScott acted normal, more or less, so I attempted the same as he and I monitored the students in the gymnasium before the morning bell. "How are the ribs?" I asked.

"Sore as the dickens. I hope they're healed by Halloween. By the way, are you wearing a costume to the carnival?"

"Of course not."

"I have to dress as a chick, you know."

"So what? I do that every day." I shifted where I leaned against the wall, and my shoulder ground against the cinder blocks.

"You could wear a costume out of loyalty to Trapp High School."

"They don't pay me enough."

"I'll pay you."

"You couldn't afford me."

Dodd came through the double doors and headed toward Grady on the other side of the gym. Once again he diverted his gaze from JohnScott and me. *Why does he do that?*

JohnScott called with a thick accent, *"¿Donde está el baño, mi amigo?"*

"Right next to the little girls' room, my friend." Dodd chuckled as he hurried by.

I frowned. "Why did you ask him where the bathroom is? In Spanish?"

"It's a joke. He visited his parents in Mexico, and *Where's the bathroom?* was the first phrase he learned, but he said it never came in handy."

I massaged my temples.

"You know, Ruthie, we've been talking, Dodd and me."

I nodded. "The Debate Club."

"The what?"

"The two of you and the ag teacher, hunched over your deep-fried burritos in the teachers' lounge. Talking, talking, talking. Maria

Fuentes and I christened you the Debate Club because you look like you're solving a complex mystery."

"You're not too far off, I suppose." A weak smile played on his lips. "Dodd's been telling us Bible stuff. It makes me think about how I treat people."

Something like fear wrapped around my neck, forcing a small puff of air through my teeth. "For crying out loud, JohnScott. You don't have to listen to that junk."

"Aw, I don't mind." He pulled at his ear. "It's pretty cool. He said Jesus forgave—"

I raised my hand to silence him, and his expression changed to guarded impatience.

"But later, Ruthie? Will you let me tell you later?"

I squinted into his eyes, one of which still had a yellowed shadow of a bruise.

He read my mind and answered softly, "I know, little cousin, but I trust him."

CHAPTER SIXTEEN

I managed to avoid further Jesus discussions with JohnScott, but I couldn't help noticing Emily Sanders had stopped ignoring me, an action I found extremely suspicious.

After school one afternoon, she entered the office, took a half step in my direction, then paused like a cornered cottontail. I raised my eyebrows questioningly, but she only gazed at the floor without speaking.

"Hey, Emily."

The girl relaxed and took a baby step. "What are you doing?"

"Spider Solitaire."

"I do Facebook a lot, but my mom said it's off limits because of one of my test grades." She twisted a strand of hair around a finger, examining the split ends. "She hired a math tutor, but I wish she hadn't. It's just more homework."

I clicked a few playing cards on the screen, and a full stack fluttered to the discard pile. "I don't know. If it helps, right?"

"Yeah, that's what Mom said." She eased forward and slipped into a chair near my desk. "Are you going to the game on Friday?"

For years little Emily had followed the church's example and given me a cold shoulder because of my mother's presumed sin. Why make small talk now? "I go to all the games."

She hugged her books against her chest. "My mom's late. She runs errands and loses track of time."

I glanced into the parking lot, scoping for Emily's mother but discovered Mrs. Blaylock instead. Emily followed my gaze and jerked to her feet as one of her books fell to the floor with a thump.

Most people had the same reaction as Emily when they came upon Fawn's mother unexpectedly—as if they'd been caught in a petty crime and would soon be punished—but not me. I simply couldn't stand her. I'd always referred to her as Mrs. Blaylock even though I called every other Trapp female by her first name. The *Mrs.* seemed to echo the distance she kept from Momma and me, but even when Fawn and I had been friends, her mother was formal and aloof.

Normally Mrs. Blaylock's presence at the high school didn't alarm me. She reigned as Trapp's unofficial civic-duty queen, volunteering her services all over town—good grief, the football stadium was named after her father—but since the new preacher's arrival, her visits charged me with apprehension. The Cunninghams sparked a certain level of static electricity, not only in the Blaylocks, but in other churchgoers as well. Whenever any of them came close, I'd feel a tiny shock, like when my socks just came out of the dryer. As I speculated about Fawn and Emily working a twisted plan, Mrs. Blaylock's entrance confirmed my suspicions and set off an electric current akin to a dry-lightning storm.

She peered down her nose at Emily before leveling her gaze six inches above my head. "I'm here to meet the principal. For a meeting about the Halloween Carnival?"

Emily coughed. "He might still be in Mrs. Morales's room. They were talking about the carnival after last period."

Mrs. Blaylock tilted her head toward Emily. "Show me?"

Good gravy, they were both obnoxious. I opted to wait for JohnScott outside.

The low brick wall west of the building was a convenient spot to meet JohnScott when he exited the side door. I sat on the wall and tipped my head back, enjoying the sun's warmth and the momentary escape from my overcast life.

JohnScott had changed, and it made me lonely. We hadn't discussed my college plans in a month, and I hadn't mentioned the scholarship rejection I'd received the week before. I could tell he wished I liked the Cunninghams, but I felt no urgent need to befriend them, especially now that I had discovered the Debate Club's main topic of discussion. JohnScott should have known his friendship with Dodd Cunningham was a time bomb set to explode … because of me. And I almost wished it would go ahead and detonate.

At least then I'd have my cousin back.

"Why are you out here by yourself?"

At the sound of Clyde Felton's low-pitched threat, every muscle in my body turned to granite. He leaned against the corner of the building, and I shifted on the wall, turning my back on him as I calculated whether or not I could make it back inside. "I could ask you the same thing," I said.

The odor of alcohol signaled his approach. "Your mom's Lynda Turner, ain't she?"

Now he stood between me and the door. "Maybe."

"You look just like her."

The fact Clyde Felton knew Momma alarmed me, but paralysis glued me to the wall. "What do you want?"

"Thought I'd be sociable, that's all." His words ran together, and the sonorous bass of his voice created a rolling echo not unlike thunder.

I bit the inside of my lip and didn't answer.

"I bet you're waiting for your coach-cousin." He sat down on the wall next to me.

"Yes, and he'll be here any minute."

Clyde grunted. "Not for a few minutes yet, unless today's different from every other day."

He had been watching me.

When I scooted away from him, he mumbled, "Everybody in this town's too good for me."

"I didn't say that." I glanced at his arms, which were possibly larger than my thighs. If I screamed, someone in the building would probably hear me, but if I screamed, Clyde might simply snap my neck in two.

He leaned toward me, and the stench of beer filled my nose. "What's your mom up to?"

I frowned.

"She live close?"

"Why do you want to know?"

He curled his lips, exposing yellow teeth, and my legs involuntarily jerked me to my feet, putting distance between us.

“I’m sorry, but I don’t know you, and as far as I know, neither does my mother.” I needed to get back in the building with Fawn’s mother and Emily. Ironic.

I tried to step around him, but Clyde gripped my wrist, his fingers tightening like handcuffs. “Wait a minute.” He spoke slowly, concentrating through the alcoholic fog. “I didn’t do nothing.”

I twisted my arm, trying to break free.

“Tell me about your momma.”

“Leave me alone. *Please.*” I leaned away from him as my heart raced. The west side of the building—perfect for avoiding Mrs. Blaylock and Emily—was also perfect for shielding Clyde’s actions from anyone who might drive past the school. His fist remained wrapped around my right wrist, and with his free hand, he grabbed my other arm. I noticed a tattoo peeking out from under the wristband of his shirt, but then he squeezed my arm so tightly, I soon lost sensation below my elbow.

A scream formed behind my diaphragm, and I felt it pushing its way up to my throat, but Clyde’s silence unnerved me. His body language said pit-bull attack, but his eyes drooped in what could only be described as disappointment. I didn’t know if drunkenness or some type of post-incarceration problem caused the inconsistency, but either way, it rattled me, and I whimpered involuntarily as I wrestled to free myself.

He held his ground with little effort, but his eyes flickered away from mine, and he glowered at something, or someone, behind me. My heart leaped. *JohnScott?* I twisted to look over my shoulder, but Clyde released my arms, and I fell to the ground, landing hard on one hip.

He spat. "I should've known *you'd* be around." He started to say something else but stopped. "Aw, forget it." Then he trudged away, cursing.

Using the wall as a support, I pulled myself up on shaky legs, ready to run to the safety of my cousin. But when I turned, it was Dodd. His arms were folded across his chest, and the tendons in his neck twitched angrily.

Instinctively I moved behind him.

The convict glanced back one last time before stumbling toward the football field, where he zigzagged across the grass and disappeared behind the concession stand. Only then did Dodd relax. He unfolded his arms and looked down at me. "Are you all right?"

The compassion on his face pulled a sob from my throat, so I pressed my knuckles to my mouth and looked away. I would not become emotional in front of him.

"Ruthie?"

I squeezed my eyes shut.

"You okay?"

A chuckle came from somewhere near my lungs, and I felt the urge to hug him. Or let him hug me. Let his strong arms ease my fears like my daddy's used to do when I was afraid.

But how ridiculous.

I inhaled deeply—sucking air all the way down to my ankles—and as I forced my breath back out, I allowed the oxygen to cleanse my fear-induced instincts. "I am now."

He studied the empty field. "Clyde's a little unpredictable."

"Unpredictable?" That wasn't the word I'd use to describe the beast.

"Has he bothered you before?"

"Not really." I chose not to admit my foolish decision to walk home alone. "I didn't know he even knew my name." *Or my mother.*

"Most likely he's upset JohnScott and I interfered that night at the elevator."

"Maybe." I felt relieved by Dodd's presence, but at the same time, his comfort alarmed me. "Thank you. I don't know what he would've done—"

"You're all right now." He sounded as though he wanted to convince both of us.

"Well, I'll be better when my legs stop shaking."

"Here. Sit down." He touched my elbow with his fingertips, then settled sideways on the wall, inspecting me as if I might collapse. "Do you want to call the police?"

"No."

We sat in silence for a few moments, and the breeze gently blew my hair across my cheek. Dodd lifted his hand as though to brush the hair from my eyes, but he rubbed his palm against the back of his neck instead.

Already the attack seemed long ago. Such a difference in only a few minutes. I studied Dodd's profile and noticed the curl behind his ear had been trimmed away with his recent haircut. "Clyde seemed intimidated by you."

His shoulders fell a half inch. "I don't know why. He could've beaten the tar out of me."

My mind conjured a prison fight, and my heart raced again. "What would you have done if he hadn't left?"

"I'm not sure." He nudged a rock with the side of his athletic shoe. "But it might have involved running."

I surprised myself by giggling.

"But I would've taken you with me," he insisted. "Or maybe we could've double-teamed him."

"Yeah, if you had tripped him, I could have hit him with my purse." For once I was grateful for Dodd drawing me into a laid-back conversation. It calmed my nerves.

His laughter faded into a thoughtful lull, and he added as an afterthought, "Clyde must be crazy to pick on someone else's girlfriend."

Confusion jumbled my thoughts. "What did you say?"

"He's an idiot to mess with another man's girl, and if I understand this town at all, he's particularly foolish to mess with the girlfriend of the head coach. He's likely to have the whole team after him." He reached for a pebble on the wall between us and scratched it against the bricks, leaving a white mark.

The intensity of my encounter with Clyde left my mind addled, and I gaped at Dodd in bewilderment. "I don't have a boyfriend."

He raised his eyes doubtfully. "But JohnScott—"

"JohnScott's my *cousin*."

Dodd froze, except for his eyebrows, which trembled once. "Cousin?"

We contemplated each other, equally perplexed, until Grady came out the door. "I've got to get home, big brother. My blasted calculus teacher gave me a truckload of homework, and I'll be lucky to fin—" He saw me and stopped short. "Hey, Ruthie-the-checker-girl." His voice held a tone of uncertainty, and it occurred to me how odd it must seem for Dodd and me to be sitting alone together.

"They're cousins," Dodd said.

"Who?"

Dodd pointed at me, and I mumbled, "JohnScott and me."

"Seriously?"

The door clanked, and JohnScott finally emerged. "Hey, bullies, are you bothering my girl?"

The brothers said in unison, "Cousin."

JohnScott put an elbow around my neck, flinching slightly from his still-sore ribs. "What's that you say?"

"You're cousins, Coach Pickett," Grady informed him.

Dodd drifted around the corner of the building toward the parking lot, but I was still so shaken, I was having a difficult time following Grady's conversation.

"Yeah, so?" JohnScott said.

Grady scrutinized him. "Are you distant cousins?"

"No, first cousins. You know, my mom, her mom, sisters."

"I understand the basic concept of cousins." Grady looked sick to his stomach. "But is it all right to date your cousin if you live in a small town?"

I gasped, and JohnScott took a step away from me. "We're not dating," he said. "She's my cousin." He grinned but dropped his gaze to the ground.

"Wow," Grady said. "How could we know you so well, yet not know this nugget of information?"

"I guess it never came up," JohnScott said. "But this is Trapp, for goodness' sake. How could you not know?"

Grady beamed as though he had never seen us before. "Right." He nodded as he turned to walk away, but he kept looking back at us. "My brother may need medical attention," he said.

JohnScott looked at me and shrugged. "City folk are so quirky."

CHAPTER SEVENTEEN

"It's been too long since I treated you, little cousin." JohnScott picked me up after work one afternoon in late October. "Let's go to the Dairy Queen and get a chili dog."

I settled into his pickup, glad to be off my feet. "If you wanted to treat me, you'd buy me ice cream."

"But you haven't eaten dinner yet."

"Minor detail."

In the past few weeks, JohnScott had taken the hint and avoided mentioning God, and I thought our relationship might get back to normal if only he would give up the Debate Club. He still considered Dodd Cunningham the best thing since Internet access, even though I insisted the infatuation wouldn't last.

As we approached the Dairy Queen, I groaned. "Tell me you didn't." The parking lot held only two cars. Dodd's El Camino and Fawn's Mustang.

"Aw, come on." He shut off the engine directly in front of the broad dining-room windows and raised a hand in greeting as four heads turned in our direction. "Humor me."

"Why didn't you just ask me in the first place?"

"You'd have said no."

"For good reason."

He opened the driver's door. "Honestly, I had no idea Fawn and Emily would be here, but you have to admit, they're getting better."

"Well, that makes it all okay, doesn't it?" My cousin was a twit.

"Fawn isn't going to stop me from getting a chili dog, but you can stay out here if you want." He shut the door, then grinned at me through the window.

I contemplated staying in the truck to prove he couldn't push me around, but since he parked right by the windows, I'd look foolish. He had planned this strategically.

I caught up to him at the front door of the restaurant. "I hate you."

"Cheese?"

"Onions, too, and a chocolate shake. You owe me."

JohnScott scrunched his face. "I probably owe you fries, too."

He ordered at the counter, and then I followed him to a booth where Dodd and Grady sat with Fawn and Emily. After JohnScott greeted them, we took an adjacent table, but he pulled his chair toward Emily when she asked him about a lesson he had assigned in history class.

The game of musical chairs continued as Grady moved to the seat across from me and plopped his cardboard container of onion rings on the table. "Hey there, Ruthie-the-checker-girl. I'm surprised you're not at work."

"I got off early."

"Of course." He stuffed an onion ring in his mouth, chewed twice, then spoke. "You work at the store most days?"

"Evenings and weekends."

"Doesn't leave much free time."

"I manage."

We reached the natural end of the conversation, and an awkward silence followed. Awkward for me, at least. Grady didn't appear uncomfortable at all. He kept munching onion rings—which smelled so good my stomach growled—while I focused on the menu behind him.

His silence finally drove me to small talk. "So how do you like West Texas?"

"I never knew land could be so flat. And barren."

"It's not barren." I frowned.

"Mesquite trees and cactus don't count."

"Of course they do."

"It's your home." His eyes were kind. "I miss the trees back in Fort Worth. We had a huge live oak with a tree swing. Pretty relaxing."

"What's relaxing?" Dodd joined us, turning a chair around to straddle it. His arm brushed mine, and I shifted away from him as a tingle shot to my ear.

"Our tree swing back home."

"I liked the porch swing better." Dodd's eyes watched me.

Touching a crumb on the table, I rubbed it between my finger and thumb before flicking it to the floor. "Well, we may not have tree swings in Trapp, but we sure enough have porch swings."

"You've got one at your house, don't you?" Dodd seemed different tonight. Something about the way he talked.

I nodded and glanced at the next table, where Emily and JohnScott flipped through a history textbook. JohnScott said something about page fifty-four while Emily nodded, but she seemed distracted by Dodd or Grady—I couldn't tell which.

Fawn squinted at Emily, which gave me the impression she was none too happy to have the teenager forcing her way into Fawn's time with the Cunninghams. I smiled in a feeble attempt to make the best of a bad situation, but Fawn didn't return the sentiment, only shifted her eyes to gaze at me with a bored expression until I looked away, embarrassed.

A few minutes later, she slid from the booth and stepped to the counter for a drink refill, which spurred Emily to abandon her assignment and scurry to the counter with her own waxed paper cup. As Emily passed our table, she poked my shoulder. "Hi, Ruthie."

She glanced at the preacher as she skittered away, hovering next to Fawn and peeking back. Curiosity compelled me to watch and see if she would keep making eyes at Dodd.

Grady mumbled without moving his lips, "Act like it isn't happening. That's what we do."

"What are you talking about?"

He put his hand over his mouth. "Emily …"

Dodd rolled his eyes. "Grady, a little discretion goes a long way."

I snickered in spite of myself, forcing my eyes away from the teenage girl.

"Like I said …" Grady raised his voice, ignoring Dodd's scolding. "There aren't many trees in West Texas that could support a tree swing."

"Except the dead tree behind the shoebox," reminded Dodd.

"True."

I lifted a hand. "What do you mean? What shoebox?"

"You've seen our house," Grady said. "It's as small as a shoebox, right? The dead tree is probably bigger than the house." He looked at Dodd. "You think it ever could have supported a swing?"

"Depends on the swing, I suppose."

The brothers continued their banter for a few moments, but when I didn't join in, Dodd leaned on his elbows. "Hey, some of the folks from the church are meeting at the Blaylocks' house after the carnival on Saturday. Would you like to come?"

I blinked.

Disbelief pressed against my eardrums, making me slightly dizzy as Fawn spun to face us, but Dodd and Grady continued to search my eyes, anticipating an answer.

"No." I shook my head. "No, thank you."

Dodd shrugged but didn't look away. "JohnScott might go. You could ride with him."

I knew what was different about the preacher. Usually his eyes bounced around the room, landing on me occasionally but looking at other people, too, especially JohnScott. He had always looked back and forth between us. Tonight he kept watching me … like he did when nobody was around. Like he did at the school office. Like at the *car wash*. Suddenly I remembered bumping into him and the feel of his arm around me.

Fawn closed the distance between the counter and our table. "Ruthie said she can't make it. Don't hound the poor girl." She reclaimed her seat at the booth just as a waitress set JohnScott's order on the table in front of me.

I considered accepting Dodd's invitation simply to rattle Fawn's cage, but I would only be torturing myself. Picking up my portion of the food, I gripped the milkshake so tightly, it squeezed out around the straw, and I glared at my imbecile cousin. "Time to go, JohnScott."

He must have sensed my determination, because he didn't argue. "I guess we'll take our grub back to Ruthie's place."

"Oh, come on, stay awhile," chimed Grady.

Dodd protested as well, but I was already pushing through the glass door, and the electronic bleeping mechanism drowned out his words.

JohnScott hurried to follow me, and when he opened the driver's door, he lowered his head and gave me a reprimanding look. "Was it that bad?"

I plopped my chili dog on the seat next to me. "Absolutely."

"Why?" His door moaned, and I wanted to do the same.

"Dodd asked me to a party at Fawn's house."

"No way." He laughed out loud. "He asked you out?"

"Not like that, you idiot. He invited me to some church thing, but Fawn told him I couldn't come."

He frowned.

"Well, not in so many words, but she got her point across." I studied the dining room, where Fawn now laughed animatedly. "I'm not part of the Debate Club, you know."

He started the truck and revved it, but then dropped his hands to his lap. "Ruthie, I don't know what's up with Fawn, but the Cunninghams are important to me."

My empty stomach reacted to the scents filling the truck, and I felt sick. "The Cunninghams or the church or God?"

"I don't know yet." He ground the truck into gear but left his foot on the brake. "But even if Fawn's a jerk, I don't think you should be afraid of her."

"I'm not afraid of Fawn Blaylock," I clarified. "Or her parents, for that matter. Or the other Christians."

"Then what are you afraid of?"

My hands trembled. "What am I afraid of?" I spit the words across the truck. "I'm afraid of good manners and fake smiles and friendly words. I'm afraid of people who don't know me but might believe any lie they hear. I'm afraid of the day they'll turn on me, because that day *will* come, JohnScott, and they'll make life in this stupid town even worse. Why can't you see that?"

"You mean the Cunninghams?" he asked quietly.

My temper boiled over. "Of course I mean the Cunninghams."

He raised his hands in exasperation, then floored the truck in reverse.

As we pulled away, I glanced into the restaurant to glare at JohnScott's important people.

And Dodd's eyes bored into mine.

CHAPTER EIGHTEEN

By the time I got to school the next morning, my temper had downgraded from a category-five hurricane to a severe thunderstorm. I grudgingly accepted the fact that my cousin would never understand, and I spent twenty minutes filling out an online scholarship application while John Mayer crooned from the speakers.

When JohnScott entered the office, he stood cautiously in the doorway as though expecting an explosion. "Still mad?"

"Pretending it didn't happen."

"Things aren't that bad, you know." His casual tone failed to mask his concern.

I pulled a tissue from a box on the corner of my desk and used it to wipe dust from the computer screen. He honestly was not the same person. "Didn't happen, JohnScott, go along with me, please."

"Done." He came around the counter, shuffled through papers in his teacher mailbox, then leaned against the wall behind my desk. "Uh-oh," he murmured. "Is this going to be a problem?"

I followed his gaze to see Dodd enter the building through the front doors and make his way across the foyer in front of the trophy cases. I growled. "Didn't. Happen."

"Alrighty, then." JohnScott raised his palms in surrender. "By the way, I can't take you to work this afternoon. I'm cutting out early to help Dad with the cattle."

"No big deal. Maria can probably give me a ride."

"Maria, the Family and Consumer Science teacher?"

"That's the one." He didn't even know me anymore.

Dodd opened the glass door and stuck his head into the room. "Morning, you guys. Ruthie, can I talk to you?"

I wanted to talk to the preacher like I wanted a bad sunburn—and JohnScott knew it—but my cousin only strolled past my desk with a teasing grin. "See you later, Ruthie."

Of course he would leave. JohnScott undoubtedly had some twisted agenda to get me to befriend the Cunninghams, but I wasn't falling for it. Just because my cousin had bought into Dodd's campaign of forgiveness and kindness didn't mean I had to.

I pushed my chair away from my desk as a subtle hint to Dodd that I would grant him no more than a few moments of my time.

His gaze dropped to my arms, crossed firmly over my chest, and he hesitated, rubbing the back of his neck. "Ruthie, I don't want you to be afraid of me. You're not, are you?"

What kind of question was that? Dodd Cunningham may have made me nervous—and irritated and angry and disgusted—but I wasn't afraid of him, and I couldn't imagine why he would ask. "No ..."

"I didn't mean that like it sounds," he said quickly. "I just want you to know I would never intentionally hurt you."

What on earth was he talking about?

He said nothing else, just leaned with his elbows on the counter, holding my gaze. He nodded, smiled gently, maybe even sighed.

I stood abruptly. "I'm on duty in the gym this morning, so if that's all you need, I should get down there." I tossed my purse in the drawer, stomped past him, and escaped to the gym before he could ask me any more senseless questions.

Dodd was acting strange today.

And JohnScott, too.

I took my usual post beneath the scoreboard and frowned at the shiny hardwood floor. What were they up to? The gym buzzed with student chatter, but my mind buzzed with apprehension, and my imagination sent possible scenarios spiraling around my body in a surge of dread.

"You look upset, Ruthie-the-checker-girl."

Grady's interruption jerked me out of my thoughts. "Why would I be upset, Grady?" I clenched my lips together.

"I haven't the slightest idea."

"I'm confused about something your brother said, that's all."

"Want to talk about it?"

Whatever happened to my plan to avoid the new guys? It had sounded simple. Stay away from Dodd and Grady to keep Momma calm. I never intended to be unfriendly or hurtful, but the droop of Grady's eyes told me I had done just that.

But I couldn't talk to him. Not about this. "I'm afraid not, Grady."

He leaned toward me. "But, Ruthie, I don't want you to be afraid."

A spark ignited. Dodd had just asked about my being scared of him, and now Grady didn't want me to be afraid. As it all began to make sense, a surge of rage flamed across my skin. What had my cousin done?

"Ruthie?"

"JohnScott talked to you about last night."

The boy's mouth hung open, but he shook his head in denial.

When the bell shrilled and students drifted down the bleachers, I locked my arms across my stomach, gripping my elbows to keep from screaming at him. "You shouldn't believe everything my cousin tells you, Grady."

Heat crept up my spine as a thought occurred to me. If JohnScott had told the Cunninghams about my fears, what else had he told them? I followed the last of the students through the doors and walked briskly toward the office, but Grady ran to catch up.

"Ruthie, wait."

I didn't slow down. If I made it back to my desk, I could drown myself in work and ignore all this mess.

"Let me explain." He reached for my arm, but I jerked away. "Coach Pickett didn't tell me anything—"

"You don't have to explain. It's between JohnScott and me, and I'll talk to him later."

"You're wrong. It has nothing to do with him."

"Grady, go to class."

One more turn and I'd be at my desk. I increased my pace, but he ran after me and barked, "Dodd can read lips."

I took three more steps, then came to a sudden stop, confusion and curiosity dampening my anger. "What do you mean?"

He took a deep breath. "Well, you see, when he was a kid, he lost his hearing and—"

"I know about that," I snapped.

"How do you—"

"Doesn't matter."

He pressed his lips together and studied me before continuing. "It took a while for anyone, including Dodd, to realize what was happening. At first he watched people's mouths to be sure of what they said, but as his hearing worsened"—Grady shifted his books—"he almost didn't recognize his hearing loss because he already read lips fluently. They say he has a knack for it."

I wavered in the middle of the hall, urging my addled brain to process what he said. "He can read anybody's lips, if he wants to?"

"As long as he can see their mouth."

The fight drained from my body. "So he, more or less, heard me last night?"

"He tries not to eavesdrop, but apparently you're a pretty big temptation." Grady shrugged. "And he's trying to figure out why you don't like him."

My mind fast-forwarded through the conversation in the truck, and I inadvertently covered my mouth with my hand.

"Please don't kill him, Ruthie-the-checker girl. Life wouldn't be the same without my big brother."

At lunchtime I positioned myself with my back to the Debate Club. Maria tried to get me to talk, but she soon accepted I didn't have it in me.

"Rough morning?" she asked.

I crinkled my empty sandwich baggie in my fist. "Rough life."

"Sounds like you need chocolate, girl." She folded her rectangular pizza and fell into a respectful silence while she ate.

Three emotions crowded my lungs. Anger was the strongest—toward Dodd for eavesdropping, toward Grady for listening while he repeated it, and toward JohnScott for taking me to the Dairy Queen in the first place. Alongside the anger, insecurity swelled in my chest, suffocating my measly self-esteem until I felt short-winded. But the dominant emotion settling into my heart, as usual, was fear.

When Dodd tossed a soft drink can in the trash barrel by the door and left the lounge without looking at me, the tightness in my chest eased, but only slightly.

Maria inspected the remaining Debate Club members. The group had grown to around five, give or take, but I still turned up the radio to avoid hearing the conversation. Maria never objected, and I liked to think she understood. "What's your favorite candy?" she asked.

"Butterfinger, I guess."

Maria dug change from her purse. "Help yourself."

I fingered the coins, clinking them against each other before picking them up. Maria really was a good person. "Thanks."

The Debate Club, short one member, took turns charting my progress, first to the trash can, then to the sink, then out the door. As I rounded the corner to the vending machines, I felt a sense of relief to have all their eyes off me. I stood before the candy machine and took a deep breath, but when the preacher appeared by my side, the tension returned, tenfold.

"Did Grady explain?" he asked cautiously.

"Yes."

"I'm sorry, Ruthie. I invaded your privacy."

"It's no problem. Really." We stood side by side, inspecting the chocolate options. He apologized, I accepted, so now he could go back to his classroom.

I noticed his reflection in the glass front of the machine. He was watching me, and I diverted my gaze when he spoke again. "I pride myself on not eavesdropping, but … suddenly you were right in front of me." He slipped quarters into the machine, then abandoned the effort and turned toward me. "This morning I saw JohnScott say you needed a ride. If you're willing to let me take you to work, I figured it might be a good chance for us to talk."

I didn't want to talk. I didn't even want to know him, much less ride in his car. I jabbed the button for a Butterfinger.

He glanced at the machine, startled. "I don't really like Butterfinger."

"I don't care."

He slowly retrieved the candy from the machine, clattering the trap door. "You're angry."

I shoved Maria's change into the slot. "I don't know what I am." My concentration couldn't keep up with my emotions, and I blurted the first thought that popped into my head. "I don't appreciate it when people do things behind my back."

He paused for several seconds, and I imagined him counting to ten. "I don't blame you, Ruthie. If I were you, I'd be angry." He pushed the button for a Reese's. "But I'd get over it so we could be friends."

I stood there mesmerized by the rotating coil releasing the candy, which dropped with a thunk. I took two breaths, then retrieved the candy and offered it to him as a trade for the Butterfinger. A chocolate-covered olive branch. He accepted the candy bar and walked away.

I listened to his slow footfalls and the thump of his classroom door as it closed, and then I returned to the teachers' lounge. My muscles turned to mush, and like a second grader, I laid my head on the table. Anger, insecurity, and fear had caused me to behave badly, and shame covered me like a damp quilt.

I knew the church would eventually pressure the Cunninghams to avoid me. But I could no longer sit idly, waiting for that to happen. Unfriendliness no longer felt right.

The shrill ring of the bell tone jerked me out of my puddle of regret, and I got up and plodded to the office. I could do better than this. I could act better. Bigger. Even though I recognized Dodd's kindness as a ploy to get me into his church, it wouldn't kill me to befriend him and Grady. After all, it was only temporary. I'd never be like JohnScott, and would never *want* to be, but I could try to be civil in the meantime.

I hesitated at the corner and looked back. Dodd stood in the doorway of his classroom, watching from halfway down the crowded hall. He leaned against the doorjamb with his arms crossed, but when our eyes met, he dropped his hands to his sides and took a tentative step.

I whispered across the expanse, "I'll wait for you after school."

He bobbed once on his heels and nodded.

CHAPTER NINETEEN

Four hours later, I waited in front of the trophy cases nibbling a hangnail while I watched Dodd unlock his car, toss trash and cups under the seat, and pull up to the entrance. I should have met him in the parking lot or at the side hallway or someplace less visible. Anywhere but the front door.

"Ruthie Turner." A mewling female voice made me wince.

It was Emily Sanders's mother, Pamela, stomping down the hall, grinning like she hadn't seen me in months. And maybe she hadn't.

"How's that mother of yours, Ruthie?" She came to a halt with her plump fingers spread across one hip. "She doing all right?"

"Yes, ma'am. Just fine." No reason to go into detail.

"We used to be fast friends, your momma and me, back in the day. Had us some good times." Pamela giggled, reminding me of her daughter.

"Yes, ma'am." We danced this conversation every time we ran into each other. Pamela asking about my mother, obviously hoping to rekindle an old friendship. Me trying my best not to hurt her feelings, since Momma never mentioned her.

I reached for the door. "I'd better be getting to work now."

She smiled, but then her eyes focused past me, and I knew she saw Dodd waiting in the parking lot. "You sure are a hard-working young lady, Ruthie." She returned her gaze to me, and her eyes changed, but I couldn't tell in what way. "You tell your momma I said hello. Tell her to stay happy."

"Will do, Pamela." I fled to the safety of the outdoors, recognizing the irony of me escaping one Christian by running to another one.

"It was nice of you to offer me a ride." I slipped quickly into the passenger side of Dodd's El Camino, hoping Pamela's were the only set of eyes watching us.

"No problem." Dodd ducked his chin slightly, and I got the feeling he wasn't too keen on being seen either. "You feel like getting a milkshake on the way?"

I shook my head. My newfound *niceness* extended only so far. "Might be late for work. Thanks, though."

As he put the car in gear, Emily jogged toward us, waving.

I thought Dodd gave a tiny sigh of frustration when he rolled down his window. "What's up, Emily?"

"I think I missed your car when I canvassed the parking lot during sixth period." She giggled as she stuck a fluorescent orange flyer under his windshield wiper, then bent to peer in the window. "Hey, Ruthie. Why is Dodd giving you a ride?"

There was no way the girl could've known the day I'd had, but the question grated on my nerves just the same. Besides, it annoyed me that she called her algebra teacher by his first name. "Why shouldn't he?"

She froze. "Uh … I don't know." Then she bounded toward the building, calling over her shoulder, "See you guys later."

Dodd stared after her, not moving for several seconds.

I smiled. "Counting to ten?"

"Twenty-five," he said as he exhaled.

"Did it help?"

He didn't answer right away. "I guess so."

Emily Sanders could test the patience of Mother Teresa herself, but still, I found it funny the preacher would be so irritated.

He glanced at me, and his face reddened. "My door handle is broken." He quickly opened the door from the outside and removed the paper from his windshield. When he returned to the car, he held up the flyer. "At all costs, don't miss the Halloween Carnival this Saturday."

A thought occurred to me. "You don't like it here, do you?"

He laughed, sounding guilty, as he pulled out of the parking lot. "This place is growing on me, but when we first moved here? No, I didn't like it."

"What's not to like?" I knew countless answers to the question but wondered how the preacher would answer.

"It's just different than the city. Not as many opportunities."

Once again, his easy conversation clouded my judgment like Uncle Ansel's stock tank after a summer rain, but I forced myself to remember who he was. "Elaborate, please."

"For starters, the stores are limited. No mall. No real restaurants." He chuckled. "No doctors or dentists or hospitals."

"We have all that in Lubbock, though."

"Sure."

He sounded as if he was leaving something out. "And ...?"

"At first I felt there weren't enough people here. Or, you know, not enough to make a community. I worried I wouldn't share the same interests with anyone." He pushed at the sun visor. "Thought I'd be lonely."

"That's Trapp for you."

"I'm surprised to hear you say that." He squinted at me. "I don't feel that way now. Not about the people anyway." He seemed to wait for a reply, but when he didn't receive one, he added, "I still wish Trapp had a CiCi's, though."

"You like cardboard pizza?"

"I do." He grinned. "As a teenager, I couldn't wait to leave for college so I could eat at CiCi's whenever I wanted."

I dug in my purse for chewing gum. "I say that a lot."

"You like CiCi's?"

"No, I can't wait to get to college."

He quieted as he slowed for a stop sign, and I could hear several questions in his silence, but he asked only one. "Where do you plan on going?"

I exhaled, not comfortable discussing my plans with him. "Tech," I said shortly, wondering if the Christians in Lubbock would be like the Cunninghams.

"I figured you for the type to leave the area."

I expected to see cynicism in his eyes, but all I saw was interest. I rubbed my thumb along the seam of my jeans as Dodd stopped at the traffic light. "Well, I won't be able to afford anything else. And even then, only if I get a scholarship."

"Um … isn't that your mom?"

My body went rigid. Sure enough, the hatchback was stopped at the red light, and when Dodd turned left, Momma's gaze followed the El Camino through the intersection.

In the split second our eyes met, her expression changed from surprise to disbelief to fury. I gripped the hand rest but refused to turn and look out the back windshield to see if Momma was following us. I knew she was.

Dodd mimicked my silence until he stopped at the front doors of the United, where he called out a polite comment—have a good day, or see you tomorrow—just before I jumped out of the car.

"Thanks." I said the word, but my body shrieked for me to hurry, run, escape, and I didn't take the time to muster a smile or a nod or any other appropriate action to express my gratitude. Instead, I rushed headlong into the store, catching the reflection of Momma's hatchback in the front windows as she sped into the parking lot, tires squealing, and slammed to a stop next to the El Camino.

I sought sanctuary in the break room, bracing myself against the back wall while I waited for the storm to hit.

Momma burst through the swinging doors. "Ruth Ann Turner, what are you thinking?"

"He gave me a ride, Momma. It's no big deal." Punching my employee code into the time clock, I willed my hands to stop shaking.

"Those people aren't like us, Ruth Ann. You can't trust them."

Even though I agreed with her, I didn't appreciate the uncontrolled intensity of her emotions. "JohnScott trusts them."

She narrowed her eyes. "What do they want with JohnScott?"

"Nothing. They're friends." I threw my purse in a locker and clanked the metal door, keeping my back to her.

"Well, what do they want with *you*?"

What did Dodd Cunningham want with me? Maybe he thought I needed a friend, maybe he thought I needed Jesus, maybe he just wanted somebody who would listen to him whine about Trapp.

"He gave me a ride to work, that's all." I tied my apron.

"Ruth Ann." Momma snarled as though she wanted to spit. "Next time? *Walk.*"

CHAPTER TWENTY

I completely ignored the preacher for two weeks. At least I tried. He insisted on talking to Maria and me, but I only ever gave him short, curt responses in an attempt to discourage his small talk. After Momma's outburst at the store, I briefly questioned my decision to befriend him. Was *befriend* even the right word? Our friendship would be more of an *acquaintanceship*. Nothing more.

Maybe not even that much.

So when I met Maria at the Halloween Carnival that Saturday night, I hoped to avoid Dodd altogether. I had agreed to work with Maria at the cakewalk, and at the risk of appearing silly, I wore a costume. Since we both lacked courage, we opted for the basic 1950s sock-hop look. Rolled-up jeans with tennis shoes, untucked shirts, and ponytails tied with scarves.

In the back of the gym were three long dessert tables stacked with cakes, pies, and cookies that filled the room with a sugary scent. I took my post at the CD player for the first round of the cakewalk as Emily approached, dressed like a little girl. *Appropriate costume.*

"How long are you working, Ruthie?"

Even though I had come to expect her to speak to me, it still felt strange. "An hour." I noticed Emily's mother a few booths over, nodding encouragement to her. I bit my tongue.

"I'm not sure why I play this game," Emily said. "I like cake, but I don't want to carry one around for three hours. You know what I mean?" She stepped onto a colored paper square next to nine other people as I punched a CD player to blare a few bars of "Monster Mash."

She needn't have worried about winning. The first cake went to Luis Vega's little sister.

During our shift, children and adults continued to parade through the cakewalk while I pondered Emily. Not only was the girl talking to me, but now her mother was prodding her to do so. It didn't take a genius to recognize Dodd's influence, but the preacher and his God would have to be a little more creative if they expected to wipe away thirteen years of hurtful actions.

Our replacement workers arrived, and Maria and I ventured to the elementary cafeteria for the fashion show, performed by JohnScott and his athletes. Every year they were the highlight of the carnival, drawing the largest crowd and bringing in the most money.

We found two chairs near the front as Roy Orbison crooned "Pretty Woman" from the speakers, and football players, dressed as women, swaggered down a makeshift runway wearing wigs, evening gowns, and enhanced undergarments. After each "girl" was introduced, the team performed a Rockettes dance routine, complete with hairy-legged high kicks.

As we left the stage area, JohnScott, sporting a feather boa and heavy makeup, flirted into the audience and planted a waxy kiss on my cheek. I could feel his lipstick smear onto my skin.

"Ruthie, you've got something on your face."

"And now I'll have to get soap to get it off. Thanks, JohnScott."

He fluttered his fake eyelashes. "Aw, just leave it."

"Goodness, Coach Pickett," Maria said, "how long did it take you to apply all that makeup?"

"Better part of an hour. I don't know how you ladies do this every day." He quickly kissed Maria on the cheek as well, but then a beefy lineman picked him up beneath the armpits and carried him away for the next show.

"See you later, Ruthie," JohnScott called. "You, too, Maria."

As I watched him wave his feather boa, my uncomfortable feelings toward the Sanders sifted from my mind like so much face powder, and I turned toward Maria and smiled. "How about a snow cone? They're set up on the baseball field." I led the way outside, filtering through the crowd to take our places at the end of the snow-cone line, where we started people watching.

"The fashion show was good this year," I said.

"I loved the quarterback's wig." Maria surveyed the baseball field and the various games and booths. "Hey, look over there."

I searched the crowd until I noticed Dodd near the baseball toss, dressed in a tuxedo with tails, and talking to someone over the fence. *Big deal.* Right before I turned back, he shifted to one side, and I did a double take.

"Clyde Felton?"

Maria faced me. "Now that's just creepy."

The convict had a rubber ghoul mask pushed back on his head, and he was listening attentively to whatever Dodd was saying.

"Ruthie, your mouth is hanging open. Stop it." Maria examined me. "Tell me what they're doing. Both of us can't stare or they'll notice."

I positioned myself so I could watch them over Maria's shoulder. If either Dodd or Clyde glanced our way, I would shift my eyes to Maria. "Talking."

"About what?"

"How should I know?"

"Sorry."

I considered them for a few minutes, wishing I had suggested a hot dog instead of a snow cone, because I could smell wieners grilling in the outfield. "They're still talking. Dodd mostly. I think he's holding a top hat."

"The tux is cool. What's Clyde doing?"

"Shaking his head. Shuffling his feet. Looking nasty." We stepped forward in line. "Now he's saying something." I shifted again, waiting while a group of people moseyed past. "Dodd's throwing the baseball."

"Thrilling."

"He knocked the bottles down the first time. Won a pink toy."

"And?"

I waited. "They're leaving now, but not together. Dodd's going the other way, and—" I focused my gaze on the snow-cone stand.

Clyde drifted past us, the sinister mask hiding his face, and I felt a tiny bit of security from the chain-link fence separating him from the festivities.

The snow-cone line moved forward, and we ordered. Blue coconut for Maria, and cherry for me. As I crunched the syrupy ice crystals, curiosity nagged my thoughts, and I wondered about the preacher's relationship with Clyde Felton. *Weird.*

After Maria and I washed the sticky syrup from our hands, we tossed basketballs, threw darts, and fished for candy. When closing time approached, we headed to the high school parking lot for the hayride. As we neared the trailer, I noticed Dodd helping children climb onto the hay, and my skin tingled.

"Incredibly nice tux," Maria said under her breath.

As much as I hated to admit it, I agreed with her. Even though ancient and tattered, the suit fit Dodd well, and the top hat cocked to one side only added to the image. I absentmindedly pressed a palm against my naval as we climbed onto a hay bale at the back and swung our bobby socks behind the trailer. The sweet scent of hay flashed me back to summers at Ansel and Velma's, and I pulled a dry straw from my makeshift seat and twirled it between my fingers.

Dodd noticed us when the tractor pulled away from the school, and Maria greeted him from our backseat perch, prompting him to match the slow pace of the tractor. "Y'all having fun?"

"*Y'all?*" Maria asked.

He smiled broadly, flashing his teeth. "I'm attempting to blend into society." He took one long stride and settled on the corner bale next to her, holding his top hat in his lap.

A strong survival instinct entered my lungs with a short gasp, but I told myself not to jump off the back of the trailer. That would never do. Friends—or acquaintances, or whatever Dodd and I were—didn't behave that way.

Maria nudged him and then whined, "You weren't in the fashion show. Why not?"

He shrugged. "A little too wild for me. I'd rather be out here with the kids, I guess. I watched it, though." He leaned forward to look at me. "Your cousin is going to die."

"I thought he might," I said. "I noticed your lipstick."

Maria and I both turned our cheeks and pointed at our own lip prints.

"You're not serious." He wiped at his face.

Reaching across Maria, I grabbed his wrist. "Stop. You're making it worse. You've got to use soap."

He held my gaze for a beat longer than necessary, until Maria raised her voice. "So … did you do the baseball toss?"

I elbowed her.

"Yes, I did, and I won a teddy bear."

Maria squealed. "How fun. Can I have it?"

"Actually, I already gave it to another young lady, shorter than you and dressed like a princess."

"Must've been Bethany," I said. "Isn't she cute?"

"How old is she?"

"Around four, I guess."

The tractor puttered back to the school, and Dodd stepped off to help the children. He swung a little boy into the air before setting him on the sidewalk, as three other kids pulled on his coattails. You'd think they preferred Dodd over the hayride.

A crowd streamed out of the high school, and Maria and I made our way across the parking lot.

"That guy has it bad for you, Ruthie." She sighed dreamily. "I think it's your hair."

"What about my hair?" I felt my scarved ponytail, wondering what she was going on about.

"Well, it's long and shiny, and most guys go for that, you know. I've seen him staring at you. His gaze begins at your face and slides all the way down your hair to your backside." She giggled. "Then, being a preacher, he embarrasses himself and looks away."

I halted in the middle of the parking lot because my legs stopped working properly. My neck seemed to be malfunctioning as well, but I managed to swivel my head and look at her. "Dodd Cunningham?"

"Yes, Dodd Cunningham." She put a hand on her hip. "He's crazy about you."

"That's absurd."

"He sat by us, didn't he?"

"He sat by *you*," I protested. "Now that I think about it, he's been talking to you at lunch a lot lately."

She stared at me with her bottom lip hanging half an inch below the top. "You honestly don't see it? Ruthie, he doesn't talk to *me* all the time. He talks to *you* all the time. I just happen to sit next to you … all the time. He never talks to me if you're not around." Her eyebrows lifted into two sharp spikes. "But I bet he talks to you when I'm not around."

I held my breath while her words tumbled in my head like wet sneakers in a dryer. *Whoosh-bang. Whoosh-bang. Whoosh-bang.* She was wrong, of course. Dodd Cunningham only wanted to preach at me like he preached to the Debate Club, nothing more.

"He can't be interested in me, Maria." I shook my head. "Absolutely not."

CHAPTER TWENTY-ONE

Sunday I woke up with a headache and stayed in bed till early afternoon.

After Maria made her ridiculous declaration, I had refused to discuss it. Dodd Cunningham? Not in a million years. If he had any interest in me at all, it was only as a missionary project. But JohnScott would know what I should do. He may have changed in the past six weeks, but he still represented my tether to sanity.

Slipping into a pair of worn sweats, I shuffled to the kitchen and grabbed the cordless phone, but it was dead. Apparently Momma had forgotten to pay the bill again.

She was banging around in her bedroom, getting ready for a late shift, and I called to her. "Could you drop me at Uncle Ansel and Aunt Velma's?"

A dresser drawer slammed. "You could've asked a little earlier."

Ansel and Velma lived less than ten minutes away, but Momma had a point. She wouldn't make it on time. "Sorry."

"What good is an apology, Ruth Ann? It won't get me to work on time." She hurried into the kitchen, where she smeared peanut butter on a slice of white bread. The smell reminded me I hadn't eaten, but I didn't want to take the time. "Can't JohnScott pick you up?" she asked.

"I wouldn't know. The phone's out."

She picked up the phone, listened, then punched it off. "Shoot. I forgot."

I replaced the lid on the peanut butter and tossed it in the cabinet while Momma reached for her purse and sweater.

We didn't speak during the short drive. Instead, Momma tuned the radio to her favorite country-and-western station, and I speculated about how to tell JohnScott the preacher might have feelings for me. This was impossible. I wished my cousin weren't such good friends with Dodd, because he would have a better perspective if he weren't.

I glanced at Momma. She never listened to my problems, but I knew how she would react to Maria's news. It wouldn't be pleasant.

I shuddered.

"What? What's wrong with you?"

"Nothing, Momma."

"You in some kind of trouble?"

Her usual question. "I'm not pregnant."

"Don't get sassy with me, Ruth Ann."

I sighed. "Just drop me at the end of the drive."

"I was planning on it." She stopped the car just long enough for me to get out, then did a three-point turn and headed back to town.

I stood knee-deep in johnsongrass near my aunt and uncle's mailbox and watched the hatchback sputter away. Why couldn't God help her be happy when I needed her so badly?

"Love you, too," I mumbled.

Ansel and Velma lived on a small farm a few miles outside of town. The older, ranch-style home, set back from the road a hundred yards, had been filled to bursting when all my cousins lived there, but I had always considered it a cozy safe haven.

JohnScott's double-wide lay fifty yards past the house, but I had a feeling he'd be at Ansel and Velma's. Normally, he ate Sunday lunch with his parents and then lay around talking to Ansel about livestock all afternoon.

As I tramped up the gravel drive, Ansel's old blue heeler came trotting around the end of the house, silently wagging his tail. "Hey, Rowdy." I scratched behind his ears, and then let myself in the front door instead of going around back, where we usually parked. I hadn't been in through the front door in years. Nobody had, yet it remained unlocked.

The house felt abnormally still.

My family wouldn't have seen my approach because only the dining room had windows facing the front yard, and that room went unused except for Thanksgiving Day. I expected Velma to be in the kitchen, so I stepped through the living room, but before I could call to her, I heard a voice.

Dodd's voice.

My chest tightened with a strange mix of hope and terror, but then I realized the sound came from the back porch, and I'd only heard him through the open windows. Creeping to the corner of the room, I glimpsed Dodd sitting at the old wooden picnic table with JohnScott and Grady. Rowdy was just settling down at JohnScott's feet.

What in the world? I scanned the living room, searching for Velma even though I could feel the emptiness. Ansel's two-toned Silverado could be seen out back with the El Camino, but the absence of Velma's car made me wonder if my aunt and uncle had made a trip to Lubbock. They might not be home for hours.

I hovered behind the recliner, searching my mind for a possible solution, prepared to bolt to the back bedroom, if necessary. Common sense told me I was overreacting, but the knot of anxiety between my shoulder blades insisted otherwise. I didn't want to talk to them. Not like this, but eventually they would come in the house and find me. And I'd look like a fool.

I sneaked a look out the window again while JohnScott was speaking in his slow drawl, "… need to wait until I get my life right, don't I? I'm not a very good person on the inside."

Grady shook his head. "Coach Pickett, no matter how long you wait, you'll never be good enough. That's the point."

JohnScott leaned his elbows on the table. "How can He love me with all I have in my past?"

For crying out loud, they were talking about Jesus stuff. I knew the Debate Club discussed the Bible, but why on earth would JohnScott have them over to the house?

The preacher shrugged. "His love is bigger than your sin."

My cousin let tears fall down his cheeks unashamedly, but his fists clenched on the table. "I don't think she'll ever be able to forgive me." His voice broke.

Dodd leaned toward him. "Your mother?"

JohnScott ran his fingers through his hair. Whatever was wrong, I hurt for him and wished the Cunninghams would leave.

I dug my fingertips into the velour headrest of the recliner as JohnScott slid his arms into his lap, defeated. "Not Mom." He met Dodd's gaze. "Ruthie."

Understanding hit me with all the force of a softball sailing over home plate, and I pressed my palms against my heart, almost feeling the pain of impact. JohnScott wasn't just talking about Jesus or the Bible. He was talking about *the church*. I paced across the room and back again.

He held his head in his hands, but if I knew my cousin, any minute he'd chuckle and say, "Naw, not for me."

He lifted his head. "I guess there's no reason to wait."

"There's no hurry, Coach Pickett."

"No, I'm ready." JohnScott wiped his cheeks. "Do we have to go to the church building, or can we do it here?"

"Water is water." Dodd scoped the yard. "What do you have in mind?"

JohnScott swung his legs over the splintery bench of the picnic table. "We've got a holding tank across the way over there."

Dodd and Grady asked in unison, "What's a holding tank?"

"You guys are such city boys." JohnScott laughed. "Big, round cement basin full of well water, like an above-ground pool."

"Slime?" Dodd stepped off the porch.

"And maybe a few goldfish."

As they moved out of sight, I stumbled down the hall to the back bedroom, where I lifted the curtain at the window overlooking the side pasture.

JohnScott and Dodd kicked off their shoes, then sat on the side of the holding tank and swung their legs over and stood in the thigh-deep water. Dodd gripped JohnScott's shoulder, and my cousin nodded. When the preacher dunked him under, the block of ice between my shoulder blades melted into a slushy pool of emptiness, and I closed my eyes.

Why did he think this would hurt me? I didn't care.

I fingered the rubbery lining of the curtain before letting it fall back into place, and then I wandered down the hall and waited in the entryway with my back pressed against the wall and my palm gripping the doorknob. When I heard them in the mudroom, I slipped out the front door as they came in the back. They would never know I had been there. I would see to that.

Trudging down the highway on my way back to town, I hugged myself not only to ward off the brisk fall wind but also to fill the loneliness in my heart.

CHAPTER TWENTY-TWO

I knew JohnScott would come.

I waited for him on the couch, entranced by the blank television screen. Thirteen years before, I had curled up on the same couch watching the *Power Rangers* while Momma and Daddy argued in the bedroom. When I turned up the volume, Momma had yelled at me to turn it down.

"Don't holler at her, Lynda. She didn't do nothing." Daddy had been in a dark mood that day, and so weary I remember thinking he needed a nap. He had long stretches, days at a time, when sadness seemed to consume him body and soul.

Momma followed him into the living room, then leaned against the doorframe. "You're right, Hoby. She didn't do anything."

Daddy knelt in front of me and took my face in his hands. I smiled at the attention he gave me, but the longer I looked into his eyes, the more my mood mirrored his own. His sorrow warmed my cheeks as he examined my eyes, lips, and nose. His fingertips trailed across my forehead, and I felt his tension—studying, hunting, searching … but for what?

"It's her eyes, Hoby," Momma had pleaded with him. "Remember, babe? It's her eyes."

He shook his head and sighed, then plodded past the *Power Rangers* and out the front door.

"Daddy, wait." I ran after him.

"I've gotta go to work now, Ruth Ann."

"But you don't have your work shirt."

He glanced down. "Yeah, I guess it's in the laundry. You be good, okay?" He grasped my miniature hand with his calloused one and kissed it before climbing into his truck. His whiskers tickled, and I pressed my palm against the leg of my cotton shorts to still the sensation before returning to the couch for the rest of my show.

Daddy never came back.

For two days I asked Momma when he'd be home, but she had only gazed at me with a lost expression. Finally Aunt Velma sat me down and explained.

A rapid knock jolted me out of my memories, and I lifted my eyes to see JohnScott's curls through the diamond-shaped window in our front door. Inhaling a ragged breath, I steeled myself for the inevitable confrontation. "Come on in."

He opened the door hesitantly, but he smiled. "Hey there, little cousin."

He had changed into dry clothes, but his hair was still damp, and I pretended not to notice the peculiar expression on his face as he followed me to the kitchen.

"You want some chocolate milk?"

Normally he would have sprawled in one of the mismatched maple chairs at the table, but instead he stalled at the counter. "I've got something to tell you, Ruthie."

"All right." I reached into the refrigerator for the milk, hugging it to my hip while I grabbed two glasses off the drain board. The coldness remained on my shirt and stomach even after I set the jug on the counter.

"I need to tell you something, little cousin."

"You said that."

He took a step toward me. "I got baptized this afternoon."

Pausing in my preparations, I intended to acknowledge his statement, but he rushed on.

"Dodd has been talking to me, but I'd been waiting because I thought I wasn't good enough. Then today it just felt right, you know?"

I scooped Nesquik into the glasses, inhaling the chocolaty powder.

"Dodd and Grady explained I don't have to be good enough. God wants me the way I am." His voice drifted to a murmur. "Cool, huh?"

The spoon tinkled hollowly against the sides of the glass, mimicking the void in my spirit. One good whack, and everything would shatter. "I guess so."

"We did it out in the holding tank." He shivered. "I thought Dodd would turn blue from the cold. You should've seen him."

A drop of guilt splashed in my heart.

"He and Grady came over to the house for lunch, and we talked for an hour or more. I feel so clean, Ruthie. Like I'm a different person."

I handed him his chocolate milk.

"Afterward I cried, Ruthie. Can you believe that? JohnScott Pickett cried." He raised the glass to his lips but lowered it before drinking. "You're not mad?"

Of course I wasn't mad.

I took a sip of my drink, and the coldness crept from my throat, behind my heart, and into my stomach. "I shouldn't be surprised. After all, you've been meeting with the Debate Club."

He slowly turned his face to the side, but his eyes remained fixed on me.

"It's no big deal, JohnScott." I settled into a chair at the kitchen table, wishing for the first time in my life that JohnScott would go home. What good would it do to talk about it?

"Ruthie, I want you to feel this good too." He sloshed milk on the table as he sat down. "Will you let me tell you about Jesus?"

I pulled a paper napkin from the plastic holder, laying it over the spill to soak up the milk. Then I wiped the vinyl tablecloth and wadded the napkin in my fist. *If only the messes of life could be cleaned so easily.*

"I remember Jesus … from Sunday school when I was small."

He rotated his glass, exposing a ring of milk, which we both studied to keep from looking at each other. "So you know He died for you?"

I nodded, but indignation lifted my chin stiffly.

"Do you believe it?"

"It makes sense." His questions goaded my patience like an electric cattle prod—*zzt, zzt, zzt.*

"Then why—"

"Because of the people." The words clunked across my tongue, and I imagined the low echo of an angry fist pounding a pulpit.

"The people?"

I slapped at a tear but refused to let a second escape. "JohnScott, *Jesus* may love you even though you're not good enough, but I'm not good enough for the *church*." I gave a sarcastic chuckle. "And they *don't* love me in spite of it."

My statement surprised me as much as him.

"The people aren't important, Ruthie."

"The people are *everything*." I rose and dumped both glasses in the sink, slamming the faucet back and forth as I rinsed them.

He waited until I settled, until my mind returned to my present-day kitchen and the weight of thirteen years lifted from my chest, until I could breathe again.

"It's about you and God," he said, touching the brown ring on the tablecloth. "But I suppose people can get in the way."

I straightened the glasses in the sink. "That's a fact."

CHAPTER TWENTY-THREE

Over the next two weeks, JohnScott and I redefined our cousinship. While the Panthers won the district title and were solidly throttled at bidistrict, I realized my relationship with JohnScott had become strained, if not remote. Uncle Ansel and Aunt Velma had yet to voice an opinion about his baptism, but they seemed to have made an unspoken agreement not to mention it to Momma.

Gradually I spent less time with him and more time with Maria, even though he still gave me rides to and from work. Dodd offered me rides too, but I wouldn't agree to that again. I stayed a safe distance from the preacher, assuming he'd get the hint and stop offering, but one day in mid-November, I realized my assumption was flawed.

I sat in the teachers' lounge picking at my peanut-butter sandwich while Maria rattled on about a weight-loss program. When Dodd sat down next to her, she slapped her palm down on the table. "Are you lost, Mr. Cunningham? The Debate Club meets at the back."

"Very funny, Maria. Or should I say Ms. Fuentes?" He smiled. "I heard a rumor we were being called a debate club."

"Well, you know what they say," Maria said. "If the boot fits ..."

It shamed me to avoid eye contact, but I hadn't yet figured out my relationship with my own cousin, much less how the preacher fit into it. I reached for a saltshaker and tilted it until a steady stream flowed onto the table.

"Do you have plans for Thanksgiving?" Dodd directed the question to me, but I didn't respond. Instead, I scooted the salt into a pile with my fingertip.

Maria bumped my knee and answered the question. "I'm visiting my folks in Amarillo. What about you?"

"We'll make a trip to Fort Worth. Both sets of grandparents are there. And about five hundred cousins."

His gaze prickled my skin uncomfortably.

Maria looked between the two of us, shrugged, then lifted her lunch tray. "Be right back."

With my pinky, I made a well in the top of the salt pile, forming a volcano. I felt like a volcano. My impertinence built up so much pressure, I thought I might explode. Maybe I should tell him I didn't need a ride to work and get it over with. To ease the tension, I lifted the corners of my mouth before returning to my sculpture.

My feeble smile must have increased his confidence, because he leaned across the table. "I wondered if you might want to go to a movie with me. On Saturday night? In Lubbock?"

I held my breath.

"Mom's going." His voice carried a frown. "And Grady." His hand brushed mine as he slid a finger into the salt, denting it. "We'd be back before late."

Unbelievable.

Maria was right after all, and I had been so upset with JohnScott, I hadn't asked him about it. What could I say? Going to a movie with the Cunninghams would either turn Momma into a dust devil or send her tumbling into depression again. And I had no idea how a date would affect Fawn and her parents. Maybe even Emily.

I raised my gaze with the intention of setting him straight but lost my train of thought when I looked into his eyes. He held me motionless with an expectant expression, his eyebrows raised.

Had I never noticed his eyes? They were blue. Startlingly blue with dark lashes, and when he smiled, they crinkled at the edges. But more than anything, I noticed how near they were to my own eyes. As we hunkered over Mount Vesuvius, his breath warmed my cheeks, sending a flame of panic coursing through my veins like molten lava.

I leaned away from him, brushing salt in his lap. "I've got to work on Saturday … Sorry." Grabbing my trash, I stumbled out of the room, and when I pushed through the door of the teachers' bathroom, I still held my lunch sack and half a sandwich. Peanut butter smeared my thumb.

Maria pounced. "Well?"

I slumped against the wall next to the paper-towel holder. "He asked me out."

"You lucky dog. Where is he taking you?"

"I'm not going."

She gawked at me as if I'd turned down a million dollars. "The church thing?"

Moving to the sink, I squirted vanilla-mint soap in my palm and washed away the peanut-butter oil. "Forget about it."

"Forget you turned your nose up at the best-looking bachelor in town?" A tinge of anger colored her words.

"He's not that good-looking." I examined my reflection in the mirror, searching for whatever Dodd saw in me.

"You're weird, Ruthie."

Her attitude irked me, and if I didn't get away from her fairly quickly, the volcano churning inside me might blow its top.

But when we exited the bathroom, JohnScott ambushed me. "What was that about?"

I shook my head and hurried toward the office and away from both of them.

JohnScott followed. "Go out with him, little cousin. He's a great guy."

Halting in the middle of the hallway, I confronted him face-to-face. "What about Momma?"

He pulled his earlobe. "Yeah, I don't know."

I yanked him toward the wall when a flood of students came around the corner from the cafeteria. "The preacher shouldn't even be interested in me. I'm not his type."

"How do you know his type?"

"I'm not a church girl, you dufus. Why doesn't he like Fawn? Or Emily?"

"Fawn has a boyfriend, and I refuse to even make a case for Emily."

"What about Maria?"

His head lolled. "Maria's even less of a church girl than you."

"Well … okay. But Fawn would dump Tyler in a heartbeat if Dodd took a shining to her."

He shrugged. "Maybe."

"So why don't you mention it? Get him off my back."

"Somehow I don't think that will make a difference."

I squeezed my eyes shut to block out my cousin and his senseless rambling. If Maria had been blinded by the probability of romance, JohnScott was handicapped by the possibility of salvation. I didn't even know him now, and he obviously didn't know me. If he did, he would recognize I'd rather walk barefoot over a cluster of devil's-head cactus than go on a single date with Dodd Cunningham.

For a week the preacher continued to seek me out despite my efforts to avoid him. He casually invited me to the Dairy Queen after school one afternoon, which reminded me that he had asked me before. When I thought back, I realized he had been asking me out for a while. Unofficially. Always with a group. How had I been so blind? It made me queasy to think I may have unintentionally encouraged him, and I felt obligated to set things straight even though I dreaded the inevitable conversation.

It happened the day school let out for Thanksgiving break

As I exited through the side door of the high school, Dodd and several male students came around the corner of the building, traveling in the direction of the weight room. An icy gust whipped my hair around my shoulders, and I pulled my jacket tight and ducked my head.

"Ruthie, wait up." Dodd jogged after me while the boys made catcalls.

I stopped but didn't turn around.

As he stepped around me, he motioned for his students to go on. Thank goodness.

I clasped my hair with one hand to keep it out of my eyes. "Yes?"

"I can't believe it's already Thanksgiving. It seems like we just moved here yesterday." He grinned, and his eyes did that crinkle thing.

"Yeah … I guess I'd better be going. It's awful cold out here."

"Oh, right." He glanced at the sky as though he were just noticing the weather. "I'm going to JohnScott's later with Grady. Some of us are planning a bonfire out in the pasture. Might eat s'mores." His hand brushed the back of his neck. "I don't know, but I thought you might come. It ought to be fun."

At least his strategy had improved. Inviting me to Ansel and Velma's house increased the odds I'd agree. But I couldn't. No matter how beautiful his eyes were, no matter how easy he was to talk to, he was still the preacher. "Dodd …" I shook my head. "You and me? It won't work, you know?"

He blinked into the wind. "Why do you say that?"

"I don't think of you like that. We're friends." I tried to sound confident but stammered instead. "Good friends … but nothing more."

"Sure." He nodded. "Sure, Ruthie." He took a few backward steps down the sidewalk. "That's fine." He raised his hand. "Have a good Thanksgiving." Then he disappeared around the corner of the building.

Just like that. It was over. I had finally done it … and I felt like a jerk.

Trudging through the parking lot, I climbed into JohnScott's truck and flopped across the seat to lie on my back with an arm over my face. Even the dusty farm scent embedded in the seat cushions didn't comfort me.

I didn't move. Not when my purse slid to the floorboard. Not when I shivered from the cold. Not when I heard the athletes filter through the parking lot, calling to each other, slamming car doors, driving away.

JohnScott must've been the last one out of the weight room. He opened the door of the truck and tossed his briefcase onto the floorboard on top of my purse.

"Little cousin?" he crooned. "You got something on your mind?" He lifted my arm from across my face.

I groaned. Why was this affecting me? I should have felt relieved.

Leaning over to make upside-down eye contact with me, he whispered, "I told him why you keep saying no."

"You what?" I rolled over and lifted myself up on my elbows, almost knocking JohnScott's nose with the back of my head.

"I had to. You're killing him."

"How?" I demanded.

"He's been nuts about you since the first time he laid eyes on you, but the goof thought I was dating you. Now he's found the courage to ask you out, and you won't go. He thought there was something wrong with him."

"There is. My mother despises him, and his family would never accept me." I collapsed onto the seat again but immediately sprang back up. "Wait a minute. What did you tell him?"

JohnScott slid behind the wheel and closed the door, blocking the wind. "That the church kicked you out after Uncle Hoby ran off. I didn't go into detail."

"You know I don't appreciate gossip behind my back."

"Oh, give it a rest, Ruthie."

I stared at a deep crack in the dashboard where too much sunshine had hardened the vinyl. "Well, how did he not know before? I thought church people discussed those things."

"I guess not. He seemed shocked." JohnScott's bottom lip pulled tight. "And angry."

I absorbed the information for a moment. "What did he say?"

"He wants to ask the elders about it, but I don't think he had ever heard of anything like that happening before."

"The *elders*?" Weary exhaustion made it hard to breathe. "Well, this is it, then."

The Cunninghams would find out the truth. They'd leave us alone now. Just like the church leaders, like the Blaylocks, like the rest of the congregation. I cringed when I thought of those men talking about Momma and me, but I wanted to destroy something when I considered they might turn on JohnScott, too.

The fatigue in my chest relaxed, and I focused on the one comforting thought in the entire scenario. "At least Dodd won't ask me out again."

It should've been a consoling balm, a breath of new air, a cleansing solution to my tumultuous problem. But it was none of those. Because the sinking feeling deep in my stomach weighed me down with despair and drowned me in self-doubt.

Typically my work distracted me from worries, but that night at the United, I could barely concentrate. Thanksgiving shoppers crowding the store didn't help matters, and after my dinner break, I worked with Luis on carryout because the lot overflowed, and people were parking at the side of the building. I loaded groceries into a customer's car and was pushing a shopping cart back to the front entrance when Milla and Dodd came around the corner. All three of us jerked to a stop, and Dodd's eyes found mine.

Milla spoke first. "Ruthie, I hoped to see you, but now that you're here, I don't know what to say."

My thumb fiddled with a piece of loose plastic on the handle of the cart.

She squeezed my arm. "Please find it in your heart to forgive." Then she lowered her head and drifted to her SUV, leaving Dodd peering down at me. Again.

How many times did I have to do this? Every ounce of emotion had been drained from my body, and I no longer felt anything for this man, good or bad. I merely wanted it to be over. Done with. Back like it was before. I studied my hands, pink from the cold.

"Ruthie?"

His compassionate tone prompted me to look at him, but I forced myself to look without seeing. Without thinking or feeling.

He squinted into my eyes, then down to my mouth, then to my hair hanging in a sloppy braid. "I understand now," he said softly.

The fact that he cared surprised me. Despising the wetness in the corners of my eyes, I turned away and studied the sand blowing across the side lot. I didn't look at him again because I knew the tears would come. "I'd better get back to work."

I set my gaze on the corner of the building where I could escape to my job, but my feet wouldn't move, wouldn't cooperate. It was as though my body wouldn't agree to take me away from this man.

He watched me for an endless time, then put his hand on the small of my back and nudged. The warmth of his hand penetrated my sweatshirt near my waistline. As I walked, he shuffled at my side, glancing at me every few steps.

More than anything in the world, I wanted him to turn around, get in his car, and drive away. I don't know why I let him lead me. *Stupid.* I could manage on my own.

As we rounded the corner and came under the bright store lights, I mentally shook myself and took several quick steps away from him, but when a car pulled up beside me, I recoiled.

Momma.

She rolled down her window and called to me. "Don't forget to bring some Cool Whip, all right?" Then she noticed Dodd, and her eyes narrowed into determined slits. "What are you doing out here with the likes of *him*?"

CHAPTER TWENTY-FOUR

Dodd knew the Turners and Blaylocks had friction between them, but he never imagined anything so broad as to include the entire congregation. He desperately needed guidance, and he'd already put a call in to Charlie Mendoza, asking him to meet him at the church building before the Thanksgiving song service.

In the meantime, Grady was craving details as they hashed it out over the phone. "Tell me Coach Pickett's exact words."

"He only said Ruthie and her mother were kicked out of the church."

"What did he mean by *kicked out* of the church?"

"I assume they were asked to leave, but he didn't say that." Dodd pinched the bridge of his nose. "It's possible the church is practicing First Corinthians, chapter five, by not speaking to Ruthie and her mother."

"Wait a minute. There's a Bible verse for ignoring people?"

"It's meant to be a discipline for those who sin blatantly."

"What's that got to do with Ruthie and her mom?"

"I'm not sure, but I'm hoping Charlie can shed some light on the situation."

Grady hummed. "I hate to say it, but Lynda Turner may have blown this out of proportion. From what I hear, that wouldn't be surprising."

A tap on his office door prompted Dodd to end the call as Charlie ducked through the doorway. He smiled warmly and gripped Dodd's hand. "Hello there, brother."

In Dodd's mind, Charlie represented the typical Trapp resident—laid back, friendly, and honest to the core. He wore freshly starched Wranglers and a crisp plaid shirt, and Dodd could see the faint dent in his hair where his rancher's cap had recently rested. His strong Old Spice aftershave battled to overpower the comfortable scent of the outdoors, and Dodd couldn't keep from grinning. "Charlie, thank you for coming."

The older man eased into a chair, which moaned as his weight distributed over the leather. "What can I do for you?"

Dodd straightened a stack of papers on his desk. There was no delicate way to broach the subject, so he went right to the crux of the problem. "It's come to my attention that Lynda Turner was removed from the church several years ago."

"Sure enough, she was," Charlie said. "That's been nigh on ten years back. Maybe more. Why do you ask?" His forthright acknowledgment pinched Dodd's stomach. He had expected regret. Or possibly shame.

"Her nephew is a friend of mine. You know JohnScott Pickett?"

Charlie laughed deeply. "Sure, I know JohnScott. The boy sported diapers a few days ago, and now he fancies himself the head coach."

Dodd wondered if the elder was taking the conversation seriously.

"Did you know he was baptized?"

"You don't say." Charlie frowned. "Now that's a surprise to me."

Dodd reached for a pen and doodled parallel lines in the corner of his Sunday sermon notes. "Do you suppose JohnScott would be welcome here? In spite of his aunt?"

"Well, now … I don't see why he wouldn't be. Is he thinking on visiting?"

"Not that I know of." Dodd tossed the pen aside. "What caused the excommunication, anyway?"

"Goodness, Dodd. I wouldn't go so far as to call it an excommunication."

"So what happened?"

Charlie rose from his chair, seeming to move in slow motion because of his height. He stepped to the window and gingerly rotated the rod to open the blinds. "Brother, there's not much to tell. Gerald Blaylock handled that mess. Neil's daddy? One of the wisest men I've been blessed to know. Pity when he passed. Anyhow, he felt it prudent to avoid gossip, so he took care of the details." He peered at Dodd, hesitating before adding, "You've heard about Hoby and Lynda Turner's separation?"

"Some." Dodd massaged his tight neck muscles. "The church disfellowshipped the whole family?"

Charlie turned, and his eyes filled with compassion, concern, and something else … *wisdom*. It was then that Dodd knew the man was more than he seemed. "Now, Dodd, keep in mind a lot happened back then we don't know about."

"You're right, and I'm trying to make sense of it. You said JohnScott would be welcome here … but would the Turners?"

Charlie's expression grew distant as he gazed at the bookshelf. "There's been a lot of water under the bridge." He sat down, rubbing his chin with a knuckle before settling his sober eyes back on Dodd. "Some of the congregants are set in their ways, if you know what I mean." He squinted. "Has Lynda indicated she'd *like* to come back to the church?"

Hopelessness pushed a sigh from deep in Dodd's abdomen. "Not at all."

"Well, you've got to consider the flock. Dredging up issues from the past could cause a passel of new problems."

Charlie had valid concerns, and Dodd had no idea how to address them. "I don't want to cause problems, but I don't think it's right to have friction between the congregation and the Turners." Dodd ran his palms over his face. "Charlie, I'm frustrated. And confused."

Charlie leaned forward with his elbows on the desk. He spoke low, his voice taking on a paternal tone. "I can tell you are, but let's keep this in perspective. From your point of view, it's a fresh wound, but remember, it happened a long time ago, and the Turners may not appreciate having the bandage ripped off." He rose, and Dodd did the same. "Tell you what, I'll talk to Neil and Lee Roy and see what they know about it. But I'll tell you one thing for sure. No matter what, I'll be praying for the Turners and JohnScott."

Dodd clasped Charlie's hand, partly in thanks and partly in desperation, but even though he hadn't gotten many answers, Dodd felt more at peace with the situation knowing Charlie was praying about it too.

Twenty minutes later, church members began arriving for the song service, and since he had the evening off from preaching duties, Dodd chose to sit with his mother instead of at the front. While Milla leaned forward, listening to a conversation in the next pew between Neil Blaylock's wife and Pamela Sanders, Dodd marveled at the normalcy of their conversation. Even though Ruthie's pain invaded his thoughts so thoroughly that his vision blurred, idle chatter carried on as though nothing had happened.

"How are your plans for the fund-raiser?" Pamela asked.

"The silent auction will be amazing this year." Neil's wife held a small mirror in front of her face, moving it here and there to check her reflection from different angles. "The garage is already full of donations, and Neil gave me the front barn for overflow."

Milla placed a hand on the back of the pew. "What's this fund-raiser for?"

"Volunteer fire department." She snapped her mirror closed. "Every year in December, we make a day of it. There's a parade, a silent auction, and all kinds of food and crafts."

Pamela giggled. "Later that night, after they announce the amount of money raised, they'll have fireworks at the stadium."

Fireworks for the fire department? Irony drifted through Dodd's clouded mind, but he pushed it away. Were these people so concerned with menial details, they couldn't see the pain of those around them?

Emily plopped next to her mother even though she normally sat with the other teenagers. She glanced back at Dodd, and Pamela spoke to her in a loud whisper. "What a sweet girl to sit with your mother."

A gentle slap on his back caused Dodd to look up. It was Neil. Dodd stood and shook hands as the elder leaned in to speak softly. "Did Charlie answer your questions about the Turners, son?"

"Yes ..." Talking to Charlie had helped matters, but Dodd still had unanswered questions. "Can we sit down and discuss it sometime? I'd appreciate your perspective as well."

Neil nodded briskly. "Yes, let's do that. One day next week." He took his seat next to his wife as Lee Roy Goodnight puttered to the front of the room to lead the opening prayer.

Neil's reassurance brought additional peace to Dodd's troubled nerves, but he still needed time to think. He studied the people in the pews around him. Every woman on the church roster had phone-called, visited, and casseroled him and his family, and he was beginning to feel like he knew their families—most of which were intermarried to the extent of confusion. As he surveyed the church, Dodd couldn't see how the faithful Christians aligned with what JohnScott had told him.

Fawn sat a few rows up, alone tonight, since Tyler only came to Trapp on weekends. But Grady sat with her. Dodd had questioned Grady about the attention he gave Fawn, but his brother insisted his interest only went so far as friendship.

Dodd took a deep breath, exhaling as they rose to sing "Come Thou Fount of Every Blessing." The tension in his neck radiated down his spine until his lower back cramped from the stress. He needed a release. Maybe he would go for a jog later. A long one. So he could think about the Turners. And the congregation. And how to handle all of it. And frankly, he could use some advice regarding personal matters, which were woven through it all.

He hadn't planned on getting attached to this tiny town, and he certainly hadn't planned on getting attached to a woman, but the more he got to know Ruthie Turner, the more he was drawn to her. Granted, she had rough edges—How did Grady put it? Prickly—but she'd been through a lot with her parents, and from the sound of it, she'd been through a lot with the church.

Emily glanced back at him again with her usual bashful smile, but when she looked past him, her eyes widened. She jerked to the front with a tiny hiccup of a gasp. Curiosity tickled Dodd, but he didn't look behind him. Instead, he kept an eye on Emily, waiting to see what she would do when she turned around again.

She never did. The song ended, and she perched on the pew as stiff as one of the towels his mother dried on the clothesline. But after a few verses of the next song, Emily's shoulders relaxed, and she whispered to her mother. Pamela Sanders spun around and gaped toward the back of the room.

What in the world could be happening back there? Corky Ledbetter typically occupied the back row with her three little kids. Maybe one of them was causing mischief. It wouldn't be the first time.

Neil must've been curious too, because he stretched his arm along the back of the pew and casually swiveled his head. He gave no reaction except to stop singing, but a muscle twitched in his jaw.

That did it. Dodd didn't feel comfortable turning around after so many others, so he feigned a restroom break. Standing, he took one step up the aisle and almost shouted for joy.

Clyde Felton sat on the back pew, singing from a hymnal.

CHAPTER TWENTY-FIVE

"I told you to stay away from those people, Ruth Ann."

Irritation spiraled in my rib cage as my paper plate rotated in the microwave. Most years, Momma and I spent Thanksgiving at Ansel and Velma's crowded ranch house with my cousins and all their kids, but this year the Picketts had traveled to Tucumcari, New Mexico, to visit Ansel's kinfolk instead. That left Momma and me home alone, reheating leftovers from the diner. We had done this before with no complaints, but on that Thursday, we spent most of the day arguing.

Her constant insistence that I stay away from *those people* now sounded like screeching babble in my ears, and I wanted to scream. Because I kept picturing Milla Cunningham in the parking lot of the United with tears on her cheeks.

"You don't even know them, Momma."

"I don't have to. They come in the diner with all the other goody-goodies, and I sure as heck know *them*."

I spooned gravy over my turkey and mashed potatoes. "What if the Cunninghams are different?"

"They're not."

"JohnScott thinks so. He even got baptized in the water." Instantly I regretted my words.

Momma's movements stilled, and she paused, holding a two-liter drink. "Why would he do that?"

"I have no idea, but the Cunninghams talk to him about the Bible all the time."

"You can't be serious." She opened the drink, which protested with a belch of foam. "Does Velma know?"

"I suppose." I scooped cranberry sauce out of a miniature paper cup and waited for her reaction.

"JohnScott's a fool."

"Momma …"

She carried her food to the living room, pulled up a TV tray, and settled on the couch to watch a football game, curtailing the discussion so she could simmer alone.

I poured myself a Dr Pepper and spent the rest of Thanksgiving Day in my bedroom, counting the days until I could leave for school. My temper flared, intense and invasive, like the streak of sunshine slicing through my curtains. Momma had no right to talk about JohnScott that way, and her words increased my determination to leave home. But whenever I thought of my cousin, my heart drifted to the bottom of a deep, dark well, and I wished God—or somebody—would pull me out.

Why did I tell her about JohnScott? He may have been driving me crazy, but he didn't deserve Momma's wrath. Nobody did.

By Saturday morning, my irritation had calmed to a manageable numbness. Momma left for work, but I stayed under the covers listening to rain patter on the roof. When I pulled myself out of bed, I saw the fog hovering outside my window. *How appropriate.*

I dressed in old jeans and a sweatshirt before eating the last of the Rice Krispies. As I stood in the kitchen holding my crackling cereal bowl, I noted our bare cabinets. I'd have to make a trip to the United, on foot, to pick up my paycheck … just to spend half of it on groceries. At least the rain had slacked off.

I twisted my hair in a bun and slipped into Momma's old letter jacket, hoping it would keep me dry as well as warm. Then I set off down the street through the fog's eerie quiet. By the time I got to the store, visibility had improved enough so I could make out Grady and Milla loading groceries into her SUV. That woman was always at the store. I thrust my hands under my armpits and quickened my pace in a feeble attempt to avoid the Cunninghams along with the sense of obligation gnawing at my conscience.

"Hey, Ruthie-the-checker-girl. Where you headed?"

I paused, hoping they wouldn't mention Momma or the church. "Picking up a few things. I've got the day off."

"Big plans?"

"Not hardly."

Milla pulled her raincoat tighter. "We have a quiet day planned too. I'm making a pot of beef stew for lunch, and then we'll rent a movie."

I reached for the door. "Sounds fun."

"We'd love for you to join us."

I didn't move, didn't blink, didn't breathe. How did I get myself into these situations? If I so much as entered the Cunninghams' house, Momma would never speak to me again. I shook my head. "Oh, I don't know. I wouldn't want to invade."

"It would be a welcome invasion." Grady grinned. "You should come."

Good gracious.

Milla opened her car door and smiled over her shoulder. "Just think about it. If you decide to invade, come on over to the house around noon."

"Better yet," Grady said, "give us a call, and I'll come pick you up. This weather's nasty."

"You're not on foot, are you?" Milla said. "Goodness, Ruthie. Let us give you a ride home. We'll wait here while you pick up your groceries."

"No, I'm fine. Thanks, though." I escaped into the grocery store, not giving them a chance to press the issue. Beef stew was the last thing I needed.

As I wheeled a shopping cart through the aisles, I wondered if Dodd had told them about Momma's reaction when he gave me a ride to work. And her reaction when she caught us in the parking lot. Probably.

Guilt crept through my heart like the low-lying fog. Milla Cunningham had always been kind to me—polite, smiling, thoughtful—and she even hugged me sometimes. Momma, on the other hand, was habitually the opposite.

As I pondered each grocery item, careful not to buy more than I could carry home, Momma's whiny voice echoed through my mind, and I grew more and more upset with her.

She insisted I stay away from *those people,* yet she offered no words of encouragement about how to do so. She couldn't even manage to pay the phone bill on time so I could discuss my problems with the only person who understood me—JohnScott. But, of course, JohnScott spent all his free time with the Cunninghams—whom Momma insisted I avoid. The screeching babble in my mind rose to a crescendo but muted when I approached the checkout. I slowed my steps.

Maybe I'd go to the Cunninghams after all. Homemade stew sounded good, and after lunch I could make an excuse to leave.

I smiled, feeling the cleansing breeze of self-assuredness that comes with a plan of action.

Momma would be upset if she found out.

But Momma needn't know.

At noon, on the dot, I rapped on the Cunninghams' door and crossed my fingers that Grady would answer. The boy would jabber nonstop, saving me from conversation, but Milla opened the door instead. After a chocolate-scented hug, she led me to the kitchen, where she resumed stirring a brownie mix.

"Dodd should be back any minute," she said. "He's working on tomorrow's sermon down at the church. But Grady drove Emily out to the Blaylocks' ranch. Fawn asked them to help her and Tyler hang Christmas lights."

Super. "It's a cold day for that."

"Exactly what I said, but nobody listens." She slid the brownie pan into the oven. "Let me show you around. I want you to feel right at home."

The small, two-bedroom house barely accommodated two people, much less three, and I could see why Dodd and Grady dubbed it the shoebox. The church ought to have sold it years ago or added another bedroom. The living room held a couch and love seat with signs of family life peppering the crowded area. A deck of cards left under an end table, unfinished needlework in a basket, a folded newspaper on the couch.

We took a few steps down a short hallway and peeked into the first bedroom.

"This is mine." Milla gestured into the room, which held a quilt-laden bed, a small dresser, and a rocking chair. Then she stepped across the hall. "And this is the boys'."

The room had been designed to hold a twin-sized bed, but it now held two. One neat, one disheveled. On the nightstand between the two beds rested a lamp, two Bibles, and several Dr Pepper cans. I recognized Grady's tennis shoes on the floor next to the unmade bed and suddenly felt as though I was stealing an intimate glimpse of their family life. Was this truly a welcome invasion?

We turned to go back to the kitchen, but the pictures hanging in the hallway caught my attention, and Milla began narrating them one by one. While inspecting portraits of Dodd and Grady at various ages, I found myself captivated by a baby picture of Dodd. *Those blue eyes.* They were like the eyes of his father, who smiled at me from another frame. After ten minutes, Milla and I still stood in the hallway while she told me stories, and somewhere on our trip down memory lane, my nervousness evaporated like steam from a cup of hot chocolate.

"The best story by far," she said, "happened when Dodd was three years old. He and his dad sat on the back porch eating Popsicles.

Dodd couldn't pronounce all his sounds yet, especially the Rs and Ls." She gazed at a picture of Dodd in a plastic, backyard pool. "My husband said the Popsicles tasted yummy, and Dodd replied that he *wuved them*."

I smiled at the visual image.

"And when Russ asked him his favorite flavor, Dodd thought for a minute, then said, 'Aw, Daddy, I wike *wime* … and *wemon*.'"

My remaining discomfort dissolved with a burst of laughter.

"Then they proceeded to discuss the positive attributes of wime and wemon."

I was still giggling when the front door slammed, sending a jolt of apprehension up my spine as though I had been caught breaking and entering.

Dodd strolled around the corner, but when he saw me, he froze. His gaze met mine, and I got the impression he might be holding his breath. His smile quivered. "Now, Mom. Not the pictures."

"I couldn't help it." She pointed at me. "Blame Ruthie."

Dodd shook his head, then studied me, and his facial expression, his posture, even his silence asked an unspoken question that sent a hum of electricity through my fingertips, still touching the frame of his baby picture.

I dropped my hand, stifled by the lull in conversation, and in a split second, I asked myself three questions. What would happen if I stopped running away from the preacher? Would it send Momma over the edge? Was it worth the problems it might cause? My decision was instantaneous and impulsive.

"Not only pictures," I said, "but also the stories to go with them. Prepare to be blackmailed."

Dodd lowered a disapproving gaze to Milla. "Mom, say you didn't."

She held up her hands in surrender, laughing as she slipped to the kitchen.

Alone with him, I crossed one arm over my stomach and pinched the loose skin behind my elbow while he stared at me as if I were an apparition.

What was I thinking? I just jumped feet first off the high dive and wasn't even sure there was water beneath me. "Well, Dodd." *I might as well break the ice.* "Tell me about your wine and women."

His eyes widened as he joined me in front of the pictures. "I guess you could say I've come a long way since my youth." He straightened the swimming-pool picture. "So … you're … *here*."

I tilted my head indifferently. "Is that such a shock?" Of course it was. Even I was surprised.

He released a long breath as though he'd been holding it since he moved to town. "Yes. It's quite a shock actually."

His laugh made me want to laugh too, but I felt the overwhelming burden of Momma and what might happen if she knew where I was. And when I considered how the church might treat Dodd and his family, the combination of worries made my stomach go queasy.

I glanced back at the preacher, whose expression had shifted to match my own.

"It's good that you're here, Ruthie."

I nodded even though I wasn't sure I agreed.

When Milla called us for lunch, Dodd moved aside to let me pass. Neither of us smiled.

The nervousness I felt earlier had been replaced with doubt, and the short prayer Dodd said before the meal made me uncomfortable, either from the praying or because Dodd and Milla each held one of my hands. But during the meal, they joked so much that I relaxed again, laughing more than I'd laughed in a long time. In fact, I had so much fun, I abandoned my plan to sneak away after lunch, and I stayed for the movie.

Milla sat on the love seat, and Dodd and I took opposite ends of the couch. When the movie began, his nearness paralyzed me, and he seemed to have the same reaction. But after thirty minutes he slouched, crossing his socked feet on the coffee table, and when my back began aching, I leaned an elbow on the armrest. By the end of the feature, I had my feet tucked beside me.

Grady came in as the closing credits rolled, and when he spotted me curled on the couch, his mouth fell open dramatically. "Ruthie-the-checker-girl? At the shoebox?" He nodded knowingly. "I see how it is. You won't go out with us if Dodd asks, but you will if Mom asks."

Milla gasped. "Grady!"

I looked between the three of them as a breath of realization blew all the fog out of my muddled brain. No matter what Momma said, these people cared about me. I raised my eyebrows. "Duh, Grady, I like her better."

Dodd snorted.

Grady scratched his chin. "You know … I do too."

Milla rose from the love seat. "You boys are impossible. Ruthie, if you'd like to get away from them, you're welcome to help me in the kitchen."

I followed her for no other reason than to escape the scrutiny of Dodd and Grady, even though it meant another one-on-one conversation with Milla.

She took a small knife from a block in the corner to cut the brownies. "Sorry, Ruthie. Grady's really missing his dad, and I think he talks more to make up for it." She chuckled. "We never know what he'll say next. You'd be surprised at some of the things he comes up with."

"Yes, I help in his computer class, you know."

She flinched. "Tell me."

"Let's see ..." I picked up a stack of saucers and spread them on the counter. "One day he quoted an entire scene from *Monty Python*."

"No, he didn't."

"Something about the velocity of a swallow?"

Milla groaned. "He did."

"And another time he took great pains to explain the difference between a buffalo and a bison—with a visual demonstration of the horns." I raised my hands to my head, forming horns with my fingers.

"Ah yes." Milla made finger horns on her own head. "Buffalo." She repositioned her hands. "Bison."

I nodded. "And of course, there's the daily commentary on his emotional adjustment to small-town life."

"He doesn't hide much, does he?"

"Not Grady."

She paused as we both heard my unintentional implication. "Do you see much of Dodd at school?"

I laughed a little too loudly. "Oh, of course we both eat in the teachers' lounge. He sits over by JohnScott, but I usually sit with Maria. She's the Family and Consumer Science teacher, but you probably knew that already." My mouth bubbled out of control. "I mean, there are other times he talks to me, but not like Grady does. When Dodd talks, he gets right to the point and doesn't use extra words. He's more reserved." I had to shut up. Determined to change the subject, I blurted, "Too bad you don't have ice cream."

Milla had been smiling knowingly, but now she lifted her head. "What?"

"Brownie-bottom pie would be tasty."

"Brownie-bottom pie?"

"You know, brownie in the bottom of the bowl, then vanilla ice cream and chocolate syrup. Whip cream on top. Nuts, optional."

Milla stared at me for several seconds, then yelled, "Ruthie and I are running to the United. Be right back."

We scurried past Dodd and Grady, and as we sped away in Milla's SUV, Momma crossed my mind for only a fraction of a second, and then I giggled.

Fifteen minutes later, we returned to the kitchen to assemble the desserts.

"So, did your mother teach you this recipe?"

"Oh no. Aunt Velma is the chef. Momma cooks frozen food."

Milla's eyes twinkled as she drizzled chocolate syrup on top. "Well, ice cream is frozen."

"You're so different from her." I said it before I thought.

"We view the world differently, that's all."

"You live in different worlds."

"Yet we're both right here in Trapp, Texas." Her expression held understanding and compassion mixed with a touch of sadness. Then she sprayed whipped topping with a flourish.

JohnScott once told me God oozed out around the edges of the Cunninghams and rubbed off when anybody got close. Now I understood what he meant. The three of them were unmistakably encouraging me toward God—without ever mentioning His name.

Dodd and Grady drove me home in the late afternoon, sandwiching me in the front seat of the El Camino. I leaned toward Grady to avoid touching Dodd, who leaned against the driver's door to avoid touching me.

As we pulled up to my house, I nudged Grady to let me out, but he didn't budge.

"So, Ruthie, does Mom need to ask you out again, or can I send my big brother?"

Dodd slapped a fist against his forehead.

I formed my lips into a syrupy smile. "I'm not sure, Grady, but thank you for asking. You're ever so thoughtful."

As Grady grinned, I scooted a half inch toward Dodd, who rolled down the window and opened the door in one fluid movement. I had never seen him so flustered. He stood with one hand on the door while I slid out of the car, but he didn't look at me. After asking me out for all those dates, how could he be bashful now? I paused in front of him until he lifted his gaze. Then I smiled.

What had come over me? Just that morning I had been determined to stay away from the preacher at all costs, and now I was smiling at him and getting all goose bumpy when his eyes widened. This was a bad idea, but for such a rotten idea, it sure felt good.

He followed me halfway across the yard. "I'm glad you came."

"Me, too." At least I thought I was glad. When I stepped onto the porch—home turf—reality gripped me like an offensive lineman. Momma could be home anytime.

Dodd stood at the bottom of the steps, smiling at me with straight, white teeth. "Ruthie, I hope you'll consider Grady's question."

I shook my head, lighthearted from the fun I'd had. "I don't want to go out with Grady."

He laughed, then said softly, seriously, "I hope you'll consider going out … with me."

The cold air seemed to drop ten degrees, and I hugged myself, stifling the emotions building inside me. The tremor in my stomach was telling me one thing, but my brain had another agenda. The Cunninghams pushed me toward God, and I wasn't sure how I felt about that, because the Big Man and I hadn't talked much lately. But if being with the preacher meant going back to the Trapp church, I could live without Dodd Cunningham. "I need to think about it." I glanced at the door behind me. "It's complicated."

"I'm in no hurry."

Neither of us remembered the car window being down until Grady said, "Dodd, you dork. It's forty degrees out here. Let's go."

Dodd rolled his eyes, then held my gaze for a count of five before saying quietly, "See you, Ruthie."

I slipped into the house and leaned against the door, listening to them drive away and wondering if I had started something I would regret. Right then I said the first prayer I'd prayed since childhood.

I thanked God for not letting Momma come home yet.

CHAPTER TWENTY-SIX

On the first night in December, cold mist pelted me as I walked from the United, but I found little refuge when I got home, where the thermostat only registered a few degrees warmer than outside. JohnScott would have gladly picked me up, but lately we seemed to be growing further and further apart, and I wondered if he wouldn't have added to the iciness.

After changing into dry jeans and a sweatshirt, I raised the setting on the heater, but only slightly. A high electric bill would wreak havoc on our makeshift budget, so Momma and I tended to seek warmth next to our tiny wood-burning fireplace.

Dashing out the door, I grabbed an armful of damp logs from our dwindling woodpile by the front porch and made a mental note to ask Ansel to bring more. He was in the process of clearing a pasture and cut down several mesquite trees every week or two. The wet logs I held in my arms dampened the sleeves of my sweatshirt before I dropped them into the box near the fireplace. I'd have a dickens of a time getting a fire started, but I knelt and began the slow process, which only darkened my mood.

For days I had been mindful of the preacher. He seemed aware of my attention even though I did my best to hide it. He would shift his gaze toward me and smile. Or wink. I could tell he wanted to give me time to figure things out, and he hadn't asked for a date again, but I had the sensation of being monitored, as if I were walking a tightrope while he lingered below, ready to catch me as soon as I fell.

I sat on the floor in front of the fireplace and stuffed wadded newspaper around the wood, pushing guilty thoughts of Dodd from my mind.

Momma came through the front door. "Thank goodness you're building a fire, Ruth Ann. I'm frozen and soggy."

"Yeah, well, so is the wood." I struck a match and held it to the paper.

She joined me on the floor, and together we watched the flame engulf the newspaper and flicker away without so much as warming the bark. "Is gasoline a bad idea?" she asked.

I enjoyed the scent of the match while I crumpled more paper. "I think so."

A tap at the door startled us.

In general we lived comfortably in our house, but it had one fault—the small, diamond-shaped window in the front door, decorative from the outside but bothersome from the inside. Anyone standing on the front porch could look into the house, and at times like this, with the porch light off, our visitors could spy on us, but we couldn't see them. Granted, we didn't get many guests, but as I knelt at the fireplace across from the door, my spine tingled.

The knock hadn't sounded right. Not that I'd ever put much thought into the sound of knuckles on wood, but I didn't recognize this particular knock as JohnScott or Velma, the only two people who ever came to see us. It was just three light taps, tapering off toward the end, and if a knock could sound hesitant, this one did. It put me on edge.

Momma stepped to the door and flicked on the porch light, then peeked out from an angle. "What does *he* want?"

My nerves coiled like a roll of barbed wire as I prayed it wasn't Dodd or Grady. Or even JohnScott.

Momma opened the door three inches, prompting me to try harder to light the fire. I could already feel the icy draft.

"Hey, Lynda."

The man's gruff voice sounded familiar, but I couldn't quite place it.

Momma leaned against the doorframe, still in her work clothes. They weren't as wet as mine had been, but she looked damp. "What do you want, Clyde?"

Clyde? Sweat moistened my armpits, and I abandoned the fire and scrambled on all fours into the hallway where he couldn't see me.

"Thought I'd pay you a visit," he said. "Been a long time."

"You sober?"

He cleared his throat and mumbled a yes.

"Well, you might as well come in, then."

Curiosity and apprehension rooted me to the spot, and I stayed in the hall even though my gut suggested I hide in my room with the door locked. *Why would Momma let Clyde Felton in the house?*

"Sorry it's so cold in here. Ruth Ann's having trouble with the fire."

"Ruth Ann?"

She huffed. "Well, the girl's hiding now."

Clyde's shoes scraped the hardwood floor, and after a pause, I heard newspaper tearing. "Can't blame her. I scared the daylights out of her a while back."

"For crying out loud, what'd you do?"

A match struck. "Aw, I'd been drinking. Didn't mean nothing by it."

Silence followed, filled by the sound of scrunching paper. I hoped the man wouldn't feed newsprint into our fireplace for the next hour, because that's how long it would take to get the wood burning.

"I guess prison's awful." Momma's voice wavered slightly, reminding me of every tale I ever heard about prisons.

"You get used to it."

The couch creaked as Momma sat. "I wouldn't have come back to Trapp if I were you."

"You might if you'd been where I've been."

I peeked around the corner. Clyde squatted by the fireplace while Momma lounged on the couch with one leg draped over the armrest. Obviously they had known each other before Clyde's imprisonment, and even though their conversation sounded harmless, the idea of a convicted rapist in my living room made me sick to my stomach.

He continued to mess with the fire, and I wanted to scream at him to give up. Go home. *Leave.*

He surprised me by saying, "I've been to church a couple times. Expected to see you."

"*You* went to *worship*?"

"Does that surprise you?"

"Under the circumstances, yes." She chuckled bitterly. "How'd it go?"

"Last time most of them were frosty. Pretended not to see me." The fireplace tools clanked as he replaced the poker. "Tonight Neil asked me not to come back."

Momma grunted. "Ah, yes. Midweek service."

"He said I'd be more comfortable at the congregation over in Slaton."

"Well, surely you didn't expect him to send out the welcome wagon."

Clyde hesitated so long, I looked around the corner again. Momma had a sad expression on her face.

"You wanted to see them, didn't you?"

Clyde shifted. "I learned a lot in prison. A couple missionaries came every few weeks and talked to us about Jesus. And I listened."

Momma cackled. "You got religion?"

"I know it's hard to believe." Clyde laughed a little too, but his suppressed cheer tapered. "The religion here is different than religion in prison."

"The religion here is different than religion anywhere."

"You didn't used to feel that way." He paused. "You ever see Hoby?"

Momma didn't answer, but I knew she must have given him a gesture to indicate the negative.

"You know where he is?"

"No idea."

"You should find him, Lynda." A long silence filled the room, seeping into the hallway, before Clyde asked, "How are things between you and Neil?"

Momma spoke quickly. "What are you doing with yourself anyway? To keep your mind off the bottle?"

Clyde hesitated. "I got me a job at the Dairy Queen, flipping burgers in the back. Why won't you give me a straight answer?"

The springs in the couch squeaked, and the front door opened. "Ruth Ann and me—we've got work tomorrow. We should call it a night."

Yeah, right. Momma never made it to bed before midnight, but her lie calmed my nerves because it meant Clyde would get away from us.

"I guess that's good-bye," he said softly.

Then he left.

I crept back to the living room and glanced at the door, thankful Momma had left the porch light on.

She stood in front of the fire, which now burned steadily, but she didn't look at me. "How do men get fires started so easily?" she asked.

"Must be in their genes." I held my cold fingers toward the increasing warmth as a million questions ran through my mind. My heart felt like a balloon, filled to near bursting, then quickly deflated into a misshapen form that would never be quite as strong.

"What's the deal with you running off?" Momma demanded. "You too uppity to talk to my friends?"

I found her question humorous, since she hadn't had a friend in years. Not really. The humor died when I remembered Clyde had asked me almost the same question on the wall at the school. "He's your friend?"

"I don't know." She shrugged. "He used to be."

I rubbed my hands together, unsure of how to talk to Momma but desperate to know what Clyde Felton had to do with my daddy. "What happened with him, Momma?"

She opened her mouth to speak and then snapped it shut. "Aw, it don't matter."

When she turned and shuffled to the kitchen, she effectively shut me out of her mind with all the finality of a slamming door.

CHAPTER TWENTY-SEVEN

Clyde still gave me the willies, even if Momma considered him a friend. After all, rape was rape, and I didn't trust him. Momma wouldn't tell me squat about what happened to him before his conviction, so I asked Velma about it the next Saturday as we dragged furniture around in her living room, clearing a spot for the artificial Christmas tree.

"Momma just sat on the couch and let him build a fire in our fireplace. They talked like old friends."

Velma slid an end table over a couple of feet. "Well, honey, they are old friends."

"How can she be friends with somebody like him?"

My aunt scanned the room, seeming to decide if we had moved enough furniture, then she made a puffing sound. "Don't believe everything you hear, Ruthie. Clyde Felton wouldn't hurt a flea."

"What do you mean? He was found guilty."

She shook her head. "Of statutory rape, not assault. You don't need to be afraid of the man."

Easier said than done.

The back door squeaked, and a moment later, Ansel came through the mudroom carrying a dusty box. He set it on the kitchen table. "Ornaments."

He and JohnScott had set a goal to extract the Christmas decorations from the shed, and I knew the driveway would soon be covered with random boxes pulled out during their search. This happened every year.

"Thanks, Uncle Ansel," I called as the back door shut.

Velma opened the box and shook her head. "I suppose they'll unearth the tree sometime this afternoon. These aren't much good till then."

I reached for an ornament nestled in the top of the box, a homemade angel one of my cousins had made from a ping-pong ball, a cupcake liner, and a toilet-paper roll. *First grade, room B.* I had made the same angel in first grade, but mine disappeared long ago. "I can't believe you still have this, Aunt Velma."

"I keep waiting for it to fall apart so I can throw it away." She hobbled to the mudroom and returned with a sweeper, which she wheeled back and forth over the carpet where the couch had been. One of my older cousins had bought her a vacuum cleaner for Mother's Day the year before, but she continued to use the old sweeper. As she bustled around the living room, the contraption rattled right along with her.

I inspected the faded angel, smiling at the places Velma had repaired it over the years. The original school paste, smeared all those years ago, was now discolored and useless. In its place, a fine line of Elmer's glue held the pieces together for a while. The latest improvement, a few pieces of cellophane tape, would crisp and pull away in a few years, but I had no doubt Velma would keep the angel alive somehow.

I set it on the table and unwrapped another and another, laying them out until I had an entire ping-pong-ball choir. Apparently all nine of my cousins had passed through room B in first grade. I formed the angels into two even lines like carolers in the snow. Five in front, five in back.

Hold on.

Velma continued to sweep, working her way around the room and into the entry hall, while I flipped each angel upside down and around, searching the names scrawled on the back. Then I found it.

Ruthie T.

I returned the angel to its place on the back row. "Aunt Velma, I've seen these angels on your tree every year since I can remember, and I never knew one of them was mine."

She clacked the sweeper back to the living room, glancing toward the table. "Sure enough. We've got a nice little crowd there, don't we?"

"Thank you for keeping it."

"Aw." She waved away the gratitude as she leaned the sweeper against the table. "Your momma does the best she can."

I busied myself unpacking the rest of the box.

"Sometimes she gives me things, Ruthie. Asks me to take care of them for her."

A sarcastic grunt slipped from my throat. "Like me?"

Velma placed her wrinkled hand over mine and gave it a squeeze as the back door burst open again.

"Here comes the tree," JohnScott called from the mudroom.

We pulled the kitchen chairs back so JohnScott and Ansel could squeeze by with the enormous box. I heard them bumping the walls of the mudroom as they maneuvered their awkward cargo to shut the back door, but the tight space prevented Velma and me from rendering aid.

JohnScott stumbled backward through the door, having let Ansel take the forward-walking end. But when the other end of the box came into view, Ansel wasn't holding it. Dodd was.

He wore a black hoodie, and when he smiled, I clutched a string of wooden cranberry beads, hanging on for dear life while my anticipation soared to the top of a roller coaster, leaving my insides quivering somewhere near the ground.

"Dodd Cunningham," Velma said. "Is Grady here too?"

"Yes, ma'am. He's straddling one of the rafters in your shed, searching for the outdoor lights."

The two men thumped the box down on the floor in the middle of the room, and JohnScott said, "He's right at home up there, swinging around like a monkey."

"Sounds like Grady." I laughed, but my voice came out airy and forced.

Velma looked at me, then swiveled her head to peer at Dodd. "Well, you boys best get back out there before Ansel climbs up the rafters too."

As they made their way outside, Dodd glanced at me, and his eyes crinkled.

Instantly a warm burst of happiness or nervousness or dread surged through me, undoubtedly coloring my cheeks with embarrassment.

When we were alone again, Velma's expression fogged. She folded her hands and held them at her waist, one thumb rubbing thoughtfully across its twin. "Well." She chuckled. "I didn't see that coming."

"What?"

She tugged on the huge box until all four flaps popped open. "You with the preacher. Makes sense when I think about it." She removed the tree stand from the top of the box, plunked it down in the middle of our desired location, and grabbed the pole for the trunk. "Not sure how your momma will handle it, but she'll get used to the idea." She shoved the pole into the stand and tightened the bolts. "Stop biting your nails, Ruthie."

I hadn't bitten my nails since childhood when Velma painted them with Tabasco sauce, but now I could have readily nibbled each one of them down to the quick. "Is it obvious?"

"Like a horsefly in a bowl of mashed potatoes."

"What should I do?"

She adjusted the greenery on a wire branch before poking it into the trunk. "It's not the end of the world, Ruthie."

She motioned to the box, and I reached for a branch and began separating pine boughs.

We worked in silence for several minutes, adding branches to complete the tree. Then we surveyed our work, and I shifted a few wires to cover holes.

"Darlin', it'll never be perfect."

"I know, but it's close."

"I'm not talking about the tree." Velma eased into her rocker by the fireplace, and I sat in Ansel's recliner and prepared for a minisermon. "I know you, Ruthie." Her expression calmed my fears. "You'll try to make everybody happy till the day you die, but some things you just need to let go."

"Let go?" She made it sound so simple.

"Sure. Don't worry about everybody else." She stretched her legs out and pointed the toes of her Naturalizers toward the fire. "Two adults have a hankering for each other. So what?"

A sliver of hope deep inside me tried to latch on to her encouraging words, but reality yanked them away. "But … *Momma*. She was upset when she found out about JohnScott's baptism. She called him a fool."

"JohnScott's no fool. In fact, I'm beginning to wonder if he can't teach me a thing or two." She raised her voice. "But I know what you're thinking. Your momma won't be any too keen when the preacher comes to call, might even hole herself up for a while, but you can't go on living your life to please her." She fumbled with the bib of her apron. "She's sure not living that way."

I sat in stunned silence. Velma had given me hundreds of sermons, but she rarely spoke ill of Momma. And she never told me to do something that might upset Momma's apple cart.

"Oh, that stinking church." She blew air through her teeth. "Enjoy yourself for once and don't worry about the rest of it." She hauled herself out of the rocking chair. "How about some cocoa? I think I'll take some outside to the monkeys."

She drifted into the kitchen, but I leaned back in the recliner, my mind whirling. Did I really try to please people? Everyone in my life seemed to hold an opinion about what I should do and who I should be, but I had never thought much about it. Amid the jumble of confusion, I recognized one feeling deep inside. *Relief.* Velma had more or less given me permission to date Dodd when I hadn't even asked for it. Or knew I wanted it. But Velma's prompt acceptance of the relationship made me feel light as a tumbleweed bouncing down the highway. She had cleared some of the brambles away from my decisions. *Don't worry about it,* she had said.

Well, maybe I wouldn't.

"Ruthie, come carry these mugs. I'll get the pot and open the door."

I stepped into the kitchen and wrapped my arms around her neck.

"Aw, now. You're going to make me spill."

Slipping into my coat, I followed her into the deceptive sunshine. It looked like seventy degrees but felt like thirty. JohnScott and Grady sat in the brown grass at the side of the house, leaning against the butane tank as they untangled strings of lights.

"Ruthie, help us," Grady whined.

JohnScott pulled the cord out of Grady's grasp. "We've got to find the end and work from there."

I gave each of them a mug and sat on the grass between them.

Across the yard, Ansel and Dodd strolled out of the shed, and Velma took them the rest of the cocoa. Soon the three of them rested in iron lawn chairs, making small talk. I could only hear an occasional muffled word on the breeze, but I knew Velma wouldn't embarrass me.

Dodd fluttered a smile before tilting his head to respond to something Velma had said. He had removed his hoodie to reveal a long-sleeved pullover with sweat marks on his chest and underarms. I pulled my coat around me as a shiver went up my spine.

"She's staring at him, Coach," Grady whispered.

"I see that."

I set my mug in the brittle grass and popped Grady on the back of the head.

He pretended to spill his cocoa. "I think you burned me."

"Liar."

"Coach, she's not being nice to me."

I looked to JohnScott in defense. "I brought the cocoa."

"Mom brought the cocoa."

"Ruthie brought the mugs, though," Grady said.

As we sipped our drinks, they struck up a conversation about off-season practice. Didn't they ever get tired of talking football? I looked across at Dodd, who gave a slight shrug and rolled his eyes.

"She's doing it again," Grady sing-songed.

"I am not."

Grady covered his head with his arms. "I see you with my eyes. It's as clear as day."

"And cute," JohnScott added.

"Say it, Ruthie," Grady commanded.

"Say what?"

"Say you like my big brother."

Plucking a few blades of grass, I mumbled, "Yes, I like your brother." I snapped the grass into smaller and smaller bits before peeking at Grady.

After all that work, he only stared at me. "You don't sound happy about it."

"It's complicated."

JohnScott picked up a string of lights, so I pulled some into my lap while Grady peppered me with questions. "Will you go out with him?"

"I'm not sure how that would work."

"You mean your mother?"

"And others."

"So, Ruthie ..." Grady reached for his mug, swirled the last of his cocoa in the bottom, then slung the cold liquid into the grass. "Do you think it's worth it?" His eyes held compassion, and I knew, in spite of his teasing, that he respected the domino effect our relationship might cause.

I looked across the yard at Dodd. "I think so."

Dodd nodded, but he had a funny expression on his face. Anticipation, impatience, and apprehension, all mixed together.

My exact feelings.

Grady yanked several blades of grass and held them in his fingertips like a miniature bouquet. "So, does this mean you're ready to date him?"

I looked directly at Dodd. "I don't know, Grady, but I think so."

"Little cousin?" JohnScott peered at me. "Will you talk to Dodd about it?"

"He already knows," Grady said.

Of course he already knew. Dodd had been reading my lips the entire time, and our silent interaction felt surprisingly personal. Collecting the mugs, I said, "I'm going inside to work on the tree. You guys want to come?"

JohnScott grunted. "I'm banished to the backyard for the day. Grady, let's climb on the roof with these lights."

As they untangled the last cord, I called my intentions to Velma.

"I'll be along directly." She waved from the shed.

I opened the back door and gave one last glance in Dodd's direction, but his lawn chair sat empty. He was following me into the house.

CHAPTER TWENTY-EIGHT

When Dodd entered Ansel and Velma's living room, I was about to start stringing lights on the tree and wondered what I'd gotten myself into. Admitting my feelings to JohnScott and Grady—and indirectly to Dodd—didn't begin to solve the problem of what to do about them. I sighed. "Want to help?"

"Sure." He reached for a cord, then wove lights through the branches without hesitation. We had them installed within minutes.

"I noticed you were eavesdropping again."

He stretched and placed the angel on the top branches. "I'm sorry about that. You're proving to be a challenge."

I laughed as I retrieved the box of ornaments from the kitchen table, placing them on the floor between us. "Don't blame me."

"I've never had this much trouble fighting the temptation to read someone's lips."

Good gracious, Momma would have a fit if she could hear this conversation. When I thought about her, my stomach cramped as if I'd swallowed a chunk of cactus, but there was no going back now. *Was there?* "So I guess you heard what I said to Grady out there."

Dodd peered at me from between the branches of the tree, the twinkle lights transforming him into a Hallmark greeting card. He raised one eyebrow and smiled. "You like me."

This man affected me more than I wanted him to know, but I shrugged as though I hadn't put much thought into it. "Oh, I don't know. I had fun with your mother the other day."

He nodded knowingly. "So it's Mom you like."

"And Grady."

He crossed his arms. "You like Mom and Grady."

"I'd like to get to know them better." I reached for another ornament. "Gradually."

"They can work with gradual."

I secured a Coca-Cola polar bear to a branch, then dropped my hands to my sides. "Dodd, I'm afraid this is a huge mistake." I had an overwhelming urge to bolt out the door and sprint home.

He shook his head. "I don't see it that way."

Of course he didn't see it that way. He stood on the other side of the problem, where everything was rosy. I moved away from him, escaping across the room where I plopped into a chair at the kitchen table, right in front of the ping-pong-ball choir. "Momma won't understand."

He followed and sat down across from me, straightening the two lines of ornaments. "Has your mother always been unhappy?"

"Before Daddy left, she laughed a lot. And wore makeup and nice clothes. I remember them swinging a jump rope for me in the driveway. Like real parents."

He flinched. "But now she's bitter toward the church, isn't she?"

"Bitter? She *despises* the church." I searched for words to convey the magnitude of what I was considering doing—what he was asking me to do—to my mother. But I was at a loss for words. I shook my head hopelessly.

"I know more or less what happened—I talked to Charlie Mendoza about it—but it doesn't make sense. I feel like there's something I'm missing." Dodd frowned. "They should've told me about it from the start, and I wanted some answers."

"I bet you didn't get any."

"Well, no. Not really."

Footsteps traveled across the roof above our heads, and I peered at the ceiling. "After Daddy left, the church branded Momma an adulteress. She always blamed Neil for the church's actions, but I don't know why."

"Neil Blaylock? But he wasn't even an elder then."

"His daddy was. Same difference. The Blaylocks have had it out for us ever since we left the church. They go out of their way to be rude." I picked a chunk of glue off a ping-pong ball. "Usually they just ignore us, but sometimes Neil talks to Momma."

"Well, that's something, right?"

"No." I'd seen Neil appear out of nowhere and stand too close to her, saying things I could never quite hear. "Whatever he says makes her pretty angry."

Dodd's brows bunched. "That seems out of character."

The naivety of Dodd's attitude annoyed me. "People aren't always what they seem, or have you not noticed that?"

He smiled. "I know you're not what you seem."

My nerves relaxed, and I rubbed a hand across my face. "I admit you're not either."

"You weren't expecting to trust me."

"I'm still not sure I do."

But I knew the day would come when I did. Already it seemed I could talk to him about things. For crying out loud, I couldn't remember ever having discussed that horrible Sunday with anyone except JohnScott. And here I was telling the preacher about it.

Dodd leaned forward. "So … Neil's father suggested you and your mom go to another congregation?"

"Um … no."

"Charlie thought that's what happened."

"Charlie Mendoza isn't a liar, but it's odd he remembers it that way. Shows how little he's thought about it since then."

Dodd massaged the back of his neck. "How old were you?"

"Seven." I twirled one of the handmade choir members. "At the time I didn't understand it, but I remember it like it was last week. It was a few months after Daddy left. Momma kept taking me to church. Her friends were there, you know? She and Pamela Sanders did everything together. And Fawn and me." Thinking about that day made me sad and angry, but Dodd's eyes urged me on. "We entered the building on Sunday morning, and Momma took a program. Everything seemed normal. We sat behind the Blaylocks, and Fawn turned around and made faces at me while Momma opened the handout to read over the announcements. But all of a sudden, she crumpled it, grabbed my hand, and dragged me out the door. Fawn's parents never even turned around."

Dodd waited. Swallowed. Whispered. "What did she read in the program?"

"That morning's sermon topic." I snickered. "Adultery. I still have it at the house. I figured I'd keep the silly paper, since it made such an impact on our lives."

He ran his index finger along the edge of the table. "And your mother? She assumed the sermon was directed at her?"

I huffed. "The congregation is small, Dodd. It was no secret what everyone was saying."

"Sorry." He raised his palms. "Remember, I'm not from around here."

I inhaled deeply, regretting my tone. I hadn't yet told him everything. "Besides, there was a notice about a business meeting to be held after services." I made quote marks in the air with my fingers. "To discuss the need to withdraw congregational fellowship from a member of the flock. It was right there before the blurb about Pyrex dishes left behind from the last fellowship meal."

He stared at me, disbelief etched on his face.

"Gerald Blaylock came by the house a few days later."

"Oh. Ruthie, I'm so sorry."

His compassion made me uncomfortable as I felt the intimacy of all I'd shared, and I rose, taking two ornaments to the tree.

He followed with more, and after three trips back and forth, we had them distributed over the branches.

Dodd adjusted a string of lights, then returned them to their original position. "I know the church's actions seem extreme, but I'm sure they thought they were doing the right thing." He added quickly, "I don't agree with them. But there's actually a verse in the

Bible about disciplining a sinner in the church." He ducked his head.

"Give me a break. I doubt Momma ever did anything wrong. Besides, even if there's a handy little verse about discipline, there's also a verse that says sinners don't have the right to cast stones at other sinners." My face warmed as my voice rose. "Either the Christians down at your stupid church think they're actually sinless, or they've scribbled that verse out of their Bibles with a Sharpie. Which is it?"

When I finished my backlash, he didn't answer, only stared with his mouth hanging open.

"What?" I demanded.

He blinked twice, then looked at the tree and back to me. "I never expected you to quote Scripture."

My anger dissolved in a silent poof. "Why … why not?"

"I didn't assume you were one to read the Bible."

Clearly I had misrepresented myself. "Only the New Testament and Psalms. And not very often. That one verse sort of stuck in my mind, you know?"

He looked at me as if he was seeing a completely different person. "Does your mom study the Bible?"

"Of course not." He really didn't get it. "And I wouldn't call what I do studying. More like searching for ammunition. But no, Momma would never read. All the Bibles disappeared from the house years ago."

His smile softened. "But she let you keep one. That says a lot for her."

"Actually, I think she forgot about it. It's just a baby Bible."

"What do you mean 'a baby Bible'? One is just as good as another."

I laughed. "You know, a *baby* Bible. I got it when I was little, from a Bible-class teacher. It's probably three inches tall, pink, with a lamb on the front."

"Oh." He grinned. "Gotcha. Mine was blue. Might've had *Doddie* engraved on it."

Outside, Velma called to JohnScott, but Dodd didn't seem to notice. His smile faded, and his expression became a mixture of confusion and pain. "I never knew anyone to actually read those little Bibles. They make them small for a baby's hands. The print is tiny."

"Yeah, well, I have good eyesight." In the bottom of the ornament box, I discovered a Ziploc baggy filled with silver tinsel, and I pinched a few strands, then draped them on the tip of a branch. Dodd hadn't moved in a few seconds, so I looked back at him.

"Ruthie, you're fascinating."

I froze. "Um … okay."

"You work harder than anyone I know, you're patient with obnoxious students and coworkers, and you're fearless in the face of danger. But if that weren't enough, you also read the Bible. I know countless Christian women who never even crack open their Bibles." He reached for a handful of tinsel, then held my wrist gently. "How am I supposed to be *gradual* knowing all this about you?"

His soft voice shook my senses, but when I didn't answer, he released my wrist with a grin and went to work on the tinsel.

I breathed again. "I work because I have to, and I'm patient because it makes life easier. I'm not going to acknowledge the Bible remark because I've already said I hardly ever read it. But fearless in the face of danger?" I shook my head. "I don't think so."

"What about Clyde Felton? That day at the school?"

"That wasn't fearlessness. That was terror."

"But you were brave. You stood up to him."

"I almost wet my pants."

He laughed gently, and then we worked in comfortable silence for a while until he said, "I don't know about Clyde. I think he's teetering on the fence, trying to decide if he's going to be a bad guy or a good guy. But either way, he's got to stop scaring people like that. I've been talking to him."

"Not about me, I hope."

He chuckled. "You're a little testy when you think someone's talking about you."

"Wouldn't you be?"

"All right. You deserve to be testy."

As he put the last sparkling strands on the tree, I stood a little behind him, suddenly wondering why I had shared so much. "You won't talk about me, right?" I knew I whined when I said it, but there was no other way for it to come out.

He turned to face me, so close I could feel his warmth. "You can trust me, Ruthie."

"I don't really do trust."

He pulled a strand of tinsel from my hair. "I know you don't." He flicked the foil toward the tree without breaking eye contact. Those beautiful eyes that were so tempted to eavesdrop now traveled around my face until they were staring at my lips. He fingered a strand of my hair and then lifted a corner of his mouth. "Ruthie, if I were to ask you out again, would you say yes this time?"

I sighed with the intensity of a leaf blower, knowing I was in so deep, I would eventually suffocate.

He chuckled but kept his voice lowered. "You really do like my mom better than me, don't you?" He looked at my left earlobe, then inspected my bangs.

"It's just that I need to get to know you gradually." I lifted a shoulder. "And quietly."

"You mean secretly?" His smile disappeared.

"Maybe at first, yes."

His eyes clouded, and he stared at me intently, not quite frowning. I met his gaze placidly and held it a few long moments, but soon my resolve wavered, and I looked away.

After a silent pause, he exhaled. "All right, secretly." He sounded as though he were giving in against his better judgment. "At first."

CHAPTER TWENTY-NINE

Never in my life had I done something so senseless. It had been a week since my discussion with Dodd, and even though I lay awake at night thinking about the way he looked at me, I spent the daylight hours mentally berating myself. My frustration with Momma had evolved into a relationship with Dodd that could hurt her.

So when he cornered me Friday in the teachers' lounge after everyone had gone, I didn't hesitate to turn down his request for dinner and a movie, maybe dancing. "Someone would see us, even in Lubbock," I protested.

He grinned as he threw away his lunch trash. "Who said anything about Lubbock?"

"Well, we certainly can't be seen in Trapp," I quipped. "Not that we have a movie theater."

"You have no imagination."

I rinsed my morning coffee mug at the sink. "Dodd, I've been thinking this isn't such a good idea."

"I know."

Relief and disappointment simultaneously swept through my lungs. "So you think we shouldn't see each other either?" I dried my mug with a paper towel and avoided his gaze.

A low chuckle came from deep in his throat, and he moved closer to me. "I meant I know you've been thinking it's not a good idea." He took the mug out of my hands and set it on the counter. "It's sort of obvious. You avoid me in the hallways, sit with your back to me at lunch, and never, *ever* make eye contact. But I happen to disagree with you. I think spending time with you is an awesome idea."

His nearness, coupled with the teasing look in his eyes, addled my tongue, so in lieu of an intelligent response, I crossed my arms.

He ignored my attitude and laughed again. "JohnScott will pick you up from the United tomorrow afternoon and take you to the Picketts'. He can stop by your house on the way. If anyone asks, tell them you're at Ansel and Velma's. We'll leave from there."

"Dinner and a movie?" I huffed. "How?"

He walked to the door. "Trust me, Ruthie."

The next afternoon, JohnScott picked me up from work and took me home, where I ran through the shower and pulled on clean jeans. My hair had been in a bun all day, but when I pulled it loose, it fell in soft curls down my back. Thank goodness for a good hair day. I touched up my mascara and squirted perfume on my wrists, and at JohnScott's suggestion, I wore boots and a warm jacket. A herd of butterflies fluttered in my abdomen. This date would never work.

I interrogated JohnScott, but he refused to give me any details and insisted everything would be fine.

As I slid from his truck, Dodd came out of the Picketts' back door with Ansel's old dog right behind him, and the two seemed out of place. Like they didn't really belong together. "Ready to hit the road?"

The butterflies in my stomach thundered into flight. "Okay." My voice quivered as he opened the passenger door of the El Camino.

"Have her home before curfew." JohnScott cleared his throat. "And don't do anything I wouldn't do."

"Wouldn't dream of it." Dodd closed the door, but I could still hear him as he walked around the car. "Don't wait up for us, J.S."

"I'll be right here, cleaning my shotgun."

Dodd opened his door. "You don't scare me, Coach."

My cousin's voice changed. "Seriously, you guys have fun. And honk if you need anything."

Dodd peered into the car at me. "I've got everything I need."

JohnScott ogled us as though watching the calf scramble at the Sheriff's Posse Rodeo, but then he ducked his head and shuffled into the house.

I looked at Dodd hesitantly as I buckled my seat belt, but he only grinned and shifted into first gear. He eased his foot off the brake, but instead of pulling toward the highway, he bumped across the pipe cattle guard into the back pasture.

"What are you doing?"

"Taking you to dinner and a movie." Dodd followed the gravel road behind the barn. "And if I'm lucky, dancing."

My hands relaxed, and I realized I'd clenched them so tightly, they were cemented together. Maybe this would be all right after all. The farther we got from the house, the calmer I became, and my brain began to function normally again. Momma wouldn't find out about this date after all, and in a few minutes, I could simply explain to the preacher I wouldn't be able to see him again. Surely he hadn't thought it through like I had. Not only would Momma become irrational, but the church wouldn't take kindly to the situation. Dodd could even lose his job at the church.

He stopped the El Camino in a low spot behind the stock tank, where we were sheltered by the dam on one side and thick mesquite trees on the other. I sighed. Nobody driving down the highway would be able to see us. But what were we doing in the middle of the pasture? It was almost freezing.

I turned in the seat to ask, but Dodd was pointing to a pile of wood nearby. "I thought a candlelight dinner might be overkill, so I opted for a campfire."

I studied the logs, neatly positioned and ready to be lit. "I'm grateful for the heat source, but …"—I raised an eyebrow—"dinner and a movie?"

He motioned to the back of the car. "Brisket sandwiches compliments of your Aunt Velma, chocolate-chip cookies from Mom, and my laptop computer for the movie."

I squirmed uncomfortably. "*Everyone* was in on this?"

"You worry too much." He opened his door.

When I met him at the tailgate, I realized the back end was filled with supplies I hadn't noticed earlier. Aunt Velma's wicker picnic basket, two camp chairs, and an old quilt. Dodd's laptop lay nestled between two cushions. I smiled in spite of myself. Even though this was our first—and potentially *only*—date, it might be a fun evening.

Twenty minutes later, we were eating sandwiches on the quilt by the fire, the picnic basket between us. The sun had set, leaving us in darkness, but the fire cast a warm glow twenty feet around. I shifted closer to its warmth and decided to wait until the end of the night to tell Dodd this wouldn't be happening twice.

"You cold?" he murmured.

"Only my back. I may have to turn like a rotisserie every few minutes."

"The camp chairs might be warmer. Besides I thought our backs might start hurting if we sat on the quilt for the entire movie."

"Sounds like you thought of everything."

"We'll see." He put an entire wavy potato chip in his mouth and smiled.

None of this made sense. I didn't have a lot of dating experience, but Dodd felt more like a brother or a cousin—my lips quivered into a smile—except when he didn't.

"What's that smile for?" Dodd popped the top on a can of Dr Pepper and handed it to me, then reached for another.

"I was wondering if JohnScott built the fire for you."

He snorted. "I'll have you know I earned Boy Scout merit badges for camping as well as fire safety. You're in good hands."

I raised my eyebrows. "I never figured you for a Boy Scout."

"It was something my dad and I did together." He gazed into the fire and sipped his drink. "I didn't follow through with Scouts in my teen years, though."

His reminiscent tone hinted I might not be out of line asking about his father, so I tested the waters. "Sounds like he was a good dad."

"The best." He opened a Cool Whip container and offered me a chocolate-chip cookie. "When I was young, he would set up a tent in the backyard, and we'd sleep out there. It was against city ordinance to build a campfire, but we'd have a couple of gas lanterns going. And we'd roast marshmallows on a camp stove."

"S'mores?"

"Sometimes." He chewed a bite of cookie. The way the fire reflected in his eyes made them look gray, and I hoped he'd tell me more. He wiped the corners of his mouth with a paper napkin. "He always wanted the best for me and encouraged me to make something of myself. Even when I didn't know what I wanted to do with my life, he told me to take my time and follow the Lord's guidance." He chuckled. "He always wanted me to preach, though."

After stirring the fire, I added another log.

"When he died, I think part of me died too, you know?"

I turned my back to the fire then, and my face tingled in the coolness of the shadows. "I know exactly what you mean."

He moved the picnic basket and scooted across the quilt until we were facing each other cross-legged. "Your dad?"

I nodded. "He's not dead, but sometimes it feels like it." I leaned back, resting my weight on my outstretched palms. "He spoiled me. Momma ran the discipline, but whenever I got in trouble, Daddy would sneak around and let me off the hook. She hated that." I wasn't sure why I was telling him about Daddy, but I couldn't think of a reason not to. It seemed fair somehow.

"I'm sorry." He said the words simply, as though he would undo the hurt if he could.

"I still love him." I shrugged. "Though sometimes I wish I didn't. I daydream everything would be better if he were here, but then I feel guilty, as if I'm unsupportive of Momma." I exhaled with a slight laugh. "But his memory is so much better than her reality."

"Do you ever see him?"

"No." The word sounded too loud and stark for the conversation, and I shifted awkwardly. "For the first few years, I watched the mailbox, but nothing ever came, and after a while, I stopped hoping." My voice trailed off and hung in the night air.

Dodd reached for my hand and held it between the two of his, rubbing my fingers with a thumb. I didn't mind. It felt natural, and I had the urge to curl into a ball with my feet toward the fire, and fall asleep dreaming about my daddy ... while Dodd held my hand. What was it about this man?

He squeezed my fingers. "Ready for a movie?"

"Sure." That might have been a lie. I would've been happy talking to him for another two hours. Or holding hands. Or staring at the fire. But a movie was fine too. "What have you got?"

"Mom sent *Les Misérables*, and Grady insisted I bring *Monty Python*." He pulled three DVDs out of the picnic basket.

"And what did *you* choose?"

He ducked his head. "*The Notebook.*"

"Thank goodness. You had me worried for a minute."

"You like Rachel McAdams?"

"No, I like Ryan Gosling."

He inserted the disk into his laptop. "Quilt or camp chairs?"

"Chairs. But we're going to have to build up the fire before we start the movie. It's getting colder out here."

We worked our makeshift campsite for ten minutes, and when we finally hit Play, we were cocooned in the camp chairs with the quilt draped across our backs and shoulders. Our chairs were so close they were touching, and the chocolate-chip-cookie container balanced on the chair arms between us, with the laptop nestled in the top of the picnic basket. One lone butterfly remained in my stomach, and when Dodd moved the cookies into his lap so he could lean across and hold my hand, the butterfly flittered across my midsection, releasing pleasant warmth. "Thanks for all this, Dodd."

His eyes teased. "Thanks for finally saying yes."

I remembered my determination to never say yes again, but I forced it out of my mind. I'd have plenty of time to deal with that on the way back to Aunt Velma's house. For now, I was planning to enjoy the movie.

About the time Rachel McAdams's parents dragged her away from Ryan Gosling, we turned our chairs because we were both broiling on the front and freezing on the back. I transported the picnic-basket entertainment center while Dodd maneuvered both chairs, but neither of us stood up completely because we didn't want to readjust the quilt. We hobbled a one-hundred-and-eighty-degree shift before flopping back in place.

When Rachel finally returned to Ryan, we both stood and stretched. I snuck another cookie. "Should we stir the fire so it'll burn down?"

He moaned softly. "I guess it's about time, but it'll be a while before we can leave it."

I didn't want the evening to end. "Did you say something about dancing?"

"Yes, I did." He chuckled. "We've got to do *something* while we wait for the fire to burn down."

"We do."

Dodd clicked his laptop a few times, and the opening notes of "Waiting on the World to Change" tinkled from the speakers.

"John Mayer. Are you serious?"

He paused, caution etched on his face. "Is John good or bad?"

"John is good. Mostly. This song is good." I rested my palms on his shoulders, and he touched my waist lightly. "I've never danced to him, but that's not saying much, because I hardly ever dance."

"I usually just sway."

"But if you sway to the beat, it counts."

As my boots crunched dried grass, I stared at his Adam's apple. I felt drawn to look into his eyes but worried he would think I wanted him to kiss me. I wasn't sure if I did or not, but I knew I didn't want him to *think* I wanted him to.

Dodd cleared his throat, and his Adam's apple quivered. "Can I ask you something?"

He sounded nervous again, and I risked looking up. His eyes were troubled, and when I made eye contact, he glanced at the fire, then back to me.

"Of course." I tried to sound encouraging, but I worried what he'd ask.

"How do you feel about God?"

"Oh." I returned my gaze to his neck. "Him?"

"I mean … you believe in God, right?"

"Of course."

He sighed. "Well, that's a relief."

"Is it?"

"God is pretty important in my life, and you know … I was hoping He was important to you, too." One of his thumbs circled my hipbone lightly.

"I do believe in God …"

He peered down at me and laughed. "I sense a *but* coming."

"But the church is messing with Him. I'm surprised He puts up with it, really."

He paused, then moved one hand to my neck and rubbed the back of his fingers against my jaw. "Ruthie, you're fascinating."

I rolled my eyes. "Don't start that again."

"No, seriously. You've nailed it. Sometimes Christians are a mess."

"Yeah, my dad was a Christian." I shrugged. "He had this enormous Bible with some kind of Western cowboy cover on it with leather laces around the edges. I always thought it looked like a rectangular saddle. He used to read it all the time, but look how he turned out." I blinked the memory away. "Anyway, God and I have an understanding, but it doesn't include going to worship services, and it doesn't involve hanging around with Christians."

He pushed my chin up until I was looking at him. "None of them?"

"You're different." I wrinkled my nose. "I suppose I could hang out with you if I had to."

His fingers were still on my chin, and he held me there as he brushed his lips against mine. He tasted of chocolate and smelled of mesquite smoke, and when he pulled away, I stood on tiptoe and found his lips again. His hand slid to the back of my neck, and his fingers twined through my hair. I forgot I was cold. I *wasn't* cold. Warmth spread through my body, radiating from his hands and mouth all the way down to my frozen toes.

I'd never been kissed like that before, but not because his technique was anything special. It was *him*. The whole of Dodd Cunningham as a man. The way he worked to provide for Grady and Milla, his easygoing conversations that always drew me in and made me forget I was nervous, that curl behind his ear that was finally growing back, the way he ate potato chips whole, even his influence on our little town.

That's what was different about Dodd.

His lips touched mine one last time before he pulled me close.

As I lay my head against his shoulder, John Mayer's next song began playing, and I knew I had been wrong.

I would definitely say *yes* when he asked again.

CHAPTER THIRTY

I asked him out myself. By Thursday I was tired of waiting and invited him to drive around and look at Christmas lights that night when I got off work. He gave the impression he'd been waiting for me to ask, and I had the urge to pop him in the arm. He only grinned and nodded and said sure, he'd pick me up at the United. His eyes held mine, and my heart quivered, and the sensations and feelings running through my mind and body were foreign to me. To say the man was under my skin would've been putting it mildly.

For a while I stopped thinking about the conflict between my family and the church. I seemed to be held captive by Dodd's personality, his smile, his casual familiarity. I didn't care if he was the preacher. I didn't care if Momma despised him or if the church scorned me. I wanted to be with Dodd Cunningham—*the preacher, for heaven's sake*—and nothing would stop me.

Dodd glanced across the seat of the El Camino as he sped down the highway, following my directions to the next Christmas-light display. "Ruthie, I'm really not comfortable sneaking around behind your mother's back."

Suddenly the conflict mattered after all.

"I can't do that to Momma. She couldn't handle it." The dashboard cast a yellowish glow across Dodd. He wore a sweatshirt. Either he wasn't concerned with impressing me or he was attempting to level the playing field by not outdoing my work clothes. I chose to assume he was concerned about my feelings.

He squinted. "What do you think would happen?"

"Oh, I don't know." Highway reflectors sped past my window, and I absentmindedly counted them. One, two, three, four, five. "She struggles with depression and anxiety. Mostly depression. She's all right if the status quo doesn't get rattled, but if she feels overwhelmed, she'll freak out."

"What does her *freak out* look like?"

I crossed my arms, but then lowered them deliberately to my sides. "Best-case scenario, she would go to bed for a few weeks. Worst case? Fits of rage followed by intense remorse … which could lead to self-injury." The volume of my voice decreased gradually. "And sometimes attempts at suicide."

His head jerked to look at me, and then he slowed the car and pulled to the side of the road as the hum of tires on pavement lowered a pitch. "She's attempted suicide?"

"Twice. The first time was after Daddy left. She was in a treatment center in Lubbock for the better part of a month. That's when I started staying with Uncle Ansel and Aunt Velma a lot."

He reached over and laid a hand on my shoulder. "I didn't know."

I wished he'd keep driving. If another car happened along and saw us on the side of the road, they would undoubtedly stop to render aid. "The next house is just around the corner."

"Time to bottle up those emotions again?"

I slid across the seat and pressed my lips against his, obviously surprising him. "Yes. It's that time." His eyebrows lifted, and he leaned toward me, but I returned to my side of the car and pointed down the road. "After you round the corner, you won't be able to miss it. Just pull over in front of the house."

He chuckled low and let his foot off the brake. "Yes, ma'am." He cleared his throat softly and seemed about to say something, when the Christmas lights came into view. "Whoa!"

It was the Coulsons' place. The house was set near the road, and we had an excellent view of their plastic, antique yard art. "They've been working on this collection for years. From garage sales and eBay mostly, and every trip they go on, they bring back another addition."

Flanking the front door were soldiers and three-foot candlesticks. On the roof was a Santa complete with his own plastic chimney. Next to him was another Santa with a sleigh and eight reindeer in flight. The yard lay utterly filled with every possible decoration. Elves, snowmen, candy canes, presents, teddy bears, angels, carolers, and a complete nativity scene, including camels. Each plastic treasure was illuminated from the inside with a lightbulb.

Dodd pointed to a Snoopy figure at the corner of the house. "Peanuts. Ruthie, this is great."

I giggled. "I know."

He pointed again. "What's that one near the porch?"

"Maybe an elf next to a mailbox? Looks like he's sending a letter to Santa."

"And look, there's Tigger."

I searched the yard. "I don't see Winnie-the-Pooh anywhere."

"No, he's not here." Dodd studied the yard slowly, then muttered, "Oh, now … *no*." He leaned toward me, placing one hand on my shoulder and pointing with the other. "Look at the side of the house. They've got two pilgrims and the Easter Bunny. That's just wrong."

I smiled at him. So much light shone from the yard, the interior of the car was lit as brightly as the afternoon sun. "At least they tried to hide them around the side."

A curtain moved at the front window, and Dodd shifted the car into gear. "Looks like it's time to go. Where next?"

"Back to town, actually. But drive straight through, because we're going about ten miles west this time."

We had already been to the fire department, where the volunteer firefighters had set their lights to music. And on our way to the Coulsons' plastic explosion, we stopped by a farmhouse bedecked in blue lights reflecting in a small lake.

When I first suggested we drive around looking at lights, Dodd had been leery, speculating there weren't enough decorated houses, but now I felt pleased to see him enjoying himself. Even though we had to drive twenty minutes between houses, the results were worth it.

I pointed to a large two-story lit with multicolored bulbs. "Not my favorite, but it's nice just the same."

"What? Oh, right." Dodd frowned slightly.

Whatever distracted him was about to work its way to his mouth.

"What was the second time your mother made an attempt?"

I flopped my arm on the edge of the window. "Are we still talking about Momma?"

"Not if you don't want to, no." He shook his head and smiled sheepishly. "I'm sorry. Let's talk about something else."

But of course, neither of us could think of anything else after that. We rode in silence for a few minutes, with Dodd humming purposefully, before I caved. "Three years ago, Neil Blaylock cheated Uncle Ansel in a cattle deal." I glanced at Dodd. "He sold Ansel twenty heifers that ended up sick. My uncle spent a lot of money on the veterinarian, but he still lost five or six head."

Dodd's elbow rested on the doorframe, and his fingers pressed against his temples. "I know I'm not a cattleman, but how could either of them know the cows were sick when Neil sold them to Ansel?"

"It was just too convenient. Momma said Neil did it to get back at her for some reason. She never told me what." I fiddled with the radio, trying to tune in a local station but getting only static. I clicked it off. "She was in treatment longer that time."

Dodd spoke quietly. "Three years ago. Your senior year?"

"Summer before. I was already working at the United, but I upped my schedule to thirty hours a week, and after graduation, the school board hired me to work days at the high school." A sarcastic laugh slid from my throat. "It's a good thing everyone in town doesn't treat me like the Blaylocks do, or I probably wouldn't have a job."

Dodd gripped the steering wheel and stared down the highway. He didn't speak.

"What?" I asked.

His expression softened, and I knew he hadn't meant to let me see his reaction. He spoke smoothly as though to buffer his words. "It's just that I can't picture Neil Blaylock deliberately hurting your family. He's a strong Christian man with high morals. None of it makes any sense." He glanced at me. "Is it all right if I pull over so we can talk about it?"

"We're almost to the next location, so just keep going." I wasn't sure I wanted to talk about it. Not if he was going to defend Neil Blaylock. "Turn on that gravel road after the mile marker." When I looked his way again, his face was so downcast, I couldn't stay irritated. Maybe he really couldn't make sense of things. I couldn't either. The Blaylocks, especially Neil, never made sense to me.

Dodd's expression shifted to wonder as we came close to the next light display. "Where's the house?"

"It's just the Christmas tree." A hundred yards away, Old Man Guthrie's evergreen stood smack in the middle of a cotton field. White lights twinkled from its branches, shedding an eerily festive glow across the moonlit landscape.

"Stop the car at this gate. We can walk in or just look from here."

Dodd turned off the car and stared. His eyes drifted across the field before he slowly rolled down his window and opened the door. "How is that done?" He stopped near the front bumper.

"I'm not sure. Mr. Guthrie used to be an architect. He designed a lot of buildings in the Panhandle." I shrugged. "His house is three or four miles from here." I pointed. "You can see the porch light."

Dodd stood in the moonlight and ran a hand over his mouth and chin. "I don't hear a generator, so he must have an electric line out here." He glanced at me as though he had forgotten I was there. "Can we walk over there? Do you mind? Would the owner care?"

"No, he's a friend of Uncle Ansel's. I called this afternoon." I smiled. "At least, I have permission. I don't know about *you*."

Dodd grabbed my hand and laced his fingers gently between mine. "Thank you for bringing me here. And I'm sorry about before."

I pulled him through the gate. "So, your fascination with this tree. Is that the mathematician in you?"

"I guess." He chuckled. "I always love figuring out how things work or trying to make things work better, or more efficiently, or more productively."

As we approached the tree, Dodd jogged ahead of me, walking in a circle, studying the trunk and the illuminated ground beneath the branches. The tree was much taller than it appeared from the road. "This is a ponderosa pine," he said. "The owner must have some kind of lift equipment to get the lights up there. Even an extension ladder wouldn't work. And he definitely has an electric line out here. Do you suppose he ran it all the way from his house?" He didn't wait for an answer. "But I can't figure why he'd do that just for Christmas decorations. He must need electricity for something else. Or maybe the electricity was here before the fields." He stared at the neat rows of plants as a slight wind whistled through the evergreen needles.

"And you thought no big trees grew around here."

"They don't. Obviously he waters regularly, which is why he planted it so close to the well."

I followed his hand gesture to a metal pipe I hadn't noticed, and then I leaned against the tree trunk and laughed out loud. "You're like a five-year-old at the science museum."

"Actually ..."—the tempo of his voice increased—"when I was little, I'd take Mom's appliances apart, figure out how they worked, and then put them back together. Well, mostly I got them back together."

"I'll ask your mother for her version of the story later." I looked up into the canopy of branches above my head, losing myself in the mass of twinkling lights.

"Do that," he challenged, stepping closer.

"You need to quit teaching high school and get an engineering degree."

He rested his forearm against the tree just above my head and gazed into my eyes. "I don't know about that."

His nearness relaxed me, and the back of my head bumped lazily against the trunk. "You should obey me."

"I'll think on it." He leaned down and covered my lips with his.

As we kissed, my brain whispered a warning, but my heart was far louder, and I lost myself in his touch. When he pulled away with a smile, I could still faintly hear the echoes of doubt, but I desperately shoved them from my mind.

CHAPTER THIRTY-ONE

I wasn't able to keep the seed of doubt dormant for long. By Saturday—the day of the craft fair and silent auction—it had blossomed into a deceptive flowering plant akin to the sweet clover growing in Ansel's pasture. Sure, the yellow blossoms were pleasant, but if they went a little moldy, they could poison the herd. Maybe I leaned toward the melodramatic, but I saw no reason to push my luck and risk being seen with Dodd.

Momma was working at the diner, so I decided to skip the parade.

I opened a book and curled up on the couch as the high school band marched down Main Street. I could hear an occasional air horn and lots of yelling. Dodd would wonder where I was. Even though we hadn't planned to walk around together, we had discussed spying on each other throughout the day. His easy smile had become a tonic to me, dulling my problems like an anesthetic, but his words from our Christmas-light adventure still stung. *I can't picture Neil Blaylock hurting your family … He's a strong Christian man.*

Yes, I wanted to see Dodd, but at the same time … *I didn't.*

Resting my head on the back of the couch, I hugged my book against my chest. JohnScott would also wonder about me. I told him I would meet him at the post office before the parade, and I didn't often go back on my word. I closed my eyes. Neither of them truly understood me.

I wasn't even sure I understood myself.

A loud knock at the door jerked me upright, and I stumbled to my feet.

"We know you're in there, little cousin." JohnScott's face pressed against the diamond window.

His voice made me smile, but when I realized Dodd was with him, every muscle in my body tightened. *Holy cow.* The preacher was standing on my front porch in front of God and everybody.

I yanked the door open and pulled the two men inside.

"Good to see you, too," Dodd said, his eyes dancing around the living room inquisitively.

Crossing my arms to ward off my panic, I ignored him. "Sorry I didn't meet up with you, JohnScott, but I figured you'd manage without me."

"I managed just fine, little cousin, but it's time for you to vacate the cave."

I tied my tennis shoes ferociously, anxious to get Dodd out of my house. Even though Momma was safely away at work, I feared her walking in unannounced. *That would be just my luck.* "Okay, I'm ready. Let's go." I hurried to the door.

JohnScott grinned as he stepped onto the porch. "I get the impression you want us out of here."

Dodd took my hand and pulled me back into the house. *"Relax."*

"I don't want people to see us together, Dodd." I gritted my teeth. "I can't do that to Momma. Not yet."

"I know." He kissed my cheek. "This afternoon I'll admire you from a distance, but will you meet me tonight after the fireworks show?"

He looked into my eyes and waited until I finally softened. "Of course. Now go away, you twit."

"I'm parked down from the high school parking. Meet me there," Dodd called over his shoulder, then took off at a brisk trot in the opposite direction from JohnScott and me.

Soon we jostled from booth to booth in the crowded downtown area. Banners flapped overhead, meat sizzled on grills, and Christmas songs rang out from a public-address system. We spent hours creeping up and down the streets, browsing the craft items, and eating nonstop. I made a few Christmas purchases, and JohnScott sampled tamales, turkey legs, funnel cakes, and hot wassail.

Occasionally Dodd would pass by, nonchalantly bumping me in the crowd, and several times I caught him reading my lips from a distance, and I took the opportunity to say things to embarrass him.

By evening my cousin had gained five pounds, and I had a stomachache. We waddled through the fire department garage, perusing the silent-auction bid sheets to see how the prices had climbed throughout the day. The two of us had offered a gift certificate for an afternoon of Christmas-light installation, Velma contributed a cookie jar shaped like the Pillsbury Doughboy, and Ansel donated several bags of feed.

As I pulled cotton candy with sticky fingers, I became aware of someone standing next to me. I ignored him but couldn't help smiling.

"Excuse me."

The deep voice didn't belong to Dodd, and I glanced up to discover Clyde Felton at my elbow.

My skin prickled.

When JohnScott took a step toward me, I relaxed and looked more closely at the convict. His eyes weren't bloodshot, and he didn't reek of alcohol, but his movements weren't natural. He shuffled his worn Adidas in the sawdust, then thrust his hands in and out of his pockets.

"Hey, Ruth Ann."

I raised an eyebrow. Apparently he thought he could call me Ruth Ann, since he knew Momma.

"I know you don't want to talk to me, and I don't blame you." He fingered a set of crocheted pot holders on the table next to him and took a half step toward me.

I shifted an equal distance away.

My body language seemed to cause him to hesitate, but he gave a slight nod of acceptance. As though he didn't deserve better. "That day at the school?" he said. "I was just curious about your momma." His gaze bounced from the pot holders to my face, and then he turned to peer behind him.

I followed his gaze and noticed Dodd standing near the auction announcer, who droned details into a crackly microphone. Probably the preacher was reading our lips, and it comforted me to know he was there, keeping an eye on me. When Dodd gave me a thumbs-up, my nerves settled.

Clyde turned back to face me. "I just wanted to say I'm real sorry, Ruth Ann."

The sincerity of his words surprised me, and his eyes held mine for a few seconds.

"Um … that's okay."

Clyde nodded, peering at me as though I might say something else, but when I didn't, he slowly turned around. From the back, his shoulders seemed even broader, and I shivered as he walked away. He may have been Momma's friend, but he still scared the life out of me. He picked his way around the tables, stepping cautiously to avoid the crowd, and then strode directly to Dodd who slapped him on the shoulder.

Needles of doubt prickled across my scalp.

"Well, that was unexpected," JohnScott said.

I gawked at the two men across the garage, and when Dodd followed Clyde through the breezeway into darkness, I realized his thumbs-up hadn't been intended for me. "What in the world?" I quizzed my cousin. "Did Dodd put him up to this?"

JohnScott squirmed. "I know he's been talking to Clyde about straightening up his act."

"His act?" I shoved my cotton candy back in its bag and squeezed it into a blob, my fingers sticking to the plastic.

"Laying off alcohol mainly, but Dodd's also been reminding him there's something worth living for."

"You mean God."

"Yep."

I didn't know what to think. Who would've dreamed Clyde Felton would apologize? A teeny part of me was irritated with Dodd for talking about me, but on the other hand, I was shocked. Not only because of Dodd's willingness to befriend someone like Clyde but because of his undeniable influence on the ex-convict. And others.

I shook my head and muttered, "Let's go to the stadium and find a good seat for the fireworks."

As we walked through town, JohnScott seemed to sense my mood, and instead of heading toward the bleachers, he led me to the high school parking lot, where we climbed to the top of his truck, sitting with our feet dangling in front of the windshield. We'd be able to see perfectly and yet still have some privacy.

Simultaneously JohnScott nudged my shoulder and I popped his knee. We sat silently for half an hour, watching the crowd gather in the distance.

"Why do you suppose he apologized?" I finally asked. "He doesn't seem like the type."

"I get the impression Clyde's not what he seems."

I laced my fingers together and hooked them over my knee. "Why does he care?"

"I guess because he's a Christian."

My breath caught slightly. Clyde had told Momma he got religion in prison, but somehow I'd never attached the term *Christian* to my image of him. I figured *got religion* meant he went to the prison worship because he didn't get any visitors otherwise. But now I began to wonder. Obviously he wasn't a Trapp type of Christian, looking down on the rest of us, but he wasn't the Cunninghams' type of Christian either, goodness oozing out of their every action. It didn't make sense, really. Clyde was an obvious sinner, tried and convicted. How could he be a Christian?

The fireworks burst over the stadium, illuminating the shadows in the parking lot. At first I squinted at the brightness, but as my eyes adjusted, I watched in fascination. The same fascination I felt every year, energized by the rumble of the detonations, the vibrating boom of the explosions, and the acrid scent of gunpowder hanging in the air. With each flash of color, applause rose, and the hardness in my soul softened.

"JohnScott ..."

"Hmm?"

"Tell me about Jesus."

JohnScott exhaled softly, relief seeming to seep out of his lungs. "It's simple, really. He loves you, and He wants to take care of you."

A few last explosions held my attention before I looked at my cousin. "I know He's there and all that, but I think I'm okay." I blinked at the smoke hanging in the air. "I'm not sure it's worth the trouble, you know?"

"You mean the church?"

"Mm-hmm."

He gave a tiny huff, and then smiled, trying to hide his impatience. "I won't ever worship in Trapp either, but it's not about them."

JohnScott was wrong, but I didn't expect him to understand. Even though he'd seen how the church treated me, he didn't feel it. He didn't know how it stung. I bumped my shoulder against his, ready to end the conversation. "I'm doing all right, JohnScott."

"Are you?"

He whispered the words, yet they hung in the air as though he had shouted.

CHAPTER THIRTY-TWO

My muscles were jelly as we climbed down from the truck after the fireworks display. Clyde's apology, coupled with JohnScott's Jesus discussion, left my brain muzzy. Both incidents prompted countless questions, but I had no energy to ask my cousin for answers. Instead, I found myself wishing for a quilt and a laptop movie in Ansel's back pasture. With Dodd. That first date seemed like an escape from the real world and all its problems.

Dodd and I planned to meet at his El Camino, but for the time being, I waited with JohnScott, hovering behind Corky Ledbetter's full-sized van as the crowd cleared. Dodd's car was parked on a shadowy side street—conveniently hidden from curious onlookers—but when I saw the preacher coming from the stadium with Clyde by his side, I groaned. "He's not going to apologize again, is he?"

JohnScott laughed. "Probably not, little cousin."

He started to say something else, but a loud bang distracted him, and we both peered around the van. Tyler and Fawn were arguing, and apparently, Tyler had kicked JohnScott's truck.

"Oh, come on, Fawn. You know you want to." Tyler's words ran together.

"No."

When I heard the pitch of Fawn's voice, my sides tightened. It was only one word, but it sounded whiny and weak, without a hint of her usual confidence.

"We never should've let it go this far." She turned away from him. "Just take me home, okay?"

Tyler grabbed her arm. "That's not what I had in mind, babe."

"Everything all right out here?" Dodd walked hesitantly around the truck, with Clyde right behind him.

"Brother Cunningham." Tyler drew the name out into several syllables, arrogance dripping from his words as he released Fawn. "You brought a registered sex offender on school property?"

Dodd didn't reply, but Fawn mumbled, "Come on, Tyler."

"Why do we keep running into you, Felton?" Tyler's voice rose. "Wherever we are, you're bound to show up."

Clyde gazed at him steadily. "Coincidence."

"You sure you're not following us?" A threat lay just beneath his words.

"He's not following you," called JohnScott as he stepped around the van. "Clyde's been with Dodd most of the day. They're headed back to his car. See?" He pointed, even though the only part of the El Camino that was visible was the corner of the front bumper.

Fawn looked between the three men, and her cheeks flushed. "Let's just go, Tyler."

In first grade, her jeans had ripped during recess, and Fawn had the same humiliated expression. That day I had given her my jacket to tie around her waist.

"You need a ride home?" asked JohnScott.

Tyler snickered. "Like I'm going to leave her when the jailbird's around."

Dodd hung back, scanning the parking lot until he located me, and then he gave a nearly imperceptible nod, indicating I should stay where I was.

Clyde took a step forward. "You're the one that's not good for the girl."

"I'm not good for her?" Tyler's words slurred again. "But I suppose you are?"

"That's not what he meant," Fawn said.

"Oh, shut up." Tyler sneered. "Why don't you go ahead and hang with Clyde. He's a rapist. Maybe he can get something off you."

The sound of her palm striking Tyler's cheek carried high on the breeze, and when Tyler's returning blow thudded, all three men rushed forward.

With mixed feelings, I silently urged them on. Even though Fawn represented most of the problems in my life, no woman deserved to be hit.

Instantly Clyde pinned Tyler against JohnScott's truck. "You're way out of your league, boy," he growled.

Tyler's eyes grew wide, but Clyde seemed to instantly regret his actions, and his shoulders fell as he pushed away. He clenched his fists at his sides as though holding back a torrent of anger. "Don't touch her again." He accented each word as he leaned within inches of Tyler's face, and then Clyde turned and strode quickly into the shadows of the bleachers.

The farther Clyde walked from the parking lot, the more Tyler seemed to regain his courage, and by the time the ex-convict disappeared, Tyler's face held no trace of the terror that had been there moments before. He mimicked Clyde with a high-pitched whine, "Don't. Touch. Her. Again."

"Dodd … Coach Pickett … I'm sorry," Fawn said. "I'm so sorry about this. It's my fault."

I had only ever heard Fawn apologize like that to one other person. Her father. During our freshman year of high school, I had walked past them at the livestock show, behind the barns. Neil had leaned against one of his enormous horse trailers, his arms crossed, while Fawn cowered in front of him. "I'm so sorry, Dad. This is my fault."

"Well, of course, it's your fault," he'd agreed. "As usual."

That day I sped past them, not wanting to hear more. And now as Tyler glared at her with the same scorn, I didn't want to hear it again, but I couldn't get away. I paced behind the van like a caged animal, trapped.

"It most certainly is not your fault," Dodd said.

JohnScott used his calming voice. The one he used so often on me. "I could take you home, Fawn."

I peeked from behind the van in time to see Tyler slam his fist against the truck. "If you go with the coach, we're finished."

"Stop hitting my truck." JohnScott sounded as though Tyler were an annoying insect.

"Fawn?" Tyler's hands were on his hips, and even though he

swayed, he still reminded me of Neil Blaylock on that day at the stock show. His body language screamed that Fawn was unworthy.

She lifted her chin. "I don't need a ride, JohnScott, but thank you. My parents are still over at the silent auction, so I'll walk over there." The way her shoulders slumped made her back appear hunched, and she didn't look like herself. "I'm sorry, you guys."

"You'll ride with me, Fawn," Tyler said.

She shook her head, uncharacteristically defiant. "No, Tyler. I'm not riding with you."

Tyler watched as she made her way through the remaining cars in the parking lot, and then he spun on his heel, letting his arms swing. "That's it, then," he called after her, even though she was probably too far away to hear. "Don't be calling me tomorrow, Fawn." He stomped toward his truck, but his fourth step turned into a stagger.

Dodd groaned. "We shouldn't let him drive."

"I got this." JohnScott trotted after Tyler. "I'll drive him to Snyder and call Grady to come fetch me in my truck."

"What if Tyler won't let you drive?"

JohnScott grinned. "It's me or the police, right?"

"Ah, the power of persuasion."

Dodd watched them for a few seconds before he turned and ambled toward me. He smiled sadly, then took my hand and led me to the El Camino. We sat side by side in silence, staring out the windshield at a shadowy hedge that jiggled when the breeze hit it, and it occurred to me that Dodd hadn't spoken much during all the commotion.

I cleared my throat. "So they broke up?"

"I guess." He stared blindly, as though deep in thought, and I studied him as he seemed to search for answers. Finally he exhaled and rested his elbows on the steering wheel, letting his head drop into his hands. He didn't move for several minutes, and I wondered if he was praying, but then he moaned. "I'm in over my head, Ruthie."

His insecurity startled me, and I hesitated before answering. "You mean with Clyde?"

"All of it." He shrugged. "The church, these people, they need more than I can give them." He peered at me through the half darkness, still slumped over the steering wheel. "I'm not big enough for this. I don't have the wisdom."

I ran the fingernails of my left hand up and down his back, trying to ease his tension. "God is bigger than all of this, right?"

Dodd leaned back and slipped an arm around my shoulders. "Of course He is. You're a smart woman."

His transparency drew me in as his soft words comforted my doubts. I snuggled against his shoulder, burying my face in his neck until I imagined I located the exact spot he applied his cologne. I inhaled deeply and lost myself in his scent, his warmth, his touch.

In the dim light, I noticed circles under his eyes, and I ran the tip of my finger from the bridge of his nose to the corner of his lashes. He smiled, and the skin crinkled beneath my fingertip. I wanted nothing more than to comfort his stress away, so I slipped my hand behind his head and pulled his lips down to mine. He moaned softly, and his weight shifted toward me as he relaxed.

We kissed tenderly, without the uncertainty of the other times we had been together. And after five minutes, or ten, or thirty, he leaned his head against the back windshield and nestled me beneath his arm. "I got you something for Christmas." He reached behind the seat and pulled out a medium-sized box.

Its weight surprised me as I tore off the paper. Lifting the lid, I felt smooth leather, so I turned the box over, its contents falling hard against my lap as my spirits fell heavy against my heart. "You got me a Bible?"

"If that's all right." Dodd's voice questioned me.

I stroked the cover, wanting to be with Dodd, and at the same time, wanting to be far away from him.

It was too much. Clyde's apology, JohnScott's impatience, Fawn's insecurity. *Now a Bible.*

Movement in the parking lot distracted me, and I took advantage of the opportunity. "Is that Grady?"

Concern covered Dodd's face, but he rolled down the window, and I followed him out on his side of the car.

"I'm sorry, Ruthie." He took my hand. "I'm rushing you."

I shook my head, unable to speak and not knowing what to say anyway. How could I verbalize the loneliness I felt? I tugged him toward JohnScott's truck, but when we walked out of the shadows, Grady was nowhere in sight.

Instead, we came face-to-face with Fawn.

Her eyes mirrored my panic. I thrust Dodd's hand away from me, but Fawn had already seen. I expected her to cock her neck to the side with a calculated smile, but she only gazed nervously toward JohnScott's truck … and lowered her head like she was the one who had been caught. Like she was the one who should be ashamed. I realized she wasn't thinking about how quickly she could spread the rumor that Ruthie Turner had been holding hands with

Dodd Cunningham. She seemed consumed by humiliation. Tyler had treated her like dirt in front of the preacher. He had talked to her like a tramp. He had struck her.

"I think I left my purse." She edged away from us, grabbed her bag from the bed of JohnScott's truck, and scurried back toward the stadium.

Dodd called, "Fawn? *Wait.*" But she didn't answer. And when he jogged after her, she only moved faster.

I stood motionless, watching her as in a dream. This couldn't actually be happening. Fawn Blaylock running away. *From me.* An involuntary chuckle escaped my lips, but then I sucked in a ragged breath as a foreign sensation welled up in my heart. I held both arms across my stomach, overwhelmed by a realization so absurd to me it stung.

I felt sorry for Fawn Blaylock.

CHAPTER THIRTY-THREE

Dodd sped down the highway, gripping the steering wheel. When Neil Blaylock called and asked him to come by the ranch on Sunday afternoon, Dodd felt a simultaneous surge of apprehension and relief. He was grateful Neil was finally following through with his promise to sit down and discuss Lynda Turner's situation, but he worried about running into Fawn.

As he pulled the El Camino through the iron gate of the Blaylocks' ranch, Neil waved from the open door of a warehouse-sized barn, motioning for Dodd to join him.

"Mind if I abuse my good manners and put you to work?" Neil powered on the overhead lights. "I need to get some feed out to my horses."

"I'd be offended if you didn't."

"That's what I like to hear."

The barn's cement floor and buzzing caged lights reminded Dodd of the gymnasium back in his elementary school, but the comparison stopped there because the barn was much larger. Dodd always imagined barns would smell like cattle, but the only animal-related scent was the hay piled in a corner. The predominant oiled-machinery smell came from two tractors, one smaller than the other, and several strange contraptions that Dodd assumed were designed to be pulled behind.

Neil noticed him looking. "You ought to see the cab of the Kubota over there. The thing's got a dashboard that puts my desktop computer to shame. I'm considering installing a DVD player."

Dodd's eyebrows shot up with interest. "You don't say." He took the pair of soft-leather work gloves Neil offered him and followed the rancher's example by stacking bales of hay in the bed of Neil's double-cab pickup.

Suddenly he missed his dad. Dodd shoved one of the bales and heard the echo of his dad's voice. "No matter the task you're up against, remember two things. Enjoy the experience, because you might never do it again, and learn from it, because you probably will."

He peered at Neil sheepishly, knowing there was only one way to learn. "I'm sure this is a stupid question, but don't horses eat grass?"

"They do." Neil nodded. "But a norther's coming, and they don't take kindly to digging in snow to get their dinner. Besides, you're in West Texas now. In case you hadn't noticed, there's not enough ground cover out here to support a jackrabbit, much less twenty horses and seven hundred fifty head of cattle."

Dodd whistled. "It must take you all day to feed them."

"Well, I've got round bales for the herd, and they go much quicker with the tractor."

"And the DVD player." Dodd felt like an ignorant city slicker, but it was worth the opportunity to spend time with Neil and pick his brain. As they climbed in the truck, he said, "I've been looking forward to talking to you."

Neil glanced at him with an indecipherable expression as he eased the pickup across the cement incline leading out of the barn and then accelerated down the gravel road, sending dust scurrying across the pasture in the wind. "Ah yes. The Turners."

Dodd dreaded bringing up the subject but knew it was the only way to help Ruthie. "Can you tell me what happened between them and the church?"

"I thought Charlie talked to you about that."

"He didn't know much. He said your father handled it."

"That he did. Tried to keep it hush-hush." Neil adjusted the heater control. "Hoby and Lynda struggled in their marriage for years. But when he found out she'd been unfaithful, it proved more than he could handle." He slowed the truck as they vibrated over a cattle guard.

His frank tone stunned Dodd into silence as the truck stopped near a cluster of metal feeders. *So the rumors were true?* Prickly-pear cactus clustered among bare mesquite trees, accentuating the stark wind pressing against the truck. A gust swirled a few snowflakes onto the warm hood, where they melted instantly.

"Lynda committed adultery, son, and never once showed a penitent heart. The church had no choice." Neil opened his door, and a whoosh of cold air cleared the stiffness in the cab. "Here come the horses. Let's get this done."

Ten more questions popped into Dodd's head as he hastened to catch up with Neil, but he opted for the safety of small talk. "The horses act like you've got candy."

"Yes, they come running as soon as they hear the truck."

Neil hefted a bale and tossed it into the feeder, where a pale horse began pulling straws from beneath the tight wires. Four other horses did the same, unable to get a good mouthful but tugging for their dinner just the same. Impatient animals.

Dodd knew how they felt, because his own impatience made him feel starved for information. He reached for another bale as Neil eased between the horses.

"I bet you've got a few more questions." Neil snipped the wires with a pair of wire cutters.

"Well, yes." Dodd rested his elbow on the top of the feeder, but the coldness of the frozen iron penetrated his jacket, and he crossed his arms instead. "JohnScott seems to think Lynda never had an affair. It seems like he would know."

"Lynda's a proud woman, son, and she knew she was in the wrong. She probably denied it to her family."

Dodd reached toward one of the horses and hesitantly rubbed a gloved hand across its neck as the animal's muscles jittered. "So how did the church find out, then?"

Neil finished removing the wire, then frowned at the remaining bales, still in the truck. "Lynda and I were good friends back then. Had been since high school. When she confided in me, I encouraged her to repent, but she wouldn't have it." He grimaced. "Stubborn pride."

"So you went to your dad?"

"Had to." Neil folded the baling wire and tossed it in the back of the truck. "Never dreamed the church would react that way, though."

Dodd threw him another bale. JohnScott and Ruthie were adamant there was no infidelity, and Dodd knew telling them wouldn't be easy. But if he didn't, Ruthie would never understand the church's actions.

"What are you thinking about, son?"

Dodd slumped against the feeder. "Ruthie. Should I talk to her about it?"

Neil paused in his work, then reached for a bale and yanked it toward him. "You're becoming good friends with Ruthie and JohnScott." His words sounded stilted, and Dodd sensed disapproval.

"Yes."

Neil folded the remaining wires and peered at a horse that was champing noisily. "Son, how long has it been since your daddy passed?"

The change in topic startled Dodd. "About a year."

Neil ran a gloved hand across the back of the pale horse and down its rump. "You've had a lot of changes. Losing your dad, moving out here, new job, new church, not to mention taking the reins with the family. That's a lot for a man to handle."

The verbal acknowledgment of his burdens caused some of the weight to dissolve from Dodd's shoulders. "It's been a challenge."

"Ever feel like things are happening too fast?"

Dodd chuckled. "Like a whirlwind."

Neal slapped his gloves against a thigh. "Might not be a bad idea to slow down. Do what you can to keep life simple while you heal from your father's death. You've already had a double dose of adjustments—some good, some bad—and you deserve to rest a spell. Get your feet under you." His lips curved. "Your family and your church need you to take your time."

Dodd's heart sank. "You're talking about Ruthie, aren't you?"

"Among other things." Neil reached for the door handle. "Let's get back to the house before we freeze."

The conversation hadn't gone as Dodd had anticipated, and instead of feeling better about the Turners, he was more confused. As he and Neil returned to the warmth of the truck, he sensed the man holding something back. "Neil? When you said 'other things,' were you referring to something in particular?"

Neil flashed a you-caught-me grin as he pulled out of the pasture and steered down a rutted lane on the edge of a field with neat green rows. "I hated to bring it up, but Lee Roy called a meeting of the elders last night. He's miffed about that ex-convict showing up at services."

Dodd's mouth fell open in surprise. "Clyde? I'm thrilled he's been there."

"Now, see ..." Neil scratched his temple with a thumbnail. "Lee Roy, Charlie, and me? We've got nothing against the man, but as shepherds of the flock, we've got to consider the congregation."

"I'm not following you."

Neil removed his cowboy hat and wiped his forehead. "Aw, Dodd. It's just that Clyde Felton is a risk to the weak."

"The weak?"

"Not everyone is as strong as you and me, and some of our members could easily be led astray. Besides, most of the women are scared of him."

Dodd didn't like the sound of Neil's explanation but respected him enough to give the benefit of the doubt. "Clyde doesn't appear to be a threat."

The truck bumped over another cattle guard. "But, son, you can't always read a person by first impressions."

Dodd shook his head. "My opinion of him is not based on an impression. I've spoken to him at length on several occasions."

"Have you?" Neil slowed the truck to peer at him momentarily.

"Yes, and he speaks highly of the prison ministry. It's because of those saints he even knows the Lord at all. In my opinion, we should gather him into the flock like one of those weak members you mentioned. He needs encouragement as much as the rest."

Silence.

As they drove past another field, the evenly spaced green rows slithered and coiled against the ginger soil. Dodd looked at Neil. "Can we discuss this with Charlie and Lee Roy? I'd appreciate hearing their views on the subject."

"We discussed it last night at the meeting, son, so I already know their views. You'll have to trust us on this one, not merely because we're your elders, but because we're your employers. If your daddy were alive, he'd tell you the same thing. Put some distance between yourself and Clyde Felton." He reached over and slapped Dodd's leg with a grin. "Good Lord, son, you're the preacher. Time you started acting like it."

Confusion crowded Dodd's thoughts. "Is the church laying out an edict for me to stay away from him?"

"Don't think of it that way. We simply think our young man ought to spend more time with those inside the church than those outside." He stopped the truck at an angle behind the El Camino. "No matter who they are."

CHAPTER THIRTY-FOUR

"Ruth Ann, stop biting your nails."

It was Monday, just after New Year's, and I was stuck reading a novel in a booth at the diner while Momma rolled paper napkins around silverware.

That morning I had awakened to six inches of snow, raised the blinds to marvel at the whiteness, and discovered ice on my bedroom window. On the inside. Our old heater was on the blink again—which happened frequently—but we always managed to keep warm by the fire until Ansel could get over to repair it. This time things weren't working out so well. As luck would have it, my uncle came down with the flu the same day we ran out of wood, forcing me to seek refuge at Dixie's Diner.

I groaned inwardly as the Blaylocks' black-and-gray pickup pulled to the curb, and Neil and the Mrs. stepped onto the sidewalk. Fawn followed behind them, and from the looks of it, she had the flu just like Ansel.

When the bell above the door jangled, Dixie called from the kitchen, "Hey there, Neil."

"Dixie, you up to no good?" he teased.

They were related somehow. Cousins, maybe.

"As usual." Dixie went back to her work, and Neil opened his menu. I wondered if the two of them ever spoke outside the diner.

Neil glanced around the room. Other than Old Man Guthrie sipping coffee on a stool by the counter, the Blaylocks were the only customers. Apparently people weren't getting out in the snow.

I pretended to read, and Momma ignored them as long as possible before sidling up to their table. "Drinks?"

"Bottled water," Mrs. Blaylock said. "And Fawn wants a Sprite."

"I'll have an iced tea. Sweet." Neil leaned back in his chair. "With a couple of lemon slices on the side."

"Coming right up." Momma ambled behind the counter to assemble the drink order but soon put their glasses aside to brew a fresh pot of coffee for Mr. Guthrie. I couldn't blame her for stalling. *Lemon slices on the side?* Dixie's Diner didn't rank as a lemon-slice establishment, and Neil knew it.

Out of sheer boredom, I studied the Blaylocks over the top of my book. As Momma took them their drinks, Neil was texting on his phone while his wife tweaked her lipstick in a compact mirror. Fawn looked as if she might pass out.

After Momma served them, she brought me a plate of chicken-fried steak, and I welcomed the distraction. Ever since the drama at the fund-raiser, Fawn had been on my mind, but the pity I initially felt had been replaced with skepticism. I'd glimpsed a side of her I hadn't seen since we were young, and I speculated how she would handle the exposure. Truth be told, I puzzled over how to handle it myself.

I drenched my steak in peppery, white gravy, sopping the remainder with a dinner roll. Nothing hit the spot like comfort food, and I managed to ignore the Blaylocks while they ate their meals.

Soon Momma paused again at their table. "Dessert?"

"Not this time. The wife and I are stuffed. And daughters are impossible." He motioned toward Fawn's untouched plate, but then he leaned back in his chair, crossed his arms over his ample chest, and slowly let his head fall back until I thought his neck might snap. "By the way, Lynda, have you had a chance to meet the new preacher?"

My fingers tightened around my fork, and my gaze jerked toward Fawn, who immediately ducked her head.

The glare Momma leveled at Neil could have melted concrete, but he merely picked his teeth with his thumbnail.

"I'll get your check," she said.

Dread bubbled up from my core like the clay volcano JohnScott made in eighth grade. *Why would Neil ask Momma about Dodd?*

His wife and daughter made their way back to the truck, where they started the ignition to warm themselves, but evidently Neil was in no hurry. He sauntered toward the register, scraping his boots on the linoleum flooring like an arrogant cowboy in an old Western. He gazed at me with laughter in his eyes.

He knew.

Momma punched buttons on the calculator Dixie kept on the Formica counter. "Twenty-five dollars, eighteen cents."

Neil leafed through his wallet and pulled out two bills, but when Momma reached for them, he tightened his grip and mumbled something I couldn't hear. He held the money a foot above her hand, then let it flutter to the counter.

Momma clenched her teeth and scooped the bills into her fist, but Neil, after glancing out the window, leaned toward her. He rested one elbow on the counter and spoke directly into her ear, and when he walked away, his fingertips trailed across her whitened knuckles.

She opened the register and robotically made change, which she shoved into the pocket of her apron. When her eyes bored into mine, my stomach wadded itself into a panicked pile of anxiety, and I thought I might toss my lunch.

This was it. She would yell then scream then cry then shatter, and I could do nothing but brace myself against the cushion of the diner booth and wait for her storm to pass. And suffer through the silence and pain and withdrawal and despair that would surely grip her for months afterward.

She stomped around the counter, trembling from the rage she felt toward me.

I shouldn't have done this. Shouldn't have gone out with the preacher. Shouldn't have pushed her so close to the edge. It wasn't worth it. It wasn't worth her lapsing back into herself.

I gripped the edge of my seat and held on tight.

"How can JohnScott associate with those people?" she asked.

I glanced out the window to the parking space, which recently held the Blaylocks' truck. A small square of asphalt was visible where the snow had melted. "I don't know, Momma."

"They're all the same. Can't JohnScott see it?" She sighed a short puff of frustration—a muted explosion of air from her lungs, which seemed to release a stockpile of energy and tension—then she plopped down across from me.

My hands loosened their grip on the seat, but my fingers stuck to the vinyl as though they had recently been dipped in plaster that had already begun to set.

I slowly exhaled.

Apparently Dodd and I were still safe. I bowed my head, surprised to find my forgotten plate still sitting on the table in front of me. I touched the edge with my palm and pushed it six inches to the right as Momma mindlessly chewed her fingernails.

She scowled at the snow on the other side of the window, staring without seeing, but when the door jangled the entrance of a new customer, she rolled her eyes, shook her head, pulled herself wearily to her feet, and got on with life. Taking my messy plate with her as she went.

I opened my book again, but I couldn't focus on the words for thinking about Momma.

If Neil hadn't told her about Dodd and me, what had he said to make her so angry?

CHAPTER THIRTY-FIVE

"Cows are such stupid animals," Momma declared as we drove through the snow toward Ansel and Velma's house the next afternoon. She had gone into a tizzy when Velma reported Ansel and JohnScott were ignoring their flu symptoms and braving the weather to feed their small herd, and she hadn't stopped griping since she got off the phone. "What are they thinking? They're too sick to work."

As we parked the hatchback behind the house, I spotted my uncle's two-tone Silverado protruding from the louvered metal barn, so I headed across the pasture while Momma went in the house to check on Velma.

"Hey, y'all," I called.

No reply.

Squeezing past the truck, I peered into the shadowy barn expecting to see Ansel and JohnScott, but the only trace of my uncle and cousin was a few bales of hay on the tailgate. The wind whistled through gaps in the sheet metal, and a rank odor swirled around me.

I discovered a puddle of vomit near my foot and kicked sand and straw to cover it.

The back door slammed in the distance, and Momma appeared. "All three of them are down. They tried to do chores but couldn't muster the strength." She stomped snow from her shoes and glared at the haystack as if it were a demon. "I detest hay."

My gaze swept the amber tower. I wasn't crazy about hay either, but we both knew what had to be done. "If I climb to the top, I can push the bales into the back of the truck." I looked at Momma. "Can you arrange them in the bed?"

She gave a determined nod. "We'll have to make two trips. One to the home pasture and one down by the pond."

"Three." I hated to tell her. "Ansel moved a few head to the back last week. Something about heifers."

"I detest hay," she repeated, but she climbed into the truck as I shimmied up the haystack. "We'll also have to break the ice on the holding tank. Wouldn't do to go to this much trouble to feed the cattle just to have them die of thirst."

"Then we'll have to check the tanks in the pasture, too." Sliding my fingers under the tightly bound baling wire, I realized I should've gotten gloves. I hefted the bale, lifting it a few inches as the metal dug into my fingers, but I managed to drag it to the edge of the stack, positioning it above the truck. I gave it a shove, and it landed in the bed, bounced toward the tailgate, and slid to the barn floor.

Momma lunged for it and cursed.

"Leave it," I said. "Let me try again."

I attempted to ease the next bale over the side so it would slide into the truck, but the fingers of my left hand got stuck under the wire, pinching me as the bale fell. "Ouch!" I twisted my hand free, which caused the bale to steer to the side, missing the truck altogether. Then I echoed Momma's curse.

She climbed down from the truck to retrieve the bales, heaving one to her thigh before shoving it onto the tailgate with her knee. "Why does Ansel have to stock alfalfa? Coastal is so much lighter."

I kneaded my fingers, which were already bleeding and beginning to swell. "Do you want me to get the other one?"

"No, you stick to your target practice, but let me find you some gloves."

She rummaged in the cab and produced two filthy leather work gloves, then tossed them up to me, the odor of dirt and sweat coming with them.

I dropped one back down. "I need a left."

She reached into the truck again and chucked another glove, this one hardened by years of use.

When I slid my fingers under the wires of a bale, the stiff leather folded, rendering my grip useless. It took several tries before I had a good hold, and when I finally maneuvered the bale to send it over the side, one of the gloves sailed with it, still wedged under the wire, but at least the bale stayed in the truck. "Third time's a charm."

Momma didn't comment, just wiped sweat off her forehead and threw the glove back up to me. When I landed two more bales on the ground, I plopped on my bottom and leaned against a bale, with my feet dangling above Momma's head.

She withered into the bed of the truck, leaning her head on her arm. This was going to take us all day.

We both jumped when we heard a man's voice calling Ansel's name, and then Dodd appeared at the barn entry, silhouetted by the snowy brightness behind him. He shut the door of the truck so he could slide past, and Grady followed on the other side of the cab.

I stifled a squeal of relief.

"Ruthie-the-checker-girl? I didn't know you were a cowhand."

"Clearly I'm not."

Dodd nodded to Momma. "Ansel must be worse off than we thought."

I spoke up, since Momma was trying to figure out how to behave appropriately. "He and JohnScott are both stuck in bed."

Dodd's gaze swept my face, my hair, my King Kong–gloved hands, and he puckered his lips to keep from smiling. "Why don't you let us finish up? Mom's in the house."

My eyes shot to Momma, and when I saw her relief, I began my descent down the stack.

"Thank you." Momma slid from her perch in the truck, landing beside Grady. "Thank you both." She slipped quickly out of the barn.

Whoa. Momma said thank you. Twice.

I could feel dust and bits of hay embedded in dried sweat on my face and neck, and I still wore the huge gloves. I jerked them off and tossed them to Grady. Most likely my hair resembled a bale of hay, and no telling what I smelled like. By the time I had my feet on the ground, Dodd and Grady had loaded my wayward bales, tightened the others in the truck, and were stacking more. I ducked my head to scurry away.

"Hang on there," Dodd said as I passed him. He craned his neck toward the house and then reached down from the back of the truck to pull a few straws from my hair. "I knew you were a hard worker, but you've surprised me again." His eyes teased unmercifully, and I shook my head to protest, but before I could speak, he cupped my chin in his hand, lifted my face toward his, and kissed me firmly on the lips. Then he lingered. Not so long my knees got weak, but long enough Grady gave a low whistle.

Dodd plucked still more hay from my hair, then winked at me.

I hurried to the house with mixed emotions. Dodd produced a gentle flurry of happiness around my heart, but Momma and Milla created a swell of panic that made me sick with apprehension. There was no telling what cheeky things Momma might say to Milla, warping whatever good impression I may have made on Dodd's mother. And to make matters worse, I had no way of knowing if Milla would mention I had been in her home, a tiny fact that would put Momma into a tizzy.

I washed my hands and face in the sink in the mudroom, then stumbled into the living area, where I found both of them. Together. It struck me as peculiar not only to see them in the same room but in a place as warm and cozy as Velma's kitchen. Milla stirred a bubbling pot on the stove, filling the room with the scent of chicken and vegetables, while Momma leaned against the refrigerator, fiddling with a cup towel.

"She brought soup." Momma's skill at small talk lacked finesse, but at least it appeared she was trying, and my panic subsided slightly. Maybe she wouldn't make a scene.

"Smells wonderful."

"I hope it helps." Milla gave me a lingering look. "My bunch had a round of flu last year, and a friend brought this over. It revived us.

Got us through the worst of it." She laughed. "But now when I make it, we remember the sickness, and it doesn't taste as good."

My nerves settled slightly as Milla and I filled three bowls and roused the patients enough for them to sit up in bed and feed themselves, and then I fixed each of them a glass of Sprite to leave at their bedsides.

While we tended them, Momma scrubbed the bathrooms. She spent more time cleaning those two rooms than she had spent cleaning our house all year, but she accomplished her dual purposes—to rid the house of influenza germs and to avoid Milla Cunningham.

Dodd's mother showed no indication of unease despite the sights and odors of illness. "Ruthie, would you like some hot tea? I think I'll take some out to Dodd and Grady now that they're back."

"I'm not normally a hot-tea drinker," I said, "but the heater is out at our house, and Momma and I need to absorb as much warmth as possible." I started to mention she could find the tea bags in the cabinet by the oven, but she was already reaching for them.

"This is a terrible time for your heat to go out. Is the repairman scheduled to come soon?"

"The repairman is laid up in the master bedroom." I laughed. "Tonight will be better, though, since we're snitching the last of Uncle Ansel's woodpile. It'll be like camping."

Momma finished the bathrooms and flopped on the couch as Milla picked up three mugs with one hand.

"Let me help you," I said quickly, partly because I wanted to see Dodd again and partly because I didn't want to be alone with Momma, giving her the opportunity to squawk about the Cunninghams.

But Milla waved me away. "I used to wait tables." Then she maneuvered through the mudroom and out into the snow.

After shutting the door behind her, I joined Momma on the couch, handing her a cup of tea. "They're pretty sick, aren't they?"

"Ansel and Velma are on the upswing, but JohnScott's still in the thick of it. He'll be down a while longer."

"Do you think Uncle Ansel will be able to feed the cattle tomorrow?" I asked.

"Maybe, but he'll have to move slowly so he won't get overtired."

With nothing left to say, I sipped my tea, waiting for the spiteful words I knew would come. Bitter phrases that sprang from Momma's mouth every time she came in contact with Christians.

But she only gazed down at her cup as though she were startled by its contents. Her eyebrows gently pulled together, but other than that, her face remained unusually void of emotion.

A few minutes later, Milla came in and placed the mugs in the sink. "We're heading back to town."

"We'll be going too." Momma reached for a broom on the way out so she could dust snow from Ansel's woodpile, and each of us gathered an armful of firewood while Dodd and Grady transferred the remainder into our trunk.

The awkwardness of being with Momma and the Cunninghams wore on me, and I realized with surprise that I wanted to get away as much as she did.

"Thank you again." She didn't look at any of them. "We'd better be going, Ruth Ann."

Dodd followed us to the car, and my pulse beat like a bass drum. Surely he wouldn't do something stupid.

"We'll check on Ansel tomorrow," he said, "to make sure he's able to get the feeding done. If not, Grady and I will take care of it."

Momma's graciousness was beginning to give way to her normal curt tone. "No need, Mr. Cunningham. I'm sure he'll be all right by then."

Her ill-mannered remark shamed me, and as I pulled the door closed, I glanced at Dodd and mouthed, "I'll call you tomorrow."

My boldness surprised me, and I felt like a rebellious teenager going against Momma's wishes with her right there next to me in the hatchback, but I had lost the ability, the need, the *reason* to be unpleasant like her.

We eased down the snow-covered highway, the short trip taking twice as long as usual. Momma fell silent with a puzzled expression.

I wondered what she was thinking, so I probed.

"That was real nice of the Cunninghams, don't you think?"

"I suppose."

Irritation prickled my skin along with the hay in the fleece of my sweatshirt. "You suppose?"

"Oh, Ruth Ann, come on." She suddenly spewed a few clipped words that seemed to release the tension she had stifled during the past hour. "Those people are only being nice because JohnScott is one of them now."

I gazed out the front windshield, weary of the snow-covered landscape and weary of the helter-skelter ride of my careening emotions. As we pulled under our carport and darkness filled my mind, I thought I recognized God in the Cunninghams' actions.

But maybe Momma was right.

Maybe it was only churchiness.

CHAPTER THIRTY-SIX

The telephone turned out to be a pleasant option. In Momma's absence, Dodd and I talked on the phone for hours, taking advantage of our last day before school started. Our conversation spanned every topic from childhood phobias to far-fetched dreams. I shared my plans for college and my desperation for a scholarship, and by the end of the call, I felt I had known him for four years instead of four months.

And whatever doubts I had felt when we pulled away from Ansel and Velma's house evaporated as Dodd spoke of Trapp residents husbands and wives, parents and children, old folks—all of whom hadn't attended worship a day in their lives. Dodd made it sound like he was truly friends with all of them. This wasn't churchiness.

A tiny concept niggled my conscience, and I wondered if JohnScott could have been right when he said it wasn't about the church. Dodd made it seem as if God was all over town.

I smiled as I hung up the phone with a promise to call him again later, but then the front door opened and slammed shut, startling me.

"Momma?"

Her purse hit the hardwood floor with a thud. "Dixie Edison got a bee in her bonnet. Something about the cash register left unattended."

I crept down the hall as alarm shimmied up my spine. "So … why are you home early?"

"She blamed me, and I don't even know what I'm accused of. She said she can't have dishonest employees working in her restaurant, but I have no idea what she's talking about." Momma threw herself onto the couch. "If Dixie hadn't always been such a fair boss, I'd say she made it up."

Realization dawned on me. "She fired you," I whispered.

"On the spot." Momma spat the words like bullets. "Said I'd be lucky to get a job anywhere in Trapp once this gets out."

I shut my eyes. Momma was already lucky to get a job anywhere in town. "Can't you tell her you didn't do anything?"

"I tried." She looked at me pointedly. "I know what you're thinking, Ruth Ann, but I didn't throw a fit." She shook her head. "Not at first anyway, but I don't think it would've mattered. She wanted me out of there."

I leaned against the jamb of the kitchen door, and a splinter, many times painted over, dug into my shoulder. What had Momma done this time? As she sat rigidly on the couch, I sensed her anger morphing into despair, but I had no clue how to comfort her. Or if I even wanted to.

When the phone chirped, I didn't react. Didn't even think for a second or two, and then I lunged to get it before Momma.

But she had already picked up the living-room extension.

I clung to the back of a kitchen chair, studying her through the doorway.

"Who wants to know?" She tilted her head to peer at me through squinted eyes, and her voice turned to syrup. "Hang on, and I'll check if she's *available to talk* … Dodd."

I snatched the kitchen line and waited until I heard Momma disconnect. "Hello?"

"Ruthie, I'm sorry. I didn't expect her to be home. I should've hung up."

"It's okay," I replied automatically.

Momma came in the kitchen and stood over me, arms crossed.

Dodd exhaled. "So …"

One little word, but I knew what he meant. He wanted me to tell Momma the truth. Tell her I'd been lying and sneaking behind her back with someone she had no respect for. With the preacher. "I'll let you know tomorrow once we're back at work, all right?" I hung up the phone, avoiding eye contact with Momma.

"You'll let him know what tomorrow?"

I stuttered, paused, took a shallow breath. "He needed to know something about a teachers' meeting."

She stared at me for what felt like hours, and I bumped around the kitchen, knowing I couldn't escape. Finally she declared, "He asked you out."

He hadn't asked me out. Not just now, anyway. I wouldn't have been lying if I denied her accusation, but a tiny part of me wanted to come clean. I wanted to look her in the eye wanted to confidently take responsibility for my actions, my decisions, my feelings. "Yes." It came out louder than I intended as I scrambled to mask my insecurity. "He did."

To my shock, Momma cackled. "Well, who does he think he is? Mister high and mighty thinks he can date anybody he pleases, but he's got a thing or two to learn about this town." Her eyes still laughed, but she hadn't diverted her gaze from me. "Ain't that right?"

I moved two dirty glasses from the counter to the sink, one of which contained curdled chocolate milk.

"Ruth Ann?"

I lifted my chin, daring her to challenge me, yet terrified she would. "No, Momma."

She recoiled as though I had slapped her.

Before I lost my nerve, I added, "Dodd and I have been together almost a month."

Her face was transparent. At first she seemed surprised by my boldness, then confused as she tried to figure how this had happened. Next came fury, the expression I expected her to embrace, but she didn't. Instead, she scrunched up her nose as if she smelled something foul. "You *want* to go out with him?"

I nodded, hesitantly at first, then firmly.

"Why?" She drawled the word with such revulsion I felt the urge to toss the congealed milk in her face.

"He's nice to me, Momma."

"Nice?" Her words dripped sarcasm. "Sure, he'll be nice to you, as long as it's convenient for him, but then he'll cast you aside like a piece of trash."

A tear slid down my cheek, but I wiped it quickly. "Dodd's not like that."

"Oh, of course not."

I felt naked when she gave a disgusted grunt and turned her back on me, stomping down the hall to firmly shut herself in the bathroom.

I stood frozen in the middle of the kitchen, my heart pounding. What would she do? I glanced at the phone but immediately discarded the notion of calling Dodd back. The phone had already caused enough trouble. I took a deep breath and pulled my jacket closed over my chest, suddenly cold. Maybe she wouldn't overreact. She seemed to have taken it all right, all things considered. Besides, Velma had told me to stop living my life to please Momma, and it was high time I took her advice. Dodd would be happy now too. He always felt like we were lying, and I suppose we were. My right foot took a tentative step, but I couldn't take another because my legs were trembling.

My reaction was ridiculous, of course. Momma had ranted and locked herself in the bathroom. Typical behavior for her, so I had no need to panic.

After a flush, the bathroom door slowly creaked, and I heard her cross through the living room in socked feet. She appeared in the doorway of the kitchen with her arms crossed, glaring at me with a rabid expression. "You've been with Dodd Cunningham for almost a month," she purred.

I didn't respond.

"I bet Neil Blaylock is as pleased with your romance as I am."

Of all the comments she could have made, why did she mention Neil?

She took a menacing step. "And Neil Blaylock and Dixie Edison are second cousins."

My heart slid to my stomach.

"You fool. You got me fired from the best job I've had in years."

CHAPTER THIRTY-SEVEN

"You all right, Ruthie?"

Saturday afternoon, Dodd picked me up at the United and drove me to his house where we attempted to work a puzzle on his coffee table. But I was decidedly not all right. I'd spent two days robotically performing my tasks at the school and the store while wondering what on earth to do about Dodd. I lifted a shoulder and repeated what he already knew. "Well, Momma won't speak to me, and she's hardly come out of her bedroom since your phone call."

"Ruthie, I'm sorry."

"Why did you do that? I said I would call you back."

"I've told you. I didn't know she would be home."

The puzzle pieces were dumped in a pile, and I flipped a couple of them right side up. "It's my fault she lost her job."

"Don't be ridiculous. It has nothing to do with you. Or Neil. She got fired. It happens."

"What makes you so sure?"

"Well,"—he swept a palm across the back of this neck—"regardless of whatever happened between Neil and your mother, I don't think he would do that. The man's not evil, Ruthie. He wouldn't jeopardize the livelihood of a family."

I disagreed, but talking to Dodd about it was like screaming into the wind during a dust storm. He simply couldn't—*wouldn't*—hear me. So when Milla and Grady came in the front door with Dairy Queen hamburgers, I embraced the interruption and stood to leave.

"Hello, Ruthie." Milla addressed me but frowned at Dodd's back. "Everything all right?"

"Super." I stepped to the door as Milla and Grady took the burgers to the kitchen.

Dodd looked at me wearily. "Stay."

His voice said stay, but the look on his face said he needed a break as much as I did. The two of us weren't going to see eye to eye regarding Neil Blaylock or Momma or the church, and I began to wonder if there wouldn't be a score of other topics just as insurmountable. I hadn't even pointed out the fact that Fawn obviously told Neil about seeing us holding hands. But now wasn't the time.

I reached for the doorknob, but just as my palm touched the cool metal, someone pounded on the door from the outside, and I jumped as if I'd touched a rattlesnake.

Dodd was equally startled, and only after another loud knock did he step around me to open the door.

What I saw on the porch shook my nerves.

The pounding had come from Clyde Felton. "I didn't know where else to take her." He had his beefy arm around Fawn Blaylock's waist, supporting her as she shook from deep sobs. Her tangled hair fell across her eyes, and she wore jeans and a sweatshirt, but no coat or footwear, except quilted house shoes crusted with mud and ice.

Dodd pulled both of them into the house while Milla enveloped Fawn in a hug.

"Oh, sweetheart, whatever it is, it'll be all right."

Fawn clung to her, and I noticed a red welt on her left cheek.

"Calm down, now." Milla set Fawn on the couch and began tracing rhythmic circles on her back.

I stared, slack-jawed with surprise, until Dodd brushed past me to close the door. He positioned himself at Clyde's side while Grady stood halfway in the kitchen, gaping.

"Clyde?" Dodd searched his face for an explanation.

"I found her wandering down highway eighty-four." His eyes were desperate. "I had just drove over to Snyder … but that don't matter." He shook his head. "The girl hiked half a mile from her car. Flat tire. She's been like this since I picked her up, but she got worse when I suggested taking her home. Started hollering she didn't want to go back there." He scanned the room, making eye contact with each of us. "I didn't know what else to do. Where else to take her. I could've changed the tire, but she's in no shape to drive."

Dodd squeezed his shoulder. "You were wise to bring her here. Come in the kitchen and get some hot coffee." He glanced at me, silently conveying his intention to leave Fawn alone with his mother, and I moved quickly to the kitchen to escape the awful sound of Fawn's tears.

She wasn't just crying. Her sobs wrenched from deep in her throat, sending unpleasant shivers down my spine, and between each wail, she inhaled as though she had been holding her breath underwater for too long and had finally come up for air.

I pulled the kitchen door closed behind me, even though it obviously hadn't been used in years. The door hung on a warped spot in the floor, and just as I yanked it free, Fawn moaned desperately, "I'm pregnant, Milla."

The click of the door shut out sounds from the next room surprisingly well, and we were left in startled silence. I turned slowly and leaned against the wall. Grady's eyes widened, and he looked down at the floor. Clyde sighed so heavily, his massive form seemed to deflate and crumple.

Only Dodd spoke. "Well, that explains it."

Grady lowered himself into a kitchen chair. "Neil will not handle this well."

"From the looks of the girl," Clyde said, "I'd say he's already not handling it well."

Dodd shook his head. "The slap could have been from Tyler."

My throat tightened. Did Dodd actually think Neil Blaylock could do no wrong? I studied the preacher as he leaned against the back door, and suddenly I didn't like him very much. "Neil will turn his back on her," I whispered.

Dodd's gaze fell on me with the same weary expression I'd seen all day. "You don't know that, Ruthie."

Clyde cleared his throat. "She may be right."

"Surely not," Grady said. "Neil may be strict, but he wouldn't do that."

I peered at the ceiling as the oniony hamburgers on the counter made my stomach churn.

Dodd's tone softened. "Ruthie, just because you've seen bad things happen doesn't mean they'll always be that way."

Clyde fell silent as the air hung heavy between us, but Grady said, "We should pray."

I bowed my head, grateful for a reason to close my eyes and shut off at least one of my senses.

Dodd prayed peace for Fawn and her parents, health for the baby, and understanding from the community. He prayed for compassion, patience, and wisdom as the four of us, and others, ministered to her. When he said *Amen*, Grady took up where Dodd left off.

I slid to the floor, hugging my bent legs as the coldness of the linoleum penetrated my jeans. When Grady prayed for forgiveness for Fawn and Tyler, I rested my forehead on my quivering knees and covered my head with my arms. Then he prayed for healing for whatever had passed between Fawn and her parents, but that didn't make sense to me. *Why would Fawn ever want to forgive them?*

After Grady, Clyde said a brief prayer, followed by silence.

Grady started a fresh pot of coffee.

The ex-convict sat at the table.

Dodd hadn't moved from the corner, where he leaned against the back door. I noticed his slumped shoulders and sad eyes, but he didn't make eye contact, so I laid my head on my knees again and stayed that way for the better part of an hour. When Milla finally opened the door, it seemed all the oxygen had drained from the room.

"She's lying down in my bedroom." Milla snatched a tissue and blotted her tear-streaked cheeks. "We need to talk."

Grady spoke first. "We heard Fawn say she's pregnant, but that's all we heard. How is she?"

"She's devastated." She shook her head. "Fawn finally worked up the courage to tell her parents, but they reacted negatively."

"She's been slapped," Clyde said.

"I get the feeling it may have been more than that, though Fawn didn't say as much. Her mother conveyed her disappointment by refusing to hug or console her. I'm not sure she even spoke. Neil did the opposite, calling her a worthless tramp—and I don't know what else—and told her to get out of his house."

Milla paused as Grady looked from me to Clyde then back to me. "Anyway, he refused to let her take anything from the house, even threatening to rip the clothes off her back. She drove away with him bellowing he would track her down to get the Mustang back."

"She can stay here for now," Dodd offered.

"She can *not* stay here." Milla trembled, then gripped her elbows as if in an attempt to keep her hands from shaking. "Neil is accusing Grady of fathering the child."

"What?" Grady grasped the back of a wooden dining chair as if he might pick it up over his head and slam it against the wall.

"Fawn said Neil has become paranoid about the two of you, and he accused her of breaking up with Tyler to throw herself at you."

"She broke up with Tyler because he's a louse."

Dodd inspected his brother for a count of five, and then seemed to slip into the role of supervisor. "Grady, even though I don't doubt the baby is Tyler's, it would be best if the Blaylocks didn't see you with Fawn over the next few weeks. It could cause more harm than good."

"Ruthie?" Dodd hesitated at first, but then said in a hopeful tone, "Can she stay with you?"

The air left my lungs as I pictured Momma discovering Fawn Blaylock in our house. I looked him straight in the eye, irritated he would even ask. "Not in a million years."

"Call Coach Pickett," Grady said. "Ansel and Velma will understand."

"Oh, thank you, Lord." Milla sniffed. "Velma will take care of her."

The room seemed to darken around me. These people didn't understand anything. Having Fawn shacked up in my aunt's house was almost the same as having her in Momma's own bed.

Dodd stepped to the middle of the room and barked orders. "I'll call Ansel and Velma and tell them Ruthie and I are on the way with Fawn. Clyde, do you mind changing the flat tire? Mom can go with you and return Fawn's car."

Clyde nodded once.

"Grady?" He took a deep breath. "Pray."

After a moment's hesitation, we all began to shift into action, but Milla's soft voice got our attention once again. "There's something else, Dodd."

I covered my face with my hands, exhausted from so much bad news.

"Neil has called a meeting of the elders."

Dodd's eyes were a mix of confusion and apprehension. "To pray for Fawn?"

"No," Milla said. "Based on his accusation against Grady, he's petitioning for your termination."

CHAPTER THIRTY-EIGHT

Velma met us halfway across the yard. "Dear girl, you come on in." She curved her plump arm around Fawn's shoulders. "Make yourself at home, you hear?" Dodd and I followed them into the house, where Velma placed Fawn at the kitchen table and started setting food items around her. "After you have a bite to eat, you'll feel better."

I eased into a chair, awkwardly sitting next to Fawn, and realized Dodd and I never ate our hamburgers. No matter. Food sounded terrible at the moment.

Velma flurried around the kitchen. "Dodd, you best head down to the barn. JohnScott could use your help with the chores. Ruthie and me? We'll take care of things here."

He touched my shoulder as he stepped past me, his fingertips trailing across my neck. Our eyes met for a split second as he disappeared into the mudroom.

My aunt rambled about nothing in particular, and Fawn picked at a muffin. A faint bruise rose along her cheekbone, and I caught myself before I shuddered. Surely the baby would be all right.

Velma must have been thinking along the same lines. "In the morning, I'll call Dr. Tubbs in Lubbock and make an appointment to have everything checked out. Get you started on some prenatal vitamins."

Fawn's brow wrinkled. "Dad took my credit card."

Velma shooed the thought away with both hands. "Aw, now, don't worry. Dr. Tubbs is good people. He'll treat us fair, and if need be, he'll know where you can get more affordable care." Her leathery hand patted Fawn's porcelain one. "The important thing is to make sure the two of you are up to par. You'll feel ten times better once you know your baby is healthy." A tear balanced on Fawn's bottom lashes as Velma continued. "The rest will sort itself out. One way or another. Now let's get you settled in the girls' room. Ruthie can show you the way."

Grabbing two extra quilts from the linen closet, I led Fawn to the back bedroom. Velma had already pulled the covers down, and on the pillow rested an old bicolored wind suit and a pair of socks. "Looks like Aunt Velma scrounged some clothes."

Fawn surveyed the room with empty eyes.

"The bathroom's right across the hall. Clean towels in the cupboard beneath the sink." I stalled at the bedroom door. "You might need the quilts because Uncle Ansel lowers the heat at night."

"Thanks." She stood motionless in the middle of the room.

"No problem." I waited, feeling a surreal urge to hug her but an even stronger urge to hurtle away from her like the proverbial bat out of hell. "Well, if you don't need anything else …"

I almost had the door shut when she blurted, "Would you mind staying? For a minute?"

"Um … okay." A stray dining-room chair stood against the wall next to the door, and I rested a knee on it but didn't sit.

Fawn perched on the edge of the bed, seeming to search for something to say. She noticed her soiled house shoes and slipped them off. "So, I guess you've stayed here a lot over the years."

Were we going to shoot the breeze? I traced my finger along the back of the chair, leaving a trail in the dust. "Valerie and Teresa shared this room. I used to sleep on their floor." I studied Fawn, recognizing her attempt to hold herself together.

"I remember them." A faint smile flickered across her face. "When we were little, I thought they were the most beautiful girls in the world."

I rubbed the dust on the leg of my jeans. "Now that you mention it, they did have a lot of boyfriends."

A pause followed, and I pulled at a lock of my hair, wondering if I should leave. When I shifted, she spoke quickly to halt my exit. "It must've been nice to go through high school with a sister. Don't you think?"

Strange question. Over the years, I spent a lot of time wishing for my dad, maybe a different mother, but I never thought much about a sister. "Yeah, I suppose it would. My cousins are the closest thing I have to siblings, but if JohnScott had been a girl, he would've been almost like a sister."

"I can't picture Coach Pickett as a girl." Fawn chuckled, but her smile faded, and she looked lost, staring at the threadbare carpet. "Ruthie, what am I going to do?"

My foot tingled as it fell asleep, and I wiggled my toes. She didn't seem to expect an answer, so I stayed quiet.

"I have two years left before I graduate, and now I don't have a place to live. No money. No future. I don't even have any shoes." Her tears had dried. "Milla says my father will reconsider, but I don't know about that. And Dad has such an influence on the church, they'll agree to whatever he says. My friends may not be my friends anymore."

I searched my mind for words and my heart for compassion but found neither, even though I ought to have had a good dose of empathy. Fawn was in the same spot I had been in when I was seven. Her world was about to change, and she had no control over the results. I felt sorry for her, but pity wasn't the same as compassion. The two emotions were different at the core, and even though I knew the pity I felt for her could possibly, eventually, thaw the ice in my heart … it hadn't yet. And because of that, I faltered at the notion of sitting in my aunt's spare bedroom while my childhood nemesis sorted through her problems.

But Fawn needn't know that.

I eased down to sit on the chair, stretching my numb leg out in front of me. I might not have had enough compassion to say all the things Fawn needed to hear, but I had enough pity to keep my mouth shut and listen.

When Fawn finally stopped talking, Dodd and JohnScott were waiting for me in the backyard. Dodd pulled me into a hug, and his embrace settled my nerves like a drink of warm milk after a nightmare. "I'm sorry I got your family tangled up in this," he said softly.

Rowdy sat at JohnScott's feet, looking as weary as I felt, and my cousin reached down to scratch behind the dog's ears. "I'd say Fawn got us tangled, not you. Besides, we want to help."

"Velma's looking after her like a mother hen." Dodd smiled.

"That's Mom. I better get in there and see if she needs anything else."

Dodd tightened his arm around my waist and kissed my temple. "We'll come inside in a while."

It seemed a strange time for him to show so much affection, but I figured we were both emotionally wrecked from the events of the day. I gazed at the pasture, enjoying the cold wind in my hair. "Want to go for a walk?"

Dodd opened the metal gate into the side pasture, still spotted with snow, and we walked slowly, crunching pebbles into the damp sand. It seemed we were both lost in thought.

I assumed he was contemplating Fawn's predicament, but he surprised me. "Can we talk about us?"

"Us?" I reached for his hand, but he didn't say anything else until we were leaning against the cement walls of the holding tank. Either he had something important to say, or he was nervous. Or both.

I peered into his blue eyes, not sure I wanted to be having this conversation.

He used two fingers to push my hair out of my eyes and behind my ear. "I'm falling in love with you, Ruthie." His grin flashed, then instantly vanished. "You're fascinating … and adorably spunky. You're constantly surprising me with your cleverness and independence, yet I fret about your college plans and worry about your mother because I want everything that involves you to be happiness."

His flattery sparked a warm glow of contentment inside me, yet at the same time, I felt exposed. I looked away from him with a smile, studying the brown moss waving in the water.

His voice slowed. "I lay awake at night dreaming of spending the rest of my life with you—watching romantic comedies by the fire, putting up Christmas lights that make the neighbors jealous … raising kids."

My heart raced. He was saying more than he loved me. Good gracious, did I love him back?

He pressed his palm against my cheek, bringing my gaze back to his face, and his eyebrows floated up momentarily before returning to their starting point. "Is there any part of you that wants to be with me like that?"

The crinkles around his eyes made it impossible for me to concentrate. I searched my mind, trying to piece together a response. How did I feel about him? He was obviously very important to me—I'd risked Momma's wrath to be with him. And his kind heart pulled me like a magnet. Even his love for God attracted me because of the way he went about showing it.

But he was the *preacher*, for heaven's sake. Not only did he lead the congregation that had caused Momma so much pain, but he supported them one hundred percent, to the extent he was blind to the faults of its members. I pictured Neil Blaylock leaning over the counter at the diner, whispering in Momma's ear, trailing his fingertips across the back of her hand. And Fawn—poor miserable, pregnant Fawn—who had caught Dodd and me together and couldn't manage to keep the information to herself, even as her own life unraveled.

I didn't know what to say, so I returned my gaze to the water.

Dodd's hand traveled down my back questioningly, but he forged on. "But I also dream of you sitting on the front pew as I preach." He hooked a finger through the belt buckle of my jeans and tilted his head, imploring me to make eye contact. "Ruthie, I know you're not ready for that yet, but will you study with me? God is the most important thing in my world, and I want to share that with you." When I didn't respond, he added softly, "I can't go on not knowing if it's a possibility."

The cold concrete, coupled with the air blowing over the water, chilled me as I slowly formed my thoughts into words. "I know God should probably be the center of my life, and I honestly would like to get to know Him better. But until the church, especially the Blaylocks, stop throwing stones at me, I don't see how I can reach out to Him." I finally looked into Dodd's eyes again. "That would be sort of hypocritical, don't you think?"

He chuckled. "You're worried about being a hypocrite?"

We were both silent for several minutes before he bumped my shoulder with his own. The action normally would've come across as a laid-back action, but this time it was awkward and forced. "I wish you wouldn't let the church come between you and God. The people may never change, but that doesn't mean you can't."

My scalp prickled. Did he just tell me I needed to change? Breathlessness washed over me as though I had submerged myself in the icy water of the holding tank, and my heart hardened into a frozen block. God may have been alive and well outside the church, but as long as I was with Dodd, the congregation and all its judgment would be inescapable.

He smiled, oblivious to his piety. "They may be throwing stones, but admit it, you've thrown a few bricks back at them as well."

"What do you mean?"

"You judge the church." He sounded tired. "It's pulling you down."

A puff of air erupted from my throat, followed by a sharp intake of breath. "You can't be serious. I don't judge the church, Dodd. *They judge me*. And they judge Momma. And from what I hear, Clyde Felton, too."

"But you never take into consideration the motives behind their actions. Maybe they believe they're doing the right thing. Maybe some of them *are*."

I gripped my elbows, digging my fingertips into the fleece of my jacket.

His shoulders fell. "Ruthie … the world isn't as bad as you make it out to be. You'd be a lot happier if you'd admit that."

"Happy like Fawn?"

"Fawn's in the middle of a mess, but overall her life has been happy."

"I guess it depends on your definition of happiness. She's lived with an overbearing father who set her up for failure."

Dodd's voice leveled. "Neil may be off track on some things, but he loves his daughter. He'll come around."

"The man is deceitful."

"No, he's human. Just like the rest of us." Disappointment smeared his words. "Surely you have compassion for Fawn, at least."

I raised my palms, then let them fall to my sides. "I feel sorry for her, I do. But if she hadn't told Neil about you and me, Momma never would've lost her job. And now you may lose yours, too, and I can't help but think it's all connected."

Dodd turned away from me then and placed his hands on the edge of the holding tank, bending at the waist as though he were about to push the cement walls across the yard. He stared at the ground between his boots, his arms rigid and his jaw tight. He remained paralyzed that way until I wondered if he intended to answer.

"Fawn didn't tell Neil." He finally answered without lifting his head. "I did."

His words made no sense at first. I had been expecting him to argue about whether or not Neil got Momma fired, not this. My mouth went dry, and I licked my lips. "What are you saying?"

He swallowed. "A week or so ago, I talked to Neil about the church's actions against your family. I told him I cared for you and asked his advice."

My tongue could form no reply as I studied this man who, only moments before, had almost spurred me to declare my love. He still gripped the concrete, staring at the ground between his feet. With his right boot, he pressed a patch of slushy snow into the sand.

What did he expect from me?

I pulled my gaze away toward the gray lines of the old windmill behind the holding tank, lifting my gaze to the sky where its blades once rotated. When I was a kid, JohnScott and I would climb up there where we could see for miles, but now the windmill was only a useless skeleton, replaced by an electric pump. Things changed.

"This is not going to work," I said quietly. "*Us.* You talk about loving me, but you don't listen to what I'm saying or validate my problems. Even your love for me hinges on *them.*"

Out of the corner of my eye, I saw him slowly lift his head. "That's not true, Ruthie. I want to spend my life with you."

"No, you don't." My lips curved into an empty smile. "You don't want me. Not really. You want a shadow of who I am." *The new and improved version.*

My heart didn't want to be having this discussion. I didn't want to say these things to him, and I certainly didn't want to hurt him. Truth was, I wanted Dodd Cunningham as much as he wanted me, but I had no choice. It was wrong to keep pretending things were going to be all right.

Steeling myself, I whispered, "You don't need a wife, Dodd. You're already married to your church."

I turned to face him then, but the man staring down at me didn't even look familiar. I'd never seen his eyes without at least a hint of humor around the edges, and I realized my statement had wounded him deeply.

He spoke in monotone. "Is that really how you feel?"

I nodded, not daring to speak lest my words give me away. I wanted to scream, "Of course that's not how I feel!" But feelings didn't matter anymore. Our relationship was no longer about butterflies fluttering in my stomach, or warm kisses shared beneath a Christmas tree. Now it was all about logic. And circumstances. And expectations.

And it simply wasn't going to work.

His jaw moved back and forth before he asked, "Can we just take a break? Talk about it again later?"

The shrug I gave him was crueler than I intended.

He stared at me for a long time while the rejection in his eyes melted into sadness. Finally he turned away and plodded across the pasture to the El Camino, not once looking back. The blue heeler met him halfway across the yard, following behind with his tail wagging.

When Dodd's headlights turned onto the highway, I collapsed into a dirty metal lawn chair on which melted snow left a slimy surface, but I didn't care. Loneliness floated over me like a snowdrift. Loneliness so thick I could smell it. Taste it. Hear it. Not even when my daddy left had I felt anything like it. Not even when the church shunned us. Not even when Momma became a ghost.

But when Dodd Cunningham walked away that afternoon, he left me with no one.

CHAPTER THIRTY-NINE

"You broke up with her?" Grady called over the noise of the chain saw.

Dodd didn't like the accusing glare in his brother's eyes, but he shut off the saw and shook his head.

"So Ruthie did the breaking up?"

"No, not really." Dodd gathered an armful of logs from the ground around the dead oak tree in their backyard.

"Generally, it has to be one or the other, so if it's all the same, I'll blame you."

"Whatever."

Their mother shushed Grady as she followed Dodd to the El Camino parked in the alley behind the house. "Are you all right?"

"Just confused." He neatly stacked the logs in the back of the car. "And stressed."

"Ruthie's bound to be upset too. When things settle down, the two of you can work it out."

"I'm not sure there's any way."

She shook her head. "You have differences, but you're good together."

He wanted to believe that—he *had* believed it, had bet everything on the relationship—but now an overwhelming sense of emotional vertigo told him he had miscalculated the odds. "Her way of viewing life runs contradictory to mine."

"Not surprising, considering your backgrounds."

"But Ruthie expects the worst. *Every time.*"

His mother smiled. "And you expect the best. From all of us."

Dodd settled on the tailgate and removed his gloves. "I know it's crazy, but I thought Ruthie was special. You know ..." He picked up a piece of bark and crumbled it. "Now I'm not sure either of us wants to make it work."

"Don't underestimate her."

Grady approached with more wood. "Mom's right. You never know what God has in mind."

Dodd knew his family meant well, but they didn't know Ruthie like he did. They didn't understand her insecurity. She had forgiven Clyde for scaring her, but she might never forgive the church. Or the Blaylocks. And the root of her bitterness was her father. She hadn't ever forgiven him for abandoning her.

From across the yard, the gate clinked, and Dodd's hope plummeted even further as Charlie Mendoza came around the side of the house.

"I thought you might be back here. There was no answer at the front."

Dodd rose, stuffing his feelings to the far back corner of his mind. "You're just in time, Charlie."

"Looks like I missed the worst of it. Mind if I help you wrap things up?"

All three Cunninghams knew exactly why Charlie was there, but they appreciated his offer to pile brush and load wood, not because they needed the help, but because it softened the blow he had been sent to deliver.

They worked alongside each other for an hour, talking about nothing in particular and cracking jokes. When the brush was piled in a mound in the middle of the yard, Dodd set fire to it, and the two men and Grady sat on stumps warming their hands while Milla excused herself to tend to dinner.

"I suspect you know why I'm here," Charlie said.

Dodd picked up a stick and broke it in half. "You mean you didn't come for the manual labor?"

"I wish that were it, son."

The fire flickered as Dodd stared into it, and a surge of injustice swept through him, and with it a flash of cynicism. "There's a lot happening in this little town, isn't there?"

"Unfortunately, it seems to have started when your family arrived."

"Not a coincidence, I suppose."

Charlie peered at him. "I don't take the situation lightly."

"Neither do I." Dodd tossed the stick into the fire. "Let's get it over with, Charlie. Just give me the bottom line."

The older man leaned his elbows on his knees. "There are three areas of discontent." He removed his cap and held it with his fingertips, lending the lanky man an air of delicacy.

Dodd finished his thought. "Fawn's baby, Clyde Felton, and the Turners."

Charlie withered. "Are you proud of what's happened?"

"No, I'm not, but I don't see where my family has done anything to be ashamed of." He waited until Charlie nodded. "Fawn made a mistake. She sinned, but my family had nothing to do with it."

Charlie's gaze flickered to Grady, then back. He said nothing.

Dodd studied his brother. "Is that baby yours?"

Grady ducked his head. "Of course not."

Charlie's gaze fell to Dodd, and his eyes held an apology. "Neil heard differently."

"If Grady says it's not his baby, it throws doubt over Neil's accusation, but the fact Fawn says it's not his baby blows the accusation out of the pond. After all, she should know."

Charlie squirmed. "Well, what about Clyde Felton? Neil talked to you about that, yet you continue to socialize with him."

"After the reception he received, I don't think there's any danger of him disrupting services again. Do you?"

Charlie frowned, but there was desperation in his voice. "Dodd, I don't fully agree with the charges Neil brought against your family, but your attitude is wrong, brother."

Dodd fingered the bark of the stump beneath him, recognizing bitterness in his heart. He sighed, wishing he could go in the house and lie down on the couch. "You're right, Charlie. And for that I apologize."

Charlie scratched his head, mussing his hair. "And then there's Lynda Turner and her daughter. I know you want to do right by them, but until Lynda humbles herself and talks to us about what happened, our hands are tied."

Dodd felt the urge to grasp his own forehead to keep it from exploding. His inability to do anything for Ruthie was driving him to madness. "But Lynda's hurting, Charlie. I'm not sure she has the emotional strength to come to us, even if she wanted to. The only way we'll ever reach her is through Ruthie."

"Could be, but with the whirlwind we've got swirling around us now, we need to let things settle."

"Let them settle?"

"Everything's upside down. The congregation is upset, wanting to know what's going on. They're ruffled."

"I find that encouraging."

"But surely you can see how it would help if things slowed down a bit."

Dodd gazed into the fire, remembering his conversation with Neil. The two men voiced similar words of wisdom. "Yes, I do see." He turned his head toward Charlie. "But you didn't come here to tell me to slow down."

Charlie rubbed the side of his hand against his jeans. "No."

"Before you ask me for a letter of resignation, can you do something for me?"

"Anything," Charlie blurted, but then he caught himself. "I'll … I'll try."

"Think about what's happened the past few days, the past few months, and even years ago. Search your heart for the truth, and call on the Lord for His guidance."

Charlie thought for several minutes before he said, "You've made a valid point. We need to slow down just as much as anyone, but in the meantime, I'll get one of the men from the congregation to preach for you, and Lee Roy can teach your Bible class." His gaze bounced to Grady, then back to Dodd. "But I ask you and your family to show respect in the meantime and avoid interaction with those we've discussed today. A two-week time-out would be healthy for everyone."

Dodd glanced at the firewood in the back of the El Camino as a fresh wave of exasperation flooded over him. "We'll do our best, Charlie. That's all I can promise."

CHAPTER FORTY

"Ruthie, why on earth would you break up with a hunk like Dodd Cunningham?"

It never ceased to amaze me the speed news traveled in our little town. Maria barely let me get my front door open before throwing more questions at me. How did she even hear about it? "Come on in."

"Tell me everything."

Slouching on the couch, I pulled a quilt over my legs and wondered what I should tell her, and how much she had already heard. For this very reason, I'd called in sick to both jobs. I didn't want to answer questions about Dodd, or Fawn, or any of it. Tucking my feet under me, I said, "It didn't work out, so we're taking a break. That's all."

"But why?" Maria had never been in my house, so her gaze shifted around the room, inspecting every detail. "Does it have anything to do with Fawn Blaylock being pregnant?"

"I don't know. Not really. It's everything. Dodd and I are different."

"And?"

"Maria … we're just different."

She slouched, defeated. "Why is it so cold in here?"

"Our heater's out." I tossed her an afghan.

Momma's bedroom door opened, and she dragged through the living room on her way to the kitchen, looking at Maria with hollow eyes. "Hey."

"Hi, Lynda."

When Momma busied herself at the kitchen sink, I asked Maria, "How was school?"

"Weird. Teachers and students gossiped about Fawn's baby and her parents kicking her out. JohnScott tried to squelch most of the rumors, but you can imagine the luck he had." She glanced around the room hopefully. "Does your cousin ever come by here?"

"You just missed him, actually."

She continued with the previous conversation as though she had never interrupted herself. "And since you didn't show at school, people speculated about some sort of twisted connection. I assured them there wasn't one. And of course, the rumor about Grady being the daddy made its way through the halls, but nobody bought it." She raised her eyebrows questioningly.

"No." I lowered my voice, conscious of Momma in the next room. "I mean yes. I mean it's ridiculous to even think that. Of course Grady's not the dad." I kicked her from under my quilt. "Give me a break. You know Tyler Cruz."

Maria pointed toward the kitchen and mouthed the words, "Does she know?"

"Fawn's camped out at Velma's house. What do you think?"

She didn't answer because Momma padded into the room, carrying a tuna sandwich. "We need eggs, Ruthie." She slipped her boots on over her socks and went out the front door.

The fishy scent of tuna hung in the air as Maria asked, "Is she going for eggs?"

"No. Mailbox."

Momma let in a whirl of frozen air when she came back in. She flipped through envelopes as she crossed in front of us, and then we heard her bedroom door click.

"She's lively," Maria said.

I didn't answer.

Maria darkened my mood. It took every bit of energy I possessed to hold myself together, but I had determined not to repel the only friend I had left.

"So, about Dodd." She began again. "Tell me one more time why you broke up with him."

I pulled my quilt higher on my shoulders. "Do we have to beat it to death?"

"Couldn't hurt."

I threw a pillow at her, and as it bounced to the floor, a thump sounded from the wall behind her.

"Did you hear that?" She leaned forward. "You don't have rats, do you?"

"The way this week is going, it wouldn't surprise me." Two more thumps got me curious. "Sounds like it's coming from the front yard."

Maria stood and peeked out the curtains, then giggled. "I'm not sure Dodd's *taking a break.*"

"What do you mean?" I rose, careful to keep the quilt around me, and looked over Maria's shoulder. Dodd and Grady were right outside the living-room window, stacking firewood while pointedly diverting their eyes from us. My legs trembled, and I pressed my knees together to keep Maria from noticing. "Why is he doing that?" I demanded.

"Because you're cold, you dufus."

I bit my lip. This didn't change the impossible mess. It didn't change anything.

Dodd flashed his eyes toward the window, and I pretended not to notice, but a bit of the tension in my neck relaxed. It felt good for him to take care of me even if I didn't want him to. He wore an unfortunate crocheted hat, and I tightened my lips to keep from smiling. "What on earth has he got on his head?"

"A Christmas gift from his grandmother." Maria pulled the afghan farther up on her shoulders. "If he knew how cold it is in here, he'd loan it to you." Maria contemplated Dodd and Grady for a few moments, then muttered, "You'd look good in Dodd's hat, Ruthie."

I returned to the couch, curling my feet beneath me, and wished Maria would get away from the window. What if Dodd read her lips? "Close the curtains, Maria."

"Tell me what happened."

I rubbed my eyes, wishing she would leave but praying she wouldn't. "It doesn't matter."

"You matter to him." She continued to watch from the window. "There's something you're not telling me. Out with it."

My irritation mounted, and I ticked items off my fingers. "Let's see. There's Momma who despises Dodd. And then there's the church that despises me. There's the Blaylocks. And somehow Clyde Felton is mixed up in all of it. Then there's Fawn. And we might as well count her baby, too, right? That certainly threw a kink in things." I glared at her. "That's what happened, all right? And the one thing that surprises me is that it didn't hit the fan sooner." I covered my face with my arm and leaned my head back. "Ruthie Turner dating the preacher? What a joke."

I had forgotten about Momma, and when her bedroom door banged against the opposite wall, I jerked to a sitting position.

"What's that blasted racket?" she called from the hallway.

Maria and I stared at each other.

Momma wandered into the living room and scrutinized Maria, who still had one hand on the curtain. "Maria, what's going on out there?"

"Oh, it's nothing." She cast worried eyes toward me.

"I'll handle it, Momma. You go back to bed." Standing up, I tried to get between her and the window as more thumps sounded against the front wall.

"Who's out there, Maria?"

"Nobody."

I looked at Momma closely. Her eyes were bloodshot with emotion. "What's wrong?" I panicked. "What's happened?"

Momma's depression turned to fury in a heartbeat. "What's wrong is there's someone in my front yard, and you won't tell me who it is."

She shoved past me and looked through the diamond-shaped window in the front door, surveying Dodd and Grady. Her hand clenched the doorknob in a fist. "We don't need charity, Ruth Ann. Are you responsible for this?"

"No."

She was drunk with rage, and I knew without a doubt something had changed. Something had driven her over the edge of the precipice of depression she had been balancing on, and now she was in a free fall of emotional turmoil. She flung the door open, stepped out onto the damp porch in her socks, and screeched at the Cunninghams to go away.

Maria stood paralyzed at the curtain as I pulled on Momma's arm. "Stop yelling."

"I'll yell if I feel like it, Ruth Ann. I don't want these people here. They don't belong here."

Dodd and Grady didn't pause in their work or even show they heard her.

The tears I tried so hard to keep hidden now surfaced, and I hated myself for it. I'd look as hysterical as she did. "Momma, please," I begged, "don't do this."

She cursed at Dodd and Grady between half screams. "Get out of my yard. Get out of my life!" Her voice grew hoarse. "And Ruth Ann doesn't want you here either."

Dodd and Grady threw the last logs onto the stack.

"You take your blasted firewood back where you got it, 'cause I don't want your charity." Her words began to slur. "We're fine, you hear me?"

As they pulled away from the house, Dodd's eyes caught mine. I swiped my hand under my nose and dried it on the leg of my sweats. "Get in the house," I growled at Momma. *"Now."*

I managed to shut the door, only to have her turn on me. "Why were they here, Ruth Ann?"

"I don't know." My tears were securely stuffed in my heart again, and I spoke clearly. "I haven't talked to them. You can ask Maria."

"I really should be going …"

"Ruth Ann, I've told you a million times, *stay away from those people*." The way she emphasized the last statement sparked a fire under my temper, which soon flared into a rage that matched her own.

"I am, Momma," I yelled back at her. "I'm not with Dodd anymore. We broke up. You get your way. You and everybody else in this stupid town." I raised my voice even louder. "So leave me alone for once and give me some peace."

She gave a silent, tearless sob, then fled down the hallway and shut herself in her bedroom again.

I stared at her door, took three deep breaths, then put my hand against my forehead and turned to Maria. "I'm so sorry."

"It's no problem. Really." She tossed the afghan on the couch. "I should be getting home, but call me later, okay? No matter what you need, call me." She scurried out the door.

Bending over, I picked up my quilt where it had fallen to the floor. No warmth remained in its fluffy layers, but I wrapped it around me anyway and fumbled with the heating pad, my fingers so cold they wouldn't obey. Lying down on the couch, I pushed my stocking feet under the couch cushion, inhaling deeply to settle my nerves.

What had set Momma off? Even though her anger wasn't out of character, the intensity of the episode, and the visible emotion, certainly were. She hadn't gotten a call. Both cordless phones were in sight. Other than her trip to the kitchen, Momma had been in her room all day—except when she made the outing to the mailbox.

I wiped my face on a corner of the quilt, tasting salt on my lips. Had she gotten a letter? That seemed unlikely. Everybody she knew lived within walking distance.

Dragging the quilt behind me, I stepped down the hall and eased her door open.

"Go away, Ruth Ann."

I shut it again, accepting the fact I would never know because she would never tell me. Kneeling in front of the fireplace, I considered building a fire but couldn't muster the energy. Instead, I plopped on my bottom, resting my elbows on my thighs.

I leaned over until my head lay on the hardwood floor and closed my eyes. Maria didn't want to stick around, and I couldn't blame her. I didn't want to be home with Momma either. A minuscule breeze fluttered my bangs, causing me to open my eyes. Sure enough, the weather stripping on the door had come loose. Only half an inch at the bottom, but enough to mess things up. The draft fluttered a crumpled paper near the curtain.

I crawled over to investigate, leaning against the door so my quilt blocked the airflow, and reached for the paper.

It was a sheet of business stationery with the flamboyant letterhead of the Blaylock Cattle Ranch. Having been folded for mailing, the paper wanted to curl in on itself, but I pressed it flat against the floor with my palms. Black scrawl ran across the page in Neil's handwriting.

Since you won't talk to me, I've resorted to the postal service. Lynda, he would want you to let go of the past. You know he would. Let me help.

I had no idea what the letter meant, but I knew Momma and I didn't need Neil Blaylock.

Taking a deep breath, I willed myself not to call JohnScott, not to long for Dodd, not to consider Maria. I didn't need them, either.

I didn't need anybody.

CHAPTER FORTY-ONE

Since Momma lost her job, my days of hitching rides came to an end, but only temporarily. I drove the hatchback to and from work for only a few days before it broke down. On the evening of its death, the car coasted into our carport and sputtered to a stop. My emotions were already so battered that the development didn't register as a letdown. So I'd have to get around on foot again. *Oh well.*

I struggled with the lock on the front door and bumbled into the house, surprised to see Momma on the couch. "You're up."

She grunted.

"Did you eat something?"

"Did you?"

Actually, I had hardly eaten all day. At school things were still unbearably awkward, so I didn't go in the teachers' lounge. I spent my lunch hour surfing the Internet in the library instead. And at the United, I had eaten only a package of crackers on my break.

"You talk to JohnScott today?" Momma flipped channels with the remote.

"Some."

She didn't continue the line of questioning, but I recognized it as her way of saying she wished things would get back to normal in our family. Well, so did I. JohnScott and I still spent thirty minutes together before the first bell, but our conversations had become testy.

The library had become my sanctuary.

But on the bright side, Momma lay curled on the couch, a drastic improvement from being shut in her room, and I couldn't help wondering if she needed me, a little. Not that we discussed our problems like a functional family, but at least we occupied the same room.

Crouching at the hearth, I stirred the fire she had built earlier in the day, digging for red-hot coals, which gave off more heat. I added two logs, then leaned back to warm myself. No additional snow lay in the forecast, but temperatures would still dip down to freezing after dark.

A knock at the door sent a nervous jolt up my spine. Which of my friends was it, coming to tell me what I should do? I didn't want to speak to any of them.

I reached for the fireplace poker and resumed stirring.

Momma huffed. "Fine, I'll get it." She peeked out the window before opening the door.

Clyde Felton strode past her as though we were expecting him. "Freezing out there."

Momma replaced the bed pillow we now kept in front of the door to ward off the draft. "You can warm up by the fire. Ruth Ann, scootch over."

I didn't want to *scootch over*. I wanted to hide in the hall like I'd done before, but that felt disrespectful now, even for Clyde.

He knelt next to me and held his hands near the fire. "I'm glad your momma's up and about."

I frowned. "What do you know about Momma?"

"Watch yourself, Clyde," Momma muttered under her breath as she sat on the couch and tucked her feet between two cushions.

"It's been a long time, but we used to hang out in school." The ex-convict shook his head, assuming my next question. "I don't mean like that. She ran with Blaylock back then."

"Neil?" A red light flashed in my mind.

"It's nothing, Ruth Ann," Momma snapped.

Clyde lowered his eyes as if he'd been sent to the principal's office, but I restated my question. "What do you mean, she ran with Neil?"

"Lynda, I didn't mean to stir up trouble," Clyde said quietly. "I figured the girl knew."

I shifted, wondering what he meant.

"Oh, Lord," Momma growled.

A corner of his mouth lifted as he peered at me. "She's got Hoby's eyes."

Momma pulled an afghan over her legs, not looking at him.

"You knew my daddy."

His gaze swept to Momma, but when she didn't acknowledge him, Clyde answered, "Sure. Back in school, we played football together. Then after we graduated, we'd get together for dominoes." He chuckled, but it sounded forced. "I'd usually win."

Momma hummed a reprimand. "You know you and Hoby split the wins. You both cheated, though."

"Aw, Lynda. Don't go telling the girl I'm a cheat. You're looking at a reformed citizen."

"Ruth Ann, don't get all judgmental," Momma said. "Clyde may have spent twenty years in prison, but he didn't do one blasted thing to deserve it."

I remembered him building the fire for us after Thanksgiving, remembered him breaking up Fawn and Tyler at the fund-raiser, remembered him finding Fawn on the side of the road and bringing her to the Cunninghams.

For once I agreed with Momma. Clyde Felton didn't seem dangerous after all.

"How did it happen then?" I asked hesitantly.

"He doesn't like to talk about it."

Clyde cleared his throat. "She probably ought to know."

Momma snorted. "Everybody ought to know. Not likely to happen, though." She focused on me and exhaled. "Back in the day, Clyde had him a girlfriend, sixteen years old. Pretty little thing, smart, and I don't often say this, but she was a sweet girl—back then anyway. You can see why she hit it off with Clyde."

He lowered his head.

"Anyway, her daddy wasn't too keen on him. Told her to break up—you know the type, father knows best—but she wouldn't do it." Momma cackled. "I'd have loved to see the look on that man's face."

"Why didn't he like Clyde?"

Momma lifted her chin, seemingly proud I would defend him. "He was from the wrong side of town. And if that weren't enough, Clyde had reached the ripe old age of twenty-one." Her smile faded into an empty stare. "And when the girl ended up in the family way, her daddy charged Clyde with statutory rape."

"No matter, Lynda," mumbled Clyde. "It's in the past. Let's leave it there."

"As long as you're in Trapp, it won't be in the past." She softened her voice in wonder. "You ought to go away and start over some place."

"Aw, Lynda, this is home." He bent down and stirred the crackling fire, sending a shower of sparks onto the hearth. "Besides, I don't want everybody around here thinking poorly of me for the rest of my life. I want to set things straight."

"You can't set things straight, though, and you sure can't change anybody's mind."

"I don't expect to. I just want to live so they'll know I'm a good person."

"Maybe in fifty or sixty years. The people here are awful, Clyde, plum awful. If it weren't for Velma, I'd have left by now."

"Naw." He shook his head. "People are no different here than anywhere else. No different than me. No different than you."

Momma sat up straight. "I am *not* like those people."

"You don't act like them, but deep down inside, we're all the same, you know? We all have problems. We just mess up our lives in different ways."

"I disagree."

He rotated to warm his other side. "You never could forgive people, Lynda."

"You've got to be kidding me," she snapped. "After what they did to you? Twenty years of it, and you're willing to forgive them?"

Clyde swallowed hard. "I know you've had a hard time, and people treated you bad, but they weren't the ones who soured your life. You did that by yourself."

She lifted her eyebrows and blinked at him.

"Aw, Lynda ..." He laughed softly as he rose and stepped to the door. "I'll be seeing you in town." Then he was gone.

I diverted my gaze from Momma as my problems faded into triviality. Clyde's story outweighed my dating troubles with Dodd, or my edginess around JohnScott, or even Fawn's untimely pregnancy.

Momma dragged herself off the couch, replaced the pillow by the door, then plopped on the hardwood next to me.

We gazed into the fire, and I sorted through the information she had dumped on me. *Strange.* Momma didn't often tell me about the past, and it occurred to me she felt more secure speaking about someone else's memories than her own.

A question nagged at my brain, but I feared she would shut down again or, worse, get angry. The more I thought about it, though, the more my curiosity itched.

"Momma?"

"I know what you're going to ask me," she said quickly.

I looked at her out of the corner of my eye.

"I ought to tell you it's none of your business, except of course, it is." Her face flushed, but then she shook her head as though to settle into her typical bland numbness. "Don't worry about it, Ruth Ann. You're better off not knowing the details."

I clasped my hands together, willing them not to shake. "Tell me what happened."

But Momma only answered by jabbing the fire, taking out her frustration on the red-hot coals.

CHAPTER FORTY-TWO

In town the next week, I viewed each person in a different light and caught myself classifying them as those who might know about Clyde and those who did not. Older people would have known, but not the Cunninghams. Probably not JohnScott. Definitely not Maria. But what about Fawn?

Such a heavy secret caused me to ponder life in general, and surprisingly, I found myself overwhelmed with sympathy. This new-found emotion manifested itself in mercy for Clyde because of the injustice of it all, but occasionally my thoughts landed on Fawn and her predicament. If I dwelt on her for more than a few moments, I felt shame at my attitude over the past two weeks. Perhaps hardship acted as an equalizer.

Fawn's mother transformed much more dramatically than I did. She showed up in the school office one afternoon, awkwardly pulling a couple of wheeled suitcases behind her. When she asked if I could deliver the clothing to the Picketts' house, I grudgingly agreed but wondered why she didn't do it herself. Apparently Mrs. Blaylock had enough heart to give her daughter a wardrobe but not enough gumption to stand up to her husband.

After school, JohnScott loaded the luggage into the back of his truck and asked if I had time to go to the Dairy Queen before my shift at the grocery store. He explained that Fawn planned to meet him there because she needed to get out of the house for a spell. I inwardly cringed, but since I'd discovered the evil surrounding Clyde's verdict, I had become more charitable toward my family, and I realized how I took my cousin for granted. It was high time I started acting like a grown-up. I called the store manager and asked to come in thirty minutes late.

"So, what's your take on Fawn now?" I asked as we sat at the sticky Dairy Queen table.

He shrugged. "She's definitely still a Blaylock, but she's in a pickle, and I don't mind helping."

I smiled at his words. "How is she getting to the Dairy Queen?" I asked. "She has no car."

He shrugged. "Mom's Chevy."

"Fawn Blaylock is driving Aunt Velma's old tank?"

"I know," he admitted. "Doesn't really fit, does it?"

I giggled when I looked out the window and saw Fawn in the Chevy, but honestly she didn't look as out of place as I had imagined. Maybe because she still wore my aunt's recycled wind suit, but she also toned down her makeup so she looked more like a real person than a plastic doll. The effect made her more approachable, but at the same time, more vulnerable.

"Why do we eat ice cream when it's cold outside?" JohnScott mused as the three of us picked at our desserts and tried to act normal.

Fawn set down her caramel sundae and breathed into her folded hands. "At least we had sunshine today."

I tried to sound normal, but my words still came out in a tumble. "We almost hit fifty degrees yesterday."

"Oh, of course," JohnScott said. "It's perfect weather for ice cream."

I sensed the conversation stilting. They were keeping things light because of me, but we could only talk about the weather for so long.

Fawn looked apologetic. "I heard you and Dodd are taking a break."

"Probably longer than a break."

"You seemed good together."

I scanned the parking lot. "Things aren't always what they appear."

"Tell me about it." She poked a plastic spoon into her ice cream. "I can't help but think you and Dodd had a misunderstanding."

I smiled at the irony of her words, since she represented our biggest disagreement, and Dodd would be thrilled to see me befriending her. I shrugged. "It's not worth the trouble. I'll be at Tech soon." She needn't know my plans were currently on hold again because of Momma.

"Lubbock is only an hour from here, Ruthie. Dodd could visit on weekends."

JohnScott wadded his paper napkin. "It's not about the school. It's about the church."

Fawn's expression fell blank, and the silence that followed was filled with the sizzle of french fries being lowered into hot oil.

I picked a chunk of chocolate off my dipped cone.

"Can I ask you something?" Fawn said softly. "Why did you stop attending church in the first place? Was it just too hard without your dad?"

Chill bumps crept up my back and across my scalp. "You don't know?"

"Should I?"

JohnScott crunched his cone between his front teeth and answered while he chewed. "Well, sure. Your church practically kicked Ruthie and Aunt Lynda out."

"Kicked them out?" Fawn looked between the two of us, her gaze landing on me. "So your mother had an—" She shook her head. "I'm sorry. It's none of my business."

The chill bumps that so recently had formed on my skin flared into angry heat, because labeling conflict as *none of her business* was cowardly. "Well, Fawn, apparently the rest of the congregation thought so too, because none of them asked Momma about it."

My subtle remark sailed over her head. She had the same expression on her face as when she worked calculus problems back in high school, and I realized how little she knew about what happened back then. I released a breath, letting air smooth across my lips like a chain-smoker. While bitterness hovered around me in a smoky haze, I wiped my eyes to keep them from burning.

"It's been different since the Cunninghams moved here." I thought of Emily Sanders's peculiar behavior. "But I'm not sure it's any different for Momma."

"But they wouldn't do that unless—"

"Oh, Fawn, think about it. You know everybody in town. Who would Momma have an affair with?"

Her eyebrows slowly rose as the solution to the calculus problem came into focus. "Then why?"

"I've been trying to figure that out for thirteen years, but Momma won't talk about it."

"I never knew." Fawn gazed at the tabletop, as though not seeing it. "I remember Mother telling me I couldn't be your friend anymore because Lynda decided not to go to church. She made it sound like your mom had done something bad." She lowered her voice and peered at me. "I was seven, Ruthie. I'm sorry."

My milkshake was melting, and I swirled my straw through it as I brooded on what to say to her. *It's all right. No big deal. Don't worry about it.* Was that what she expected? JohnScott cleared his throat—a simple sound, but the equivalent of anyone else screaming a reprimand. I debated punching him in the ear. Wasn't it enough that I was here at all?

The electronic mechanism above the door beeped, and Milla and Grady entered the restaurant. An intense fight-or-flight instinct came over me, but I rooted myself to my seat. I could handle this. At least they distracted Fawn from our trip down memory lane.

"How are you feeling, Fawn?" Milla touched my shoulder but otherwise gave me a fair amount of space as she pulled up a chair.

"Good," Fawn said. "I have another appointment with Dr. Tubbs tomorrow."

"How's everything else?" asked Grady.

She lifted a shoulder. "Emily still calls me—even more than usual—but most people are keeping their distance. Maybe they don't know what to say."

JohnScott shot his napkin into a trash can several yards away. "Don't take it personal. You know people in this town are persnickety."

A million snarky comments came to mind, but I kept my mouth shut.

"I've thought the same thing," Grady said, "but then someone will come forward with a penitent heart, sorry for something they've said or done." His voice softened. "I can't help but think God's working here."

Milla rested her chin on her palm. "The other day, a friend called and asked me to pray for her. When people openly refer to their prayer lives, they're usually living what they preach."

Frustration picked at my nerves. *God* … *prayer* … such soft, fuzzy explanations. Fawn's life lay shattered in pieces all around her, and they had the nerve to suggest the church might practice what they preached. I felt like pounding my fists against my skull, or shaking Milla by the shoulders, or simply curling into a ball until all this conflict had passed.

But Momma had already tried that. And it hadn't worked.

Fawn's gaze fell to her sundae, where the caramel swam through the melted ice cream like swirling mud.

Milla touched her hand. "I talked to your mother. She's worried sick and wants to call, but—"

"Dad won't let her."

"Yes, well … she also mentioned Tyler."

Fawn tensed. "And?"

"Your mother called him."

"Of course. It's all right for her to call *Tyler*."

Milla tilted her head to the side and bit her bottom lip. "He denied the baby is his."

Fawn's face paled, but she didn't comment, didn't really seem surprised.

JohnScott leaned forward. "Can the doctor do a test or something to prove Tyler is the father?"

Milla nodded, but Fawn shook her head wearily. "I don't want him in my life anyway. Is that awful of me?"

"You don't have to figure it out today." Milla patted her arm. "Those questions can be answered months from now. Like the Scriptures say, each day has enough trouble of its own."

That's for sure.

Grady's attention shifted to the back corner of the dining room, and he lifted his chin in a greeting. "How you doing?"

Clyde, filling the napkin dispenser two tables over, nodded. "Fine. You?"

"Not bad."

I speculated whether the four people sitting in front of me had any idea about Clyde and the scandal surrounding his imprisonment.

"How do you like your new job?" Milla asked.

Clyde moved to the next table and tore open a package of napkins. "It's a paycheck."

"Do you get free food?" Grady motioned for him to join us.

"I do." He stepped as far as the table next to ours and shoved a stack of napkins into the spring-loaded holder. "Though after cooking all day, it's not as good as it sounds."

"Free ice cream would make it worth it." Grady rubbed his stomach.

"Sure enough. That part's nice."

My chest ached out of pity for him. I'd always wished no one knew my business, but Clyde made me wonder if that would be more of a curse.

The door beeped again, and JohnScott pushed his chair back briskly. "Time to go."

His abruptness startled me, and I frowned at my cousin's rudeness, but Clyde only shuffled away to work on his napkins. Milla, in contrast, put her arm around Fawn, and Grady thrust out his chin, eyeing the front counter.

I followed his gaze, and my nerves turned to granite. Neil Blaylock gazed at the lighted menu on the wall, calmly placing his order as if he were the only customer in the place.

CHAPTER FORTY-THREE

"Your mother dated Neil Blaylock?" Maria's mouth hung open in surprise.

"Creepy, huh?" We met in the gym for Friday night's basketball game against Ballinger. Grady had played a few minutes of the game, and JohnScott and Dodd sat on the bench, assisting the head basketball coach.

Maria's face furrowed. "I can't picture your mother with Neil. Did you ask her about it?"

"Even better, I asked Aunt Velma."

"And?"

Dodd glanced casually into the stands, his eyes searching, and I waited until he turned away.

"She said they dated in high school, and it lasted a couple years after they graduated."

"What happened?"

"Neil broke up with her." And Momma had been heartbroken for months after, but I left out that part, since I was none too proud of it.

Maria lowered her head, obviously not as concerned with Momma's past as she was with my present. "Dodd Cunningham has been looking at you for the entire game."

I had already noticed, but I chose to ignore him along with Maria's comment. When the final buzzer sounded, I stood. "Want a Coke?"

"Dr Pepper."

"Let's go."

Maria could easily be distracted with food and drink, but of course she was right. As much as I hated to admit it, every time Dodd turned around, my insides leaped like a large-mouth bass at Lake Alan Henry, but then reality splashed into the depths of the cold, dark water, suffocating me.

Because things couldn't work out between Dodd and me. They just couldn't.

The soft-drink machine lay in a broad hallway leading to the locker rooms, and fans and players congregated there after games. Maria and I were retrieving our drinks when JohnScott came up behind us. He nudged me with his elbow. "Ruthie, give me a drink."

"Get your own."

"I don't have a dollar."

"Okay, but just one sip."

He nodded, then chugged my Dr Pepper like a desert dweller.

"Stop it." I laughed.

He shook the can and handed it back. "There you go, little cousin. I left you a sip like you said."

"It's all spit now."

JohnScott's banter soothed my nerves like soft music, and I punched him in the chest. I had missed him.

His gaze swept over my head. "Dodd, want the last of Ruthie's D.P.?"

I didn't hear Dodd answer because Maria crooned in my ear, "Well, if it isn't Mr. Stare-at-Ruthie."

"I'll take it," Grady called. "I'm parched."

JohnScott took the can from me, swept it out of my reach, and handed it to Grady.

"It's empty, Ruthie," Grady complained. "Why would you offer me an empty drink? I'm appalled." He tilted his head back and let the last few drops of liquid fall into his mouth. "Ruthie-the-checker-girl, did I just drink your spit?"

"No, JohnScott's." I dragged the words out, enjoying the look on Grady's face.

He froze for a split second, then threw his arms around my cousin. "We're blood brothers now, Coach Pickett."

We wandered into the parking lot, where the frigid air took my breath away. JohnScott looped his arm around my neck, making it easier for me to ignore Dodd. "Need a ride home, little cousin?"

"I rode with Maria."

"Ms. Fuentes, I'll take Ruthie home, 'kay?"

"Sure thing, Coach. I'll see you both on Monday."

Tension slid from my shoulders, and I breathed deeply for the first time all evening. I had my cousin back.

Gradually, Panther fans drifted to their vehicles until the only cars remaining in the parking lot were JohnScott's truck and Dodd's

El Camino. When it was only the four of us, it became more difficult to ignore Dodd, and I was ready to leave.

Apparently Grady was too. "Dodd, throw me the keys. I'll pull the El Camino down here and pick you up." He lifted his hand and caught the keys as Dodd tossed them. "And give me your cell phone. I'll text Mom."

"I need to get home too," I said. "I've got work tomorrow."

I reached for the passenger door of JohnScott's truck, surprised to find it locked.

I waited, listening to JohnScott and Dodd discuss the game, until Grady arrived.

"Hey, Coach Pickett," Grady called, "do you have a copy of the study guide for history? I can't find mine."

Dodd tapped the passenger window of the El Camino. "Open up, Grady."

His brother didn't notice.

"I think I've got it right here in the truck," JohnScott said. "Hold on a minute."

Dodd knocked again. "Grady, unlock already."

I peered into JohnScott's cab and jiggled the door handle so he would think to let me in. He didn't even look up. Disbelief paralyzed me as JohnScott shut the driver's door, started the ignition, and drove away.

Grady followed him, honking as he pulled out of the parking lot, and Dodd and I stared after them as their taillights disappeared down the street.

An apprehensive vibration inched its way from my knees to my stomach to my heart, sending an unwanted blip of anticipation into my bloodstream. I shoved it away. My back was toward Dodd, and I didn't want to turn around, but it would be childish to walk away. I turned, and his expression told me none of this had been his idea. The warm vibration drained from my heart like the trickle of our kitchen faucet during a freeze.

He thrust his hands into his pockets. "I guess they think this is funny."

"They'll be back."

The emptiness of the lot made the air feel colder, and the smoky scent of a nearby fireplace reminded me how warm it would be at home by the fire. A breeze stirred my hair, sending a whisper of icy air past my neck, and I pulled my coat around me, dreaming of ways to torture and kill my cousin. It would be a slow death.

A car horn echoed from downtown, less than a mile away, and I sighed helplessly.

"Sounds like they're at the car wash." Dodd's boots crunched gravel as he studied the school building. "Sorry about this, Ruthie. My brother's sense of humor sometimes gets the best of him." He laughed a little, then cleared his throat. "And I'm sorry … about everything."

I pointed my face into the wind, letting air slide past my cheeks and cleanse my mind. "Me, too." How long would JohnScott leave me here? It infuriated me that he and Grady forced this. I tapped my foot. "I could've been home by now if I'd started walking." I took three steps toward the street, then glanced back at him.

He followed.

We trudged in silence for the first block, and as we approached the corner where he would turn toward his house, I blurted, "Well, bye," afraid he would insist on seeing me home.

He did.

"You don't have to."

"I know, but it's the right thing to do."

In the moonlight, all I could make out was his silhouette. "Do you always do the right thing?"

His answer was immediate. "Obviously not."

An animal rustled in a bush next to a house, then darted across the street. A cat.

Dodd slowed his steps. "I'm sorry about the church, Ruthie. It's a mess down there right now. Lots of the members—like Emily Sanders and her family—don't know what to do. *Who to follow.* They're confused." He paused, and the weariness in his voice pulled at my compassion. "Neil's wife is upset because of the way he's treating Fawn."

My heart hurt. Dodd wanted to fix it, but there was no way he could.

He stopped in the middle of the street. "But most of all, I'm sorry about the way I handled our relationship."

We stood face-to-face beneath the glow of a streetlight, and my darkness began to crack until a sliver of light illuminated my hopelessness. *This man.* This man had wrapped me in warmth since the first day we met. I looked into his sad eyes, but a tear slid down my own cheek, not his.

His thumb wiped at the wetness, and I leaned my cheek against his palm.

He inhaled slowly, but his breath caught. "I love you, Ruthie."

"I know."

When his lips brushed mine, I didn't protest, couldn't even if I'd wanted to. My arms slipped around his waist, and his fingers meshed through my hair. He gripped the back of my head, and I sensed his desperation as he pressed his mouth against mine and walked me backward. I don't think he realized what he was doing until I was pinned against the light post, his body pressed against mine.

He pulled away, ducking his head apologetically, and then traced his finger along the path where my lone tear had fallen. "Ruthie, forget about the church. Talk to God."

A car turned at the corner, and its headlights blinded me back to reality. "God?" I slipped away from him and crossed my arms against the cold.

"Don't go." He leaned against the post. "God wants to help you, Ruthie. Why won't you let Him?"

I took a deep breath and let it out in a frozen mist. "I'll talk to Him about it … but I can't go to your church, Dodd."

"I know." He pulled me toward him and held me against his chest, kissing the top of my head. "I'm not asking you to."

CHAPTER FORTY-FOUR

When Lee Roy Goodnight and Charlie Mendoza dropped by the parsonage on Saturday afternoon, Dodd had no doubt he would lose his job. The elders' request for his family to stay away from Clyde, Fawn, and the Turners had been blown apart by his mom's and Grady's visit to the Dairy Queen earlier in the week, and Dodd felt certain Neil had driven past Ruthie and him the night before.

He didn't regret his actions any more than his family regretted theirs, but his attitude regarding the church leadership shamed him. He hadn't turned out to be a very submissive minister—or Christian—but given the opportunity, he'd continue talking to Ruthie. If she let him.

Lee Roy and Charlie sat in the living room, avoiding eye contact. Dodd pulled a couple of chairs from the kitchen, and he and Grady settled into them as his mother removed a pie from the oven. The scent of meringue followed her into the room.

Lee Roy cleared his throat. "Dodd, I'm sorry we're not here under more pleasant circumstances." He reached for a needlework magazine on the coffee table, absentmindedly laying it across his knees before fingering the corner.

Charlie withdrew a folded paper from the hip pocket of his Wranglers. "We thought it would be easier to communicate in written form." He opened the paper and glanced at Dodd as he rested a pair of lightweight glasses on the end of his nose. "Do you mind if I read it aloud?"

"Please do." Dodd remained calm, but his heart cramped. He had put a tremendous amount of energy into the little congregation and had planned to do much more. He felt his family was being sent away before they had finished the job.

Charlie's cheeks turned rosy as he read.

Brother Cunningham,

As shepherds of the Trapp congregation, we would like to thank you for the service you have granted our flock. You and your family have been a source of encouragement not only to our congregation but also to our community. Your sermons are doctrinally sound and always ring true. Since your arrival, our congregation has seen spiritual growth unparalleled in the history of our church. Your effort, talent, and love are to be commended.

Because of the bond each of us feels, it is difficult for us to breach the current situation with you, and much time and prayer have gone into our decision. We regret to inform you that, as of today, you are dismissed from your position as minister of the Trapp congregation. As is customary, you will receive two weeks' advance salary. You are at liberty to remain in the parsonage until you acquire alternate living arrangements, not exceeding eight weeks' time.

We pray blessings on future ministries to which the Lord may lead you. We have enclosed a letter of recommendation for future employers.

Sincerely,
Lee Roy Goodnight
Charlie Mendoza
Neil Blaylock

Charlie folded the letter, then handed it to Dodd as though it might burn him if he held it any longer.

Dodd leaned with elbows on thighs, holding the paper. When he looked up, he thought the sadness in Charlie's eyes would break him. "Charlie? Lee Roy?" He hesitated before asking softly, "Do you support this decision?"

Lee Roy dropped his gaze and blinked at the magazine in his lap. He frowned and returned it to the table. "Dodd … so much has happened."

"I know, Lee Roy. The decision couldn't have been an easy one."

Charlie let his shoulders relax. "We talked until we were blue in the face. Lee Roy and me? We're caught in the middle. We don't want to see you go, but it came down to Neil's word against yours." He shook his head. "Roots run deep."

Lee Roy wheezed a small cough. "We had to stand behind our man. Neil's going through so much turmoil right now, he's about to break in two."

Dodd felt the effects of too many sleepless nights catching up to him, and he blew out an exhausted breath. "I understand, but I hate it for the church."

Charlie rose slowly. "This has been difficult for everyone involved."

"Sure has," Lee Roy said as he patted Milla on the shoulder.

"There's something else." Charlie paused at the door. "Neil requested you clean out your desk … today."

Dodd's jaw tightened. Up until then he felt sorry for the men delivering such bad news. Now his pity ran short, and he stifled his frustration. "No problem. Grady and I will go right now."

"We'll go with you," Lee Roy said.

Dodd scrutinized him, wondering if the old man meant to keep an eye on him. He picked up his keys and switched into autopilot. "I'll need to go by the United and get a few boxes out of the back Dumpster. I've got a lot of books."

"Let me help," Charlie said. "We can take my truck."

Dodd shrugged and then told Grady to bring Lee Roy to the church building in the El Camino. They would meet there and get this over with.

He rode in the passenger seat of Charlie's truck with his mind surprisingly vacant. Maybe being released from his preaching position cleared his head—if only for a few seconds. His thoughts drifted away from the church and all its drama. All he could think of was Ruthie and what she must think of him. He sighed as they pulled into the parking lot of the grocery store, but when he saw her standing by her mother's car, his mind jerked to attention and his pulsed raced.

"Well, don't that beat all," Charlie said as he maneuvered his truck behind the Dumpster, blocking their view of the parking lot.

"What?" Dodd reached for the door handle, anxious to get one more look at Ruthie before she and her mother drove away.

"I could've sworn I saw Neil over there talking to Lynda Turner."

CHAPTER FORTY-FIVE

As I ambled out the back door of the United with two trash bags, I spotted Momma's car in the side parking lot, thankful Uncle Ansel had gotten it running again. I threw the trash up and over the side of the metal Dumpster but stopped abruptly when I noticed Neil Blaylock's pickup angled behind the hatchback.

The two of them were talking.

Neil Blaylock and Momma. Talking in the parking lot of the United.

I stared at them before edging forward, itching to hear what they said. Neil and Momma hadn't spoken to each other in years. Not really.

Momma leaned against her driver's door with arms clenched over her stomach while Neil rested one boot on the rear bumper, elbow to his knee.

Neil's voice was controlled and smooth. "You should talk it over with Ruthie. Maybe she has more sense."

I stepped onto the sidewalk in front of our car, but Momma didn't acknowledge me.

"I don't need to talk it over with anybody, Neil."

His name sounded strange on her lips.

"I think you do." He chuckled. "Ruthie, I've been telling your mother you'd be better off in Lubbock. The old-timers in Trapp will never treat you like you deserve." He straightened his cowboy hat. "Some of them have trouble letting go of the past."

I tensed. "What are you talking about?"

"I'd like to make your lives easier." His smile seemed out of place. "There's a nice apartment complex on Lubbock's west side. It's clean, comfortable, homey."

A tractor roared past the front of the store, and I waited for it to pass before snapping, "You know we can't afford that."

"Stay out of this, Ruth Ann," Momma said.

Neil dropped his foot from the bumper and leaned on the car door next to Momma. "Lynda, I can take care of the rent, and Ruthie could afford Tech if she lived with you." His gaze traveled in a circle, starting at the top of her head, falling down her hair to her shoulders, then up her neck to her mouth and eyes as though he were breathing in the parts that pleased him.

Nausea inched toward my throat, but Momma only stared at the ground six feet in front of her.

Neil tilted his head into her line of vision. "I know I should've offered to help you long ago, and I apologize. Can you forgive me?"

My heart bounced and fluttered in a haphazard confusion of repulsion and desire. Neil Blaylock had just given me a way out of Trapp. Even if it came from him, I could humble myself and accept his gift. Maybe this was the forgiveness I'd heard so much about.

Momma seemed paralyzed, but when I noticed her fist clenched around her car keys, I recognized it as the silent fuse sparking toward a cluster of dynamite. "Momma?"

"Don't listen to him, Ruth Ann. He's a snake."

Neil's shoulders drooped dramatically. "Can't you see I have your best interests in mind?"

Momma's fingers gripped her elbows so tightly, the keys dug into her skin. "If you were thinking of me, you wouldn't be talking about this in front of my daughter."

"Your daughter is old enough to be part of the decision, since it affects her as much as you."

"You can't stand the guilt any longer, can you?" Momma's voice was acid.

The muddled meaning of their words drove me to step off the sidewalk. "What are you not telling me?"

"Nothing, Ruth Ann."

My anger, familiar and ever present, simmered just below the surface, but I redirected it from Momma's refusal to answer and instead turned to Neil.

He inspected his boots, unflustered. "We dated back in high school," he admitted. "And a while after."

"I know that."

Momma jerked her palm to silence him. "What he's not saying is he couldn't stand it when your daddy put a wedding band on my finger."

"Now, Lynda … life is no fairy tale, but I reached out to you and Hoby. I fulfilled my Christian duty."

"Christian duty? Is that what you call your actions when Hoby left?"

"I stood by you." He rubbed his palm across his mouth.

"You stood by me, wrapped your arms around my waist, and pulled me close." Momma trembled with rage.

"Maybe you read more into it, but that's understandable." Neil shifted away. "You were desperate."

Suddenly Momma shot words at him. "Yes, I was desperate. And I looked to my friends and my church for help, but you took them away from me with your lies. You convinced them to turn me away so you could hide your own lust."

"I protected you."

She made a spitting sound with her mouth. "Oh, please. You were afraid I'd tell your wife."

He paused, with some sort of twisted love painted across his face, and my stomach rolled into a tight ball of disgust.

"Lynda, be reasonable." He spoke softly, leaning into her. "Take the place in Lubbock."

"Do you expect the church to be reasonable about it?" Momma shook her head.

Neil flicked his hand through the air. "The church will follow my lead like stupid sheep. Besides, they don't have to know I'm taking care of you."

Heat washed over me as I envisioned Dodd worried about the church. "What do you mean, they don't have to know?"

"I can get the two of you set up in an apartment, register you for school, buy enough groceries to stock the pantry." He rested his arm on top of the car behind Momma's shoulders. "I never stopped loving your mother, Ruthie. Not this whole time."

Momma closed her eyes.

I gaped at the two of them. I hadn't even known Momma dated Neil until recently, and now he stood in front of me declaring his love for her?

He touched her cheek with the knuckle of his middle finger.

Momma's eyes snapped open, and with a growl she swung wildly, scraping her keys across his face like a weapon.

Neil cursed and stepped back to gain leverage, sweeping his arm back to slap her, but I yanked Momma out of the way.

"You little—" He swallowed, then spoke low. "Lynda, if you refuse me again, I won't handle it well."

"Once and for all, get over yourself," Momma lashed. "I haven't been tempted by you since I discovered what you're made of." She held her fist with keys sticking out in all directions. "Hoby still owns my heart, Neil. He always will."

Neil's gaze drifted above our heads as though we were invisible. As though he hadn't just been emotionally involved in a conversation. As though he had temporarily lowered himself to the level of swine simply to smear manure across our self-esteem. When he strode to his truck and drove away without a backward glance, the air in the parking lot snapped with silence, and for a speck of time, it hadn't happened.

Momma didn't move.

Neil's truck disappeared around the front corner of the store, but what if he came back? What if he tried to hit her again? What if he continued to pelt her confidence with spikes? My body surged with instinct, urging me to escape, but questions ran through my mind, stalling my actions. "Momma?"

"*What?*"

She stared straight ahead, eyes unfocused, as I lay my hand on her shoulder. "You all right?"

"Of course I'm all right," she snapped. "Get in the car."

Her face reflected the usual mixture of anger and bitterness, but there was a subtle difference. Now, layered on top of her brashness, I recognized … determination.

I gripped the armrest as the car careened out of the lot. "Can we talk about this?"

"No reason to."

"But Neil did wrong when Daddy left."

"Of course he did, but talking about it won't change anything." She ran the stop sign at the corner.

"The church needs to know." Dodd needed to know.

A sarcastic chuckle spit from her lips. "I don't give a horse's backside what that blasted church needs."

"But they were your friends. They should know the truth."

"Great friends." She slammed on the brakes in front of our house. "Get out. I need to drive."

"No. Tell me what happened with Daddy."

Her face was blank parchment as she stared blindly through the windshield, her shoulders melting. The pulse in my ears flumped two times as I realized Momma's exhaustion from hiding the truth finally outweighed her resolve to do so. When she spoke, her voice conveyed irritation, but I saw something significant in the droop of her shoulders. Something other than her habitual dreariness. Something masked as indifference … but more like acceptance. Peace.

She spoke without looking at me. "A hundred-pound load has been lifted from my shoulders, now that you know about … *Neil.*"

She flicked her fingernail against a seam in the vinyl steering-wheel cover. "I suppose I should tell you the rest."

The engine idled high then low as she drifted into her thoughts. "Your daddy suffered from depression, Ruth Ann. All his life. His family hurt more than helped, but I thought after we married, I could boost him up, you know? Back then, I *didn't* have the blues." She chuckled. "Clyde says I caught it from Hoby, and I don't know but what he's right."

Momma's words were salve on dry skin. All I had ever known about my daddy's departure I heard from Aunt Velma, who sugar-coated the details.

She turned the ignition off and clinked the keys onto the seat between us. "When you were born—" Her voice caught, and I realized, with amazement, she had a tear in her eye. "I never saw him so happy, Ruth Ann. He loved you. So much."

The memory brightened her face, but then her eyes clouded again. "Neil couldn't stand it." Her jaw hardened. "He claims he loves me, but actually he just wants what he can't have. He's always been that way."

"But if he loved you so much, why did he break it off in the first place?"

"I can't explain that, Ruth Ann." Her voice calmed. "I can, but I shouldn't. Just let me finish."

"Okay."

"The Blaylocks married before your daddy and me, and for some reason Neil thought we could remain friends." She blew air through her teeth. "But he expected something more than friendship. It was subtle at first, but after a while I realized his intentions, and I avoided him. He wouldn't back off, though, and after a few years, it was so bad your daddy began to notice." She closed her eyes, seeming to will the pain away. "Hoby began to question my loyalty, and over time, his insecurity gave way to paranoia. His depression got worse than ever."

Momma's shoulders trembled, and I wanted to slide across the seat and hold her, but we weren't used to talking to each other, much less hugging.

"I didn't know how to encourage him, and he wouldn't let me get close. He didn't believe anything I told him. I felt very alone, and Neil knew it. So he took it upon himself to flirt with me every chance he got, which, of course, only made things worse for your daddy."

She turned to look directly into my eyes, and I held my breath, terrified of what she would say next.

"Ruth Ann, I'm so sorry. I'm sorry about all of it. If I had done things differently, it wouldn't have happened the way it did. I was so alone. I didn't know what to do."

I leaned toward her and touched the back of her hand. "Whatever happened, it's all right, Momma. Really."

She turned away and spoke quicker, as though to get it over with. "One night when your daddy was at work, Neil came by the house. He made a blatant pass at me, and I told him to get away and never touch me again. You can't imagine how I hated that man." She laughed harshly. "But he was still there when your daddy got home. You'd think Neil Blaylock would be confident enough not to care when I turned him down, but he lashed out at me in the most effective way he knew."

"What did he do?" I whispered.

"He told your daddy I'd already been unfaithful."

"But why would he believe Neil?"

"You know how evil the monster of depression can be." She stuck the keys back in the ignition, signaling she couldn't take much more. "But that's not all Neil told him, Ruth Ann."

I rubbed the toe of my tennis shoe against a daub of dried sand on the floorboard. An inch to the left. An inch to the right. Back again. The gritty rasp echoed the coarseness of her words against my heart. A heart that couldn't bear the weight of another stone intended for Neil Blaylock. The acidity of my feelings slowly reached an overwhelming peak, and I felt myself sliding into the safety of indifference.

"What did he say?" I asked numbly.

"He told Hoby I'd been unfaithful before you were born. After that, your daddy never believed you were his child." Momma started the car. "He was gone a month later."

CHAPTER FORTY-SIX

Dodd couldn't fathom whom Charlie had seen with Lynda Turner, but it couldn't have been Neil. Maybe it was the middle school principal who had a similar truck. Either way, it didn't matter. Dodd pulled at the door handle of Charlie's truck, itching to run after Ruthie … but then what? He thrust one foot to the ground and stopped.

Charlie sat motionless in the driver's seat, seeming to weigh their options, obviously convinced he had seen Neil. "Well, we came here for boxes. Let's see if we can find any."

Dodd bolted around the truck but slowed before peeking around the edge of the Dumpster. He did a double take. "It really is him."

Neil leaned leisurely on the bumper of the hatchback, but Lynda and Ruthie both hunkered as though face-to-face with a wolf. Their posture worked like a magnet, tugging at Dodd's insides and urging him to post himself between the women and danger.

But he couldn't.

He no longer had the right—either as a friend or a minister—and Ruthie would undoubtedly view his actions in a way he didn't intend. Besides, he couldn't be entirely sure a genuine danger existed.

Charlie stepped to the end of the Dumpster in full view of Neil while Dodd gawked from the corner. Instinct urged him to rush to Ruthie's side, but Charlie calmly stuck a hand in the opening of the Dumpster and grabbed two boxes, then paused to contemplate the scene across the parking lot. "Dodd? You're friends with Ruthie. You ever known her or her mom to shoot the breeze with Neil?"

"Not hardly."

Charlie reached for another box in slow motion. "What do you think they're talking about?"

Neil had his face turned slightly, but Dodd could make out his lips. "Neil is saying their life could be easier."

"What makes you say so?"

"He's found them an apartment in Lubbock." Dodd's fist clenched involuntarily. "He says Ruthie can go to Tech."

Charlie slowly rotated his head to inspect Dodd. "What in the world?"

"Neil says it's his duty to help them get out of Trapp." Dodd lifted a palm. "Lynda's understandably skeptical."

Charlie looked back across the parking lot as though to verify the possibility of Neil saying such a thing. "How are you doing that?"

"I'm reading their lips. Lynda called him a snake."

The older man leaned an elbow on the Dumpster and lowered his head. "Dodd, I don't know how you're doing that, but it don't feel right listening in on them. Or whatever you call it." He stepped in front of Dodd to block his view.

Dodd slouched against the pickup, rubbing a hand over his eyes. "I know. It's been a curse ever since I lost my hearing." He breathed deeply, trying to slow his pulse. "But something isn't right over there."

Charlie shook his head. "There's nothing we can do. Let's get what we came for and go."

They dug for the last few boxes, but Dodd inadvertently glanced at Lynda again. "Wait a minute … Neil and Lynda dated?"

"Well, yes. Back in high school." Charlie's eyebrows lifted, and the two of them silently contemplated each other before the elder stepped aside. "Well, don't just stand there. Find out what they're saying."

Dodd faced the taller man, peeking around his shoulder. He eavesdropped briefly before he paraphrased. "Neil did something when Hoby left."

"What did he do?"

"He made a pass at Lynda?" Dodd shook his head, not believing what he was hearing. "Then lied to the church so no one would find out."

"Oh, dear God. Which one of them said so?"

Dodd frowned. "Does it matter?"

"Unfortunately, it does."

"Neil more or less said he had her shunned to protect her."

"Well, that's possible, isn't it?"

"He called the church stupid sheep."

"I think we've heard enough," Charlie said.

"He's touching her now. He says he never stopped loving her."

Charlie spun in time to see Lynda shove Neil's hand away from her face and scrape him with her keys. "He's going to hit her."

They both jerked toward the women but stopped when Neil backed off and walked calmly to his truck.

"What's the man thinking?" Charlie whispered.

Dodd couldn't answer. Ruthie had never looked more lost or alone, and Dodd had an overwhelming urge to wrap his arms around her and never let go.

And apologize. Oh, how he needed to apologize.

Ten minutes later, they stood in Dodd's office while Lee Roy and Grady quizzed them.

"That doesn't sound like Neil. Could you have misunderstood?" Lee Roy eased himself into a chair next to Dodd.

"No, I'm positive."

Charlie laid a hand on Lee Roy's shoulder. "With my own eyes, I saw him try to strike Lynda Turner."

The baggy skin around Lee Roy's eyes quivered as he blinked. He turned to contemplate Dodd, but then he lowered his head. He stayed there for several minutes while the space heater cycled on and off, and then he raised his gaze to Charlie. "What should we do?"

"I'm afraid the damage to the Turners may be hopeless."

Lee Roy moaned, pain etched on his face. "The poor woman."

"But our God is a God of miracles." Grady muttered the words as though trying to convince himself.

Dodd dropped his head in his hands, picturing Ruthie's face—a blend of anger and isolation. "I'm afraid it'll take a miracle."

"We'll do everything we can." Charlie wiped a fist over his parted lips. "We may not ever make it up to them, but we can try."

Lee Roy raised quivering hands, holding them in the air as though beseeching the Lord. "What have we done?"

"You did what you thought best," Dodd said. "You and Charlie trusted Neil—and his father—to help you with decisions, as you should have." Dodd made eye contact with each man. "Now it's time for you to make decisions without him, but you're both wise. I have faith you can do this."

Lee Roy rose and hobbled to the window, leaning heavily on his cane. "But what will the church think of us?"

"They'll think no less of our actions than their own." Charlie gently blew air through his moist lips. "Neil misled us all."

"We'll have to confront him with what we know," Lee Roy said.

Charlie nodded. "We should go to him. I'm sure these sins have been weighing on his heart."

As if on cue, the door opened abruptly, and Neil stood in the doorway, his eyes narrowed. A dead silence enveloped the room, but Neil strolled in confidently. "I thought this office would be cleared out by now."

Charlie motioned to a chair. "Come in, brother. We need to talk."

Neil lowered himself into the chair, leaned back, and crossed an ankle over his knee. "What's this about, Charlie? You look like you just came from a funeral." He scowled at the Cunninghams, compelling Grady to slip out the door, but Dodd held his ground.

The two elders positioned themselves in chairs in front of Neil.

Charlie clasped his hands together, and for a moment the tall man seemed small under Neil's scrutiny, but then he straightened with a forceful yet compassionate expression. "This afternoon I drove to the United with Dodd to get boxes from the Dumpster."

"Okay ..." An unsure smile played on Neil's lips, and he looked at Lee Roy as though Charlie were speaking nonsense.

Charlie lowered his voice. "We saw you there with Lynda Turner and her daughter."

"Yes, I was there." Neil hesitated before nodding. "She asked me for money, said she and the girl are having trouble. I explained the church could help her with some groceries."

"*Brother—*" Lee Roy's tone was uncharacteristically stifling.

Neil quickly motioned to the mark on his cheek. "She became angry and struck me."

Charlie stared at him as though seeing him for the first time, and not liking what he saw.

Lee Roy turned his head away.

"We know you've been under a lot of strain on account of Fawn," Charlie said, "but the church is here to support you."

Neil screwed up his face. "What are you saying?"

Dodd took a step toward them. "When I was young, I lost my hearing. Did my parents ever tell you about that?"

"Lee Roy, I'd like to know what's going on." When Neil didn't even acknowledge his statement, Dodd realized how wrong he'd been to trust him at all.

"Our minister is trying to explain." Charlie motioned to Dodd. "The boy can read lips. He witnessed your conversation with Lynda this afternoon." His voice fell. "He told us everything."

"And you believe him?" Neil's voice rose frantically, and Dodd wondered if he had ever truly known the man.

Lee Roy reached for a Bible on Dodd's desk and pulled it into his lap to stroke the leather cover.

Charlie's face flushed. "I saw you touch Lynda Turner."

"She threw herself at me." He flicked his wrist. "You know the woman she is."

"Actually, most of what I know about her is what you've told me, but I plan to have a long discussion with her in the near future." Charlie's eyes held tears, yet he looked stronger than Dodd had ever seen him.

Neil rose abruptly, toppling his chair. "I can't believe you're treating me like this. I'm an elder of this congregation. My family's been here for generations. Send the preacher out so we can discuss this properly."

Lee Roy's gravelly voice smoothed as he said, "Neil, admit your sin, repent, and we can help you."

Neil paced the floor like a caged tiger. "I have nothing to confess, Lee Roy, and if you had any sense, you'd see Dodd's judgment is tainted because of the Turner girl. He's the one who needs to repent." Neil pointedly refused to look at Dodd, but the skin on each side of his nose puckered as though he smelled the stench of rot. "Lynda Turner's an easy woman, and her daughter's just as deceitful. Your preacher boy came to town in the shadow of his father's reputation, but he simply doesn't have what it takes. A faithful minister would never have been led astray by a girl with loose morals."

Dodd felt as though a vice were clamped to his forehead. "Ruthie does *not* have loose morals. And neither does Lynda."

Neil continued as though Dodd hadn't spoken. "The fact he got involved with Ruthie Turner tells me I can't trust anything he says." He lifted his chin and peered from Charlie to Lee Roy. "You'd be wise to do the same."

Every muscle in Dodd's body tightened with rage, and he fought to maintain control. Neil had insulted him in the worst possible ways—through his father and through Ruthie—but Dodd stifled the urge to attack the man. Even in the midst of his anger, he knew violence would only make matters worse. His arms crossed, and he held himself back by gripping both elbows until his knuckles turned white.

Lee Roy sighed wearily. "Son?"

Dodd jerked his eyes toward the old man, thinking Lee Roy was talking to him, but the sad, wrinkled eyes were fixed on Neil. "In the past, it's come down to your word against Dodd's. But this time it's different." Lee Roy gestured to Charlie. "This time it comes down to your word against Charlie's." One of his shoulders lifted slightly, and he turned his face toward the window. "And Lynda and Ruthie Turner."

The stillness in the air pressed on Dodd's shoulders as he glared at the man he once considered a mentor. Neil's face became pale, but his fury hadn't abated. He seemed even more livid, and Dodd imagined his own face might be a mirror image.

When Neil finally spoke, his voice was the low growl of a mad dog. "If this church is going to stoop so low as to take into account the word of a woman not fit to worship with the saints"—he swallowed as though he had a rancid taste in his mouth—"I cannot continue to fellowship here."

A chair stood between him and the door, and he shoved it out of his way, never looking back at them as he filled the narrow hallway with a booming threat. "May God be your judge!"

Dodd felt a pang of angst, fearing how God might judge Neil Blaylock.

CHAPTER FORTY-SEVEN

When Momma drove away, I had no idea where she went. Probably Ansel and Velma's, but if so, she'd regret it. After all, Fawn was there.

I went to the bathroom and turned on the shower. Momma's words saddened me, but I felt dirty—*filthy*—from Neil's. His accusations and suggestions, his penetrating eyes and body language. I wanted to cleanse myself of his memory, and as I waited for the water to heat, I studied myself in the medicine-cabinet mirror. My face reflected back at me, pale and death like, and I wondered when dark circles had appeared beneath my eyes. They made me look even more like Momma.

I stepped into the shower before adjusting the water, and my left side scalded, but I didn't care. At least I felt it. At least I felt something. My heart, which normally beat heavily with bitterness, now felt like a stone in my chest—a weight to be lugged through whatever trial came next.

The soapy washcloth wasn't sufficient, and I reached through the shower curtain to fumble under the sink for Momma's old loofah sponge. I never used the thing because of its coarseness, but suddenly I wanted it desperately. After saturating it with shower gel, I scrubbed my arms, legs, and body until my skin stung. Half the bottle of shampoo went onto my hair, and I clawed at my scalp, not slowing even when the soap trickled into my eyes. The burning under my lids eventually released pent-up anger, and I slammed my fists against the tile and screamed. The sound more closely resembled that of a tortured animal than a human, and it caught me so off guard that I halted my tantrum.

I stayed in the shower for what felt like hours, letting the water wash away the soap, the shampoo, the disgrace. Then I gently dried myself, wrapping the towel around my pinkened skin. I still felt dirty. Wiping the fog off the mirror, I peered at my reflection once again and even though the dark circles remained, I looked different. I stared at myself until I figured out what it was.

My eyes.

The emptiness had lessened, and my determination had increased. *What had changed?*

A gentle stirring prickled my heart, and I realized I wanted to talk to God. *Needed to*. After all, there was no one else left. Every person in my world had pulled away in one way or another, but strangely, I didn't feel alone. I leaned toward the mirror with scrutiny. My eyes really were different. Lowering the toilet lid, I sat on the seat and rested my elbows on my knees.

And I prayed.

I told God about Momma's anger and Fawn's pregnancy and JohnScott's distance. I explained my jumbled feelings for Dodd and asked what in the world I should do, and then I begged for a way to get out of Trapp. When I griped at Him about Neil's behavior, I felt like a tattling preschooler, but then I lashed out at God for allowing that man so much power. Grief and anger bubbled inside me, and I embraced their familiarity like an old friend.

When I opened the bathroom door, cold air chilled my moist skin, and I quickly pulled on sweats and socks. I towel-dried my hair and pulled it into a bun, envisioning Neil's fury as he swung at Momma. None of it made sense. Or maybe it made too much sense. I stumbled to the kitchen table and sat down. What would he do now? Neil had already taken the Cunninghams away from me. Momma's job from her. Years ago, he took our church, our friends, our reputation.

And he took my daddy.

A whimper came from the depths of my lungs. One solitary sob that seemed to die from lack of energy.

As I positioned the salt-and-pepper shakers in the middle of the table, side by side, my hands shook. I pressed my palms on the table and studied them. Knuckles, fingernails, cuticles. My nails needed to be filed.

A knock sounded, and Dodd called to me as the door opened. "Ruthie, you okay?"

Why was the preacher here? Even though we had talked, and kissed, the night before, I made sure he understood my feelings hadn't changed. I couldn't go to his church or be what he wanted me to be, and I rested my forehead in my hands to avoid looking at him. "I've been better."

He sat next to me at the table and trailed a finger across my arm. "You're shaking a little."

I shrugged.

"Ruthie, I owe you another apology."

I lifted my head to look at him then.

He leaned back and ran his hands through his hair, pausing to grip the back of his neck. "You were right."

"About what?"

"Everything. I didn't listen to you, not really, and now I see how blind I was to what you were going through." He pulled his chair close to me and took my hands in his. "I know what Neil said. Ruthie, I'm so sorry."

"What? When?"

"At the United. This afternoon."

The dirty feeling crept across my shoulders again. "You were there?"

"Charlie and me. Over by the Dumpster. We were getting boxes."

I stared at the ceiling. The corner above Dodd's head had browned from a water spot. "What did you overhear?"

"All of it, I guess. Neil talked about an apartment in Lubbock, and college … and your mom."

My entire life was soiled. "There's more," I whispered. *He might as well know everything*. "Momma told me more."

He squeezed my hands.

"Neil lied. He told my daddy I wasn't his daughter. That's why Daddy left us. Momma couldn't convince him otherwise."

Dodd didn't move for several seconds. "So … your mother didn't have an affair, with Neil."

"No." I paused to consider it, answering slowly. "I don't think she had an affair with *anyone*."

"Should we ask her?"

I laughed bitterly. "She won't be ready for an interrogation anytime soon."

He studied me intently, then asked the question that had been running through my mind. "Do you believe Hoby is your dad?"

Another sob slipped from my lips, and I clamped my fingers over my mouth. Neil had already taken my daddy once. He wasn't taking him again. "I do. I believe that."

Dodd pulled me toward him, cradling my head against his shoulder. He brushed aside a wisp of wet hair that had pulled loose from my bun. Then he prayed.

His prayer was different than mine had been. He prayed peace for Momma and me, and understanding and strength. He prayed Momma and I would learn how to communicate again. That we would heal and be blessed. Then he prayed forgiveness for Neil. At first I cringed, but then I realized I no longer had the capacity to withhold it from him. Even though his actions infuriated me, I would not allow him to control my anger any longer.

As Dodd continued to pray, I cried.

Thirteen years' worth of tears. Thirteen years of bitterness and frustration, confusion and anger—all blustering out of my heart in one explosive stream of forgiveness. I had never cried so hard, not even as a child—never knew it was possible for my body to react in such an involuntary way. In fact, trying to stop my blubbering would have been like trying to hold back the West Texas wind. I don't know how long it took, but Dodd never left my side or stopped praying, except to occasionally whisper words of comfort.

Eventually my sobs diminished to whimpers, and I wilted into a heap, laying my cheek flat on the kitchen table. "So what happened? After?"

Dodd wiped beneath my eyes. "I told Charlie and Lee Roy everything."

"They believed you?"

"Why wouldn't they?"

I sighed. "What about Neil?"

Dodd shook his head. "Charlie and Lee Roy confronted him, but he couldn't repent. He stormed out of the building."

I closed my eyes. "The Blaylocks won't have a friend left to their name." Somehow the thought of the Blaylock women being knocked down a few notches satisfied me.

"Is that really what you want?" He spoke so softly, I could barely hear him. "To punish them for Neil's sins?"

My hand trembled as I pressed a fist against my lips, wishing my words could be taken back. I sat up and shook my head.

"The man is black with sin, Ruthie."

I nodded. "Will the church push him away?"

"I get the impression Neil is gone for good, but if not, Charlie and Lee Roy won't ask him to leave." He exhaled and leaned against the wall. "God is capable of forgiving the darkest sins, and He expects us to do the same."

"If you're telling me to forgive Neil … I think I just did." I peered into his beautiful blue eyes as they crinkled into a smile.

"I'm telling you to let God forgive *you.*"

CHAPTER FORTY-EIGHT

The following weeks held so many changes, I didn't recognize my little town, much less my life. Not only did the church formally apologize to Momma and me, but a few families, like the Sanders, invited us into their homes. While Momma muddled through her feelings for the church members, I muddled through my own. I thought I had forgiven most of them, but it would take me a while to forget about Neil Blaylock and the accusations he had slung against my family.

Two things still bothered me, but I accepted it might be years before Momma explained them. First, I couldn't help but wonder about Clyde Felton. Whatever happened to his girlfriend and baby? Second—and this wasn't nearly as pleasant—I found myself wondering about Momma and Neil dating back in high school. She never told me why he broke up with her. *Thank God, he did.* But why?

In spite of my questions, peace gradually settled over Momma and me like soft music. I had discovered so much about my past, I couldn't handle any more for a while, so I ignored my doubts and embraced rest. Of course, the peace didn't make a lick of sense, but

I decided most things weren't meant to make sense, and I was better off not forcing sense into them.

Like my feelings for Dodd. He had been gracious enough to back off for a while, but never so far I had to wonder about his intentions. He would wink whenever he came into the school office, or slip me a Butterfinger in the teachers' lounge, or eavesdrop on my conversations across the gym. My feelings for him, though intense, were tangled up with my feelings for the church, and I had a dickens of a time sorting them out.

Even though Momma still begrudged Christians to a certain extent, I no longer worried about my actions hurting her. Maybe I'd cause her grief, and maybe I wouldn't, but Momma had to tend to her own pain. We formed a nonverbal truce, allowing each other to befriend, or not befriend, whomever we wanted. So far I had bitten my tongue at her impatience with the church ladies, and she had done nothing more than hide in her bedroom if Fawn dropped by the house … which happened often.

Fawn and I weren't as close as we had been when we were young, but every day, I found it more likely we would be. Ansel and Velma had welcomed her into their home for as long as she needed a place to stay, and I was beginning to view her presence as a blessing instead of an intrusion. Besides, the distance she kept from her father—and possibly her mother—seemed to gradually cleanse the spite from her heart. As she became a different person, I found my own heart overflowing with compassion for her, but I worried how she would manage. Without her parents' support, she would have a terrible time making a life for herself and her child. I wanted to help her and yet had no idea how to go about it.

Emily Sanders also showed up at my house periodically. I assumed her mother still pushed her to befriend me, but I no longer minded. What once seemed manipulative, I now understood to be their bumbling way of reaching out in love. Sure, the whole Sanders family would always be what I called *followers,* but they no longer blindly followed the church crowd, so I couldn't fault them. And neither could Momma. Whenever she saw Emily, she would roll her eyes, but at least she didn't lock herself in her bedroom.

She tolerated both Fawn and Emily, but the ultimate test of her patience came when I invited Dodd to dinner. I knew it would make Momma uncomfortable, but I also knew I couldn't keep him waiting indefinitely.

In preparation for dinner, I cleaned the house from top to bottom, cooked two chocolate sheath cakes, burning the first, and washed all my laundry in hopes of discovering something new to wear.

Momma, on the other hand, appeared indifferent. She brought takeout from Dixie's Diner, then slipped into her house shoes.

Even though I was glad she returned to her job at the diner, I couldn't help wishing for a home-cooked meal for Dodd. I frowned at the Styrofoam containers boasting *The Best Dining Experience in Texas,* but at least we had a homemade dessert.

"What?" Momma asked. "Your preacher man too good for takeout?"

I didn't argue as I transferred the chicken-fried steak onto one of our own platters, but when I heard Dodd's knock, my stomach knotted.

What if Momma pitched a fit? What if Dodd said something to set her off? What if my life never changed, and I remained trapped in the same scenario for another decade?

I opened the door and shrugged helplessly. "Thanks for coming."

"Thanks for asking." The crinkles around Dodd's eyes settled my nerves.

"She's waiting for us," I whispered.

When we stepped into the kitchen, Momma tossed three of our flowery plastic plates on the table without looking up.

"Thanks for having me over, Lynda."

Dodd put one arm around her shoulders briefly, but she only motioned toward the table with an ice tray. "Sit."

I didn't appreciate her attitude, but I understood it perfectly. Dodd and I had been studying the Bible together. At first I tried to hide it from Momma but soon realized she might as well get used to the idea because if I started hiding it now, I'd be hiding it the rest of my life. That's how long I planned on reading the stinking book, because now that I'd begun listening to God, I didn't know how I had done without Him for so long.

I poured iced tea into glasses, which Dodd helped me carry to the table. As we sat, he habitually lifted his palms to hold hands during the blessing, but when he noticed Momma had already put a bite in her mouth, he swept up his fork before she noticed. "This looks tasty, Lynda."

She stopped chewing and glared at him suspiciously. "It came out of Styrofoam."

"Not any old Styrofoam, though." Dodd pointed with his knife. "Styrofoam from Dixie's Diner, the best dining experience in Texas."

Momma scrutinized him, probably wondering if he was making fun, but he continued. "We get dinner from Dixie's at least once a week. I'm not sure it's the best food in Texas, but it's good, just the same. The meat loaf is exceptional, and Mom loves the pork chops, but my favorite is the chicken-fried steak. I don't think anyone could beat it, do you?" He placed a bite in his mouth.

"Well … I suppose not." Momma pushed a dollop of mashed potatoes around her plate. "I do love Dixie's chicken and dumplings."

I blinked.

"How does she get them so perfect?" he asked. "Not too done, but not too soggy. And with all that gravy." He leaned toward her as though he were sharing a special secret. "We may have to get some for dessert."

"Don't be silly," I said automatically. "I made sheath cake."

Dodd held his hand to the side of his mouth and spoke to Momma in a stage whisper. "Just go along with it. We don't want to hurt her feelings."

Momma actually chuckled.

"What's a sheath cake anyway?" he asked me.

"Only the best chocolate cake in the world. Gooey, with icing drizzled on top when it's still warm."

He rubbed his chin thoughtfully. "So it's actually better than Dixie's chicken and dumplings?"

The knot around my stomach had gradually unwound, and now it did a gleeful cannonball into the deep end of my emotions, splashing my heart with something that felt an awful lot like love.

Dodd continued to carry the conversation, asking nonthreatening questions to get Momma to join in, and when he told her the lime and lemon Popsicle story, she almost spewed iced tea. Evidently the image of the preacher carrying on about wine and women got to her, and she was trying not to smile when she carried her plate to the sink.

Dodd followed with his own dishes. "Thanks again for the meal, Lynda."

Her lips parted as though she had just thought of something funny to say, but then she turned away suddenly, mumbling, "Oh, sure."

Evidently she had reached the limit of her hospitality, because she stalked to her bedroom and shut the door.

Dodd sighed. "Should I go?"

"Not yet." I felt my expression changing into what JohnScott called my spoiled-brat face, but I couldn't help myself.

"Okay, then," Dodd said. "Should we do the dishes or sit on the couch and talk?"

"Couch, definitely."

He reached for my wrist and pulled me into the living room, where I silently studied Momma's bedroom door, closed like so many doors in my life. Closed doors, closed minds, closed hearts. But I was learning to make peace with the closed doors and climb through the windows.

He leaned back on the couch and slipped his arm around my shoulders, sending chills down to my elbows. When I smiled up at him, I was surprised by his grave expression, and a thin shadow fell across my happy mood.

"What's wrong?"

He opened his mouth. Closed it again. Rubbed the back of his neck. "Ruthie, you need to register for classes at Tech this fall." He sounded like a parent telling a third grader to brush his teeth.

"What? Why? I'm not sure it will work out with Momma."

His eyebrows met in the middle. "It's time for you to make it work out."

I raised an eyebrow playfully. "Are you telling me what to do?"

"It's only fair." He ran a finger across the velour of the couch cushion. "You told me what to do."

"I don't know what you're talking about."

He pulled my hand onto his knee and traced my fingers. "Remember that night at Old Man Guthrie's ponderosa pine? Before Christmas?"

"What about it?"

"You told me to quit teaching and get an engineering degree." He smiled. "Then you told me to obey you."

He tickled my hand, and I had trouble focusing on the conversation. "And ..."

"Well, you were right. So really, I should thank you." He picked up my hand and ran his lips across the tips of my fingers. "So in light of your revelation, I decided not to renew my teaching contract for next year."

I gasped. "You can't do that. What about your mom and Grady? You need the income. You've got to consider the possibilities and not make a hasty decision."

He laughed out loud. "This hasn't been a hasty decision. I've been thinking about it since that night in December. Mom will still be at the middle school in the fall, so that will be a steady income for her. Grady will be at Tech"—he raised an eyebrow—"with *you*, and like you, most of his tuition will be covered with grants and loans. You won't want the loans, but that works out because you can live here with your mom. Of course, you won't mind evenings in Trapp because I'll be here." He rubbed his lips across my cheek, and an electric current spun down my neck, but he only grinned. "Any questions?"

"What was that you said about engineering?"

"This is the best part, Ruthie." He chuckled. "I'm going back to school with you and Grady, to get my bachelor's in engineering. Tech agreed to let me work part-time in the math department for now, and when I start my master's, I can probably teach a few freshman-level courses."

It was almost too much information to get my mind around. "Dodd, that's … that's amazing. I don't know what to say."

He laughed. "Say you'll register."

Momma remained shut up in her bedroom, bumping around in there noisily, and I stared at her door, searching for an answer.

"Hey," Dodd said softly, "I listened to your advice. The least you can do is listen to mine."

He was right. I could take college classes. I could study the Bible. I could date the preacher. I could do whatever I wanted. And suddenly I knew what I wanted to do. What I was ready to do. What I *needed* to do.

Placing my palm against his jaw, and ignoring the tears in my eyes, I said, "I want to go to church with you, Dodd."

He melted. "All I asked for was a few college classes."

"I know, and I'll do that, too."

He squinted his eyes softly, and I knew he was afraid to ask the next question. His voice was so light, I wouldn't have heard him if I hadn't been looking.

"Why?"

I leaned back against the couch cushions. "Well, it's complicated. First of all, I love you, and because I love you, I want to experience life with you and make you happy. But that's not the real reason." I raised my hands slightly before letting them fall back to my lap. "It's just that I love God, too, and He wants me there. He wants me at worship, even though the people are a faulty, ugly, sticky mess." I sighed. "I have a feeling He thinks I'll fit right in."

Dodd stared at me, and in his crinkly blue eyes, I saw pride. And peace. He gently leaned in, wrapped his arms around me, and nestled my head against his shoulder.

And it felt so good.

He rubbed his hand up and down my back, then ran his fingers through my hair, and I didn't care if he ever stopped. "What was that first thing you said again?"

I laughed out loud and popped him on the chest.

Neither of us heard Momma come out of her room, and we were startled when she dropped a small cardboard box on the coffee table in front of us. "I suppose I might as well get this out of storage now." My heart raced from the hollow thump the box had made on the wooden table, and I wasn't sure what to say to her.

She barely paused before hurrying to the kitchen. "Glad you came, Dodd." She grabbed the dish detergent with urgency, and then spoke again without turning around. "You should come again." She reached toward the windowsill and flipped on the CD player to drown out any further conversation.

Dodd and I watched her back as she ran dishwater into the sink. Momma had just made some kind of paradigm shift that we could feel but couldn't quite touch. We looked at each other and shrugged simultaneously, and then I remembered the box.

It was old and worn, with a thin layer of dust on top. I pulled it toward me and opened the flaps. They gave way easily, as though they had been opened many times over the years. What I saw inside made me gasp.

It was my daddy's old Bible.

Just as I remembered it. Large, with an ornately decorated Western cover and leather cording laced through holes on the edges.

"A rectangular saddle," Dodd said.

He eased it out of the box and laid it across my lap, opening to the book of Genesis. He kissed my temple as I fingered the worn pages. Dodd knew. He understood as well as I did that Momma had just opened a door.

She was setting me free.

... a little more ...

When a delightful concert comes to an end,

the orchestra might offer an encore.

When a fine meal comes to an end,

it's always nice to savor a bit of dessert.

When a great story comes to an end,

we think you may want to linger.

And so, we offer ...

AfterWords—just a little something more after you

have finished a David C Cook novel.

We invite you to stay awhile in the story.

Thanks for reading!

Turn the page for ...

- **Note to the Reader**
- **Acknowledgments**
- **Book Club Discussion Guide**
- **A Sneak Peek at Book Two: *Justified***
- **About the Author**

NOTE TO THE READER

Some books are designed for entertainment, some to send a message, others to influence or change the audience. I honestly can't say why I wrote *Jaded.* What started out as a light romance five years ago evolved into a painful story that continues to tear at my heart.

I hope it tears at yours, too, in a good way. I hope you find yourself somewhere in its pages and grow because of the journey you've taken with Ruthie and the Trapp congregation. Not all hearts are as hard as hers, but we all have room for improvement. And certainly not all congregations are as bitter as hers, but as long as we're on earth, the church will be filled with humans who have real-life flaws and opinions. I pray we have the humility and strength to forgive each other's sins until we reach heaven, where everything will be so, so much easier.

Trapp, Texas, is a fictitious town created from a blend of places I've lived and visited. It sits approximately in the same location as Post but undoubtedly shares characteristics of my hometown, Grandview. However, the culture and geography in *Jaded* are not quite true to either, and I apologize for any inaccuracies in my memory and research.

And just for the record, the Trapp congregation—bless their hearts—exists nowhere on Earth. Or maybe it exists in every town; you be the judge. Either way, Neil Blaylock and the other characters are figments of my imagination, and any resemblance they may have to members of your local congregation is purely coincidental.

Soon you will be able to find the sequel, *Justified,* which continues the story through the eyes of Ruthie's former friend, Fawn Blaylock. In the meantime, feel free to contact me online at varinadenman.com. I'd love to hear from you.

Thank you for reading,

Varina

ACKNOWLEDGMENTS

It's truly unfair that only one person's name is on the cover of this book, because so many more have contributed. Listing them here, at the very back, hardly makes up for the injustice, but it's all I've got to work with, so here goes.

Thank you to my husband, Don, for never doubting the dream. For helping me laugh at the rejections and tears, and for patiently explaining my characters' motivations when I couldn't figure them out on my own. *How do you do that?* But more than anything, thank you for being stubbornly determined to keep me home with our children and not minding that I wrote a book while I was there.

Thank you to my daughters, Jessica, Jillian, and Janae, for your suggestions about what should happen next, and how it should happen, and whether or not Dodd needs muscles after all. And thank you to my sons, Drew and Dene, for recognizing I was writing … *something* … and being proud of me. And to all five of you for allowing me to ignore you for long stretches of time—you seem to have turned out all right regardless. And to Colton and Kelsea, who joined us after the madness began—thank you for marrying into our family anyway. I promise I won't always have a deadline … maybe.

Thank you to Marci for reading, rereading, and re-rereading. And for showing me the spots where "something's just not working here." Those words are a treasure map for a writer to follow.

Thank you to all the friends and family who supported and encouraged me the past five years. Especially those who read my

original manuscript and refrained from telling me it was terrible (when it clearly was)—D'arci, Teddy, Anna, Mom, Jackie, Jill, Paula, Lance, Hannah, Kelsey, Karla (and the girls at her office who passed around a notebook copy). Your graciousness gave me courage to keep going.

To Sudona, Paula, Kathy, and Connie for propping me up during the frenzy of publication and for praying me through several bouts of temporary insanity.

Thank you to Mary and the Storytellers, for being a gentle source of praise.

Thank you to Anne Mateer and Candace Calvert, two of the most gracious, knowledgeable, and encouraging mentors a new writer could ask for. And to Nicole Deese and Amy Matayo for their empathy, their brainstorming sessions, their laughter and tears.

Thank you to Jamie Chavez and Julie Gwinn for your patience as I learned to work with professional editors. I appreciate you butchering my manuscript, teaching me the craft in the process, and inviting me to the full-on party happening in the margin notes.

Thank you to Jessica Kirkland, not only my agent but my cheerleader, adviser, spokesman, therapist, editor, fellow plotter, nutrition consultant, and sweet friend. I don't know where you find the time to do all that you do, but I'm certainly glad that you do it. By now, I owe you a truckload of gluten-free cupcakes.

And a huge thank-you to all the folks at David C Cook who took a chance on a debut author and brought Ruthie Turner to life. Thank you to John Blase for finding Ruthie and me. To Ingrid Beck for answering what I'm sure were the most remedial publishing questions ever asked. To Amy Konyndyk for going the extra mile for the

perfect cover. To Jennifer Lonas for polishing the manuscript until I could see my reflection in it. And to the entire team at David C Cook, including Nick Lee, Helen Macdonald, and Karen Athen, for the care you have shown to Ruthie, Dodd, and the Trapp congregation.

And last but not least, thank you to Chris for loaning me ten minutes of your life story and allowing me to twist it beyond recognition. This book is for you, and for me, and for others who wish the church was just a little bit different.

BOOK CLUB DISCUSSION GUIDE

1. When the story opens, Ruthie Turner has been an outsider in her own hometown for thirteen years because of an event that happened when she was just seven years old. How has her seven-year-old perception of what happened colored her adult attitudes? Do you blame her? How could things have been different?

2. Have you ever witnessed judgmental behavior by Christians? Regardless of where you stood in the situation, how did it make you feel?

3. Why do you think Lynda Turner keeps her daughter in the dark for so long? If she'd told Ruthie the truth—at some point—how might their lives have been better?

4. Being the only child of a single parent who also suffers from depression can't have been easy, but Ruthie develops coping mechanisms to make the best of a bad situation. How do these methods of coping help or hinder her personal growth? In what ways does Ruthie seem mature for her age?

5. Early conflict in the story is based on assumptions and misunderstandings—and all of the characters seem to be affected. What

are Ruthie's assumptions—about Dodd, about JohnScott? What are Dodd's assumptions—about his congregation, about Ruthie?

6. Ruthie and her mother are quite bitter toward the church. Do you think their attitudes are justified? What emotions do you feel toward those two characters?

7. When Dodd Cunningham first moves to Trapp, he doesn't recognize the judgmental attitudes among his congregants or the corruption in the leadership. How does his innocence/naiveté help or hurt the situation? What do you think he learned from the situation?

8. When Clyde Felton visits the small congregation, the members react in fear and defensiveness. Why would Christians behave in such a way? When might such a reaction be warranted?

9. Consider the character Emily Sanders. She is described as a follower. Do you view her as such? How does she appear weak? In what ways does her faith seem stronger than some of the other characters'?

10. What do you think of the Picketts' behavior compared to the behavior of the Blaylocks? One family is in church three times a week and the other is not, but which family seems more Christlike? Why?

11. On several occasions, the Cunninghams exhibit Christian love to Lynda Turner. Why might she have trouble accepting their love? Describe a time you have been on either side of this scenario.

12. Toward the end of the book, Fawn Blaylock's parents learn she is pregnant and throw her out of their home. What emotions did you feel when this happened to her? What do you think will happen to Fawn now?

13. Neil Blaylock, the villain of the story, is depicted as evil even though he is an elder in the church. This scenario demonstrates the use of irony for literary purposes. What might the author have been trying to show? How does this character make you feel? What do you hope happens to Neil by the end of the series? What do you hope happens to the other elders?

14. In the middle of the story, Ruthie wants to date Dodd, but she is afraid of what her mother will do. Do you approve of her decision to hide her relationship? When, if ever, would it be appropriate to conceal your actions for the sake of your loved ones? How did this work out for Ruthie?

15. At the end of the book, Ruthie cries out to God after she takes a shower. Have you ever experienced a vulnerable time when you needed to reach out to God in such a personal way? Have you ever been unable to do so? Explain.

16. Ruthie Turner must forgive her parents, friends, Christians, the church, and God. In what order is she able to forgive them? By the end of the book, do you feel she has completed the process?

17. The closing scene has Ruthie declaring she is ready to go back to the small-town congregation. Do you approve of her decision? What would you do in her place?

18. By the end of the story, we see a change of heart in some of the members of the congregation. What do you think the overall reaction will be when Ruthie walks into church? How would you hope to treat her yourself? How might she perceive your actions?

A Sneak Peek at Book Two:

JUSTIFIED

Varina Denman

CHAPTER ONE

My world shattered in the second week of December. A hairline crack formed, and my life perched on the edge of an abyss, set to topple at the slightest breeze. But instead of a breeze, I got a whirlwind—in the form of a positive pregnancy test.

Of course, that wasn't supposed to happen. Not to me. But when my world finally ceased its roiling, nothing was left right side up. I barely recognized myself—or my thoughts and feelings—because my new life had become an inverted image of what it was before.

Now I sat on the hood of Velma's old maroon Chevy, waiting for the sunrise, and rubbed a palm across the curve of my stomach. "Don't worry, little guy, it's not your fault." I say little guy because I had the sonogram. Saw the picture. And it figures I'd bring another man into the world. Even though I wanted this child more than I imagined possible, I prayed he wouldn't be like his daddy. Or mine.

My new rental house was perched fifty yards from the edge of the Caprock Escarpment, a chalky bronze declivity dividing the flat-as-a-board tableland of the Llano Estacado with the rolling plains hundreds of feet below. I could see for thirty miles, and I drank in the unbroken terrain as it transformed from shadows to sunshine.

And I tried to figure out my life.

I'd been trying for almost eight months, and so far I'd determined three things. I could survive without my parents' help. My heart wouldn't break if I never saw Tyler Cruz again. And I could and would make a home for my child.

I shifted on the car and peered down at the fading streetlights of my hometown. In a few minutes, the glow of dawn would eclipse the artificial light, and Trapp, Texas, would momentarily disappear. Good riddance.

Already the horizon glowed orange, and I sipped my iced coffee, letting its bitterness relieve the effects of the smothering heat. August had always been a source of pleasure with its parties and cookouts, but now that I had no central air-conditioning or ceiling fans or swimming pool, fall looked better all the time.

I opened the Bible app on my cell phone and read my new favorite verse. *Children are a blessing from the Lord.* I whispered it into the warm air, reminding myself that even though I hadn't followed the proper timeline, even though I disgraced my family, my church, my community, even though this baby turned my life upside down … my little man was a blessing.

It had taken me quite a while to accept that fact. I cried the entire first trimester and threw tantrums the second, but now that the baby could kick some sense into me, I realized that for the first time in twenty-one spoiled-little-rich-girl years, my life would have purpose.

The good Lord—cranky as He was—had gifted me with a mission I hadn't thought to ask for. Not that He was rewarding my sin. On the contrary, I felt the sting of His punishment daily when people in town greeted me, then discreetly turned away. Last week my only remaining friend, Ruthie Turner, told me I'd get used to all that. But I wasn't so sure.

The ever-brightening sky continued to pull the sun above the ground, illuminating miles of uneven pastureland and revealing

all its browns and greens, gradually appearing from the blackness. The wind whipped past me, slacking as though an oscillating fan had turned from high to low and causing my hair to hover above my shoulders before falling weightlessly down my back. I breathed deeply, inhaling the scents of cedar and sage, and waited for the sunshine and wind to erase my insecurity.

I shouldn't care what people thought, yet the pious opinions of my parents and a handful of church members chaffed my guilt like a new saddle. It didn't matter if they never spoke the words, gave the looks, cast the blame, because I knew what they were thinking. I knew they expected me to marry Tyler. I knew they thought a wedding would cover a multitude of sins. I knew, in their eyes, marriage was the only way out of my mess.

I knew it ... because I was them.

The sun poised golden above the horizon, seeming to buckle its seat belt before sliding boldly into the sky, but it didn't lighten my mood. I slid from the car, turned my back on the rising sun, and studied the house, now bathed in morning fire.

The paint had long since peeled from the wood siding, the roof slanted precariously over the front porch, and a mesquite branch rubbed against a side window, screeching like the ghost of a centuries-old resident.

If my parents ever saw this house, they'd have cardiac arrest. Their barn was nicer.

My sandals crunched dry grass as I dragged myself into my new home. My little guy deserved better than this.

But I probably didn't.

CHAPTER TWO

Tyler Cruz stalked diagonally across two plots at the Snyder cemetery. *Idiot lawyer. Senseless will.* But his *dad* … his dad had triggered a defensive reaction within Tyler that had him growling like a cornered javelina. Good thing the old man was already dead or Tyler might have taken a sledgehammer to him.

Anger pressed against him as he stood in the center of the grave, panting. A steady rhythm pounded his temples, and the skin on the back of his neck grew moist from sweat, yet he forced himself to settle down. The will didn't matter. He could work with it. When he met his lawyer that morning, he had imagined leaving the office with the bulk of his family's estate, and he still would. Eventually.

His boots sank into the soft mound of dirt, and he asked himself why he had come there. *Such a female thing to do.* Mothers or girlfriends or wives, left with empty arms, might stand by the graves of their *loved ones* and bawl enough tears to green the dry West Texas grass.

Tyler's eyes were dry.

He hadn't come because he missed his dad. He came because this was the last place he had seen Fawn. She stood near the back of the crowd at the funeral—looking as though she might pass out from the summer heat—while he sat in a folding chair under the canopy. At the time, he figured it served her right, but in the past hour, he had developed a change of heart.

He looked down and noticed two flower bouquets, now brown and brittle, left on either side of the tombstone by grievers the morning of. Tyler squatted with an elbow to his knee and pulled a stem from one of the cement vases. Without thinking, he waved the corpse silently back and forth, and remembered Fawn years ago in a high school play, dressed in pink fluff and holding a magic wand between her fingertips. *Glinda the Good Witch.* He crushed the petals in his fist.

Five months ago the woman had infuriated him as much as his father ever did. She had done it quietly out at the ranch, but she might as well have taken out a full-page ad in the newspaper. Everyone for miles around knew he had been rejected. They knew Fawn turned her nose up at his family's millions and swore a blue streak she was done for good this time. But none of that mattered now because Tyler was man enough to forgive her.

He released his grip, allowing the bits of dried flower to sift through his fingers and fall to the base of the granite marker. It might take a while, but he could woo her back.

After all, she needed him. Her privileged upbringing hadn't prepared her for parenthood, especially not as a single mother. Not that he had been raised any differently, but he would have enough money to make up for it. Fawn, on the other hand, wouldn't get ten cents from her uppity Bible-righteous parents even though they had it to give.

A chuckle rose from deep in his throat as he brushed trembling palms against his jeans. Fawn wanted him to think pregnancy had somehow made her self-sufficient, defiant, even tenacious, and perhaps he had wondered about that at first.

But when she showed up at his father's funeral, she nullified all the verbal claims she had made about their future. She exposed her subconscious feelings, her naive simplicity, her yearning for things to be set right.

And she proved to Tyler that he still owned her.

CHAPTER THREE

"I still can't believe you went to Byron Cruz's funeral."

I sat stiffly on a denim-covered futon in the waiting area of Sophie's Style Station while Ruthie Turner reprimanded me.

"You went," I said.

"I'm not carrying his grandchild."

"That's the point. I'm practically family."

Her voice lowered. "But you don't want to be part of that family."

"No, I don't, but that doesn't change the facts. My baby is a Cruz whether I like it or not."

A sarcastic snicker slipped from her lips like a stifled hiccup. "Poor kid."

I inspected a cricket near my foot before reaching for a tattered fashion magazine. Ruthie's comments rubbed, but I took the criticism as well as my pride would allow. After all, she stuck around when my sorority sisters flurried away like startled quail. But we were unlikely friends.

She was a grocery-store clerk desperately in need of a manicure, working nights and weekends to put herself through college, and I was the holier-than-thou daughter of the wealthiest man in Trapp. But somehow Ruthie found it in her heart to forgive my family of our sins against hers when I toppled from my imaginary pedestal and landed splat on the ground at her feet.

I'd say we were best friends, but that sounds all cute and confident and united in purpose, which we weren't. The only thing holding us

together was my upside-down life, because we both knew I would flounder without her by my side, tutoring me in lower-middle-class survival.

Flipping the pages of the magazine, I boasted, "I scrubbed the windows on my house."

"The place is falling down, and you clean the windows." Her tinkling laughter caught the attention of Sophie Snodgrass who paused with a lime-green roller suspended above the hunched shoulders of a tiny old woman whose name I couldn't remember.

"Fawn Blaylock washing windows? I can't picture it." Sophie's jaw worked a wad of chewing gum like one of my father's Hereford cows, and she lifted an eyebrow at her gray-haired customer.

I answered her lightly, brushing off her insulting tone. "The view is the only thing the property has going for it."

"That's not true," said Ruthie quickly. "Your place is cozy, and with your fancy things, it practically looks like something on HGTV."

Bless Ruthie Turner.

Even though she considered my house a dump—and told me so—she would never stand by and let Sophie do the same. None of my "fancy things" had been allowed to leave my parents' house. Instead, Ruthie and I drove to garage sales, collecting tacky household items, which her cousin delivered in his pickup truck.

I lowered my head. "Mother would just *die*, wouldn't she?"

"Eew, don't think about your mother."

The woman in Sophie's chair chimed in. "How's your mama doing, Fawn? I haven't seen her in town for weeks."

Her question startled me, partly because I never dreamed the old woman could hear my private mutterings to Ruthie, and partly because I had no answer for her—I hadn't seen my mother either.

A second elderly woman appeared from the corner bathroom, inching toward a hair-dryer seat with her four-pronged aluminum cane clicking along the linoleum. "That's not quite right, Sister," she said slowly. "We bumped into Susan Blaylock last week in the United grocery. In front of the freezer where they keep the orange sherbet."

"Oh, that's right. She wore high heels on a Tuesday morning."

I lifted my magazine slightly and whispered, "Remind me of their names."

Ruthie turned in her seat as though she were looking at something on the street. "No idea. I always call them Blue and Gray." She winked before wandering to the air conditioner where she held her hair away from her neck so the frigid blast could dry her skin.

Blue and Gray? I frowned, wondering if she was referencing the Civil War, but when she crossed her eyes and tilted her head toward the hair-dryer seat, it all made sense. The woman in front of Sophie was gray headed, but her sister's hair held a tinge of blue from too much dye.

I bit my lip to keep from laughing.

"Fawn, honey," said Gray as Sophie pulled the last roller from her hair, "I remember when your mama married. Seems like just last week."

Blue gave an airy whistle. "Susan and Neil Blaylock's wedding was the most highfalutin event Trapp's seen in fifty years."

"Maybe sixty." Gray scrunched her nose. "And I bet Fawn's marriage to the Cruz boy will be even fancier."

A sickening knot tightened my insides. Apparently, the news of my newfound independence hadn't completed the local gossip

circuit yet, though from the look on Sophie's face, the hairdresser was bursting to share the news.

The sweet sisters continued their conversation, oblivious to the tension in the room.

"Like mother, like daughter."

"Sure enough—the apple doesn't fall far."

I crossed one knee over the other, which sent the futon's uneven legs tapping back and forth like the pendulum on my parents' grandfather clock. The words of two batty old women shouldn't bother me. Everyone from Trapp to Tahoka had already pointed out that my unplanned pregnancy and hurried wedding plans echoed that of my parents.

Sophie peered at me with wide eyes. "Have you and Tyler pushed the big day back until after the baby comes, Fawn?"

I wanted to crawl under the futon. Or leave the building. Or move to another state. A haircut shouldn't be so much trouble.

Ruthie huffed. "Sophie, you know good and well Fawn broke it off with Tyler Cruz."

"Well." Sophie's mouth tightened into a reprimanded O. "I never heard it from Fawn herself, so who am I to say?" She busily teased a lock of Gray's hair into a tangled frenzy.

Blue sat up straight, stretching her withered frame to peek at me over the edge of the counter. "I bet he was unfaithful to you, wasn't he, dearie?" She seemed to imply that if Tyler would sleep with one woman out of wedlock, he would certainly sleep with others.

I lowered my gaze to the floor with an air of mournful loss. I didn't want to lie to the old woman, but I wasn't about to admit the real reason I backed out of my engagement. So far, the truth hadn't

come anywhere near the gossip chain—evidence of Tyler's interest in keeping it under the radar as well. In fact, I wouldn't put it past him to have started the "cheating groom" rumor. He knew as well as I did that people around here wouldn't forgive abusive behavior nearly as readily as they overlooked promiscuity.

"That's the natural way of men." Gray held up a crooked finger for emphasis. "Can't trust 'em from here to the porch and back."

She coughed as Sophie sprayed her head with a can labeled *Big Sexy Hair*.

"You're all done, sweetie." Sophie gently shooed Gray toward the door with Blue close behind. "Ladies, I'll see you again next week. Same time."

I stepped around the puttering women and wondered if the hairdresser wasn't anxious to get me captive in her chair. I muttered to Ruthie, "I'm beginning to remember why Mother always took me to the spa in Lubbock."

"Welcome to the working class."

I settled into Sophie's throne as the hairdresser approached. "What can I do for you, Fawn, hon?"

A brief explanation quickly sent her to work on my split ends, and soon her gentle combing and snipping relaxed my nerves. I closed my eyes, hoping she would let me enjoy the goose bumps tickling across my scalp.

"Oh, sorry." She yanked a tangle, and when my eyes popped open, she asked, "So you're living up on the Cap?"

"Yes, ma'am."

"But I see you're still driving Velma Pickett's car."

"Yes, she loaned it to me."

"Ansel and Velma were awful hospitable to board you while you worked things out with your folks."

What was she getting at? Not only had I not worked things out with my folks, but my moving in with the Picketts was old news. "I talked it over with Ansel and Velma, and we agreed I should have my own place before the baby comes. That's why I rented."

Sophie's response came so quickly her words tripped over mine. "Someone sat in this very chair the other day, saying they knew the reason that house has been vacant so long."

"Sophie …" Ruthie plopped into the hair-dryer seat. "This sounds like something you shouldn't bring up."

"Why shouldn't I bring it up?"

Sophie's movements grew rapid and jerky, and I began to fear for my hairstyle. "I've probably heard it already," I said.

"Oh, I doubt it. You never would have moved there."

The lingering scent of *Big Sexy Hair* stung the back of my throat, but I accepted it along with Sophie's prattle. Another layer of my sentence.

She paused in her work, clearly waiting for us to ask for details, and when we didn't, she blurted, "The place is infested with rattlesnakes. I heard the last tenants moved to Oklahoma after they found their six-year-old daughter dead one morning … with a rattlesnake coiled on her pillow."

"That's not true, and you know it." Ruthie looked as though she might slap her.

"Well …" Sophie's bottom lip pooched. "I heard there were tons of—"

"But nobody ever *died*."

The hairdresser lifted her chin. "So you admit there are snakes up there."

"Of course. We live smack in the middle of rattlesnake country, but don't start telling Fawn wild stories."

"I've heard all the stories." A small foot or hand or elbow poked my insides, reminding me to keep things in perspective. "But I've been there a week, and I haven't seen anything except scorpions and tarantulas."

"Did the owner mention snakes?" Sophie turned her head so quickly her bobbed hair whipped against her cheeks.

"I haven't met him."

She dropped her hands to her sides. "Then how did you rent the house?"

"Ansel knows him." I adjusted the plastic cape hanging from my shoulders. "I don't know where the man lives. Dallas or Austin, maybe."

"Ruthie, do you know who he is?"

"No, but if he's a friend of Uncle Ansel, he's probably supernice."

I ran my thumb across the stubble on my knee. I hadn't told them everything. Sophie didn't need to know, but I rightly should have admitted to Ruthie the sole detail that redeemed my ratty little shack on the Caprock.

It could only be called a shack, but I didn't care. The owner offered to let me stay there free of charge the first month if I cleaned the place up, so I had no choice. The financial break could make all the difference.

Sophie stood motionless with her eyebrows bunched together in concentration. "Let me see if I've got this straight. You're willing to

live alone in a snake-infested dump because you're too proud to live in Tyler Cruz's enormous mansion?"

Ruthie slapped her palms against her thighs. "Sophie Snodgrass, Fawn's house may not be as nice as what she grew up in, but she sure as heck doesn't need any help from Tyler."

"Oh, he's that bad, is he?" Sophie chuckled, then squirted gel into her palm and began working it through my curls. "Maybe that boy wants to do right by Fawn; have you ever thought about that?"

Ruthie snorted.

"He doesn't." I moaned softly. "When I broke it off with him, he didn't argue. If anything, he seemed relieved."

"Not that it's any of your business." Ruthie scowled.

Sophie's lips wadded into a tight pucker. "Well, I'd bet money you misjudged the boy. I'd wager he's concerned for his little family."

"Why on earth would you say that?" Ruthie's voice rose. "He hasn't shown an ounce of interest in Fawn or the baby in five months."

The hairdresser wrinkled her nose at Ruthie's reflection in the mirror, and then made eye contact with me. "I just think you're wrong about that." She looked pointedly out the front windows to the street. "Take a look."

The vinyl cape acted as a barrier, trapping warm air against my torso, but when I stood and looked past the front counter, chill bumps shimmied up my arms and legs, and I felt as though I had stepped outside during a cold snap.

Tyler was just outside the Style Station, leaning against Velma's Chevy, waiting for me.

ABOUT THE AUTHOR

Varina Denman is a native Texan who spent her high school years in a small Texas town. Now she lives near Fort Worth with her husband and her five mostly grown children. *Jaded* is her debut novel. Look for the sequel, *Justified*, to be released soon from David C Cook.